I Belong To Me

Louise Ayden

ISBN 978-0-9808729-4-1

9 780980 872941

For Christy

Many thanks to everyone who assisted me in the preparation of this book.

"You give but little when you give of your possessions. It is when you give of yourself that you truly give"

…..The Prophet Collection by Kahil Gibran

Part One

A Dysfunctional Family

1

CONFLICT has invaded my life for as long as I can remember, and I have long carried the emotional scars. I felt my mind resembled a room that had been ransacked, and to put anything back into its proper place was made difficult by the emotional damage. It was just too painful. Rummaging through the mental debris searching for whatever was still salvageable had become harder and harder to do, so the chaos was left for another day. Failure to tidy up the disorder had become a serious stumbling block.

I knew that eventually I would have to face the ghosts of my past and take responsibility for them. Being aware of that was one thing, knowing the remedy was another.

My childhood family life was like a battleground. My parents were continually at each other's throats and I was the referee stepping in between, desperately trying to calm the volatility. I left home a number of times, the first at age five. I wanted to escape this domestic mess.

William O'Farrell and Sarah Bernstein are my parents. They met and married in England during World War Two. My father had served in the Royal Australian Air Force as a rear gunner before his aircraft was shot down. He parachuted out of the stricken craft just before it crash-landed; severely breaking both legs, and for the rest of his life wondered why he was the only one to survive the crash.

My father endured endless operations, spending months wrapped in a plaster cast. During his long hospital confinement he kept himself amused by causing havoc in the ward. He would slip chocolate between the sheets and then wait with great expectation for the nurse's expression of utter disgust when she straightened his bed, roaring with delight at her frustration on bearing the brunt of his joke.

Although his right leg ended up permanently stiff and shorter than the left leg, Dad said he was grateful that his life had been spared and believed that his Rosary beads and his faith in God had saved his life.

The evening Dad met my mother, he had sneaked out of the English military hospital with the help of his mates and gone to the local dance. My mother accidentally bumped his leg when she passed by him and he slumped over and screamed in pain. His cheeky blue eyes and red crimped hair must have made an impression on the raven-haired beauty. They married before Dad was repatriated back to Australia.

Try as I might, I could not imagine my mother as a carefree young woman in love; she was a mystery to me. When I asked about her family, the answer would always be the same and so would the irritation in her voice, "All that is in the past, Emma. Leave things alone, why don't you?" Years later, I discovered she had two younger sisters. Her parents were Spanish and her grandfather was an Oxford University Law graduate, and her mother's death certificate was written in Hebrew. Their wedding photograph looked like any handsome, happy couple, all smiles and anticipation of a happy future. What had happened to spoil their illusion? Whatever it was, it created a great deal of unhappiness, bitterness, resentment, remorse, and heartbreak, all of which rebounded on their four children, Tina, Peter, Mary and me. When it came to parental affection and praise there was barely enough to mention.

According to the snippet of information, my paternal aunt told me several decades later, Tina May was born in England during a London air raid. Immediately after my sister's birth she and my mother were left alone in a room, the oxygen Tina needed was not administered and she ended up slightly mentally challenged. Photographs of Tina bore no evidence of any damage. She was a pretty child, with dark hair and large brown eyes.

My only brother, Peter James, arrived 18 months later. He needed three operations to correct his right eye muscle, but eventually lost the sight in his eye. After another 18 months, I was born with an inherited Mediterranean genetic blood disorder which was not diagnosed until I was fourteen. My early childhood was absorbed in hospital stays, visiting doctors, undergoing tests and blood transfusions, in search of a name for the mystery illness. At one point, it was thought that I had the dreaded leukaemia. Apart from an exceptionally pale complexion and lack of energy and a tendency to chubbiness, I appeared fine. Chubby children in the 50's were considered to be healthy.

I was six when Mary Joy was born. My mother's pride and joy had blonde curls, hazel eyes and an engaging smile that captivated everyone. Mom doted on her perfect child, but we were soon to discover that my baby sister was not perfect. Her frightening crying fits caused havoc in our household, especially when she would hold her breath and pass out. Whenever she cried, we all would stand rigid, waiting for the inevitable and heaving a sigh of relief when it didn't happen. Mary frightened me and I detested the times when I had to watch her. I didn't know what to do if she cried and was afraid I would be in trouble if something happened to her. My brother adored her though, and was happy to take her with him when he did shopping for Mom.

We lived in an outer Sydney suburb. I would often enter our red brick home with great trepidation, wondering whether or not there would be trouble brewing. Dad's alcoholism and Mom's bitterness for the life she didn't want made our home a battlefield. I was too young to understand what had caused their unhappiness, but not too young to be disturbed by it.

Sad childhood memories marred the pleasant ones. The times I recalled those years, I would see myself lying in my bed listening to my parents' raised voices. Initially, they would only be talking loudly but all too soon, it would soar into a shouting match. I would cringe and curl up into a foetal position and silently weep with my pillow over my head. Even pressing my hands hard against my ears did not block out their voices. One night I bolted up out of bed in fright when I heard screams and breaking glass. The commotion then fell into an eerie silence.

My stomach churned with fear as I quietly opened the bedroom door to see what had happened. All the lights in the house were on but no one was about. Gingerly, I crept through the still house looking for my parents. They were nowhere to be seen. The front door was wide open. I turned around and ran throughout the house crying hysterically and calling for my mother. There was no answer. In a panic, I ran out onto the front veranda and called out into the darkness for her. The commotion woke my siblings. We were three very small children crying hysterically in unison for our parents – and nobody came.

I never knew what happened that night, where our parents were, or the length of time they were away. The terror of that memory and similar memories remained with me for many years. Although I was very young, I lived with the uncertainty of what would happen to my parents and wondered which one would eventually harm or even kill the other.

Relief from the tempest of my home life came when playing in the streets of my neighbourhood. I had the best time of my young life out there, where I found fun and mischief as only a youngster could. I fondly remember the baker delivering the bread by horse and cart, and the sound of hooves clip-clopping along the gravel road and echoing up the street. I remember too the wheat-like smell of the old draught horse and the children's roars of laughter when he relieved himself, scattering them everywhere as a river of pee spilled on to the pitted ground.

My mother ordered bread daily and the baker left the fresh, scrumptious, crusty loaf on our front doorstep. The delicious aroma wafting in the air had me salivating, tempting me to eat the middle out of the bread and then mischievously deny any knowledge of its half-demolished state.

I was exhilarated by the thrill of sneaking away from the confines of our backyard with my siblings to play with the Brady boys, who lived across the street. We were forbidden to associate with those boys or anyone else in the street. 'Wild ruffians,' my parents called them, especially the Brady boys. There were seven of them.

Joey the eldest was married; next was 19 year old Ronny. I had a crush on Ronny when I was about seven years old - he nick-named me 'Sparrow'. Bobby had joined the Air Force. Paul who came next sang in a Coca-Cola Bottlers Club wireless competition. The whole neighbourhood gathered at the Brady's home that day to listen to Paul sing. Then came Jon, he was 12. Greg was eight years old and Mike, the youngest, was five.

The similarity between the brothers was amazing. They all looked alike, with the same large square head covered in thick black tresses and they all had the same blue eyes. The boys were keen footballers. Their enthusiasm to emulate their sporting heroes kept them in excellent physical shape. Teenage girls did double takes when the boys were around. Greg and Mike were closer to our age. They were our playmates. Because of my parents' disapproval, we could only play with them when my parents were out of sight.

On weekends or school holidays, through a hole in our fence, we would watch the neighbourhood kids play cricket or football and other games out in the street, wishing we could play too. If Greg noticed us peering through the cracks he would yell out, "C'mon," beckoning to us to join in the game.

Peter and Tina climbed the fence with me after I dared them to.

Cricket was the most popular game, a wooden fruit box serving as a wicket. Once it was placed in the middle of the road, the street came alive with kids eager for a game. Any idle wooden fruit box found lying around, other than the vital wicket, became a seat for a billy cart. The mere suggestion of building a billy cart resulted in the magical appearance of the items needed for construction - a long plank, 2 sets of baby stroller wheels, a skipping rope, a few nuts and bolts, hammer and nails.

The older boys supervised and yelled instructions to the younger kids to pick up bits and hold tools. Tears sometimes spilled as tempers flared in frustration when the younger ones, helping in a chaotic fashion, were ordered to get out of the way when they did something wrong. But once the billy cart was completed hurt feelings were forgotten as we eagerly dragged it to the top of a hill to take turns in a wild ride back down.

An afternoon at the Saturday matinee watching a 'Cowboys and Indians' movie had us eager to get home and drag out the billy cart for a game. It thundered along the gravel road under the steam of two energetic kids who imagined wild Indians were chasing them. We all whooped and hollered and chased them right past our front door, while Rastas, the Brady boys' little fox terrier, went bonkers running alongside the cart, barking non-stop in jubilation.

On rainy days Rastas merrily barked when our paper sailboats weaved and darted their way over and around make-shift dams in the gutter, as we cheered them on in the downpour.

Exhilarated laughter from the street, filtering in to our lounge room where my father spent his leisure hours, would have him storm out of the house. Infuriated by the disturbance, he would stand on the veranda in military style, shouting orders at us to be quiet and to get home. Dozens of children of various shapes and sizes scattered at great speed in every direction the instant they heard the sound of his fiery wrath.

The moment the door opened was a signal for Peter, Tina and I to dive behind the hedge along our front fence, hiding until our father went back inside. Our little hearts pounded with excitement as we waited for the shrill of an 'all clear' whistle from one of the boys. Once courage returned we would double up with laughter from nervous tension. We were not caught very often but when we were, the order "Get inside!" rang out through the air and our little legs ran as fast as they would carry us back to our yard to endure a long yelling rant from our parents about mixing with riff-raff.

2

I never understood my parents' strong disapproval of the neighbours, who seemed much like our family. They had their fights too, only it seemed not as often as my parents. Mr and Mrs Brady were always kind to Peter, Tina and me. When I saw either of them in their front yard I'd call out, "Hello Mr Brady, hello Mrs Brady," in singsong and skip across the road to visit them. I spent many afternoons sitting out on their front porch chatting with them when my father was away working and my mother was in bed nursing a headache.

Mr Brady rolled his own cigarettes. It intrigued me the way he made them. I watched him and curiously followed his every movement whenever he opened the small round tin he always carried with him. He took a tiny white sheet of paper from a small packet that lay on top of the brown fibres and placed it on his bottom lip before he pulled a small amount of tobacco from the tin and put it into the palm of his hand.

"And how are you today, little lady?" Mr Brady would ask, grinning toothlessly down at me. "Now what are you doing sitting down there? Come up here and sit beside me," he'd say, patting the top step and thereby interrupting the slow massaging of tobacco between his palms.

I'd jump up, grinning like a fool and eagerly climb the three stairs to sit beside him, but I never took my eyes off his hands as they kept moving round and round, pressing the brown fibres into a ball. Our conversation flowed without interruption as the delicate piece of paper sat on his bottom lip. My eyes were transfixed, watching it flap like a butterfly when he spoke or smiled. I was waiting for the paper to fall off or blow away. But it never did.

"How's your mom?"

"Hmmm, she's in bed sick...Dad made her sick."

"Oh, that's no good. How did he do that?"

"Dunno," I shrugged. "Mom just told Dad that he makes her sick and went to bed."

Mr Brady smiled and removed the delicate white paper from his lip. He held it between two fingers and tipped the tobacco on to the transparent paper. In one quick sweep, with a little more adjusting, he rolled it up. He ran the tip of his tongue along the paper in a rapid sweep and lit the cigarette.

I loved visiting the Brady's home. They welcomed me with open arms. Many times I followed Mr Brady around the yard, chatting with him while he mowed his lawn. I watched perspiration trickle from his pores under the strain of pushing his sparkling clean mower back and forth. His lawn was the neatest I had ever seen. No one in the street had grass like Mr Brady. He pulled out with contempt every weed that dared grow in his green carpet. He roared like an injured bear if he ever found anyone walking on his manicured masterpiece. Although he never seemed to mind if I did when I was with him. Just about every weekend I could find him crawling on all fours trimming the edges of the lawn with clippers. It was easier for me to talk to him when he did, because I didn't have to crane my neck to look up at him. I liked to look at him when we talked. His blue eyes sparkled when he smiled.

Mr Brady would tell me that I was a funny little thing but I could never work out what he thought was funny about me. I didn't think about it too much because I knew he liked me.

Even though the Brady's backyard was huge, the blanket of grass that surrounded their house only went halfway up the back yard. The rest was bush shrubs and gum trees, where we played marbles with the younger sons. In one of the trees, the Brady boys built a tree house. Allan Davison, Paul Brady's mate, gave an excellent rendition of Tarzan's jungle cry every time he swung from the tree house to the ground below.

The Brady's home was full of laughter and rowdy people. I knew their world was not perfect, but I enjoyed being there and secretly visited them every chance I got. Mr Brady's mother also lived with the family. We all called her Nanna. Although the years had taken her youth, turned her hair snow-white and left her frail and small, she was still a feisty little lady. Nanna turned into a spitfire and mumbled colourful language under her breath when she was annoyed with the boys. Sometimes she used the cane that supported her while walking as a missile to hurl at her grandsons whenever they playfully teased and mimicked her. Her fiery temper was reserved for those who tested her patience. The blue dress and bonnet she knitted for my doll, which my mother grudgingly allowed me to keep, was evidence of her tender side and a treasured memory.

Nanna's passing was vague, but I missed her. The little old lady with the white hair, who had always worn a long black dress and a shawl draped around her shoulders was not just the Brady boys' Nanna. I thought of her as my Nanna too and felt a deep sense of loss when she died.

I can remember how from the age of four I would squirm with discomfort at my own paternal grandparents' embrace, especially my grandfather. I hated him and the creepy expression that slowly spread across his face like a dark shadow when he looked at me.

Every chance he got he would reach out and grab hold of me and lift me up onto his lap. While caught in his vice-like grip, he would slowly rub his hand up and down my arm, moving downwards to put his hand inside my panties. I managed to break free and ran away and hid under my bed, too terrified to tell my mother what he did. I told her only that I did not like him and she angrily told me to keep away from him.

So whenever my grandfather visited our home after that, I hid under my bed, holding my breath while watching his feet come halfway into my room and then leave quietly. I was lucky my grandparents lived in another state, which prevented them visiting us often. Even at this late stage of my life, I cringe and feel trapped when a man I'm not sure of stands too close.

As a small child, there were very few people I could say I cared about. Apart from the Brady's, I had a favourite uncle, but I didn't see much of him. My brother was top of my favourite people list. He was different when away from home, far different from the quiet 'Mr Goody two shoes' my parents thought he was.

As teenagers, we learned ballroom dancing on Saturday afternoons. My mild mannered brother and his mate Trevor, who came with us, would cut loose and smoke and swear during those outings. Initially, many of Peter's friends at the Maris Brothers' College thought I was his girlfriend, because he had taken me to his school dance. Since we danced well together, he thought, why not. My brother's olive complexion, black hair and dark eyes were a stark contrast to mine, so much so that his mates were surprised to learn that we were related.

Although Peter was placid and shy he was confident on the dance floor. We had so much fun together that his classmates couldn't believe we really were siblings. But when we came together the following year, it really took some convincing to prove that I was his sister. They called me a 'cool chick', dolled up in my pink cotton frock, puff sleeves and many rope petticoats.

We managed to get tickets to the television show 'Teen Time' hosted by Lou Lewton. Peter and I had a great time showing off, doing the twist while nonchalantly trying to keep in full view of the camera, then basking in the glory of our five minutes of fame when friends told us that they had seen us on the show.

When he had enough money saved, Peter bought our grandfather's 1956 Dodge. It was huge, black and sturdy as a tank. One rainy night he almost ran over the top of another vehicle trying to stop at traffic lights. The near-miss would have had my parents cringing in horror if they had known, but I felt sure that if anyone had told them, they would not have believed Peter would have done anything careless.

I was glad my brother tested life a little and was not a mama's boy. Although he didn't walk on the edge the way I did, at least he had fun being a tad wild. As children, we sat together in our next-door neighbour's peach tree, close to our kitchen window. From there we watched our mother preparing the evening meal and heard her complaining about us being late. We ignored her calls to come inside, giggling between ourselves, quietly eating peaches.

"Where are those little devils?" she grumbled. "Just wait till I get my hands on them when they come home!"

When we heard that, we knew it was time to go. Quickly we scurried down the tree and over the high fence, trying to avoid getting splinters in our hands and feet in our haste.

My school years closely resembled my home life — turbulent. I was extremely guarded around nuns I had witnessed severely reprimanding students, ever mindful of possibly being slapped over the head for any small misdemeanour inadvertently committed. I was terrified that I would be beaten with the strap or locked in the cupboard, which I had seen happened to other students I knew.

Although I was only five, I clearly remember my first class teacher, Sister Mary, hitting Patrick Murphy with a ruler again and again until it broke, and shutting him in a cupboard at the back of the classroom for talking in class. I never liked Patrick. He was a bully. He always tried to thump my brother on our way home from school, but I do recall feeling sorry for him, and thinking how horrible Sister Mary was for thrashing and humiliating him. I wanted to yell at her and tell her to stop hitting him. Fear kept me silent. No one in the class was brave enough to look sideways.

Sister Mary also wouldn't let one of the boys go to the toilet when he asked. "No!" she screamed at him. "Kneel down for morning prayers and behave yourself."

The class obediently knelt down on the bare wooden floor with heads bowed. As we prayed, I noticed a puddle coming from the second desk in front of me. Trickles were running in several directions and one was heading for me. The girl in front of me saw it too. Pointing at the puddle, she sounded the alarm, "Sister! Sister!"

Sister Mary grabbed the boy violently by the neck and shook him. Every nerve in my stomach knotted. I thought she was going to strangle him.

I wasn't well enough to be actively involved in much of anything at school. Although I mixed with other children, I was distant from them. More often than not, I was content to stand on the sideline observing my surroundings. Some days I was invited to lunch with a group of pretty girls with ribbons in their hair but mostly I ate alone. I never minded being alone since I really didn't feel comfortable in their company or with the way they sniggered when one of them made a spiteful remark about other classmates. I would move away from them when they started to whisper to each other. It was beyond me why they could be so nasty without provocation.

Sixth class was my most challenging time. Prior to that the fear of the injustice developed from first class had slowly progressed to indifference. Sister Helen, our sixth class teacher, had an intense dislike of me. In her traditional nun's habit, she reminded me of a lifeless stick penguin. Her features were stern and pale, her thick bushy eyebrows framing her cold, dark eyes. The only time those stony features reflect a glimmer of warmth was when the parish priest came to our classroom.

During a math lesson, Sister Helen noticed that I was daydreaming, as I often did when bored. Math was my worst subject, I loathed the class and I loathed Sister Helen. In her frustration at discovering a disinterested student, the penguin commanded me to come forward and write the answer to the math problem on the blackboard. I stood a few moments in front of the huge board, gazing blankly at the numbers as if they were ancient hieroglyphics, then nonchalantly shrugged and said I didn't know how. A look of utter disgust crossed Sister Helen's face as she raised her arm that held a child tamer. In a frenzy of insults, she began to poke and prod me with it screaming, "You're a stupid ninny, Miss O'Farrell."

She clenched her jaws tighter as she pinched my arm, prodded me several times with the stick and pulled clumps of my hair, "And lazy too," she spat, "Just like your stupid sister...!"

Sister Helen's face had turned purple. The nasty names, the spiteful tugs at my hair and slaps of her cane had no effect on me, but when she resorted to taunts about my sister being handicapped and stupid, causing the class to laugh, I instantly reacted.

Humiliation drove my anger to rise like a volcano, exploding without warning. Driven by hysteria, I snatched the cane from the unholy monster's hand and struck her several times with it.

"Stop saying awful things about Tina." I yelled at her. "She can't help it!"

The room was still. Sister Helen realised she had over-stepped many boundaries and quickly ushered me from the classroom and into the nuns' lunchroom next door. The lunchroom had always been a mystery I was keen to solve. For years I had tried to imagine what was going on behind the green door at the end of the long veranda. Day after day I watched with wide-eyed, uncontrollable curiosity as the sisters flitted in and out of that room. What did they do in there? I wondered.

The nuns' long strings of large wooden rosary beads, hanging from their thick black belts, clanged against the lunchroom door every time they entered or exited. I would crane my neck as far as I could to snatch a peek inside whenever I heard that sound.

After all that wondering, my curiosity was soothed to a great disappointment. I was finally in the mysterious room with the green door. It was sparsely furnished with nothing of interest.

Sister sat me down at an ordinary old wooden kitchen table. She placed a cup of coffee and a biscuit in front of me. "Here," she said pushing them closer and then left. I sipped the coffee, which was lukewarm, then bit into the biscuit and immediately spat it out. It was stale. I sat alone staring blankly at the unpalatable biscuit and coffee, mystified as to how I was going to get myself out of this mess.

A sense of shame as much as a sense of triumph finally kicked in as I anxiously waited to be punished. Relief washed over me in disbelief when the afternoon bell rang and Sister

Helen came rushing back and told me to get out of her sight. I didn't hesitate a moment, gathering my books and belongings together and running all the way home.

When I arrived home that afternoon, I was sure that when I told my mother what had happened in class she would embrace me as a heroine for defending Tina but, quite to the contrary, she berated me for hours on end. Her response confused me. I was bewildered beyond words as to why I was in trouble and why my mother would allow the nun to belittle my sister. Her refusal to do anything about it angered me so much that it provoked a vow. I promised that if I ever have children, I will always stand by them, no matter what. No one will ever be allowed to humiliate any of them, ever.

Interacting with other families gave me insight to a fact of life; everyone, at one time or another will experience strife. I never understood my parents' attitude towards the neighbours and most things in general. I also wrestled with the ill feelings I harboured toward my mother.

When I lived at home the guilt about those ill feelings plagued my thoughts. I couldn't control my dislike of my mother. She complained about everything, my father, the neighbours, my siblings and especially me. I felt she didn't like me, even hated me at times. Nothing was ever good enough.

Regardless, I made every effort to appease my mother and failed miserably. To compensate for disliking her, I maintained the sense of responsibility I had developed towards her as a six year old, dutifully standing up to my father whenever my parents fought and demanding that he leave my mother alone. My father would glare down at me like a crazed man, but usually he simply stumbled away in disgust. Although I trembled in my shoes I didn't move, whatever the outcome.

Dad's excessive drinking drove my mother to nag him about it. I detested the constant trouble that lingered in our home like a bad odour. I felt utterly helpless that I could not resolve the situation. The abuse they hurled at each other was awful. My parents reminded me of wild dogs, eyes wide with rage, teeth clenched and foaming at the mouth. It was an ugly sight for anyone to witness, let alone children. It mattered little to either of them who witnessed their shameful behaviour and they seemed unconcerned at our acute discomfort at the times they fought in the company of friends.

Relief from the mounting pressure in our home and in our lives came when my father, a salesman, was away on business trips. During his absence my mother grumbled about her unhappy life, her complaints stirring within me a profound pity for her. I silently prayed that my father wouldn't come back home. Life was better without him. To lighten the mood I would sometimes mimic my father at his worst, sending ripples of laughter throughout the house. Unintentionally, I said and did things that often shocked people. None of my siblings dared to be so bold.

I yearned to leave home, wanting to find a happier place. Running away was a constant thought of mine. I can recall at age five, stuffing my few treasures in my tiny school case and helping myself to five shillings from my mother's purse. Slipping on my pale avocado and white spotted, hooded raincoat and my white canvas rubber tipped sandshoes, then marching defiantly out of the house. Just before closing the door behind me, I announced in a very loud voice that I was running away...and never coming back.

The reason for the escapade has faded with time, but I clearly remember the sloshing sound my sandshoes made as I trudged through the rain and muddy potholes, walking without direction along a deserted street, with only those five shillings in my pocket and my tiny case tucked under my arm.

I still remember the humiliation of falling into a mud puddle, when salty tears blurred my vision. I hated being small and helpless. I was so mad that I stamped my foot, splashing even more muddy water over myself, I sobbed louder.

Soaked to the skin and filthy, I had no other option but to return home defeated. Before I did, I spent the five shillings at the local milk bar, where I bought a huge bag of sweets to help me feel better. But I didn't feel better.

Hurt by the rejection of being ignored when I came back, I boldly yelled from my bedroom while peeling cold, sodden clothes from my chilled body, "As soon as I am big, I'm leaving this place!"

It baffled me why neither my sister nor my brother ever seemed to want to leave home too. They appeared to accept what was going on around them as normal. When Dad came home drunk, I pleaded with my mother to ignore him. She silenced me with the threat of her hand. My fathers' drinking was like a red rag to a bull.

I was twelve when Mom had a nervous breakdown and was admitted to hospital. Dad took care of us then. We were used to Mom being ill, especially me. She was always ill in the winter, the month of my birthday.

Dad still drained his whisky bottles, and apart from the usual sibling disputes over whose turn it was to do the dishes, trouble was almost non-existent. We had united and looked after Dad and ourselves without any mishaps.

When we visited Mom, she quizzed me the moment Dad left the room about what was happening at home without her. She glared at me when I told her we were managing just fine and not to worry about us. Dad was a different person without Mom at home - nicer. His angry outbursts and cranky moods had stopped. He was actually good fun, even though he was still drinking. I loathed seeing him stumbling around the house drunk. My feelings for my father were a mixture of pity and disgust.

In my mother's absence, I gained new insight into my parents and my attitude towards my father changed dramatically. He no longer appeared to be a villain, simply a man who carried a huge burden upon his shoulders and didn't know what to do with it. Never did he say a bad word against

Mom while she was away. He once told me that she had come from a well-to-do family and he felt he wasn't good enough for her. When I asked questions, all he would say was, "She's a classy woman, too good for him."

I can't remember the length of time Mom was away, but I can remember not missing her. Dad drank less and our home was more settled without her. I wished she had stayed in hospital...forever. Mom returned – the moment she walked through the door, the atmosphere in our house changed. Fights began and Dad guzzled his whisky. Trying to reason with Mom was pointless.

As a diversion when Dad was drunk, I would sit and talk or spend hours listening to his jazz records with him, for we shared a love of music. It was during those times he dragged out his precious guitar and strummed along with one of his favourite musicians. One day he stacked several of his favourite long playing records, one on top of the other, on the arm of the radiogram turntable. Then he staggered back and sat down on the edge of his high-back papa chair. He lean forward and picked up the guitar from its case. His damaged leg jutted in front of him.

Nursing the guitar on the good leg, he'd tinker the strings into tune. When he was ready, he looked at me and nodded. That was the signal to release a record. With a click, a plop and then a short crackling sound from the needle on the old recording, the up-tempo tune filled the room. Dad's head bobbed in time with the music and his lower lip automatically rolled over as he concentrated seriously on his strumming, the melody carrying him to another place. I was curled up on the lounge in my pyjamas and dressing gown, watching him and listening to the music.

Suddenly, the door opened with such violence that it went crashing against the wall, startling us and sending shock waves through the peaceful ambience. Mom stood in the door-way with hands on hips. Her eyes were full of rage, as she stood there, dressed in her nightgown.

"Get to bed, Emma!" she shrilled.

"Get the hell out of here, you trouble-making bitch and leave her alone!" Dad bellowed back.

My mother glared at me as if I had spoken the words and ordered me to bed again. Dad told me to stay put as he struggled to jump up out of the chair. His stiff leg and the alcohol slowed his movements. Mom lunged at him. They stood in the middle of the lounge facing each other while I gawked upwards at them, expecting them to start punching each other.

"Mom hissed at Dad, pointing at me, "She has school tomorrow. The little trouble-maker has to go to bed!"

"Get out!" he snarled. They scuffled as he pushed her from the room. They got to the doorway and Dad tried to close the door, but Mom pushed her weight against it. He gave one almighty shove and closed the door. "Stay out!" he yelled.

We could hear her cursing me from the hallway. "This is your fault you, you, stupid little bitch... All you had to do was go to bed, you fat..."

"Don't take any notice of the old hag, mate," Dad said picking up his guitar. "Put on another record." I silently obeyed, stifling a yawn and wishing I could go to bed. I was exhausted.

My mother's hurtful and nasty words reinforced my every inadequacy and became relics I carried into adulthood. All I had ever wanted was to be accepted in spite of my imperfections. My effort to excel was marred by ill health. I eventually gave up trying, appearing uninterested and dead lazy to the less understanding. As time passed I ceased to care what anyone thought.

My mother and the holy nuns who taught me insisted I was stupid, but I knew that was not so and held dear the affirming years I had spent in the Brownies.

I was seven when I joined the Brownie pack. There I competently completed tests and earned badges and quickly became a pack leader. No favours were given to me. I worked very hard to earn every badge and my sixer (leader) stripes.

Five years of diligence had earned me the privilege of a guard of honour ceremony when I left the Brownies, and I flew up with honours to the Girl Guides, where I also earned more badges and became a group leader. I was proud to be a Brownie and a Girl Guide, and of my achievements.

Two turbulent years later I left school with the mutual consent of my parents and the holy sisters, but not before one of them said, "By the way you're going, Miss O'Farrell, I can't see your future being any better than being a common streetwalker, a prostitute."

Contrary to the reverend sister's prophetic words, I immediately started work in a leading city hair salon. Hairdressing and make-up artistry was the general direction in which I was heading.

At 13, I had earned a few shillings doing comb-ups now and then for some of the women in my street. While I appreciated the opportunity of working in a prestigious salon, I was exhausted by midday. Being on my feet for hours on end depleted what little energy I had. I was seriously ill and didn't know it.

A boy I met on the train on my way home from work took the edge off the long journey to and from the city each day. At first I thought his attention was sweet, but when he sang love songs to me in the crowded carriage and all eyes were on us, I shrank with embarrassment.

My admirer wore fashionable suits and worked in the men's department of Mark Foy's city store. Brylcreem kept his fair hair slicked down and held the peak he combed above his forehead. Although he was only sixteen, he oozed ambition and boasted future plans of grandeur in show business. I was not surprised to see my former admirer several years later, belting out a tune in front of his band on Bandstand, looking considerably different from the days when I knew him before he became as famous as he had predicted.

My health deteriorated so rapidly that I left my job and admirer behind and ended up at the children's hospital at Camperdown.

Mom refused to leave the hospital until someone told her what was the wrong with me. When the doctor in Outpatients saw my blood test results, I was immediately admitted to hospital. One doctor in particular made a huge impact on me; he had kind blue eyes and a gentle voice. I felt safe with him. He sat on the edge of my bed and explained in simple terms the procedures that had to be done to make me well.

"You have Spherocytosis, Emma. We have to remove your spleen," Dr Pennington said.

I stared blankly back at him as if to say, 'what the heck is that?'

"Your blood cells are round instead of oval," he quickly responded. "The spleen filters your blood, but because the cells are abnormal, it destroys them, which is why you have to have surgery…"

The doctor's casual and gentle manner was reassuring. Although I comprehended only a small portion of what he said, I understood enough not to be afraid. Other doctors had terrified me.

I hated the way our local doctor, a stout man with black, straight hair smiled at me and said, "This won't hurt a bit," every time he gave me an injection. The needles he used were as large as a drill and felt just as blunt. When I was seven, my foot became infected and blew up like a balloon. Mom had to call him to our home. After he looked at the wound, I overheard him say, "I'll have to give her a penicillin shot," as they walked out of my room and in to the kitchen.

The moment they were out of sight, I darted out of bed and hid behind our kidney-shaped dressing table, crawling in between the lining of the pink chiffon skirt secured around it. I froze in terror when I heard them come back to my room. They both gasped to find me gone.

"Where has that little devil gone?" Mom said irritated. "Where are you, Emma?" she called sharply. Their voices faded as they left my room searching everywhere for me.

Mom came back and looked under the dressing table. "I don't know where she could be," I heard her say. Then suddenly her voice was above me shouting, "What are you doing behind there?" pulling the dressing table out of the way.

"No! No!" I screamed full force. "I don't want a needle." I held on tight to whatever I could as both of them dragged me kicking and screaming from my hiding place. I fought like crazy when they held me down on the bed. In spite of my efforts, the doctor plunged the needle into my rigid bottom.

At age 13, the same doctor recommended that I have a series of liver injections to boost my blood. After the second one, I developed an incredible itch and my whole body swelled, starting with my face. I was supposed to go the pictures with Robbie Anderson that day. He was popular and looked like Cliff Richard's twin. It was to be our first date and he walked a long way to come to my house. By the time he arrived, I was unrecognisable. I looked like a monster. My mother answered the door to Robbie and burst into laughter when he asked for me. "She's sick," was all she could get out as she closed the door, leaving Robbie utterly bewildered.

My family could not contain their laughter. I looked hideous. I didn't have a face. It had turned into a huge melon with slits. My head had almost doubled in size and the map of India had formed on my back. Even the doctor couldn't restrain his laughter when he came to the house to give me another injection. While everyone fell about laughing, I cried, fearful I would permanently look that way. It seemed that no one really cared that my tongue had swollen so badly that I almost choked.

Doctor Pennington was the first doctor to treat me with dignity. I liked that and I liked him. He was also the first doctor with whom I had ever felt comfortable. His visits were the highlight of my day. I eagerly looked forward to seeing him, even if it was just to take blood samples. It surprised me that he was interested in what I thought. No one before had ever seemed to care how or what I felt. I was raised in the 'children should be seen and not heard' era. The doctor made me feel as if I mattered.

When I asked Doctor Pennington if I could see my spleen after surgery, he smiled and promised to bring it in to show me after I was taken back to the ward. Both my parents were surprised he did that for me. I was heavily sedated and only remember Doctor Pennington standing by my bed holding a stainless steel dish with my huge purple spleen in it. The doctor later told me that my spleen measured eight inches in length, when it should have been just two inches.

My parents had come to my room and sat with me and had even spoken to me, but I remember nothing of them ever being there.

3

A noticeable physical change had taken place in me while I was in hospital. The baby fat I had lugged around since a toddler had melted away, sculpturing my round features into high cheekbones, emphasising my melancholic, dark eyes. I was amazed to see the transformed image in the mirror. It looked like another person staring back at me, someone I didn't know. The difference was daunting as well as exciting. I didn't feel so different from the chubby girl I once was. Even though I was often complimented on my new appearance, that chubby girl still lurked inside me.

I gave credit to the doctor for my speedy recovery. It was he who had inadvertently given me the will to want to get better. Keeping his promise told me that I was worth something. I knew he must have had more important things to do than to bring the spleen to the ward to show me, but he did it anyway. What he did for me was important and it made a huge impact on my life. Two months later, just after my fifteenth birthday, I was back in hospital for more surgery. Although Doctor Pennington wasn't directly involved with this case, he made time to visit me.

My wellbeing gave me a zest for living. I wanted so much to change the things that were not working for me, and leaving home had become my strongest obsession. I dared to hope for an opportunity to come quickly.

In my recklessness I foolishly vocalised my intention to leave the moment trouble erupted. My mother saw my declaration as a threat to get my own way. While stuck in the family mire, it had occurred to me that most of the trouble was avoidable. After years of enduring traumatic fights and arguments, day in and day out, seething in frustration I told my mother just that. Her features hardened as I spewed out many years of corralled thoughts and feelings.

"Why, you ungrateful little bitch," she snarled with such force that the veins in her neck bulged. "After all I've done for you! You, you wouldn't be alive today if I hadn't taken you to doctor after doctor, persisting all those years to find out what was making you so ill. How dare you!" she repeated in fury, before storming out of the room.

For as long as I can remember, my mother held me indebted to her. Repeatedly reminding me of all she had done, so frequently that I wished she had let me die instead. The price I had to pay was too high. There was no doubt she did persist with doctors and hospitals for many years and that persistence saved my life. I was grateful to her for that, but did not believe I owed her my life for doing what a mother should naturally do anyway – care for her sick child.

While dealing with the no win situation I tried in earnest to suppress my hostile feelings towards my mother and pretended that all was well, doing my utmost to avoid dilemmas at home. But no matter what I did, it never seemed to be the right thing. Consequently, hostility outweighed any gratitude.

I was disappointed when I had lost my chance to continue working at the city salon, but after I had fully recovered from both operations, a neighbour told me about a position in the office where she worked. That job was the independence I hoped and prayed for, to make it possible for me to move away from home.

My friends and the new job were a welcome distraction from the madness of my home life. Erica Jackson was my best friend then. She was seventeen, two years older than me. We spent many of our weekends together and shared our future hopes and dreams with each other. I found it amazing that Erica's main ambition was to be married, as soon as possible.

Although I wasn't sure what I wanted, marriage was not at the top of my list.

I assumed Erica's desire to marry quickly was due to her happy home. Her family was a warm and very close-knit unit. They had welcomed me into their home, and I enjoyed being there so much that I didn't want to go back to my place, ever.

I was with Erica and her boyfriend the day Lucas Romano walked into my life. My heart fluttered and my insides went wonky at the sight of him. I had never experienced anything like that before or felt such strong feelings since. I instantly understood Erica's dream of marriage. Luc's cobalt eyes engulfed me as I looked into them when we were introduced. He was charismatic, charming and popular and cut a fine figure in his navy-blue suit. When he left, I almost drove Erica to distraction with endless questions about him, but she only knew him as an acquaintance.

I was so taken with Luc that I told my mother about him. Doubt appeared in her eyes when I told her that he was incredibly handsome. A few months later, unbeknown to me, Erica had arranged for Luc to take me to a birthday party. Initially, I thought I was going with Erica and her boyfriend, so my jaw fell open in surprise when I answered the knock at the front door and found Luc standing there. The evening was surreal. His image had been etched in my memory from our first meeting. I dreamed that he would one day take me out, and there he was standing at my front door.

By the smile on my mother's face, I could clearly see that she was impressed with Luc's good looks, but I also didn't miss her creased brow as she tried to estimate his age. She did not seem too impressed that he was a mature man, but nothing would have prevented me from seeing him, regardless of the eight year gap in our ages.

A chic, bouffant hairstyle and a winter white, gold pinstripe, three-quarter sleeve, two-piece suit gave me an air of maturity beyond my sixteen years. Skilfully applied make-up erased all traces of the naive teenager I really was. My youth did not discourage me in any way from intuitively knowing that I had found the man with whom I wanted to share the rest of my life, even though I knew he had several girlfriends.

I also had a boyfriend, and perhaps he would have been the love of my life if Luc hadn't come into the equation. I was very fond of my boyfriend and perhaps even loved him. Matt Calloway, a fun-loving Navy radio operator, viewed life as a game and was ever ready to meet the challenge of a dare. No other person had ever made me laugh as much as he had. This lean, lanky, mischievous nineteen-year-old brought a lot of sunshine into my life when I needed it most, and he cherished me.

We met at Sydney's Circular Quay one Saturday evening, shortly after my first stint in hospital and seven months prior to meeting Luc. I was with Tina and two other girlfriends at the time. We were on our way home from the pictures and heading in the direction of the train station when a small group of sailors called out to us. One was doing backflips on an overhead railing and telling jokes to get our attention.

My sister and friends giggled amongst themselves while I tried to pretend they were not there. I held my head high as we walked past the sailors, but quickly glanced over my shoulder and thought the guy doing backflips and clowning around was cute. I stopped walking and then turned around and slowly walked over to where he hung upside down and asked what he was doing.

"Trying to get your attention," he said in mid swing, leaping to the ground and landing upright in front of me, grinning from ear to ear saying, "I thought for a minute there you weren't going to stop." His cheeky grin had won me.

"What's your name?"

"Matt Calloway. What's yours?"

"Emma Jane O'Farrell. Sorry Matt, I have to go. Tina, Rosy, Mary come on!" I called when I heard our train pull into the station and ran down the stairs waving him goodbye.

"What's your phone number?"

Laughing, I yelled out the number, not really expecting to see or hear from him again. I didn't think he would remember the number. But as he promised, Matt rang the next day, asking me to meet him in the city the following weekend. I invited him to come to my home instead. Matt was delighted at the invitation and eagerly accepted, asking if he could bring a mate with him. The evening was a huge success. My family instantly liked Matt, who had everyone doubled up with laughter at his mischievous tales. He was the breath of fresh air that the family needed and he was always welcomed at our house.

I felt happy when Matt visited and missed him terribly when he went to sea. Eagerly I would wait for his poetic and very romantic letters to arrive. His words were from one lover to another, even though we had only kissed and held hands. While reading the amusing tales he so expressively wrote about, his voice and his cheeky laughter echoed in my mind. He called me his princess and carried my photograph in his wallet. I adored him and treasured his letters.

Although things changed between us after I met Luc, there was always a place in my heart for Matt. I had not planned to fall in love with Luc, it just happened. I didn't understand what love was all about until I met him, and I quickly discovered that life situations didn't make staying on track easy. It seemed that when I least expected it, a detour sign appeared in front of me and changed my direction in life. Although no longer my boyfriend, Matt still visited my family when he came to Sydney. I truly believe that if I had not met Luc, I would have married Matt.

Luc's sophistication unnerved me at times but I was determined not to become a notch on anyone's belt. My plan was to wait until marriage before exploring my sexuality and, although Luc reluctantly resigned himself to that, it didn't keep him from trying to persuade me to give in to him. I knew in my heart that he was the man that I wanted to be with, and in hope of some sort of commitment from him, I asked if he thought we had a future together.

He seemed uncomfortable and quickly told me he thought I was too young to consider anything like that. "Ah gee Doll, I don't know…"

"Well sweetheart," I said, "I'm not too young for you to keep on trying to score with me, am I? Call me when you do know."

"Why? What's going on Doll?"

"No more games honey. Either I'm your girlfriend or I'm not. It's pretty simple. You work it out and then call me," I said and kissed him on the cheek. "Bye Luc."

Breaking up with him was painful, but I wanted an answer one way or the other. I was not into playing games. It was all or nothing for me. I had no shortage of offers to go out and managed to camouflage the vulnerability I felt deep in my soul, masking the emptiness of missing Luc. The masquerade was difficult to keep up, especially since he would still call me at work and turn up in the afternoons to drive me home, as if I had not given him the ultimatum.

The first time I saw his car in the parking lot, several weeks after I told him goodbye, my heart skipped a beat. I expected him to tell me he wanted us to be a real couple. He greeted me with a kiss, as he usually did. As he opened the car door for me he said he had missed me. Our last conversation was not even mentioned. I didn't want to be the one to bring it up and so nothing was resolved.

Luc was usually alone, but sometimes Les Carter, a work colleague, would be with him. I didn't like Les. He hardly said a word to me other than hello. I felt he intruded on my time with Luc. There was something odd about him that made me feel uncomfortable. I was not sure whether or not I had imagined that he watched me more closely than he should have.

I also found Luc puzzling. I didn't know why he bothered to drive me home several afternoons a week. His actions gave me every reason to believe that he cared more for me than he was willing to admit. But he said nothing that would confirm our relationship.

It was almost December of 1965, and nothing had changed between Luc and me. I invited him to the office Christmas party but he wasn't able to go. I was disappointed and decided not to go either, then changed my mind, only because my mother had gone to so much trouble to make me a dress.

It was a pale pink linen dress. It hugged my slim body, but its revealing neckline made me feel uncomfortable. I asked Mom to make a three-quarter Chantilly lace jacket in a deeper shade of the dress, to cover a revealing neckline. I bought matching pink pigskin shoes and a pink Italian straw handbag. My shoulder length blonde hair was styled in to barrel curls and piled on top of my head and my fringe fell in wisps around my forehead.

For the first and only time in my life, Dad looked at me in utter amazement and said, "You're a beauty mate." Mom showed her approval with a smile, but I felt she was admiring the outfit she had made, rather than me.

I didn't tell my parents that I was going to the party alone. As soon as everyone went into the lounge room to watch television, I slipped out the back door and got into the cab I had ordered earlier.

By the time I arrived at the party, the room was already full of the familiar faces I saw week after week at the office. Everyone was much more relaxed with a drink in their hand, away from the drudgery of work. To begin with I felt shy being on my own but I wasn't alone for long. Several bachelors were at the party, and I felt more relaxed after a glass of wine.

Jack Weston, one of the company's salesmen, paid particular attention to me that night. He was tall and distinguished looking. In retrospect, it didn't seem unusual. On several occasions he had asked me out and was always flirting with me and the other girls in the office. Although he was arrogant and a bit of a show off, because he was attractive most of the girls fell over each other to do typing for him. He seemed harmless and I did not take his advances seriously.

As the evening came to a close, Jack gently pulled me aside and asked how I was getting home.

"By cab," I said

"Don't bother calling one. I'll drive you home," he said self-assured, in his strong English accent.

Jack's car was parked under a streetlight. Just before he unlocked the door, he turned around, and without any warning he scooped up me into his arms and kissed me passionately, in full view of everyone. Utterly embarrassed, I wriggled free, mindful not to cause a scene or draw any more unwanted attention to us. I hung my head, wishing I could disappear. Office gossip runs rampant the moment anything looks compromising and I felt certain that the people who saw Jack kissing me would make it a 'Monday morning office scandal'.

After releasing me Jack promptly apologised. I said that I should get a cab but when he promised to drive me straight home I accepted his offer because I had no reason to doubt that he would. The alcohol I had consumed that evening, in addition to the late hour, made me sleepy. In the comfort of the car seat, I laid my head back on the head rest and dozed off into a twilight sleep, while fighting the urge to fall into a deep sleep.

The car engine sounded far away. I was aware of it moving and when the vehicle had stopped, I imagined that I was home. My body felt like lead. I tried to wake up, but relaxed into Jack's arms when he lifted me from the car.

The tugging of my clothing sent a sobering shock wave through me, as I struggled under his body weight.

"Please Jack, no. I've never…" I repeatedly begged him to let me go, afraid to scream.

Jack cut me off with a mocking laugh. I kept turning my head furiously from side to side, pleading with him to let me go and screaming silently inside. I had no idea where I was but guessed he had made a detour to his flat and I was in his bedroom. I fought desperately to break free, but I was no match against his athletic physique. Still I persistently fought and pleaded with him.

The stabbing pain deep inside me confirmed the nightmare. I felt a deep shame and cried bitter tears for trusting Jack. My first time was meant to be special and I wanted my first time to be with Luc. I wanted to be Luc's wife. But now I was just another notch on Jack's bed.

"Damn you, Jack!" I screamed at him, "Damn you to hell! You…you bastard!"

Jack's selfish, barbaric act of stealing a moment's pleasure for himself had changed me. I hated him. If I had had a gun I would have shot him dead. My spirit felt lifeless. I was dirty and undignified, the common trollop my mother had called me.

A panic fear of disgrace, shame and humiliation kept me silent, just as I had kept silent about my grandfather touching me. I didn't want anyone to know. I had no time for self-pity or for any more tears; nothing would ever change what had happened. I was hard of heart and angry, and so distraught that I couldn't remember how I got home.

On Monday morning I went to work and acted as if nothing had happened. I was not about to give the office girls the satisfaction of knowing anything about me that would send a shiver of glee through their poisonous, petty minds.

To rub salt into my wounds, Jack bounced into my office, head held high and grinning from ear to ear. He announced that what happened that night was my fault for being so gorgeous and sexy. I was screaming, 'Get away from me you bastard!' in my mind while containing the goliath within me from scratching out his eyes. I carried on working stony face, as if he wasn't there. I could not look at him but wished him dead.

It was torture to crack the surface to smile, but I had to pretend that everything was normal. I trusted no one. For the very first time in my life, I fully understood what hate was, as the cancerous seed subtly ate at my soul. Everything had overwhelmed me, the rape, my mother's 'poor me' attitude and the constant turmoil at home. I longed to get away.

After another clash with my mother I found an ad in the local paper, an affordable room to rent in the home of an elderly brother and sister. It was modest, containing only a bed and wardrobe, perfect for me.

The day I left, my mother was whining as usual and anger churned deep within me. The words "Shut up!" erupted from me. The nightmare of living in hell was too much. I threw everything I owned into a sea trunk, called a taxi, and left with her scathing words echoing behind me.

4

Independence and solitude were so very precious to me. I valued peace and quiet as if they had a life-giving source all of their own, and treasured the seclusion I had fought so hard to gain. Solitude taught me that I didn't need people to make me happy. All I needed and desired was peaceful surroundings. I had hoped that it would give me an inner harmony that would help erase my past and enable me to get on with my life, but the nightmare kept resurfacing.

Alone in my room, I allowed myself to think about the office Christmas party for the first time since it had happened. I searched my mind for evidence that I had somehow invited Jack's unwanted attention. Was my smile more than friendly? Did my eyes linger too long on his? These were only some of the many questions I repeatedly ran over and over in my mind. Exhausted, I buried my head in my hands and surrendered to uncontrollable emotion, and let unfathomable tears flow, washing away the emotional pain I had so neatly contained.

A harsh reality of that night was a possible pregnancy. My concern was so great that I confided in Peter. He thought if I was pregnant the baby would be Luc's, and I didn't correct him. But shortly afterwards, it was apparent that I wasn't pregnant. The relief of the discovery washed over me like a wave in heavy seas. The dread I felt was nothing more than fear of an undesirable outcome of a horrible event. I wept an ocean of tears in relief then, pretending that everything was all right, simply got on with living my life.

Several months passed and I found living away from home a lot easier than I had first imagined. Apart from feeling mentally exhausted at times, I was fine. I had convinced myself that I was still recovering from my illness and it would take time to fully recover.

To remedy the exhaustion, a friend gave me a bottle of pills, which I naively assumed were vitamins. After taking one my energy shot up and I soared through the day. One of the side effects of the pills was a rapid decline in my appetite, but as food had never been a main focus of mine at best, I wasn't concerned that I hardly ate anything. I had already made a conscious decision to never be overweight, ever again. Another side effect was that I was rendered useless after the effect of the pills had worn off. I had to keep increasing the number I took for them to be effective.

I went through a period of partying with friends all weekend and arriving at work on Monday mornings without having had any sleep. The madness of my reckless lifestyle continued for six months, until I eventually felt persistently ill. It was during that time that I started having a dream; one, which recurred night after night but by morning, had dissolved into vague remnants and had totally faded by daylight.

Then one night, it all became very clear. I woke up to the sound of whispering. I heard, 'You must go home. You must go home'. I was more curious than afraid. The room was filled with a hazy light. While still groggy with sleep, I craned my neck and looked out of the window, thinking the light was coming from the street. It wasn't.

'That's strange,' I thought, shrugging nonchalantly, then fell into a peaceful sleep.

In the morning, without hesitation, I called Peter and asked him to come and pick me up. "I'm coming home," I said.

I had no qualms at all about returning. I certainly didn't feel the least bit concerned that I hadn't spoken to my parents in many months. I just knew that it would be all right. When I returned home nothing much was said and I didn't unpack my bag. I have no idea why I didn't, but the fact that I hadn't irritated my mother. Within a space of a few days I was admitted into hospital, the isolation ward, suffering from glandular fever.

The day I was admitted into hospital, the attending doctor, while compiling my medical history, asked if I was taking any medication.

"Yes," I said and rummaged through my bag and found my bottle of tiny white pills and handed them to him. "These."

He looked at them, raised his eyebrows, and asked, "Do you know what these are?"

"Vitamins, I think. A friend gave them to me because I didn't have any energy."

I had no idea I was taking 'pep pills,' commonly known as speed, until the doctor told me what they were and the dangers in taking them. As it turned out, my illness was a blessing. The nine weeks I spent in hospital were enough for me to recuperate from the effects of the pills, which I never took again.

While in hospital, some of my friends made a surprise visit to celebrate my seventeenth birthday. It was the first birthday party that I'd ever had. I was in isolation ward, and visitors were given hospital gowns to wear. It was also a rule that infectious patients were allowed only one visitor at a time. That evening, eight of my friends crammed themselves into my tiny hospital cubicle, with only enough room to stand.

Luc and his work mate Les Carter took a stroll around the ward, bidding patients a good evening and asking them how they were feeling. We couldn't contain our laughter when we heard other patients discussing their illness with them. Wearing hospital gowns over their suits, Luc and Les were easily mistaken for doctors. The commotion we made had the head nurse frequently running to my doorway, insisting the noise be kept down. "Otherwise," she said with authority in her voice, "all of you will have to leave. As it is, I'm already breaking the rules allowing so many visitors in at one time. So please," she said, raising her eyebrows before she left, "indulge me."

Once the nurse had vanished from sight, we looked at each other and giggled like naughty children whispering, "Oooooaha!"

"Hope I don't get the blunt needle tonight as punishment," I mocked and everyone roared with laughter and then stopped suddenly, in mock fear of the nurse.

After Luc and Les returned from their walkabout, Luc and another mate decided to lay either side of me and the portable television sitting on the trolley at the end of my bed. They pulled the TV closer but neither of them would agree on a program, and consequently switched from channel to channel. As they wrestled each other for the television, the others cheered them on and the noise carried on down the hall again.

Everyone went suddenly quiet when they noticed my family standing in the doorway, stunned to a standstill by the scene in my cubicle. My bed was in total disarray, gifts and wrapping paper strewn all over it. Luc and his mate did not move. They both smiled and said, "G'day." I'll never forget the critical eye my mother scanned over the scene. I enjoyed every minute of it, especially her surprise.

I felt a loneliness creep over me with the departure of my friends, but quickly cheered up, thinking about how wonderful the evening had been and how it would become a treasured memory to indulge in as a pick-me-up whenever I felt low.

Shortly after I was discharged from hospital I had a visitor; three earlier times he had called and each time I was sleeping. The mystery visitor turned out to be Les Carter. I was surprised to see him and thought he would have been the last person to visit me. I had secretly thought he might be gay because I had never seen him with a girl, nor had he ever mentioned one.

When I answered the door, Les fidgeted and coughed, appearing very nervous. His features seemed sullen and his eyes darted about as if looking for something. I didn't find him attractive at all. He was tall and heavy-set, and his closely-cropped hair made his large ears look even larger. The suit he wore drooped on him due to bad posture. He usually lingered in the background and often seemed invisible. At times he had tried to simulate Luc's charismatic charm but failed miserably. What struck me most about him was that he rarely smiled. He seemed an introvert among extroverts.

"Oh, it's you," I said, trying not to sound disappointed.

I did not invite him inside. Instead, we sat in his car for a while and spoke about things in general. He reeked of aftershave and seemed awkward and shy and certainly friendlier than he had ever been. The contrast in him was amazing.

"Would you like to go to the drive-in tonight?" he blurted out, as I was about to leave

"Oh, I don't know," I half-heartedly shrugged, puzzled by his visit. "Call me later tonight if you like." He did and for some reason I agreed to go.

A Patch of Blue was showing at the local drive-in that evening. During the movie Les said he was surprised I had come, "I thought you were Luc's lady."

"We've broken up," I reply staring down at my hands.

When we arrived home, he thanked me for going out with him and asked if he could call me again.

"Yes, that would be nice." I smiled politely thinking, 'I wonder what Luc will think when he finds out that I've been out with Les.'

Les wanted me to keep our friendship a secret and asked me not to tell anyone. But I was not about to keep this secret. I wanted Luc to know. As soon as he found out, he came to my house and cautioned me about Les.

"You know what to do to change that, Luc," I said with hope in my heart. "My feelings are still the same. They always will be."

He didn't say anything. He only reached out and drew me closer to him and held me tight.

'Why?' I wondered wanting to scream. 'Why won't he tell me how he really feels?'

I continued to see Les and made no secret of the fact that I loved Luc. Les gave no indication that my feelings for Luc bothered him.

My short stint at home had become unbearable and having Les' support seemed a blessing at the time. He made it obvious that he cared a great deal for me but I had conflicting feelings about him. Some days I was fonder of him than other days. Without knowing why, I felt an overwhelming sense of pity for him. Every time we were together, he told how much he needed me. My life was going nowhere and my spirit felt only half-alive and so I allowed our relationship to become more intimate and quickly regretted it.

A rueful smile touched the corners of my mouth, recalling the tail end of a conversation I had overheard in the lunchroom at the office.

"Once you open your legs," the girl complained, "they never leave you alone. I don't know," she sighed, "for a lot of huffing and puffing, it's all over in a matter of seconds. He gets his jollies and all I get is my hair and make-up messed up. And another thing..." She was about to say, but went silent when I walked in.

The girl was exactly the kind of girl my mother would have immediately tagged as 'common'. Regardless, what she had said that day was relevant to my current situation, which I thought was ironic.

When Les took me home to meet his family, I was astounded at the change in his behaviour around his mother. It was remarkable enough for me to feel concerned. I looked on in amazement as he turned from a mature man to a submissive child-like oaf. When Maude came towards him, he stooped. His jaw and arms hung limp. He dropped his head and waited for her to give him a reassuring pat as she passed by. His strange behaviour and his mother's controlling influence over him disturbed me. I wanted to end our relationship. Many times I started to tell him how I felt, but before I could, he would tell me how much he loved me. I didn't have the heart to say anything.

Dread hit me with a wallop when I discovered I was pregnant. Panic stricken and shrouded in confusion I thought, 'What am I going to do now? I don't want to marry Les. Oh God, I don't want to.'

I was totally desperate. I cut my long hair very short because I knew Les wouldn't like it. He loathed short hair. I knew an argument would give me the opportunity to end the relationship.

Just as I had hoped, he was very angry. We fought and broke up. I was relieved to see Les storm out of the house, but after he had left my momentary relief turned to despair with the concern of facing the pregnancy alone. I wiped tears from my eyes as I walked aimlessly around my parents' lounge room. The shame of being unmarried and pregnant at nineteen had overwhelmed me. In my head, I could hear my mother screaming awful names at me for my greatest sin. I felt I had no other alternative but to put an end to everything.

No one was home that day. I found sleeping tablets amongst the smorgasbord of pills my parents kept in their cupboard.

'Perhaps now I will find peace,' I wistfully hoped, swallowing a handful of pills before I made myself comfortable on the lounge and let the tension of my life leave me as I surrendered to the medication.

Bright lights overhead, loud voices and someone pulling and prodding me brought me back to consciousness. A tube was being dragged from my throat. I was in hospital.

When I was fully conscious, Les came rushing into the room. His face was wet and contorted.

"I didn't know what to do, Bubby," he whimpered. "I came back to try to patch things up and found you."

I was silent, trying to focus.

"I was so scared," he continued dribbling on. "I took you home and Mom...she, she tried to revive you. She told me to bring you here."

As he was talking my mind recalled foggy images that seemed part of a nightmare, but I later realised that Maude's distorted image and voice were real. Although I didn't show it, I bitterly resented Les for coming back and taking me to hospital. I was trying to get away from him. I wanted to escape the pregnancy but mostly I wanted to escape my life and he had stopped me from doing that. Now I was trapped.

The doctor came into the emergency room preventing Les from breaking down completely. He ignored Les and spoke to me. "Taking an overdose is very serious, Emma. Do you understand that? I really should report this to the authorities, but I won't if you promise to get help."

I timidly nodded and promised to get help and then thanked him. He released me into Les' care.

My stomach churned with the horrible tasting liquid floating around in my gut and at the thought of returning to the Carters' home and having to face them, but I had no other option. Maude was kind enough, but I felt from her critical glances that she considered me unstable.

I neglected to do anything about getting counselling. I believed I could handle my problems myself, feeling that too many people already knew more about me that I had wanted anyone to know. No one in my family ever found out what I had almost succeeded to do that day but later on, because I had no other option, I told my father about the baby. He was speechless but supportive, and even took me to his doctor.

My mother was not as obliging. The icy stare she gave me and the way her lips were drawn in a thin line echoed her thoughts. I felt her anger hit me like piercing darts. She couldn't have hurt me more even if she had physically slapped me.

The evening my father and I were in the lounge room discussing the situation. I told him I didn't want to get married and my mother overheard him say, "You don't have to marry him mate, if you don't want to. We can work something out."

She rushed into the lounge room, glared at my father and, pointing at me, said in a menacing tone, "She got pregnant! Now, she can get married. What will the neighbours think...?"

This time I felt that I didn't have the right to defend myself against my mother's insensitivity. She was right. But I despised her for failing to provide any of us with a safe loving home. I had despised her for so many reasons. I was disappointed also in my father for being weak – he didn't fight for me as hard as he could have.

So often I was told that my mother was beautiful and stylish but I failed to see that. I saw her only as a hard, spiteful woman, especially after she had repeatedly called me a 'trollop' and accused me of having sex with Matt when I hadn't. Listening to her shout all those awful accusations at me was disturbing enough that I thought marriage to Les may not be so bad. Perhaps, I thought in earnest, he would love me and want to take care of me. I knew Luc didn't.

I had not mentioned the pregnancy to Les prior to telling my father. I worried what his response would be. Times have since changed, but as an unmarried mother in the sixties, I would have been a social outcast and brought shame and embarrassment to my family. All I had at that time was some small savings in the bank, a job and a medical benefit membership. Those few things would have quickly disappeared once it was known that I was pregnant and unmarried. No decent man would have anything to do with me so I felt coerced into marrying the father of my unborn child.

The news of the baby shocked Les. Initially, he thought I had been with Luc. His reaction horrified me. I began to weep.

"What do you think I am?" I responded angrily. "This baby is yours," wishing it wasn't.

He apologised and told me that he didn't think he was capable of making a baby.

Both families met and neither liked the other. 'Good start,' I thought wondering which way to turn.

My mother held the opinion that I was marrying 'beneath me.' Although my father disliked Les and his family, he was relieved that I was at the very least marrying a Catholic. Poor Dad, he had this thing about his children associating only with Catholics. They could be bastards too, did he not know that? To avoid getting a lecture from him, I told my non-Catholic friends that if they ever met my father they were to say they were Catholic. He usually inquired by asking them which church they went to. Les, as it happened, was the only Catholic I had ever been out with.

5

News of my impending marriage reached Luc. I was caught off guard when I answered the door and found him standing on the front veranda.

"Can we talk?" he asked the moment he saw me.

"What about?"

"Not here, in the car."

We walked to his car in silence. Luc opened the passenger door for me as he usually did, and waited until I had settled in before closing it. He hurried to the driver's side and slid in beside me.

"I hear you're getting married." It was more of a statement than a question.

"Yes," I said I shrugged and waited for his reaction.

"Why?"

"Well Luc," I said half-heartedly looking at my hands, "you don't want me and it is hell living here. And…"

"I do," he whispered interrupting me.

"What? What did you say?" I looked at him in wide-eyed disbelief.

"I do want you."

At any other time I would have been overjoyed to hear Luc tell me he loved me. I ached for him to tell me, but that night he brought me to the brink of tears for not saying something sooner. I couldn't be with him – I couldn't marry him in pregnant to another man. Abortion was not an option. I wanted to scream at him for the profound loss I felt deep in my soul. There was so much I had wanted to say, but instead I said, defeated, "It's too late. I'll always love you Luc, you know that, but it's too late."

"Yes, and I love you," he said for the first time.

Although he didn't say so, I felt he knew I was pregnant. I had wished with all my heart that the baby was his. Since there was nothing left to say, we sat huddled together holding hands as we listened to the radio. The time we had together that night seemed like a few seconds in comparison to the rest of my life. Leaving Luc was so difficult; it was one of the hardest things I have ever had to do.

The wedding took place at the same church where I had attended primary school. Visiting the church to make arrangements for the ceremony with the priest reminded me of the incident with my sixth class teacher. I wondered where the nun was and if she had ever repeated history. That memory seemed a lifetime ago. Although I was only a teenager about to marry a man I barely liked, and have his baby, I felt so old and stifled. Time did not allow me to dwell on the past. The future awaited me.

Prior to the wedding, Les and I went looking for a flat and found a perfect place at Punchbowl, a short distance from the Carter's house. It was fully furnished, clean and close to public transport. We only had to secure it with a bond and the place was ours, but a few days before we were to sign the lease Les senior took me aside. He told me that Maude and he thought we should not take the flat.

"What!" I barked, looking up at the grey haired man, searching his face for humour and thinking that he was joking, "Why not?"

"Well," the old man began sucking in air as he always did before he spoke. "Les needs his family around him. He won't have anyone to talk to and besides that, he can't afford to pay out that much money each week."

Butting in, I sarcastically replied, "He'll have to talk to me then, won't he? And I'm sure we'll manage to pay the rent."

Maude was behind this, I was sure of it. Many people had underestimated Maude's iron will. She would stop at nothing to get her own way, even going as far as manipulating her family to make it happen. I knew the short, rotund woman with steel grey hair had little regard for me. She was convinced the baby I was carrying belonged to Luc and resented me trapping her son into marriage, but skilfully disguised her contempt when others were present. I didn't miss her chilly glances when I caught her looking at me.

Maude undermined our effort to obtain the flat and in his weakness Les sided with her. Instead of taking the flat, she insisted that we stay in her son's bedroom and pay eight pounds a week for board, the same amount we would have paid for the flat.

The old fellow's manner towards me was contrary to his wife's. Even in his grumpiest moment he'd always muster up a warm smile for me. At times, he would seek my company. We would sit and talk small talk. During one of those occasions he shook his head and asked, "How is it that my eldest son managed to find a girl as pretty as you, Emma? He's nothing special. I don't know what you see in him."

It was obvious Les wasn't his father's favourite and although he was not mine either, I disliked hearing his father say awful things about his son. I felt that if my future father-in-law thought me less attractive, he would not have given me the time of day, and that irritated me.

My parents were annoyed with the Carters, to say the least, for their interference over the issue with the flat. My mother was so angry that she prowled through the house like a caged lioness and eventually it became too much for her to contain her fury. She succumbed to the temptation of calling Les and giving him a piece of her mind. Maude overheard the conversation between them, snatched the phone out of Les' hand and had her bit to say also. Maude involved the whole family. That's the way it was with the Carters and the situation quickly became the Carters versus the O'Farrell's.

The situation became so bad that I was unsure if there was going to be a wedding. My mother was livid and wanted nothing to do with any of them. That was okay with me, neither did I.

As the war between the families escalated, several details of the wedding were overlooked. There were no flowers or music, but I really didn't care. I had already called my friends and told them not to come to the ceremony. I felt too ashamed to face them.

The drive to the church took only a few minutes. I wished it was longer, much longer. Fear of the unknown made me feel sick to my stomach and the urge to cry, "Please don't make me marry him!" became stronger. Defeated and on the brink of tears again I thought, 'What's the use anyway, I don't have anywhere else to go, and I have a baby to think about now.' Thinking about the baby gave me a moment's hope and enforced my belief that perhaps everything might turn out alright in the long run. A fierce determination urged me to believe the marriage would work, for the baby's sake if nothing else.

Familiar cars parked outside the church had me gasping. I could hardly breathe. I fought the urge to weep uncontrollably. My friends had come, even after I had asked them not to. They always seemed to be there when I needed them most.

The occasion didn't feel like a wedding, especially not mine. My heart was torn to shreds. The man I wanted to marry was one of my guests. He should have been waiting at the altar for me, not Les Carter.

Walking down that aisle without music, with my father limping beside me and with all those eyes upon me, highlighted my shame and my desire to run away and hide. Thankfully the knee length white linen dress and matching three-quarter sleeve lace jacket were lovely, and a multi-coloured pink floral hat substituted for the traditional veil. I could never fault my mother's impeccable and expensive taste.

Les and the best man were waiting at the altar. Les looked awful, his face ashen. Not only was he recovering from the bucks' night, it was obvious that he was just as scared as I was. With trembling hands he took my hand in his and we exchanged our vows.

'Well,' I thought half-heartedly, hardly believing what had just taken place, 'this is it. I am married, Mrs Les Carter; certainly not the way a young girl dreams about, but married all the same.'

A few weeks before the ceremony I had mentioned to Les that I wanted to keep my own name instead of taking his. The request was met with so much opposition that I gave up the idea and felt I had traded my identity for his. My name was all that I had that belonged to me. Losing my identity left me feeling that I had nothing that I could call my own. The sense of loss was highlighted by the fact that I didn't love him. I simply didn't want to belong to Les Carter as the marriage laws declared that I did. If I had married either Luc or Matt the subject would never have been mentioned.

After the ceremony everyone gathered outside the church, taking photos and acting as though it was a happy occasion. Oddly enough, not one single photograph taken that day turned out.

When I saw Luc standing with the other guests, I wistfully gazed at him, imagining I had married him. 'No!' I shook myself sensible. 'I have a baby to concentrate on.'

When I heard someone call out, "Come on everyone," my attention was suddenly jerked back to the present. I turned to see who was gathering everyone together and overheard both Luc and his mate, Leo Paddington, telling guests where the reception was.

Puzzled at what was going on, I asked Leo, "What reception?"

"It's all fixed love," he smiled mischievously. "Come on, we're all going to the Trotting Club."

I never found out who actually organised the reception, whether it was Luc or Leo or both of them. Nevertheless, I was astounded at their infinite kindness. None of our parents joined the party and the evening turned out to be enjoyable for everyone. Some of the guests even had a lucky strike with the poker machines after Les and I had left.

Les had booked a room overnight at a motel. The whole affair seemed less like my wedding night and more like a bad dream. Les was very sweet and tried to be romantic, which was just bearable. I grabbed my pillow as a sign of saying good night but later I woke up and found my new husband lying beside me, sobbing like a child into his pillow.

"What's wrong?" I asked, puzzled and concerned.

"Bubby," Les said tugging on my nightie, pulling me closer to him.

"Please never leave me," he sobbed. "You can have any man you want but please never leave me."

I was utterly flabbergasted but didn't show it. I cradled Les' head and promised never to leave him, unaware of what lay ahead of me. Seeing Les like that left me dispirited. I had thought he was going to look after me, but I knew that I would have to look after him instead. He had given up before we had even begun our life together. The sight of a large man, seven years my senior, with a wet and swollen face disgusted me. Les and I arrived home Monday afternoon, after a brief weekend honeymoon. As we turned into the driveway, I looked at the house that was now my home and thought that it had definitely seen better days. The paint was cracked and peeling, doors squeaked and rugs hid damaged floorboards. It was hot in summer and cold and draughty in the winter. The thing I liked most about the place was the doorhandles. They were low and easy to reach. I wished my parents' home had

had them. I had spent most of my childhood standing on tiptoes or climbing on chairs trying to reach doorknobs.

Les and I soon settled into a semblance of orderly daily routine. I stayed at home while he continued his career as a repossession agent, which I loathed. He had insisted that I quit my office job before we were married, stating emphatically that he did not want his wife working and only he would support his family. Even he had agreed to my working, I would have lost my job anyway, because I was pregnant.

I was uncomfortable with my husband repossessing other people's property under the threat of their hardship. I discovered Les' passion was diesel engines but it took some convincing on my part to get him to apply for a Diesel Mechanic's position.

Les confessed to me in the privacy of our bedroom, furnished with our only possessions, that he hadn't finished his apprenticeship. He said he had specifically gone to a sheep station north-west of Sydney, to do his motor mechanic apprenticeship but had to leave before he'd finished. He wouldn't say why he left, just that he was afraid to apply for any motor mechanic's position because he didn't have his papers. I asked him why he didn't finish. He just shrugged and said in a strange voice, "I had to leave."

I was sitting on the edge of the bed, watching him silently comb his wet hair flat on his head, mulling over what he had told me. I studied him and thought his hair style emphasised his large ears and nose. With a burst of enthusiasm, I said, "Don't let that stop you, Les, just bluff your way in." I knew he was pretending not to listen as I continued. "Say you've lost your papers... Once you've got the job, your boss will discover you're a good mechanic and you won't need them."

I waited for him to say something and when he didn't I added,

"Well at least try."

I rolled over on the bed, propped myself up on the pillows and gave him a questioning looked. I really didn't understand him at all. I knew I would not have suffered a job that I disliked, especially since there were so many positions to choose from.

Les' need for continued encouragement and reassurance was physically draining. I was grateful that he did at times listen to me, and eventually applied for the job that steered him in the direction of his future career.

6

Les and his family were virtual strangers to me. But they soon showed me what kind of people they really were. It came as a huge surprise to discover the car Les always drove belonged to his father and not to him, as he had led me to believe. The day I overheard Les asking his father permission to use the vehicle, I naturally asked why he was asking to use his own car. My inquiry was met with disdain and no response. Later on, Les' eldest sister, Bell, told me the car was none of my business. I reminded Bell that since I was her brother's wife, everything to do with my husband was indeed my business. The Carters hadn't counted on me being so forthright, which caused them to dislike me more than they already did.

I felt terribly isolated living in a house full of strangers. I saw no one else during the day other than them. Although they included me in everything they did, I still felt like an outsider. Perhaps I may have felt more comfortable if Maude had been less manipulating and controlling. My mother-in-law monitored my every move, making the house feel more like a prison than a home.

A few weeks reprieve from Maude came when she went away with Bell and her family, but not before she informed me that I would be taking care of my father-in-law and her youngest son Max as well as Les. I didn't mind at all. I actually welcomed the chance to put a few things in the house in order. My mother-in-law was not the best housekeeper.

During the first week I cleared away a stack of ironing that had been a permanent fixture, overflowing from an old armchair and cluttering a corner of the enclosed back veranda that served as the dining room. My industriousness had won me greater favour with my father-in-law but displeased Maude, especially since her flamboyant sister-in-law loudly praised me for my housekeeping skills. "Darling," she said, "you should have come sooner, it's been years since I have seen that corner." Then, turning to Maude who had just arrived home from her holiday that day, she continued, "You must enjoy having an extra pair of helpful hands, Maudie," forcing my mother-in-law to acknowledge me as an asset.

I didn't miss Maude's icy smirk when she said in her whiny sing-song tone, "Oh yes, the house looks so nice. Thanks love."

I knew that tone of hers so well. I also knew that I would be in trouble when my father-in-law told his wife that I was also a great cook. "The steak melted in my mouth when she cooked it, Mama," the old man said winking at me. Maude didn't say a word, but gave him a frosty look that he didn't appear to notice.

To keep from going insane, I kept a diary. When things became too much, it became my confidant and I poured all my pent up irritations into it. In secrecy I frantically penned my wild, angry thoughts and misery onto the pages. The diary was kept hidden and I never disclosed its existence to anyone. I was afraid that I would get more than I bargained for if it were ever discovered. I was certain that if the Carters read it, they would try to have me committed to a mental institution.

I knew my mother's anger and when I saw it coming I would duck for cover, but the Carters were different. I had never encountered people like them before. They acted warm and friendly towards people they called friends and behind their backs they said horrible things about them. "What will I put in the old hag's tea," Marla mocked about an old family friend, "Ground glass or arsenic?"

"But I thought all of you liked her," I said, looking utterly puzzled by Marla's bizarre behaviour.

"Nup, not really," Marla shrugged as she poured tea into the cups.

I called a spade a spade just as my parents did. The Carters played mind games with each other and with me, which unnerved me. I saw them as deceitful people, and made a special effort to observe all of them, endeavouring to work them out.

I found the family antics amusing at times. They could have been mistaken as being comical if the situation hadn't been serious, especially since most of them were puffed up with self-importance and thought they were above everything, even the law.

Les had two sisters and two brothers. Bell was the eldest, Marla, Paul and then Max, my favourite. Les was the second eldest. Everyone, with the exception of me, was wary of Bell. I found her bossy and calculating but never fearsome. She was good to her family in a controlling way. In the few years I knew her, I felt sure the short, stout, raven-haired woman, who constantly fought off kilograms, would have been a nice person if she had not taken herself so seriously.

I smile whenever I remember Bell's nasal, whining voice distinctly saying 'you know' after every sentence in her effort to sound posh. Then there was the manner in which she strutted into the room wearing the latest designer outfit, which usually cost a small fortune, attracting my attention. I looked at her, amused and wondering whether or not I should stand and salute. In a way, I actually felt sorry for Bell. She was attractive, but in a matronly way. Her smile was stiff and awkward and looked more like a sneer. She was arrogant and thought she knew everything. She raised her toddler son Ben under the strict guidance of 'Dr Spock' the renowned child expert of the sixties. Ben was totally uncontrollable. The whole family shuddered every time Bell visited and brought him with her. He was a nightmare to have around, throwing tantrums every time he couldn't get his way. But miraculously, Ben grew up to be a good man like his father.

Bell's husband, Will Brown, was the exact opposite. He was a genuine, gentle man with a heart of gold and kind eyes. Will was nobody's fool, which was evident from the fact that his astute business dealings had made him a wealthy man. He always seemed to be having fun no matter what he did. His ever-present easy smile said, 'Welcome to my world'. I liked and admired Will for the compassionate person he was.

Marla, the second sister and third sibling, left people with the impression that she was a little off-beat which wasn't altogether true. In my opinion, the tall, heavy-set, attractive woman was vivacious and very competent, but she had a profound sadness about her. I felt that Marla secretly laughed at those who believed she was off-beat. Although we were never close, we did initially like each other and got along well at family gatherings.

Paul bore a strong resemblance to his father, not only in looks but in attitude. His arrogance at times annoyed me. At least the years had mellowed his father. Paul was tall and slim, with red hair and striking blue eyes. He was more attractive than Les but just as volatile.

Drinking was Paul's favourite pastime. One evening Les and I attended an engagement party where I saw firsthand how intoxicated Paul often became. Seconds after Les had left my side to get a drink, Paul staggered over to where I was talking to friends. He stood a few paces away, swaying back and forth staring at me. Then for no apparent reason he slurred, "I can take you away from my brother any time I like."

A sarcastic smirk replaced his normally warm, friendly smile as he rocked back and forth like a puppet on a string, clutching a beer bottle in one hand and a cigarette in the other. I looked over at him, smiled sweetly and said, "Paul, I wouldn't go anywhere with you if you were the only man on earth," then turned and walked away, dismissing him. Judging by his condition, I assumed he wouldn't remember what he had said the next day. I was astounded by his behaviour because previously he had been nothing but charming and polite towards me. Fortunately he never acted that way ever again.

Max was the youngest of the five siblings and everyone's favourite. At fifteen he was gangly and painfully shy. We hit it off from our first meeting. Max playfully teased me about being a shortie when he realised that he was an inch taller than me, which automatically eliminated him from being the shortest in the family. We quickly became great mates. The weekends I visited before I married Les, he told me that I could sleep in the spare bed in his room, instead of the couch, breaking his rule that girls weren't allowed to even enter his room. He also gave me one of his shirts and a pair of shorts the weekend I got a drenching from a backyard water fight, of which, I became involved by accident. Max was a refreshing contrast to the rest of his family but sadly, time allowed the Carters to mould their youngest into their own image. Some years later, Max married a woman who was a carbon copy of his mother but a tad more evil.

On the surface Maude appeared sickly sweet and friendly, but I knew differently. My survival instincts taught me to quietly observe my mother-in-law as she systematically controlled and manipulated her family like pawns on a chess board.

Maude resented me doing anything for Les. When I rose early to prepare his breakfast and pack him a lunch for work, she usually found something to subtly criticise me for as I moved around the tiny out-dated kitchen.

"Oh Les won't eat that or he doesn't like this..." I would hear from over my shoulder. But I carried on with what I was doing at the time, feverishly gripping the butter knife I had in my hand and trying very hard to remain calm. I knew that if I exploded I wouldn't stop so I said nothing.

When Les came into the kitchen for breakfast on the morning he started his new job, Maude pushed past me.

"What would my pussy cat like for breakfast?" she asked, knowing full well that I had already prepared it.

"I have already made it!" I declared.

Maude turned and looked at me in pretend surprise and said sweetly, "Oh have you love? I didn't know."

A silent battle of wills began between us. "He's my husband and she'd better get used to it. I'll do things my way," I muttered under my breath, wishing that I had the courage to say it directly to her face.

Every night I dreamt of getting away from them and living as normal married couples should, but my husband's self-esteem was so low that he feared making any decisions on his own. I loathed the place and wanted a home or a shack, even a tent, just as long as I could call it my own.

On a few occasions, when the house was still and everyone was asleep, I left my bed and went outside. Wrapped in a dressing gown, I sat on the back step looking at the cluttered back yard, or gazed up at the stars as I walked aimlessly around in circles searching for some insight to our future. In the chilly night I had the freedom to release my tears, but even that was interrupted one night when Maude, on her way to the toilet, found me weeping. Annoyed and curious that I was there, she demanded to know why I was still up at that late hour. I told her I was upset because Les was ignoring me. "Never mind," she laughed sarcastically, "in a short time you will be thinking up excuses to ignore him."

At first I was puzzled by the comment, and then felt a burning embarrassment, when it dawned on me what she was referring to. 'How dare you,' I wanted to scream at her, 'Sex with Les is the last thing on my mind. If you only knew, you stupid old cow, I need to talk to my husband and plan a future for our baby, and to get away from you!'

Every time I mentioned to Les that I wanted a place of our own, he pretended not to hear. The longer I lived under his family's roof, the less I liked them. My beliefs were in opposition to theirs and I was unaccustomed to the high volume of prejudices and hatred directed towards law enforcement and minority groups. One scene I witnessed displayed just how low the family would sink to cover for one of its members.

Paul came home late one Saturday evening in a panic, waking the household by banging on the front door. He was heavily intoxicated and incoherent. The family first thought someone was out to attack him. He was shaking uncontrollably, but once he had calmed down enough, I overheard him tell his parents and Les that he had been in a hit and run and had fled the scene because he was so drunk.

The police had chased him home and were banging on the door as Paul was speaking. Les and his father answered the door. Les senior brazenly told the police Paul was asleep and had been there all night. Les confirmed his father's lie. What I found most amazing about the incident was that both men were calm and sounded perfectly genuine while lying to the police. That really frightened me. What they had done disgusted me enough to overrule my fear of them. Astonished at their deliberate fabrication, I told Les I disagreed with what he and his father had done.

"You lied to cover for your brother when he was in the wrong. He needed to be taught a lesson," I said shaking my head in utter amazement. "And what if he had killed someone?" I asked bewildered.

"We'd still say the same thing," he replied, without a flicker of remorse or shame.

"Well don't ever expect me to lie for any of you," I said boldly. "I won't do it!"

He leaned in closer to me and whispered, "You'll do as you're told."

The tense atmosphere in the house made it increasingly difficult for me to cope. My dislike and mistrust of my husband and his family had heightened. Les seemed comfortable and content to stay safely tied to his mother's invisible apron strings, but I had news for him. I'd decided that we were moving out of that house. Consequently, an almighty argument stemming from petty annoyances over my wanting to move had erupted between Les and I. He slapped the family dog out of his way when he stormed out of the house in a tantrum. His mother, while wrestling wet sheets flapping in the wind as she hung them on the clothesline, saw him do it and called to him, "She's the one who should be getting a beating, not the dog."

Les saw his mother's sarcastic comment as a direct order. From our bedroom window, I saw him spin around and storm back inside. I also didn't miss the glimmer of satisfaction that appeared on the old woman's face. Les threw open our bedroom door and walked calmly over to where I huddled in the corner. Slowly he removed his belt, telling me that he was going to teach me to be a good girl.

Utterly shaken, humiliated, bruised and sobbing, I threw as much of my things as I could fit into bags and hurried to the safety of my parents' house the moment the Carters were out of sight. To say that my mother was not pleased to see me arrive on her doorstep with bags in hand was an understatement. She had problems of her own and wasn't about to welcome more. Since I had nowhere else to go, she allowed me to stay a few days to decide what I should do.

After much deliberation and driven by anger, I had come to the conclusion that Maude Carter wasn't going to control my marriage or my life any longer. It was time that I took charge of it myself. I had put up with all that I was going to from that family. Once I had made a decision, I promptly telephoned Les and told him firmly that I would be returning in the morning and would talk to him then.

Next morning, I paid the cab driver, turned around and took a long hard look at the house before going inside. It was definitely an ordinary looking house. It certainly lacked personality. I was glad that I wouldn't be living there for much longer.

It was a beautiful morning, clear blue sky and sunshine, but I was about to create a storm inside. Heaving under the weight of my bags, I half carried, half dragged them up the stairs and onto the timber veranda, more out of determination than anything. I refused to ask any of them for help, even in my condition. At the front door, I took a deep breath and found courage, then brazenly entered the house without bothering to knock.

I only had to walk a few paces down the hallway to find Les and his parents sitting in semi-darkness in the musty lounge room watching television. Les was wearing the red short pyjamas that I loathed. They all turned simultaneously like robots and looked at me when I spoke to Les, who was sprawled in an old armchair in the far corner of the lounge room. I felt disgusted at the sight of him dressed like that at that hour of the day. "You have a week to find a place for us," I said adamantly, "or I'll leave you and take the baby with me and you'll never see us again."

I then turned and looked directly down at Maude as I stood beside her chair, feeling my anger rise, "Any more trouble from you," I stated boldly, "I'll take you to court for interfering in my marriage. We pay eight pounds a week for this dump," I said, pointing to the door directly behind me, "and that's where I will stay until we leave." I hurried to the bedroom and slammed the door behind me, almost shaking the house off its foundations and leaving the in-laws and my husband with their mouths gaping open.

Later on my father-in-law knocked on the door to tell me that no one had ever spoken to them the way I had. "Well, that is just too bad," I said defiantly. "I want out of this place, so either he finds another place, or I will, and it won't be with him. I can assure you of that. He has a week!" I slammed the door in his face.

I did not care one iota what they or anyone else thought. They had pushed me to my limits and now I was fighting back. The baby was my only motivation for doing so, otherwise I would never have returned, then or ever. I felt only contempt for my husband but nevertheless, was determined to make the marriage work in spite of the odds against it. I had no money and no other place to go. Divorce was out of the question. My Catholic beliefs forbade it and, as much as I loathed the church and its teachings, it still controlled my life.

* * *

The exasperation I felt towards my so called Catholic faith derived from its controlling indoctrination. From early adolescence I began to resent the Catholic Church and God. For as long as I could remember I had been brainwashed into thinking that God would punish me every time I did anything wrong, and this created in me a sense of fear. After a while, I got fed up being afraid of something I couldn't see. Consequently, resentment for anything to do with the church had set in.

As children, my father insisted we attend church services with him every Sunday morning. Many times he was so intoxicated that he would fall asleep and snore loud enough for people to stare at us. Even the priest stared down from the pulpit with a look of disdain as he preached his sermon. My father's behaviour disgusted and embarrassed me. I was 12 years old when I told him I didn't want to go to church anymore and all hell broke loose.

Monday mornings at school sent a tremor of panic through me. Father Bailey, our parish priest, made a point of coming to our classroom and asking children who had not gone to church on Sunday to put up their hands. In those days it was rare for a child to lie, especially to a priest, and the whole class was fearful of this priest. So, slowly and awkwardly up went the few trembling hands.

The priest's face would turn crimson with rage at the sight of them. "Why?" he would roar full force into the air. He would pause a moment to glare into petrified faces, then suck in enough air to bellow again, leaning forward to emphasise his point, "Don't you know it's a mortal sin to miss Mass on Sundays? God will punish you for your disobedience. You'll burn in Hell!"

The priest had at times slapped children across the face, leaving his handprint glowing red on a cheek as evidence that he had been there. I disliked him and was terrified of him. I did my utmost to avoid him when I saw him in the schoolyard, but was unable to do so on the days that the whole school went to confession.

As we filed in the church pews, one after the other, the sisters flitted about, casting their eagle eyes over all of us, ensuring that nobody misbehaved while they policed the confessionals. I really thought God was against me because almost every time I went to confession, one of the sisters would usher me into Father Bailey's confessional. I wasn't brave enough to look at him and kept my eyes lowered. His ugly chewed-to-the-quick nails were in full view. The sight of them made me feel sick. I was so uncomfortable that I was distracted from confessing my weekly sins.

"Bless me Father for I have sinned," I stammered, nervously fidgeting. "My past sins are. Ah! Um! Ah! Ah!" I could feel the priest getting annoyed as I laboured over my misdeeds. I felt like crying. I couldn't think of anything to report. Then suddenly a few wrong doings came to mind, enough to satisfy him to grant me absolution with several Hail Marys and an Our Father for my penance.

As a youngster I had repeatedly questioned whether there really was a God, due to my parents, the nuns and Father Bailey's behaviour. I also wondered whether there was any truth in what I had been bullied into believing; that God was always angry with 'sinners.' I didn't have the courage to openly challenge any of it or anyone then, but it didn't stop me from wondering. Fear of punishment kept me silent. As naïve as this might sound, I would even go so far as to say that the indoctrination of the Catholic faith led me, at one time, to foolishly believe that my marriage was a form of punishment for missing Mass.

Despite my misgivings, I thought I was making the right decision in remaining with my husband. A fear of failure also spurred me on. My marriage and the baby were all I had. Naively, I also believed it would have been unfair for my child to be raised without his father.

When Les realised that I was serious about leaving him, he pleaded with me to reconsider. "I want to move away from here," I declared in tears. "I will live in a tent if I have to, it would be better than here. Anything would be better than here, Les." I looked pleadingly at him. "This isn't our home. If you want me to stay with you we have to move, now!"

He gathered me in his arms and promised to find us another place.

7

Within a week of my ultimatum I found a tiny but comfortable garage flatette in the suburb of Bankstown. I loved it, although there was barely enough room for us to move. The kitchen was so narrow that I could touch the walls when I stretched my arms horizontally. A fibro partition separated the kitchen from the bedroom, which was only a smidgen larger, with just enough space for a bed and wardrobe.

Mr Billingsley had turned their garage into a flatette for their son. Since he had married and moved away Mrs Billingsley thought she would put it to good use and advertised the flat for rent in the local paper. Les and I were the first to apply.

"You can have the place if you don't mind using the outside bathroom," she told us. I nodded smiling. "Oh yes, and the laundry too, I wash on Mondays. You can put your washing with mine," she said warmly.

I was so elated to be away from Maude and her prying eyes that our new home felt like a palace. In my jubilation, my nurturing and nesting instincts developed. I happily fussed over my husband and home. Everything in the dwelling was fresh and sparkling clean. I washed every piece of clothing we owned, symbolically eradicating the Carters from our life and remarkably, the tension between Les and me eased. For a short period we were actually happy. We shared a few fond memories while living there.

I found it amazing how some women immediately recollect their most unpleasant pregnancy experience in the company of a new mother-to-be, painting a most unpleasant picture, endeavouring to prepare me for the worst. I listened with interest, feeling increasingly alarmed as my well-meaning landlady, while doing our laundry together, talked about all the things that could go wrong in a pregnancy.

Mrs Billingsley's practical country upbringing included our wash with hers on washing days. "No sense wasting water," she said the first morning, as I walked into her laundry carrying a basket of washing. "Water is as precious as gold in the country. Put your clothes down on the floor, love, and sort them into their piles."

I was happy to follow her advice. I liked Mrs Billingsley. Although the stout lady was bossy, she was kind and fussed over me like a mother hen. She taught me a few of her secret family recipes and showed me how to hang clothes on the line so that they would keep their shape. She was an amazing woman, full of all sorts of interesting anecdotes.

Many afternoons, the sweet lady would knock on my door and invite me to join her on the veranda for afternoon tea; freshly baked scones with lashings of jam and cream.

Mrs Billingsley's approach to just about everything fascinated me. She took everything in her stride and nothing seemed to faze her. Her faith in old wives' tales had warned me to expect strange cravings, morning sickness, swollen legs and varicose veins. But for the first time in my life I was in perfectly good health and suffered none of Mrs Billingsley's predicted nasties, with the exception of cravings. Given my medical history, the fact that I was in such good health was almost miraculous.

One particularly miserable rainy Sunday, I was overcome with a craving for chocolate and was ready to venture out in the formidable weather to buy a block. The horrible weather had held Les and I virtual prisoners in our little home, with nothing much else to do other than to lie on the bed, read, and drink coffee or tea.

"Oh gawd," I moaned all morning, "I wish I had some chocolate."

That afternoon, Les secretly slipped away when I had fallen asleep out of boredom. He walked to the corner shop in the downpour and freezing cold and bought me a box of chocolates. I woke up when he came back.

"Where have you been?" I asked when I saw that he was soaked to the skin and shivering.

"To the shop," he replied tossing a box of chocolates on the bed. I was so surprised and thrilled at what he had done that I scrambled off the bed laughing and hugged him. After he had changed, we sat on the bed and devoured the chocolates together.

Away from Maude's controlling negative influence, Les was more supportive, and I began to feel that perhaps my marriage wasn't that bad after all. I had even gone to a lot of trouble to bake roast beef, as a surprise for when he came home from work.

The small kitchen table was covered with a crisp white tablecloth. It hid the ingrained scratches and stains I was unable to remove from the laminated surface. I laid out cutlery, crockery and glasses given to us as wedding gifts. Everything looked perfect. By the time Les arrived home everything was cooked, with the exception of the meat. It was still red, when it should have turned brown ages ago. We waited a little longer. When I looked at the meat for the umpteenth time it finally dawned on me that I had mistakenly baked silverside instead of topside, and that it would never brown unless I burned the bloody thing. I felt silly, but giggled like a dizzy schoolgirl when Les playfully teased me about it. The meal was different but delicious and we had a good laugh talking about it later on.

Things began to sour again when Les became paranoid about returning home and finding me gone. One day, just on dusk and shortly before he was due home, I wrapped up warmly and walked to the corner shop to buy a bottle of milk. On my way back I turned the corner of my street and saw Les frantically running up and down the street looking in the well-groomed yards of houses nearby. I called to him and he looked up with a start. When he saw my silhouette against the twilight sky coming his way he ran to me distraught and in tears. His panicked state frightened me as he gripped tightly on my arms. "Where have you been?" He demanded breathlessly, sniffing back fluid in the back of his throat, "I thought that you'd left me. Promise me you'll always be there when I come home." I promised.

Since our marriage I'd had little contact with either my family or friends. Les was adamant that none of my family were to visit his home. He was still furious with my mother for what she had said to him during the flat incident. She was unaware of Les' animosity towards her and I saw no reason to mention it. I was not expecting her to visit me, but one Saturday afternoon she arrived out of the blue and stayed just long enough to have a cup of tea. She looked out of place in our humble home, dressed in her expensive clothes. Although the contrast was obvious, it didn't faze me. It was better than living with the Carters and I wasn't about to complain, least of all to her.

Les came home early that afternoon and found my mother's immaculate sliver Hillman parked in the street. He waited outside until she had left before he came inside. I had no idea what had put him in a bad mood. It was best to say nothing. I made him lunch and a cup of coffee, placed it on the table in front of him and then sat down opposite him after I had made a fresh pot of tea for myself.

"How was your day?" I asked warmly as I usually did and I poured the tea.

"I saw your old lady leaving here."

"So?" I braced myself for an argument

"I told you," he said, getting angrier, "your old lady's not allowed near our place. Tell her to stay away!"

"Don't keep telling me who I can or can't see," I said defiantly, ready to march out of the flat to get away from him. "I don't see or speak to anyone any more, as it is. You can't make this place my prison."

I relented and gave in for the sake of peace, but soon after that fight an invitation to Tina's wedding arrived in the post. Les refused to go and tried to dissuade me from going too. I stood firm, this time telling him I was going and that was that. He gave his permission only after extracting a promise from me to be home before he'd finished work.

On the morning of the wedding, an argument between my youngest sister Mary and me erupted at my parents' home. I innocently asked Mary, who was Tina's bridesmaid, to tone down her makeup, endeavouring to explain that the day was Tina's and not hers. Mary, a pretty teenager, looked beautiful in her cyclamen pink, bell-shaped mini dress with long bell sleeves and frill edging. She was used to being in the limelight with her ballroom dancing competitions and Tina was usually pushed into the background by most of the family. Although Tina looked beautiful in her elegant, but plain wedding dress, the comparison between my sisters was as different as night and day. I felt that Mary did not need to wear so much makeup that day.

My mother viewed my request as a personal attack upon Mary, adamant that I was jealous of her. We argued, my mother standing vigorously against me. The argument had me distraught and in no state to go anywhere, let alone to the wedding. I had intended to catch a cab home after everyone had left for the church, but felt exhausted and wanted ed to rest first.

While lying there on my sister's bed, I wept sad and remorseful tears, remembering the day I discovered that the mementos and keepsakes of happier times, I had kept hidden in a small leather briefcase in the back of the wardrobe were missing. It had contained Matt's letters, my seventeenth birthday cards, and photos of my friends and of Matt and me, and the only photo I had of Luc.

During rare earlier visits to my parents' house, I would slip out of sight to secretly browse through that briefcase, to re-read Matt's letters and gaze over his and Luc's photograph, recalling those special moments. The briefcase had housed my past and my dreams of what might have been. Those letters and photographs were my most valuable treasures, they were everything to me. I was incensed and totally crushed to discover them missing. In a panic I rushed from the bedroom and asked my mother what had happened to my letters and photos. "Oh I burnt all that stuff," she said in an off-handed way.

I was stunned, hurt and devastated not only for the loss, but also for her total lack of sensitivity regarding the sentimental value of those mementos to me.

"Oh no, how could you?" I bellowed, bursting into tears. I wanted to scream my lungs empty of the anger I felt. Punch holes in the wall...hit her!

"I thought it was rubbish," my mother repeated louder, getting exasperated.

"How could anyone think that photos and letters were rubbish?" I was red faced and vein-popping hysterical.

My mother turned to face me. She leaned up against the kitchen sink, arms folded, staring at me. Her eyes flashed cold and dark, lips straight and tight in a thin line, nostrils flaring. Exasperated, she danced around in circles waving her hands in the air and then stopped, her body rigid with anger. She had had a long day at work and couldn't be bothered with my tantrums or me. She dismissed me, totally indifferent and unsympathetic to my hysteria. Her unremorseful apology cut deep.

The memory of that day was heartbreaking. I ended up falling asleep and woke up too late to make it home before Les. It was late evening by the time I arrived home. I was surprised to find the flat in darkness and thought Les must have gone to his parents' place. I unlocked the door, stepped inside and turned on the lights, and almost passed out from fright. Les was still in his greasy overalls, sitting on the edge of the bed sobbing like a lost two year old.

'God,' I thought, feeling totally defeated looking at him, 'my life is shit.' I could have done with a little compassion myself, but I knew if I had said anything to him it would have made matters worse. So I simply encouraged him back into good humour with a few reassuring words after apologising for being late, telling him that I was unwell and didn't go to the wedding after all. I longed to run away, but where could I go?

Whenever I could, I sat alone in Mrs Billingsley's garden and wrote in my diary. Les' behaviour gave me cause for concern when I seriously considered his crying and moodiness. Realising he had a serious problem; I prayed that it wasn't a personality trait that could be passed on to my child.

Maude had often talked about Les' erratic behaviour as a child. She would laugh as if it were something to be proud of. "Les chased his sisters around the yard with an axe. He did that whenever they upset him. When they locked themselves in the outside toilet, he tried to chop down the door. Their screams excited him," she said, wearing her creepy sneer. She had taken Les to a psychiatrist, but found it amusing the way he had outwitted the doctors with his response to the tests and questions they gave him. "He is very bright you know love," she smirked, "He had all the doctors fooled."

I secretly thought Maude's comments and reaction were odd. Les' childhood antics were a popular topic at family get-togethers. They had all laughed when Maude reminisced about the time he trailed toilet paper throughout the house and then lit it. "It was one of his favourite pastimes. We had to watch him all the time. We tried not to upset him either," she said.

I was more than convinced that Maude was an extraordinarily odd person also. It was strange the way her pale eyes appeared watery. She gave me the creeps. Les physically resembled his mother. He had her large nose and droopy lower jaw.

Initially, I didn't place a whole lot of importance on the tales Maude bragged about. I did, however, think Les' actions were strange, but naturally assumed that he had outgrown his childish pranks. Now I was questioning his stability and was so concerned that I asked him to get professional help, but that proved futile. He simply refused, telling me he thought that all doctors were mad.

I spent a lot of time alone, deeply troubled about my baby's sanity and quietly praying for a healthy daughter. I dearly wanted a daughter, knowing the Carters would not take that much interest in the child and therefore she wouldn't be under their influence. Females, according to Les senior, were less significant than males.

The old fellow took great pride in his sons. He boasted about the numerous times they came home so drunk that they could hardly stand up. In his view, their drunkenness was 'manly' and he silently encouraged it.

My baby's sudden movement prompted me to hope that this child would give Les reason to take control of his life and to feel encouraged about the future. 'Perhaps,' I thought, 'he will even find the courage to stand up to his parents, now that he has a family of his own to look after.'

I didn't object to Les visiting or doing anything for his family, if that was what he wanted to do. I strongly objected to the way his father's requests sounded more like commands. "Come around Saturday and fix my car. Your mother's washing machine is on the blink, come and fix it," the old man would say.

My father-in-law expected Les to be at his beck and call. I bitterly resented that and reminded Les that he was a grown man and not a child. "Your father should remember that," I said. "Tell him," I yelled in frustration, "to ask if you are available or if you have the time, before he orders you around to be his handyman."

Les promised me faithfully that he wouldn't allow any of his family to interfere in our lives any longer. I wanted to trust and respect him, even if I didn't love him. I particularly wanted to admire him for something, even if it was just for taking charge of his own life. I hoped the baby would be the catalyst for him to make that change.

One day shortly before the baby was due to arrive, I was travelling home on the train from my weekly doctor's visit. The only seat vacant was at the far end of the carriage, facing other travellers. Squashed in between two bulky men, holding my handbag in front of me like a shield, I nonchalantly looked around the carriage, casually glancing at other commuters. Some were reading the daily paper, some read books, while others gazed about them or dozed. I couldn't help smiling at the diverse shapes that surrounded me, especially the large men with bellies bigger and firmer than mine. I was grateful that my shape wasn't permanent like theirs.

As I contemplated my gratitude, the baby gave an almighty kick and sent my handbag tumbling onto the carriage floor. At the same time, the three men sitting opposite me turned their newspaper pages in unison. They saw what had happened and laughed, sending ripples of merriment through the carriage. I shrivelled up with embarrassment and hurried from the carriage when the train stopped, thankfully at my station.

The doctor told me the baby wouldn't be born for a few more weeks. Although I was thankful the pregnancy was uneventful and I had gained only a few pounds, the last few weeks dragged on. I was eager to meet the little bundle that was stretching my body out of shape.

I felt good that day. I always felt good when I wore my chocolate-brown, A-line corduroy maternity dress, with three-quarter sleeves and roll collar. I had made it myself. Normally I would have taken a taxi home from the station, but because I felt so good I walked the three miles.

Later that evening, I started to feel strange and asked Les to take me to the hospital. Although I was not in any pain, I knew I was in labour. The nurse asked me a lot of questions and then examined and prepped me for labour, but nothing happened. Les was told to go home while I remained in hospital overnight as a precautionary measure.

The next morning the nurse told me that I could go home. I slid out of bed, about to shower and dress. As I bent down to pick up my bag, a loud popping sound startled me. My nightgown was dripping wet. The woman in the next bed to me called the nurse.

8

My first child was born in less than twenty minutes. "A quick and easy birth," the nurse said later on. Although I had wanted a daughter, the moment my son was placed in my arms, natural instincts erased any disappointment. The nurse had him wrapped tightly like a bunch of flowers, with only the top of his tiny sandy crown poking out. Lovingly I inspected his scrunched up red face and thought he was magnificent. Brad was perfect with the exception of being jaundiced, a tell-tale sign that he had inherited Spherocytosis.

The doctor assured me that my baby would be fine. "All we can do for the present is monitor his progress," he said, but his words gave me no comfort. I felt so guilty that Brad had inherited my problem and concealed my concerns from everyone. In both families, I had enemies ready to condemn me of something and they would surely hold me responsible for passing the blood disorder onto my child. But none of them could have made me feel worse than I already felt.

Les was subdued when he arrived with his parents. They were all smiles.

"Have you seen the baby?" I asked, expecting Les to be jumping for joy.

"Nup," he said, and then kissed my cheek as he took hold of my hand.

My in-laws were in high spirits. They asked if I was all right and could they go and see the baby.

"I'm fine," I said. "The birth was no trouble at all. You don't have to ask to see your grandson," I smiled, 'He's in the nursery, go on up." I looked at Les, 'You go too, honey," but he seemed reluctant to let go of my hand.

He looked at his parents and said, "You two go, I want to be with Emma."

Les' grip on my hand tightened as he watched his parents rush from the ward like children fleeing a classroom at the end of term. As soon as they were out of sight, I asked what was wrong. Choking back tears he said ruefully, with a touch of irritation, "I wanted to be the first to know when my son arrived. Dad came to work to tell me. I wanted to be the first to know."

It was difficult for me not to feel sorry for him. I was more a mother figure than a wife. Although annoyed with his parents for their interference, I knew that it was pointless to say anything. Instead, I promised Les that if we were to have any more children, no one would know before him. To compensate for his disappointment, I reluctantly agreed to name the baby Lesley Bradley. My decision pleased Les and his father enormously. "But I want everyone to call him Brad," I declared.

The first grandson was expected to carry on the Christian name of his father. It was a Carter tradition. I certainly didn't want to name my precious child after people I disliked. Under different circumstances, following family tradition would have been an honour.

Both Les and I knew that his father had gone out of his way to visit the baby and me. It surprised and delighted Les, especially since his father had refused to go anywhere near the hospital when Bell's and Marla's sons were born. Although the old fellow was fond of the boys he never considered either of them to be as important to him as Brad because they wouldn't carry on the Carter name. Nonetheless, irrespective of whether I had a son or daughter, I felt sure the crusty old man would still have come to the hospital. Brad's birth brought Les favour with his father; having the first boy born on the Carter side of the family had pleased the old fellow immensely.

The way my father-in-law responded to Brad puzzled me.

"This child I'm holding," he muttered with pride raising my son above his head, "is my real grandchild. He's a Carter."

I thought my father-in-law's comments were cruel. The idea of my son being held in higher regard than his cousins made me feel ill at ease. "I just don't understand how he could make a statement like that," I said to Les, "Especially when both of his daughters have sons." But Les didn't care one way or the other. He was too preoccupied with being pleased about finally getting into his father's good books. I shuddered. The whole family was completely beyond my understanding.

Now that Brad had arrived, the place we called home seemed to have suddenly shrunk even smaller, and we needed to find another flat. Our new home was just a few streets away and only a smidgen larger than the previous place, but it was all we could afford and I was thankful for the extra space, however minute.

I loved being a mother. The sight of my sleeping child lying in his bassinette warmed and softened my heart. He gave new meaning to my dysfunctional life. During Brad's waking hours, when we lay together on the bed, I talked to him about the wonderful life ahead of him. I told Brad that he was so special that he could be anything he wanted to be. I promised him that I would protect him from bullying school teachers and even apologised to him for not being able to love his father.

"I'm sorry little man," I said sincerely, "it just isn't there. I tried but..." I laughed and rolled over holding him high in the air, "but I love you...and Luc. That's all my heart can handle right now. "

He laughed and his big blue eyes sparkled and looked directly at me the whole time I was talking to him. At two months old and he was alert and rapidly gaining weight. He greedily suckled at every feed. Feeding Brad was certainly an experience I won't forget in a hurry. My breasts swelled out of such proportion that I looked top heavy. Huge breasts disgusted me. They were sore and uncomfortable, as well as being an unwelcome object of curiosity. While Brad suckled at one breast, the other spurted like a fountain. The flow was so fast that he coughed and spluttered for the first few minutes. I felt like a jersey cow. While in hospital, one of the nurses remarked that I had enough milk to feed several babies.

It all literally came to a grinding halt when Brad dug his first tooth into my nipple and made it bleed. I didn't know that I would experience so much pain when I stopped feeding so suddenly. My breasts swelled larger than they already were. They were inflamed and very painful to touch. I had to take countless hot showers to relieve the pressure. My chest felt like it was on fire and the pain was so acute that tears filled my eyes with the slightest bump. I could have taken medication but chose not to, after having had injections, blood transfusions and medication for most of my childhood. I avoided taking drugs wherever possible and opted for natural remedies instead. I eventually found relief by wrapping wide bandages around my chest.

9

Les spent most Saturdays working overtime. I suspected that at times he used that excuse to sneak off to his parents' house, but didn't care one way or the other. Brad kept me busy and I was secretly thankful that Les wasn't at home that much. He didn't seem very interested in Brad except when we visited his family or in the company of others.

My suspicion was confirmed the Saturday afternoon Brad was ill and I had to call Les at work.

"Um, Les left ages ago, love," the workshop foreman reluctantly said.

The next call I made was to my in-laws' house. Les' mother called him to the phone saying, "It's her."

"What are you doing there?" I snapped after hearing that. "You told me you were working all day."

"I'm fixing Dad's car," he answered awkwardly.

"Your son isn't well. Do you think you could spare time to take us to the doctor?"

"I'll be home as soon as I can," he said, irritated.

I also was irritated, thinking about Les breaking his promise once again and lying about it. "Put your mother on the phone," I blurted out before he hung up, thinking it was high time that I told his mother the facts of life.

When Maude came on the line I said in a cold, calm tone, "When are you going to realise that Les has responsibilities of his own now? He's my husband, not your handyman."

Marla was there at the time and overhearing the conversation, she took the telephone from Maude while in mid-sentence. "Just who do you think you are talking to my mother like that?" she barked.

"I suggest you mind your own business, Marla," I warned sharply.

"My mother is my business," she snapped back.

"All of you might be used to running each other's lives, which is fine with me, just as long as you keep your noses out of mine," I barked back. "Like I said Marla, butt out! This has nothing to do with you."

None of them liked being told to mind their own business, especially not by a teenager. In retaliation, Marla demanded that I return everything the family had given to my son, bassinette, clothes, toys, and so on. "That's fine with me Marla, I didn't want your charity in the first place," I replied, happy to oblige her. "Everything will be ready for you to collect when you bring Les home."

The argument continued when Marla arrived, demanding that I hand over the baby items. In silence I passed her everything. I knew she was spoiling for a fight and was utterly thrown off guard when she hurled accusations at me about Brad not being her brother's child. I was seething. "Whatever you think I am, Marla," I smiled meanly, "at least I was married before my child was born. That's more than you can say." Then I shut the door in her face.

It took a while for me to calm down. I felt a moment of satisfaction but in truth, I was sorry for what I had said and felt that my sister-in-law was also a victim of her family, which is why I easily forgave her.

Marla had fallen pregnant before I met Les. He had often mentioned her and obviously cared about his sister. I thought it unusual that he didn't visit her and asked why. I was horrified to learn that Les' father had ordered Marla out of the house and instructed everyone to stay away from her because she had shamed the family. The way Les was talking, anyone would have thought that Marla had committed murder.

"And you obeyed him?" I asked, dismayed. "She's your sister; you can't turn your back on her. For pity's sake Les, you're an adult not a child. Don't let your father make decisions for you. I want you to meet your sister," I said firmly.

A few days later we were out in the car when Les pulled up at an unfamiliar block of flats. He asked me to wait in the car while he went inside. A few minutes later he returned and opened the car. "Come on in," he said, "There's someone I want you to meet."

Puzzled, I followed Les into one of the flats. A tall, very pregnant, brunette was in the corner of a tiny kitchen making coffee. Les introduced me to Marla. It was obvious by her awkward smile that she was embarrassed at meeting her brother's girlfriend in her condition. I was genuinely pleased to meet her and said so, with the intention of putting her at ease.

Les senior had made life difficult for his youngest daughter and used Les to do his dirty work until I encouraged him to support Marla instead. Les and Paul had attacked Marla's boyfriend Ian, when they discovered she was pregnant. Every time Marla and Ian argued, both brothers would pay him a visit threatening to reprogram him. Although Ian stood his ground he was outmatched by the two larger men.

Later on, after her son Jake was born, Marla thanked me for my support. She and Ian eventually married but the marriage was doomed to fail due to the family's interference. Ian was ostracised at clan gatherings. In spite of the tales I heard about Ian, I liked him and felt that if Marla had had a backbone, her marriage would have survived. Marla and I could have become close friends but instead we became adversaries, divided by family differences.

Les was angry and hurt and deeply surprised by his family's adverse actions. Maude and Marla had succeeded in hurting him, not me. Their vindictiveness gave me the opportunity I wanted to distance myself from the family. The idea of not having to visit them any more delighted me, but I was careful to conceal my joy from my husband.

Fortunately, Brad's fever and runny nose was due to teething and was nothing to worry about, but I didn't know that at the time.

Try as I might, I couldn't feel for my husband anything stronger than cordial regard. The damage was done – he had lied and let me down so many times that the deceit had sapped whatever respect I had left for him. He couldn't even muster enough courage to dream of something better than what existed past that day. He would tell me to "get real" whenever I tried to encourage him about the future.

"There's no point to anything if you don't have a dream," I told him, bewildered that he didn't have any future goals. "Dreams keep you going and give you hope," I said enthusiastically

"Well sweetness, I don't dream. I live in the real world. You should too."

Les' cynical attitude irritated me and I could see no reason to stay around him. To escape another possible argument, I went for a walk. I wanted to be alone to clear my head. The road I walked was empty, with no signs of life other than the streetlights and lights coming from within the houses standing neatly in a row. In the distance a dog was barking. The night sky was clear and the evening air felt warm on my skin. I stood still for a moment looking upwards. The black sky was laced with a carpet of tiny lights, blinking off and on. How peaceful it looked up there, I thought, and wished I were up there too. I truly didn't want to return home and without thinking I suddenly began to run as though the devil was chasing me. Tearfully, I came to my senses and stopped running, realising it was an inane attempt to run away. Although I desperately wanted to escape my life, I knew I could never do that because I had Brad to think about. Brad was the only reason I returned home instead of running until I was far, far away from Les.

Thinking about my baby gave me hope and a sense of purpose. When I held him, he snuggled in closely to me and held a tight grip on my finger with his tiny hand. The thought of him reminded me that I had someone to love and that someone needed me. Brad was about four months old when I realised I was pregnant again and that leaving Les would only be a longed-for ambition. Much as I wanted to leave Les, I was actually afraid to, especially after the evening when, while we were watching television, he casually mentioned that he had shot and killed an Aborigine while working on the sheep station. Even though what he had said sent a chill through me, I light-heartedly asked, "Oh really, and why did you shoot him?"

I was stunned when he said without hesitation or remorse, "The black bastard was a firebug and needed to be taken care of."

Another chill shot through me like lightening, every hair on my body stood on end. My eyes widened in horror at his unemotional admission.

"So one day when no one was about, I took my rifle and shot him and then buried him under a tree where no one would find him. That bastard had been causing strife around the place for some time. He needed to be fixed."

Everything about Les' mood, expression, and body language had convinced me that he wasn't just simply telling a story to frighten me. He sounded and looked strange – creepy and frightening. Every muscle in his face went rigid. The colour drained away, leaving an ugly greyish tinge. He stared at the wall and spoke slowly and deliberately, as if watching a scene by scene replay. When he paused, a smirk touched the corner of his mouth.

Les' manner sent chills down my spine. I had no idea then that I would see that frightening expression many times during our marriage. Everything my intuition told me left little doubt in my mind that Les had certainly done something terrible to someone that day. What he confessed horrified and scared me, but I still asked, "Aren't you afraid someone will find out?"

"Nope. No one saw me and no one else knows," he replied, totally sure of himself and grinning smugly." And I never leave evidence."

"But… " I was about to remind him that I now knew.

He silenced me by putting his index finger to his pursed lips. "Shhh." He was getting annoyed so I let the matter drop. I realised then that was the reason he left the Station so suddenly, and why he hadn't finished his apprenticeship.

I didn't know for sure if Les was telling the truth, but I understood the threat of that statement enough to fear him. Les had warned me many, many times during our marriage that if I ever left him he would *fix* Luc.

The realisation of another child stirred mixed emotions in me. They varied from resentment at sharing my children with this awful family and with a father who was already showing signs of jealousy towards his son, to the excitement of the possibility of a daughter. Even though every aspect of my situation looked grim, I remained hopeful that things would one day change for the better.

My friends had warned me about marrying Les. The shame of my marriage was a huge burden and pride had kept me almost a recluse. I couldn't let anyone know my marriage had failed so soon. The world in which I existed then wasn't one I wanted to share with friends, so the best way to conceal the horrible truth was to avoid everyone.

A surprise visit from an acquaintance caught me off guard. Kay Hanes told me she was passing and thought she would call in to say hello. But I felt she had come more out of curiosity than friendship. While we drank coffee, Kay commented on my home being 'nice', adding that she didn't pick me for the homebody/mother type. Puzzled by her comment, I asked what she meant. "Well," she said rather seriously, "you were always so glamorous. I didn't take you for the marrying kind and especially not a housewife."

I wasn't exactly sure what motivated Kay to say that. But I said, "You're pretty and you keep a nice home, Kay." She squirmed in her seat and smiled awkwardly.

In the evenings, Les and I spent a lot of time talking about his precious diesel engines. He didn't want to talk about anything else and if I tried to change the subject, he would simply retire into himself. Sometimes days would pass with hardly a word spoken between us.

Brad had given me a purpose and now there was to be another child to strengthen that purpose. As a mother I felt competent and found motherhood to be as natural as breathing. Les on the other hand displayed little emotion when I told him about the second pregnancy. He acted as though he hadn't heard me.

Another child predestined another move. In the local paper I found an advertisement for a two bedroom flat in the next suburb. The flat was spacious, clean, and the only one with carpet throughout. Our few possessions consisted mainly of the bedroom suite, which was still at the in-laws. Our last two places had been furnished, making it impossible to take our belongings with us.

When we arrived to collect the furniture it was already out on the veranda. I casually remarked to Les that I was surprised his mother hadn't ordered our things to be thrown into the middle of the street. By his surly expression he was clearly annoyed at what she had done, but he said nothing.

The Carters knew nothing about my second pregnancy until months later when Maude and Bell saw me at the shopping centre. Bell ignored me, but Maude came over to speak to Brad. She asked when the baby was due. "Pa misses his grandson," she said.

"Well, I warned you that one day you would regret what you've done," I said, before walking away from her.

"Bring the baby around home," Maude called out. I didn't respond. I was engulfed with a sense of power. I had no intention of going around to that house ever again.

My marriage was in crisis and I felt that I couldn't handle any more of their interference. Apart from that, I believed it was in my son's best interest to stay as far away from them as possible.

10

I wept joyful tears when the doctor placed the daughter I had longed for into my arms.

"Hello little lady,' I said to the squeaking, squirming little mite that yawned and stretched, completely oblivious to her surroundings. " You are the answer to my prayers. Do you know that? And a very special little girl at that, my little Celeste," I said, kissing the tips of her tiny fingers. I studied her features, all crinkled, pink and puffy, and the rolls and folds of white fur that covered her perfect little body, thinking that at last, I have my precious little girl.

The moment Les received the call to tell him that I had gone into the hospital, he left work and headed straight there in his greasy overalls. It didn't occur to him to shower and change first. When Celeste arrived he was already in the waiting room. A rare smile crept across his grease-stained face when the nurse told him he had a daughter.

A baby in my arms brought the best out in me. In the joy of my daughter, I wished that I'd had stronger feelings beyond tolerance for my husband, since that moment was so precious. It should have been something to treasure and share for many years afterwards, not just for a few hours. I sighed heavily with regret, resigned to the way it was.

Like her brother, Celeste was a wonderful baby. By the time I had taken her home, her creased and puffy features had changed. Her long white lashes and large sapphire blue eyes, petite rosebud mouth and white blonde hair blended superbly with pale skin and dapple-pink cheeks, revealing her beauty.

Brad adored his little sister and eagerly welcomed her to the family. Les, however, was showing signs of jealousy towards both children, even though I tried to do as much for him as I possibly could. One particular night when I had failed to immediately respond to his request for a coffee, he bitterly complained.

"You're always fussing with those bloody kids," he bellowed. "I'm your husband. I expect you to get my coffee when I ask for it, I shouldn't have to wait."

After one particularly long day, I glared at him and snapped out of exasperation, "Oh and the babies can just wait, huh? You're a big boy Les, make your own coffee. You can see that I'm feeding Celeste!"

Les' persistent demands for attention the moment I started feeding the baby had exhausted my energy as well as my patience with him.

"Bitch!" he snarled. "I'll fix you." He ran to the kitchen, threw open the cupboard doors and began hurling crockery against the wall, one item at a time. "Maybe this will get your attention," he barked.

I was sitting on the far end of the couch, still feeding the baby. I jumped up suddenly to avoid airborne debris, jerking Celeste from my breast. She screamed and I tried to soothe her, at the same time pleading with Les to stop.

He looked me at and smirked, "Next time I ask for coffee, you'll get it won't you sweetness?"

I sat helplessly in a haze of disbelief while he trashed the place. When the cupboards were bare he went to bed.

The kitchenette was divided from the dining room by a breakfast bar, and both sections of the room were covered with shattered crockery. As I meticulously and laboriously picked up every piece from the carpet, blistering hatred slowly churned deep in my gut. The poisonous seed gnawed at my insides, at the audacity of his childish behaviour.

Les had put Brad in danger of cutting himself when he crawled around on the carpet, should I miss any of the debris.

June and Alan Taylor, who lived in the flat above us, were privy to the turbulence below them. I was thankful they minded their own business. June, although sympathetic, did not pry, realising that I wanted it that way. We had a routine of having coffee together most mornings while our children played together.

I first met June in the laundry, a few days after we had moved into the building. That day she told me that she had no ambitions other than being a wife and a Mom.

"It's good bein' 'ome. Al can look after me and our two kids, Max and Mandy, and I'll cook and clean and look after 'im. What about you, luv, you like being married? When's ya baby due?"

I hesitated. "I er…" But she had already changed the subject, prattling on about her children's bed-wetting problem. "Ah I dunno, all I seem to do is wash. Should bring me bloody bed 'ere," she joked, grinning mischievously at me through the smoky haze from her cigarette.

At twenty-three, the threads of silver that ran through June's black wavy hair, made her look older than she was. An ever-present cigarette dangled from her mouth as she sorted through her family's clothing, putting them into piles on the laundry floor.

"Do ya 'ave any other kids other than…?" she asked, pointing to my tummy.

"Yes I have…a boy."

"Well ya can bring 'im up to me flat and 'e kin play wif me kids. When are ya due?"

"Five months. Okay, thanks, that would be nice," I stuttered, but June had already changed the subject again.

I stood back and watched June pull washing out of a long pale-blue plastic washing basket, thinking that she was everything my mother would disapprove of. I wasn't all that comfortable with her overly friendly manner. We had just met and she had already told me her life story, which made me feel the need to be cautious. Since June talked almost non-stop it saved me from having to divulge much. As I got to know her, I discovered that June gossiped only about trivial matters and she was a person that I could trust.

Although Brad was much younger than June's children, he avidly romped in unison with them while Celeste lay beside me in her bouncinette. Brad adored his new baby sister and was ever mindful that someone might hurt her. Even though he was still only a toddler himself, he clearly wanted to protect her from the other children whenever their rowdiness brought them too close to her bouncinette. If they did, he would stop playing, jump up and run to stand beside her, waving his little hand in the air like a traffic cop yelling, "No! No!" I had to reassure him that everything was okay, otherwise he would become distressed.

When Les was given a company van for field service work, he was often away for several days at a time. His absence brought peace to our home and I was grateful the children didn't show any signs of missing him. The mounting stress and tension between us had left me thin and run down, and my chain-smoking habit did little to enhance my health, but it brought a temporary comfort to my nerves, as I endeavoured to hide the truth of my stormy marriage from everyone.

The weight loss emphasised the size of my eyes and defined my cheekbones. My hair had grown shoulder length and was much lighter than when I was first married. Although I was always particular about my grooming, I never felt attractive and imagined myself as ugly and avoided people as much as possible.

Les felt pressured and resented the added responsibility of the children. But I believed the children brought about a change for the better. The more negative he was, the more determined I became that our lives would improve.

Before Celeste was born we had desperately needed a car, but Les said we could not afford one. "We don't even have enough money for a deposit," he barked.

I wouldn't accept that as an excuse, and decided to do something about it without telling him. It took several months of secretly scrimping to save the money for the deposit on a halfway decent car.

"Now can we go and look for a car?" I asked, waving dollar bills in the air.

The blue and white automatic Holden instantly made my small world larger. I had never driven a car before and Les offered to teach me. Eager to get the lessons started, I asked June to mind Brad for an hour. As with everything else Les and I did together, the driving lessons turned into an argument. I resented the way he spoke and yelled at me like I was an imbecile because I was a female. In retaliation, I ordered him out of the car.

"Get out! Get out! I'll teach myself, "I yelled at him in a way that took him completely by surprise. I was usually much braver away from home, while Les usually acted as though he was a 'hen pecked husband'. He got out without saying a word, wearing an odd expression. I guess he didn't expect me to drive off slowly down the street.

"God!" I thought immediately regretting my impulsive action. "What have I done?"

At first I was very nervous about driving alone, but I was very determined to learn, even if it meant teaching myself. I gently pressed my foot down on the accelerator and the car jerked forward a little faster. Quickly glancing into the rear vision mirror, I saw my husband's large frame standing in the middle of the road, becoming smaller.

"I can do this on my own, I don't need him. Bastard!" I muttered to myself, feeling excited and taking the corner a little too wide. "Oops! Ooh wah!" The sound of squealing tyres unnerved me a little thinking that another car was close behind. I realised the sound came from my tyres. I slowed down and began to relax and work out how to handle the vehicle. Leaning forward quickly, I turned on the car radio. The bubbly disc jockey and his peppy music dissolved my fear of feeling alone.

After an hour of precariously driving up and down and around our streets, I felt I had mastered the driving technique. Bored with driving around in circles, a sudden surge of confidence pushed me to be more daring and I steered the car in the direction of my parents' home, twenty miles away. Arriving at the busy Hume Highway intersection, with 'Sweet Sixteen' blaring from the radio and my heart thumping wildly, I safely negotiated my way into the traffic and cruised along with the flow. Half an hour later, I came to a halt in front of my parents' home and slowly released my firm hold on the steering wheel. I expelled a huge sigh of relief and smiled and said, "I made it!"

My mother was horrified to learn I was driving unlicensed and unaccompanied while very pregnant, but I ignored her rebuke, busting with pride at my accomplishment of mastering the car in such a short time. It certainly never occurred to me that what I had undertaken could have had serious ramifications, if I'd had an accident. Listening to my mother go on about the seriousness of my actions, deflated my confidence and had me worrying about the return trip.

My initial impulse to drive over to my parents' house was made in anger. But after I had had time to think about the consequences, I felt anxious and was actually scared to drive the car back home, but chose not to let my parents know how I was feeling. With a burst of false confidence, I scooped up my car keys from the table, saying, "Well, I'd better be off," after finishing the last of the tea my mother had made.

All my fears vanished with the cranking of the engine, as a sense of excitement overtook me, the jive-talking disc jockey keeping me company. I arrived home to a very worried husband.

"Well Les," I said smugly, tossing the keys onto the bench, "I don't need any lessons any more. I know how to drive. Anyone can do it, even girls."

He was speechless, but smiled an acknowledgment to my mocking jibe.

That sedan stretched my world larger than ever before, providing me with the freedom to take the children on a short drive or to visit my parents. My mother was fond of her grandchildren, especially Celeste, declaring my daughter resembled me more than she did Les.

On my way home from an outing one afternoon, I pulled into a service station. As I did, I noticed a familiar car pull up behind me. My heart pounded hard in my chest and my hands began to tremble. Through my rear vision mirror, I watched the driver leave the car and casually stroll over to where I was parked.

"Hi!" Luc's handsome face peered through my window, sporting a beaming smile that said he was more than pleased to see me. My frail appearance startled him and he asked if I was okay. "I'm fine," I assured him, too quickly. Feeling uncomfortable under his surveillance, I turned his attention away from me and to my children.

Brad was standing up leaning against the back seat looking out of the rear window. He turned and responded to Luc's, "G'day mate!" with a big grin. Celeste was secured in her car seat in the front. She chuckled loudly when he tickled her tummy.

We passed the few minutes with small talk while we refuelled. Luc insisted on paying for the petrol, and before I drove away said he would call around to see me soon. I was doubtful, since he hadn't asked for the address.

In the privacy of my bedroom, I examined my reflection in the dressing table mirror and wondered what Luc had thought, seeing me so tired and sad. All that was visible of the sophistication and confidence I once had was my stance. I stood straight and as tall as my five feet would allow, in my faded jeans and tee shirt. My hair was pulled back into a ponytail. "God I look awful," I sobbed, mourning my vanishing spirit.

Trying to lift my mood, I spun around and swung open my wardrobe, expecting it to be bulging with the latest fashions. I held the doors wide open until my imagination filled the cupboard. It was a game I played many times to lift my spiralling spirits, the same sort of make believe games I played when I was twelve, after finding an American dime. Because I had the dime in my possession, I believed beyond a doubt that I would one day travel and had often said, "I will go to America someday." Although my family just smiled whenever I said it, I knew I would.

11

My inability to display or to feel any affection for my husband had caused constant friction between us. I had suggested, even pleaded that we separate after returning from the trip we took shortly after Celeste was born.

She was only a few weeks old when Les came home and announced that he was going to Port Macquarie for a couple of days to repair a truck. He wanted me to come with him. I reluctantly agreed to go, even though I suffered travel sickness. The prospect of the long drive did not excite me. Celeste's birth was still the highlight of our lives at that point and Les convinced me the break would do us good.

The drive from Sydney to Port Macquarie was long and tiring. As soon as we arrived at the motel, all I wanted to do was feed the babies and go to sleep. Les woke me in the middle of the night, groping my body and calling, "Sarah, Sarah," my mother's name. I sprang up in horror. Sick to the stomach with disgust, I shoved him. "Get away from me," I hissed at him, careful not to wake my children sleeping close by.

He realised what he had said, and quickly told me that he didn't mean it. "I don't care," I said, "just stay away from me, how could you? My mother! You make me sick!" I declared, emphasising my every work with contempt.

He frantically tried to apologise. The more he did the colder I became, refusing to listen to anything he had to say from then on. The marriage was finished as far as I was concerned. His betrayal was unforgivable. I demanded that we separate. He would not, claiming he loved me and would never let me go, ever. If only he had, our lives would have been less traumatic. His stubbornness had caused us to hurl a deluge of cruel words at each other. What a waste of our lives, and for what reason? He knew I didn't love him. I never loved him. He also knew that I wanted to be with Luc.

My feelings of abandonment and loneliness weren't due just to the betrayal, but also from self-pity at being entrapped in a nightmare of a marriage from which there seemed no escape. I was baffled as to why Les had developed an interest in my mother. Neither of them had a kind word for each other. I had to lie to him, saying that my mother admired and respected him for being a good provider, and in turn I did the same with my mother, telling her that Les admired her beauty. I thought if I catered to their egos it would keep the peace and I wouldn't have to endure Les nagging me about my mother's interference in the flat, before we were married.

Prior to the night in Port Macquarie, I had been willing to give the marriage a chance, as Celeste's arrival had given me the spark I needed to make a new start possible. But in my heart I knew the marriage was doomed. Every day afterwards I prayed for Les to be removed from my life. Then I simply gave up when nothing changed, feeling that nobody really cared, not even God.

I brought up the subject of divorce with Les again on the eve of seeing Luc. I told him that I was unhappy and believed that he was too. "We could be friends, divorced," I naively pleaded, "and you would probably be a better father, please, Les, I don't want to be married to you, please let me go."

I looked imploringly at him while he sat silently in the chair staring into space. For a split second I thought he was going to agree, since his features seemed to soften. But in a flash they changed. His eyes glazed over and his skin turned that increasingly familiar grey colour. I froze in fright at the deadly expression that emerged whenever I said the wrong thing, and wondered which way I could run when I saw him removing the belt from his trousers, saying, "I'm going to fix you and to teach you to be a good girl."

I saw a way out. Just as I was about to run for it Les lunged forward and grabbed a handful of my hair and pulled me backwards. I struggled to get free of his vice-like grip as the belt stung and bit into my flesh. The whistling sound of the belt cutting through the air just before contact increased my terror. He kept lashing at me, ignoring my pleas to stop. I wished him dead with every stroke.

The following day, the angry red welts covering my body had turned blackish-blue, and my eyes were heavily swollen from crying. The physical pain fuelled my hatred and I seriously considered killing Les. It was fortunate that he was called away on a job, leaving me to recover from the ordeal.

Luc arrived unexpectedly just a couple of hours after Les had left to go interstate. My resistance to invite him inside had alarmed him. "What's wrong?" he asked, but I remained silent, embarrassed and ashamed of my appearance. He was the last person I wanted to see me battered and bruised.

The dimly-lit hallway had concealed the reason for my odd behaviour. I hoped that Luc would just go away. "Let me in, Doll. What's wrong?" He was gently pushing on the door as he spoke. I finally gave in and let him in. "What are you doing?" he said, then went deadly quiet. His eyes widened with horror. He pulled me gently to him, wrapped his arms around me, and swore softly under his breath. I hung my head in shame. I couldn't look at him.

"Please don't tell anyone, I couldn't stand it." I pleaded, pulling away from him. "Please don't look at me, I'm ugly." He went to speak but I said, "I know you mean well, but please don't say anything, not right now. I'd rather you didn't stay. I feel uncomfortable with you seeing me like this."

"Okay darl," he said, taking a step towards me, "if you don't want me to stay I'll go, but I'm coming back, okay?" I nodded.

Luc left but made regular weekly visits to make sure the children and I were safe. He stayed only a few moments at first. Knowing that he cared for me gave new meaning to my life. Neither of us spoke of our lives, other than what we shared together. Luc and my children were all that existed for me when I was with him. Guilt had never entered my mind. His devotion to the children and me helped me to cope with living with Les.

Luc didn't openly speak of his love for me, yet in subtle ways he revealed his feelings. The way he looked at me and his kindness to my children spoke volumes. We became lovers. In my heart Luc was my husband. We should have been together but I knew we were moving in different directions and so, while I could, I enjoyed every precious moment we shared. I make no apologies for that.

12

My third pregnancy was a huge surprise. I was in awe and kept the news a secret for almost three months before telling Luc. The news shocked him.

"What are you going to do?" he asked, worried for my safety.

"Do?" I looked at him puzzled. "I'm happy about the baby. Don't worry, everything will be alright."

Luc was concerned that Les would harm me when he found out, but I reassured him not to worry, that I would deal with it. Several days later, while I was in the middle of making breakfast, I told Les.

"I'm pregnant," I said casually, and carried on with what I was doing, waiting for him to explode, expecting him to tell me the baby wasn't his, and to get the hell out of the house. But none of that happened. He acted as though I hadn't spoken. He finished breakfast in silence, kissed me on the cheek as he usually did, and left for work.

I knew Les was aware the baby wasn't his. My loathing of him was so intense that I could not bear even to look at him during a conversation, let alone allow him to touch me. Strange though it may seem, things changed dramatically. My spirits soared, fantasising about my new baby, Luc's baby. My belief in God was renewed with gratitude to at least have Luc's child. Any hope I had of marrying him was relinquished eons ago and Les seemed content to ignore the truth. His behaviour became erratic from day to day, with him keenly shadowing my every move. I could feel his eyes on me, the same way Jack Weston leered at me at work after the Christmas party.

I finally snapped, "What are you looking at?"

He smirked, deliberately taking his time to answer, "At you. Can't I look at my beautiful wife? I enjoy looking at you. I love you. You are my wife. I own you," he taunted, and then added as an afterthought. "I have something your boyfriend wants, but it belongs to me."

One moment Les was endeavouring to convince me Luc never wanted me, then the next, he gloated about the fact that he had what he thought Luc wanted. I couldn't see how Les could feel any love for me, knowing what I harboured against him, and that I was in love I with Luc.

"It's all so horribly sad and disturbing," I noted in my diary, "watching our lives being systematically destroyed with each passing day. He speaks of loving me. What utter rubbish! The creep is holding me prisoner because he believes Luc wants me. He can't have me, so in his mind, neither can anyone else."

Numerous times I had tried to encourage Les to make friends with the men at work, even suggesting that he take time off from work and go to a football game. He resisted, saying that he hated football. He also said the people at work weren't his friends. "None of them could give a shit whether I lives or die, so why the hell would you think I'd class any of them as friends?"

His interest, apart from work, related only to guns and engines. I thought that if he had other interests away from home, perhaps it would distract him from stalking me when he was at home. He worked seven days a week, only taking a Sunday off every now and then. I felt he worked the long hours to avoid the reality of our dilapidated marriage. He once confessed, "When I'm away from you," he said, "I fantasize that we are happy."

Odd though it may seem, I clearly understood how he felt. We both had unfulfilled desires.

The love I had for my children could not compensate for the absence of Luc from my life. From our first meeting, a day didn't pass without me thinking about him. I was joyful because he was back in my life again. The baby was everything to me because it was Luc's child, my only child conceived out of love.

During my sixth month I saw signs of a possible miscarriage and went straight to the hospital outpatients. Waiting in line was an agonising ordeal. Brad and Celeste sat quietly on the floor at my feet playing with their toys while I silently prayed, hoping that God would hear me.

"Mrs Carter!" The sound of my name and the sight of the oversize nurse in white, standing in front of me, snapped me to attention.

"Oh yes, that's me."

The stout woman briskly ushered me to a nearby cubicle. "In here," she said pulling back the curtain and drawing close after her. "The doctor will be here in a minute," she said, instructing me to lie on the bed. Moments later the doctor whizzed into the room as if he were on roller skates.

"Hello, how are we today?" he said, fumbling with my clothing and asking all sorts of questions while running the stethoscope over my exposed, small rounded belly. Frowning he said, "Hmm, are you sure your dates are correct?" as he gently pressed and pushed my stomach.

"Yes, why?" I replied, thinking how could I not be sure? Luc and I didn't have much time together. *Of course my dates were accurate,* I thought, a little irritated.

"Why do you ask, is everything okay?"

"Your baby is very small for the dates you've given us, that's all."

"Is my baby in any danger?" I was more concerned about my child's welfare than the stupid dates. I was annoyed with the questions and wasn't about to explain why I was certain my dates were correct.

"Hmm, no, I don't think so, everything seems okay," he sounded hesitant. "But I'm not sure you have the correct dates, your baby is very small."

I also had thought the pregnancy was unusual. It wasn't until my sixth month that I appeared pregnant and even then I was still able to wear jeans and tee shirts comfortably. Nevertheless, about the end of the eighth month, the baby grew almost overnight. My tummy was so large and tight that the simplest tasks became an effort. I was also getting weary of hearing neighbours and family ask as the pregnancy lingered, "Are you still here?"

I didn't consult a doctor in the last month as it was difficult for me to get about with the children. My health was good and I usually took care of myself during pregnancy. According to my dates, the baby was well overdue, and my belly was stretched to its limits. I looked and felt as if I was about to burst open any minute.

June's mother, who had her six children at home with a midwife in attendance, gave me some motherly advice. "Babies are like fruit," she said, "they fall from the tree when they are ripe. But if nature needs a little help, castor oil usually does the trick."

Thinking about what the woman had said, it occurred to me that perhaps I should give nature a push. I bought two bottles of castor oil but wasn't sure how much I needed to take. Just the thought of swallowing the oil made me gag. After eyeing the bottle for a very long time, I finally worked up the courage to open the lid and sniff the contents. I recoiled from its odour. It took me ages to swallow a couple of spoons full. After hours of anxious waiting nothing happened, so I consumed the remainder of the bottle before going to bed. The taste of the oil left me feeling nauseous and I ended up exhausting myself throwing up. The taste and smell of the oil was still with me in the morning. The oil was so overpowering it felt as though it was oozing from my pores.

Les had already left for work and the children were in their room when I scurried to the bathroom to throw up again. I washed my face and was about to check on the children when my water ruptured. I grabbed a clean towel from the cupboard, shoved it between my legs and discovered I was also haemorrhaging.

"God, what have I done? What is happening?" I shuddered in horror, thinking something was seriously wrong. With the towel still in place, I shuffled across the hall and banged on a neighbour's door.

Labour took less than an hour before my beautiful, seven-pound two ounce baby boy, with a mass of jet-black hair, made his noisy entrance into the world. I cherished the thought of gazing upon my son's face and seeing the image of his father. 'How fortunate am I,' I noted in my diary later on, 'to be given a gift as beautiful as this.'

Our son was a striking child and stirred a curiosity in the ward. Nurses came to my room many times to admire him and his abundant jet, black hair. Reaching Luc was no easy task, but when I did I said, "You have a son."

I could sense him smiling when he replied, "Do I? What's his name?"

I hesitated, "You know I wish I could give our son your name don't you?"

"Yes, but you can't."

"I'm calling him Cain," I said cheerfully.

I was so overjoyed that I could hardly contain myself. The moment was far too special to understate. "I want to share every detail with you," I said enthusiastically, and started with the castor oil. We talked for ages, our laughter covering the sadness we both felt. Luc approved of his son's name and apologised for not being able to come to the hospital.

"I'm glad everything went well and that you and Cain are okay," he said. "I'll come and see you when the fuss dies down."

Just before I hung up I heard him say, "Doll?"

"Yes?"

"Thank you," he said it in a way that needed no explanation.

Shortly after the call to Luc, Les arrived. He said hello and kissed me briefly on the cheek, then walked to the other side of the bed to the baby's cot. All that was visible was a mop of black hair poking out of the top of the blanket. He pulled back the blanket and looked at the baby's face and smiled, but I couldn't read his face. "He's beautiful," was all he said

"Yes, he is," I replied proudly.

Les lingered beside the cot a few minutes longer before turning his attention to me. I happily gave him an account of the birth, and the curiosity Cain had stirred. My mood was infectious because Les was obviously pleased. He liked the name I had chosen and gave no indication that he wasn't Cain's father. I was completely baffled, especially since Cain was the image of Luc, and nothing like Brad or Celeste.

My family arrived later that evening. I expected a comment about the contrast between Cain and his brother and sister, but Mary surprised everyone by innocently saying, "Are you sure this is Les' child? He's nothing like Brad or Celeste. He is so dark, and all that hair!"

The atmosphere in the room went deadly quiet for a few seconds. It was as if everyone, with the exception of me, had taken a deep breath. I was full of smiles and ignored my sister's comment, but suspected my mother and brother recognised the truth in her statement.

Cain's arrival brought a hub of activity to our home. The move from the flat to a house close by made it impossible for Luc to visit sooner.

"I knew you would know where to find us," I declared mischievously with outstretched arms when I answered the door and found him grinning broadly. He hugged and kissed me and told me that he had monitored our movements. He knew when and where we had moved to and when to visit.

"Come and see our son," I said, gently breaking free and taking his hand in mine. In my enthusiasm I half skipped across the room like a child, dragging him along behind me.

Luc leant over the cot and slowly lifted back the bunny rug. A smile pinched his mouth as his cobalt eyes studied the baby – our baby.

"Beautiful isn't he?" I beamed. "Like looking into a mirror isn't it?"

Luc's attention remained fixed on his son as I spoke, then slowly turning his head he acknowledged me with a silent nod. Slowly he straightened upright. He reached for my hand and gently pulled me closer to him. We stood beside the cot with our arms around each other, watching Cain sleeping, until Brad and Celeste came roaring into the room asking for something to eat. They had been in the backyard when Luc arrived. When they saw him, they ran to him. He knelt down and gave each of them a hug. From the kitchen I could hear the children telling Luc they had a new brother.

Once the children had settled down, Luc left them playing with their toys and joined me. He asked if Les had said anything about Cain.

"No, not a word," I said, spinning around to face him, still holding the butterknife in my hand, and then turned back to finish making the children's sandwiches. "I can't understand why. It's scary," I said, cutting the bread into small triangles.

Luc stood behind me and slid his arms around my waist. I stopped what I was doing and leaned into him when he kissed my cheek, warning me to be careful.

On his way out he noticed the telephone on the sideboard.

"Is it connected?" he asked. I nodded. "Good," he said and wrote the number on the back of a business card. "I'll call you."

13

The way Les favoured Cain over his own children was extraordinary. He practically ignored Brad and Celeste altogether. I was bewildered but reluctant to draw attention to it. In retaliation for his odd behaviour I would always refer to Cain as my son whenever I mentioned him.

Bath time was a fun time for Brad, aged three and Celeste, aged two. Cain was almost nine months old and was crawling. The three of them enjoyed playing in the bath together while I sat on the floor and watched them. They were sitting quietly when the telephone rang. I moved three metres away from the bathroom door to answer it. At the sound of splashing, a hollow thud and the roar of the tap at full force, I hurled the telephone aside and ran in terror to the bathroom. The sight I saw created utter disbelief. Brad and Celeste were playing while Cain lay face up under the water, unconscious.

Although in shock, I automatically yanked Cain out of the water by his feet, and ran screaming for help into the deserted street, holding him upside down. My beautiful baby son was as limp as a rag doll. I had no knowledge of first-aid or how to save my child, but my brain told me to keep praying and to keep screaming and holding him upside down. Within seconds the street came alive. Someone took Cain from me and tried to resuscitate him. People took turns working on him. A very long time passed and nothing happened. My reserved manner was gone; I was hysterical and calling out to God, begging him to save my baby.

The ambulance arrived and the attendants took over. Cain was blue and still unconscious and I heard someone say, "He's gone!"

"No! Noooo!" I screamed, refusing to accept it. "He can't be. Please, please God, no!" I cried and refused to move from my kneeling position, shrugging away comforting arms.

"Please God, please, let him live!" I pleaded, begging for his life. My heartache and my helplessness were beyond comprehension. Cain was my life. He had to live. I continued to pray, refusing to believe he was dead, determined not to move or to stop praying until he was breathing again.

Minutes later the attendants called out, "We've got him," and the crowd that gathered cheered. My tears of crushing despair and heartache instantly turned to euphoric joy, relief and gratitude. Losing Cain would have destroyed me. If he had not survived, then neither would I.

In the mayhem, I hadn't noticed that Brad and Celeste had followed me out into the street. They were both still wrapped in towels, standing beside me. A neighbour came forward and offered to take care of the children while I went to the hospital with Cain. I responded like a zombie.

'This is really a nightmare. I will wake up soon.' I was huddled in the corner of the hospital waiting room. The accident had highlighted that my careless action almost cost my child his life. The emotional intensity of the responsibility of that burden was unfathomable. Huddled in shame, I caught a glimpse of my reflection in one of the glass doors. At first, I did not recognise the haunted eyes that peered from a gaunt face, and the shoulder-length hair that hung lifeless, as my own image staring back at me. My spirit felt old and heavily burdened with the responsibility of my children. Three little people had trusted me, their mother, to protect them from the dangers of life. I felt I had jeopardised that trust by a split second of stupidity. Nothing was comparable to the utter helplessness that plagued my mind. Guilt at the near tragedy penetrated my soul. A profound sadness overwhelmed me when the devastation tricked my mind into imagining Cain had died and grieving quickly set in again.

The sight of Les coming towards me jolted me back to reality. The way he walked, he looked oafish. He was repulsive. I hated him and didn't want him near me. We were hardly speaking at all. His face was hard and threatening. He demanded to know what had happened, but I couldn't speak for crying. "What did you do to that baby?" he demanded

"What!" I responded as if he had slapped me, in disbelief of the accusation. "I would never hurt any of my children, I love Cain, and he is MY son, you know that, you bastard. I hate you!" I hissed at him.

"I'll fix you when we get home," he threatened.

The doctor called me over to tell me that Cain would be fine. "You can take him home when you are ready," he said gently. Concerned for me, he asked if I was okay. I nodded.

"He should sleep throughout the night. And you should you get some rest yourself."

I thanked the doctor and then picked up Cain from the hospital bed and held him close, silently thanking God for giving him back to me. Les was waiting outside. He looked at Cain sleeping peacefully in my arms.

"You're so lucky nothing happened to him, otherwise you would have been very sorry."

I was mystified at his implication and demanded to know what he had meant. But he did not answer.

"Cain is my son, Les. I would never hurt him," I said with conviction for the second time.

We drove home in silence. My mind was in turmoil, trying to analyse his reaction.

'He must be insane to think such a thing. He's acting as if I deliberately hurt Cain. He's the one who is insane, especially the way he is acting about another man's child.'

My feelings for Les had surpassed hatred – I wanted him to die.

Even though it was never mentioned again, no matter how much I tried, the nightmare of that incident could not be erased from my mind. I was alone, with no one to talk to about what had happened. I was falling apart emotionally and physically and was totally helpless to do anything about it. Subconsciously, my mind was telling me I was grieving, and vigorously fighting the idea that Cain had died. A deep depression took hold and without any warning I was literally overwhelmed, feeling Cain had really died. I fell in a heap to the floor weeping. It would happen periodically for many years after. The grief was so acute and uncontrollable that I feared for my sanity.

My babies had often found me on the floor sobbing. Brad would cradle my head and gently pat my face with his little hand, saying, "It's all right Mommy, never mind," the same way I soothed him when he was upset.

Meanwhile Celeste snuggled in close cooing, "Ah! Ah! Poor Mommy."

I knew I had to pull myself together, but didn't know how. Black moods overshadowed me and I felt the pain of living. The hatred I had absorbed from life's abrasions was destroying my spirit. I craved for peace but it never came. It had abandoned me. The children were my only saving grace. If it wasn't for them I would have given up long ago. In moments of deep despair, a smile or, "I love you Mommy," from Brad or Celeste reminded me of who I was and why I was there. Their love for me made sense of my life.

Although my faith in the Catholic Church had diminished, its indoctrination still had an impact. "I want the children baptised," I told Les after Cain's accident, but he would not agree, sending me into battle with him once again. I was determined that it would happen and made arrangements, even though he was strongly against it.

The following week, on the Sunday morning while I dressed the children, Les came and stood in the doorway of their bedroom and said, "You're not taking him," pointing to

Brad. "We are going to the zoo, aren't we mate? It will be more fun than going to that churchy shit your mother wants to take you to."

I looked at Brad; he was looking up at his father and grinning like a fool. "Yeah Dad," he said.

Brad was so excited that I knew it was useless to fight Les. I felt heartsick watching him subtly coerce my three-year-old into going to the zoo, while his siblings were baptised Catholics.

The fact that Brad was not baptised weighed heavily on my mind, so much that I baptised him in the bath that night. I poured a pail of water over his head and said, "I baptise thee in the name of the Father and the Son and the Holy Ghost, Amen." But I knew it was not enough for him to officially become a Catholic. He needed a Baptismal Certificate for that.

"Someday," I said scornfully to Les later that evening, after the children were in bed, "Brad will need a Baptismal Certificate."

He just scoffed at me. "Ah, for Christ sake get off my back, you don't know what you're talking about!"

"Oh yes I do. Today you made Brad different from the others."

"Ah, bullshit. Shut up!"

My contempt for Les was no longer hidden. Our home was a battlefield and he was the enemy. I was the prisoner. He would be nasty and threaten me at every turn and then expect sex from me. I hated going to bed when he was home. Time and time again I rebuffed his advances but later in the evening he would try again. My rejection would only start a violent fight.

"I'm fed up with you pushing me away all the time," he bellowed into my face as he forced me on to the bed one night, pinning me down with his weight, threatening to pour caustic soda over my face.

"Your boyfriend won't want you all scarred, will he?" he snarled, waving a bottle containing the dangerous chemical over my head. I fought for my life, struggling and squirming under his weight. With an almighty force I threw him off balance and broke free. In a reflex action, he grabbed my hair and violently hurled me backwards on to the bed. Terrified, I fought him like a crazed woman. He backed away from me and started trashing the furniture in retaliation.

"Stop it! Stop it, you bastard, we'll have nothing left by the time you get through smashing everything!"

"You should have thought about that before," he shouted back glaring down at me. I was crouched in the corner of the bed with my hand over my head, protecting myself from flying glass.

"I hate you. I'm getting out of here. I can't stand being with you," I yelled back.

Les dived to the floor and scrambled under the bed for what I knew was the only thing there, his rifle. I went silent and trembled uncontrollably when I saw him loading the .308. "What are you going to do with that?" I asked.

"Teach you to be a good girl and give me what I'm entitled to or I'll shoot you."

His voice was steady, but I knew by the tone that he meant what he had said. I became hysterical and buried my face in the pillow and screamed. I stopped. The barrel was against my head. He was saying that he would pull the trigger if I wasn't a good girl. I felt ill and wanted to vomit.

"This is your fault you know," he growled. "You drive me crazy. I can't help it. It's your fault."

He stood the rifle against the wall and then raped me. I was too afraid to fight him any longer. "You're mine," he muttered, pawing my body. "I can do whatever I want with you. You're my wife. I own you."

I lay still like a rag doll, giving nothing. Les was mumbling that he loved me. I cringed, feeling revulsion and disgust. Lust satisfied, he fell on me panting. I made an attempt to push him away from me and run to the bathroom to shower as I usually did. But this time he would not let me leave the bed.

"I hope you're happy," I said venomously. "I'm pregnant again."

"How do you know that?" he asked sarcastically.

"I just know," I said. "I'm not bringing another child into this hell hole. This baby will be up for adoption."

He did not respond. He rolled over and went to sleep. I lay still, clinging to the edge of the bed, quietly crying. I could see the gun in the dim light. It was still propped up against the wall in the corner, on the other side of the bed. I fought the urge to use it on him.

Hours passed before I dared leave the bed to check on the children. I was relieved to find them sleeping soundly; I went to the bathroom and washed myself. I felt dirty. Frantically I scrubbed my body to rid me of him, but still I felt unclean. Utterly helpless and alone, I sat on the cold bathroom floor, my head buried in a towel, and silently wept.

In the morning, I surveyed the bedroom, the curtains hanging by their threads and the dressing-table mirror totally shattered, fragments scattered everywhere. The room resembled just how I felt. I did not have the emotional strength to clear the wreckage away, so it remained there for weeks afterwards. Each morning I got up, walked out of the room and closed the door behind me.

As I had predicted, I was pregnant. I had no intention of bringing another child in to a hell home, and I made that very clear to Les. My spirit went numb, which helped me to feel nothing for the baby. I could not. I would not allow myself to feel anything. It would be unfair to the child if I did.

In the eighth month of the pregnancy, Les quit his job. He said he had had enough of working his arse off for nothing and refused to find another one. I was at my wits' end, utterly bewildered by what he had done. We had no money for food after the bills had been paid and Les didn't seem to care. I didn't know what to do. I was afraid I wouldn't be able to feed my children. I could have found a job if I had not been pregnant. In desperation, I called my brother and told him. When Les went out Peter came to the house with groceries and gave me enough money for that week. Although I was grateful for his help, I felt humiliated and worried what I would do when the food and money was gone.

Watching Les doing nothing other than sit in front of the television all day, snapping at the children to be quiet, drove me to ask, "When are you going to find another job?"

"I'm not." He smirked. "Why should I when I don't want to?"

"But you have a family and we don't have any money."

"So?"

"What do you mean so? How the hell do you expect us to pay the rent or eat?"

"You'll have to figure that out yourself. I'm not working any more. I don't want to discuss it. Piss off and leave me alone, I'm watching the show! Shut up you kids and sit down!"

"Don't talk to them like that. They are only babies!"

"I told you to piss off!"

I sat in the kitchen drinking the tea I had made earlier. It had gone cold. Agitated, I got up and paced the kitchen floor. 'What the hell am I going do? We don't have savings to fall back on. What am I going to do? Oh God, I've tried so hard to find something to like about him,' I thought tearfully, 'I really have.' I never pretended to love him and he knew that I didn't. He knew I wouldn't have married him if I hadn't been pregnant. He doesn't love me. All I am is a trophy. I rested my head in my hands and sobbed.

A surge of madness took hold and I rushed back to the lounge room still crying. "You bastard," I said feeling utter powerless. "You stinking bastard, I hate you Les! I won't be bringing another child into this hell that's for sure. And you made such a big deal about looking after your family. Huh, some provider you are. I told Peter what you did and he brought the food we're eating this week."

He looked up at me and glared saying, "You shouldn't have done that."

I ignored Les, turned around and went back to the kitchen. In a flash he had moved from the lounge room to the kitchen and was standing over me, holding the electric jug cord in his left hand. He grabbed me by the hair with his other hand and pushed me further to the floor with each blow of the cord. I automatically put my arms over my head to protect my face.

Les was enraged and swung the cord countless times, whipping me until I was numb. Still gripping clumps of my hair, he pulled me to my feet, then wrapped the cord around my wrists and dragged me to the garage.

"Scream and I'll break your neck," he warned before leaving the kitchen. My fear for my life overruled any thought of a challenge. I felt light-headed. Everything seemed to happen in slow motion.

When we entered the garage, Les savagely pushed me up against a post. "Put your hands behind your back," he ordered. I responded automatically, half-dazed. "You're always giving me trouble," he muttered, tying my hands tighter.

Once I was secure he put tape across my mouth. "This should teach you to be a good girl," he said and whipped me several more times. "Just so you get the message."

I can recall thinking how odd it was that I felt very little pain, especially since he was swinging the cord so hard. He left me alone in the garage for long periods at a time, occasionally checking on me.

"Thought you'd like to know your mother came around," he grinned, "I told her you were out and I'm looking after the kids."

My eyes hardened when I briefly looked up at him. He saw murder in them.

"Don't you look at me like that," he warned lunging at me, "otherwise I'll give you more of the same. Do you hear?

Want more?" he taunted, and I quickly looked down. "That's better," he cooed as he left.

As time passed, the feeling in my body returned, and with it came excruciating pain. My baby moved. It was the first time I had thought of the child as mine and I sobbed. The realisation of having to give my baby away had finally penetrated. I really did not want to do it, but I knew I had to for the baby's sake and that was that.

Ten hours later, Les untied me under the threat of another beating if I spoke or glared at him. The sight of blood and black bruises and raised angry welts all over my body took my breath away. I vomited after surveying the horror in the bathroom mirror. 'What had my baby felt?' I wondered wiping my mouth with a warm face cloth. 'It was a miracle that I hadn't gone into labour.'

Warm shower-spray stung every wound, bringing life to every nerve I possessed, and stimulating my hatred for Les. "No one has the right to inflict such cruelty," I mumbled, making a fist but stifling the urge to punch something or scream. "And this mad man says that he loves me. I could kill him! I could kill him!" My tears mingled with the spray from the shower.

When the swelling on my face subsided, I visited the family doctor in hope that he would help me. The doctor had known the Carters for many years. I was dumbfounded that he viewed my condition and Les' behaviour in such an off-handed manner. He said that I shouldn't put my husband under any strain to cause him to act like that. Bewildered, I went home feeling utter despair.

Several weeks later I found the courage to visit a solicitor. That visit was more reassuring when I showed him the remaining marks on my back when he asked to see them. But my hopes were dashed when he mentioned the fee. Sixty dollars was a lot of money in 1971, and I was lucky to have six dollars. The consultation fee was ten dollars, even that was more than I could afford.

For weeks after the visit I waited, worried that a collection agent might come to my door asking for the ten dollars that I owed but didn't have. I also lived in fear of Les discovering where I had been. But thankfully nothing happened and, as far as I knew, he didn't know that I was trying to divorce him.

I was trapped, living in perpetual fear for my life. Les wasn't about to let me go. He promised that if I did leave him he would harm Luc, as he had threatened numerous times in the past.

14

July fourteenth, 1971, at ten past ten in the evening, my fourth child and third son was born. Plans for his adoption were in progress. I braced myself for condemnation from the hospital staff, but instead they were supportive and sympathetic.

There were no tears of joy or any kind of emotion when the baby let out a cry to announce his arrival. I willed myself to feel nothing. As far as I was concerned this child would have a better life away from his family. I had adjusted myself to that. A peaceful feeling had come with the decision that I was making the right choice for his future. I even declined to see him after he was born. All I wanted to know was that he was healthy and everything was intact. The nurse assured me that he was perfect, with the exception of being jaundiced.

It was difficult to be in the same ward with the other mothers and their new babies. As a distraction, I sat outside in the waiting room and watched the passing parade of people. It was a favourite pastime of mine, trying to imagine what the people were like and whether or not they were happy. My peace was disturbed when Les loomed into view. I turned away when he walked towards me. As far as I was concerned we had nothing more to say to each other.

"Have you seen the baby?" he asked with uncertainty.

"No, and I am not going to either!" I didn't want to think about anything except going home to my children.

"Why not?" he asked. "Why not? You know why not." I tried to remain calm and whispered, "I told you what I planned to do. I don't want to bring another child into our hell. I won't!" I hissed at him.

I walked over to a vacant chair and sat down to get away from him, but he followed. Kneeling down beside me, he gripped my hand, pleading with me not to give the baby away. People stared at us. They could hear what Les was saying. The scene was horribly uncomfortable and I squirmed with embarrassment as Les begged me to forgive him, promising never to hit me again. When I whispered to him to stop carrying on and struggled to free myself from his tight grip he just protested louder, repeatedly declaring his love for me in front of onlookers. To silence him, and against my better judgement, I relented and gave in. I so wanted to believe that he was genuine. I honestly didn't want to give my baby away, although I felt for his sake, I should.

Together we went to the nursery to meet our new son, but I went with great trepidation. Gazing upon my son's tiny face, I felt nothing for him. It was as though I was looking at someone else's child. But when the nurse placed him into my arms, an overwhelming surge of emotion flooded through me, bonding me to my child.

He looked so small, the smallest of all my children. It was impossible for me not to love him. Les showed no emotion, apart from a gentle touch on the baby's cheek. His lack of response to his son puzzled and disturbed me, especially after the scene he had made in the waiting room.

Our arrival home from the hospital was also puzzling. Les usually carried the baby basket from the car and into the house. This time he did not. He left that to me. His behaviour hurt and angered me and I demanded to know what was going on.

"What do you mean?" Les asked innocently.

"The way you're acting, is what I mean!" I snapped at him, already regretting my decision to bring the baby home. "I knew I shouldn't have listened to you, I should have left him at the hospital," I cried.

"He's your kid. You want him. You look after him," he said.

From that moment on he ignored the baby. It was sad and it was cruel. He had already turned all his attention to Cain. Brad often tried to attract his father's attention but Les appeared not to notice. Celeste on the other hand cried a lot whenever Les was at home, and then seemed to withdraw from him. Cain was a bright, happy handsome child. He loved all the attention he received and there was so much of it from everyone. Benjamin John, BJ as he was affectionately known, exuded an air of serenity asleep in the bassinette. Even his cry lacked aggression and his waking hours were met with patience.

Turbulence was slowly brewing in the air once again as Les fed upon his jealousy. Indignant at his demands, I informed him that he did not deserve any of my attention. He raised his hand, ready to strike me, and I screamed at him, "Go on hit me! Where's your gun? Kill me, why don't you. Get it over and done with. At least I will have some peace and be free of you."

Les ran into the bedroom as I was shrieking hysterically and came out holding the rifle. He pointed it directly at me. I froze, fully expecting to be shot. I watched transfixed as he turned the gun around holding it by the barrel. He raised it high above his head then forcefully slammed the butt onto the wooden floor, damaging both the floor and the gun. He continued to slam the gun until he had completely destroyed it.

"Now," he said breathlessly, gathering up the pieces, "you don't have to worry about the gun anymore."

Still frozen with fear I began to tremble uncontrollably, stifling the urge to scream, 'Get out of my life you bastard, I hate you. I'll kill you!'

Every night I prayed for something to happen to Les. I prayed for his death. My nerves were shattered. I lived in fear of him one day killing me or me killing him. The possibility of losing my children prevented me from fulfilling my desire. Instincts warned me of more danger ahead and the need to escape became urgent. To finance my plan to leave I took a job at night with a catering company, until I had saved enough money to escape.

During my pregnancy with BJ I had met up with Matt Calloway again. He just turned up one evening at my parents place, after eight years. I happened to be there at the time. He had not changed at all, still full of fun and mischief. The feelings we felt for each other years ago were still there too. We wanted to talk but time wouldn't allow it as I had to go home. As I was leaving, Matt asked for my telephone number. He called the following day and we made arrangements to meet in the evening a few days later, at Circular Quay train station, where we had first met.

I told Les I wanted to catch up with a friend, knowing he wouldn't check. He did not want to know what I was doing, just as long I returned home. I parked the car across the street from the Quay and saw Matt waiting for me. I sat there a few minutes watching him, amazed at how little he had changed. I tried to imagine him older, but couldn't. He possessed a Peter Pan spirit, unlike any other person I knew. My heart skipped a beat wondering what my life would have been like with him.

Matt looked up and saw me. His smile was broad as he hurried across the road. I was suddenly fifteen, light-hearted and giddy. My heart beat so fast that I almost lost my breath. Then reality hit. I was very pregnant. I wondered if he would feel embarrassed being with me. Les could not bear to see me pregnant, it made him uncomfortable.

I stood beside the car, feeling a little awkward and grinning like a fool. When Matt arrived, he wrapped his arms around me and kissed me gently. "Hello princess," he said, as he slipped his hand in mine, "Come on, let's go for a walk."

"Aren't you embarrassed that I'm pregnant?" I asked shyly.

"No," he laughed, letting go of my hand to wrap his arm around my shoulders, "We can pretend I'm the father."

A short time later Matt stopped under a street lamp, removed a worn photograph from his wallet and handed it to me.

"You're still my princess," he said looking down at me. "I carry you everywhere I go."

I was surprised and flattered at Matt's confession. It made me feel very special.

I looked at the photograph I had given him years before and thought of my teenage image as someone I used to know. Blonde hair styled fashionably in curls piled on top of her head, a fringe draped almost into large sparkling brown eyes. Wide smile, totally unaware that that smile would not be as bright in the future. 'It was a nice photograph. I looked happy then,' I thought and passed it back to him.

"That was a long time ago, Matt," I said ruefully.

He nodded, shot a quick glance at the photograph, and then slipped it back into his wallet.

Matt took my hand and we continued our walk in silence. I felt comfortable with him. When he asked if I was happy I told him the truth that I wanted to escape from the horror of my marriage. I could not confide in Luc or anyone else. Knowing that Matt still cared a great deal for me gave me hope. He offered to help me get away. "Come to Darwin..." he said.

When BJ was born, Matt came to the hospital with my father to see me. Les was already there. I introduced Matt to Les as an old family friend. They both nodded and eyed each other with suspicion from opposite sides of my bed.

Luc's visits to the house lessened because the children had mentioned his name a few times, but he remained in contact with me by telephone and called several times a week. There was no point involving Luc in my plan to run away. Les had made it perfectly clear that he would harm Luc if I went to him. Les would not accept

that I had relinquished all hope of being with Luc eons ago. He had married and I loved him enough to let him go.

My relationship with Matt took nothing away from the love I felt for Luc. No one could ever do that. What I shared with Matt had a special place all of its own and I discovered that it was possible to love in degrees. Matt was stationed at Darwin's Naval Base. He was due to leave Sydney a couple of days after I was discharged from hospital. Because he did not know when he would see me again, he asked me to spend his last night in Sydney with him. I fabricated another story, telling Les I wanted to visit June and her husband, since they had not seen the baby. June had invited me to stay with her, but I had already visited her and had not mentioned it to Les. "I'll be home before you leave for work in the morning," I said.

Les narrowed his eyes then said gruffly, "Make sure you are," giving me a sidelong look that I ignored.

An hour later I was cheerfully driving into the city, with BJ sound asleep in his basket on the back seat. When I saw Matt waiting at our meeting spot, I stopped the car and moved over to the passenger's side so he could slide in behind the wheel. He kissed me quickly and then headed in the direction of Kings Cross. We were silent for a few minutes, then looked at each other and started laughing and giggling like a couple of naughty children

"Have you eaten?" he asked, trying to be serious.

"Yes, with the children," I replied, thinking how rushed I had been trying to bath, feed and put them to bed before I left. "Thank God my babies are well behaved," I sighed.

"Did you say something, Princess?"

I looked at him and smiled, "Not really. I was talking to myself. I guess that means I'm crazy." We chuckled again.

"I feel like a naughty kid caught with my hand in the bickie tin." He grinned and raised his eyebrows.

"Me too," I said. "But I'm having lots of fun doing it." I gave him a cheeky sideward glance.

BJ was asleep in his carry basket in the back while Matt and I acted like a pair of dizzy teenagers, laughing and giggling in the front. BJ did not stir until we turned into the motel's driveway.

I became more enchanted with Matt when he took an interest in BJ. He was fascinated with the way I handled the baby. "Can I hold him?" he asked with arms outstretched when I had finished feeding and changing BJ. Matt took BJ and looked at him and wistfully said, "I would really like to be a father."

"Would you?" I was surprised

"Yes," he said. "I thought about how this little guy could have been mine."

We looked at each other and then burst into laughter with the same thought. We had never slept together. Matt knew that we would not make love, but he still wanted me to stay with him, and I was glad that I did. Lying in his arms had softened the hard shell I had built around myself. His warmth and his tenderness, and especially the way he responded to BJ, warmed my heart. I was happy. He made me feel special.

The next morning we rose early as Matt had to be back at the ship before six am. I drove him to the dock and then left with his promise to write. The first letter arrived one week after he had arrived back at the Naval Base. With it came hope, and I was finally making plans to leave Les.

Once I knew in my heart that leaving was the only thing I could do, I contacted Bankstown Department of Welfare, and asked to speak to one of the officers there. A few hours later I was answering a knock on my door and found a very tall man of about thirty casting a huge shadow across the entrance of my home.

"Hello," he said. "Are you Emma Carter?" I nodded.

"I'm Tom Hall from Children's Welfare Services."

I invited him in. He followed me into the lounge room and sat on the edge of our black leather lounge. I remained standing. I was nervous and trying to think where to start.

"I'm not leaving my children, I'm leaving my husband," I blurted out almost too quickly. "I want you to know that. I can't take them with me when I leave in a few weeks. But I intend to get a job and get some money together and come back for them." I had to stop talking for a moment, fighting the urge to cry. I looked at the floor in an effort to regain my composure. "I want my intentions to be a matter of record so my husband cannot say I deserted my children," I finally said.

"Why are you leaving your husband, Emma?" Tom Hall asked. I took a deep breath, but as soon as I admitted out loud that I was afraid for my life and was afraid of Les, I began to sob.

"What about the children? Wouldn't he hurt them too?"

"Oh no, I don't believe he would do that, otherwise I'd never leave them, but if I don't go now, I'm not sure what will happen. I have to go," I said imploringly. "Please, Mr Hall, I need to know that you will look in on my children while I'm away."

"I'll do everything that I can," he said on his way out.

Several weeks later, everything I owned went into an old sea trunk and was sent to Darwin ahead of me. My intention was to have Les believe that I was not going to return. 'It's imperative that he believes the children are not important to me,' I thought while packing, 'otherwise, he'll never let me near them again as punishment for leaving.' It was impossible for me to take the children with me and choosing one over the other was inconceivable; I love them equally.

On the day of my departure, as I kissed and hugged the children before leaving, I hesitated, almost changing my mind, but I knew if I did not go then, nothing would ever change. I had arranged for a teenage girl to stay with the children until Les came home from work. Before leaving I told the girl where his pay packet and the letter I had left for him was, and to let him know. But later on I learned that he thought that I had taken the money. I had taken only the money I earned working part-time for a catering company at night. I knew Les needed every cent to care for the children and to pay the rent, among other things. That money was all we had.

15

The aeroplane touched down at Darwin Airport at midnight. The trip had been long, emotional and very draining. Matt and some of his mates were waiting at the airport coffee lounge for my arrival. A welcoming committee took me by surprise and immediately I felt conscious of how tired I must look when I saw them.

Several months had passed since I had seen Matt and during that time I had lost a considerable amount of weight. Matt asked if I was okay.

"I'm fine," I said, endeavouring to sound convincing. "I've been under a lot of strain lately. I'll look and feel better after a rest."

"Ok, just as long as you are okay Princess."

Sensing that I would rather be on our way than socialising, Matt took the initiative and suggested we check out our quarters. One of Matt's mates had given him the use of a Mini. As we tore along the asphalt, he leaned towards me and shouted over the noise of the engine, "Hope you don't mind living in a caravan until we find better quarters?"

"Not at all," I called back.

The moon was high when Matt turned the little car into the Overlander Caravan Park. He drove a little farther down a pitted track, and then came to a stop outside a white caravan. The park was quiet. Only our movements disturbed the silence. Just before he opened the door, Matt started to chuckle again and said, "Wait till you see what's inside."

Curiously I stepped in and looked about. To the right, my oversize trunk was jammed up against the seat, taking up half the room inside the van.

"We'll have to go outside to change our minds," he teased, "and you will have to share your bunk with me tonight, because your trunk's using mine."

Lying quietly in Matt's arms, he turned and whispered in my ear, "It's good to see you again, Princess."

Matt returned to the base in the morning without waking me. I woke up late in the afternoon in a pool of perspiration. The heat was unbearable. I dragged myself over to the shower block hoping to cool down, but to no avail. The humidity was so high that it became impossible to remain dry.

Over the following weeks I began to relax and enjoy my new surroundings and consequently, the transformation in my appearance was nothing short of remarkable. My complexion took on a glow and I had not had a headache since I had arrived. I felt great for the first time in years. Matt introduced me to his friends. All that was missing were my children; they had never left my thoughts.

The second week I had three part-time jobs. Three evenings a week I was a waitress at an Italian restaurant, and the other three nights a drink waitress at the Darwin Hotel. Saturday and Sunday mornings I served in a milk bar, across the road from the caravan park.

Matt complained that I was working too much, which left little time for us to be together. 'I'm not here to play," I told him. "I'm here to earn money so I can take care of my children."

Matt had expected me to settle down with him and start a family. "I already have a family and I want them with me." I was disappointed that he did not understand.

"What about me?" he shouted.

"What about you?" I shouted back.

Matt was hurt and angry and allowed his pride to get the better of him. He gathered his belongings together and returned to the base. I was taken by surprise when he left so abruptly. I expected him to return the next day, but he did not. I was stunned and did not know what to do when I realised he had deserted me.

A few days prior to our break up, Matt and I moved from the smaller van into a larger one. Since we were not together any more I did not need it. When I recovered from my daze and realised that Matt was not coming back, I thought the most sensible thing for me to do was to move into town and get shared accommodation. I made inquiries at the hotel where I worked and was told that one of the girls there had a room for rent.

Every cent I made, apart from living expenses, went into my savings account. My flat-mate, Kelly, noticed my frugal lifestyle and commented about it several times. To put her curiosity to rest, I finally told her about my intentions to reclaim my children. She was shocked to learn that I was married, let alone had four children.

"You don't look old enough or big enough to have four kids. Shit!" Kelly exclaimed.

"Well I am and I have, and I'm nearly twenty three," I said.

"Shit!" Kelly said again and after recovering from the shock she said, "I guess money is real important to you, huh?"

"Yes it is. I'll need a lot to get my babies back," I responded, wondering how long it would take to get together the amount I needed, which I imagined would be several thousand dollars.

"I have a friend who might be able to help you," Kelly said sounding mysterious.

"No! Don't tell anyone. I don't want anyone to know anything about me," I said alarmed. "Promise me you'll keep my secret."

Talking about the children stirred suppressed emotions in me. I did not want to think about anything I could not control. I needed to remain focused; it was vital.

My job as a waitress at the hotel was fun, once I learnt how to handle the rowdy men. Initially I felt shy and wanted to run away and hide, but I knew I had nowhere to run and no one to run to. I missed Matt but pride would not allow me to call him and apologise for the way I had spoken to him, even though I still cared a great deal for him. 'Perhaps it was the wrong time for us,' I thought and left things as they were. I knew I was on my own and the jobs I had were important to my survival.

The tips I received were generous and most nights I made really good money. One Saturday night after the bar closed off the till, an American called me over to his table and asked if he could buy a box of matches.

"Sorry sir," I said politely, "the bar is closed, but I have a box of matches you can have." I handed them to him; he lit his cigarette and then returned the box to me. Before he did, he slipped something inside. I waited until he was out of sight before looking to see what it was and found a neatly folded ten-dollar note.

Offers to go out came from every direction but I declined, not wanting to get involved with anyone. There was one guy who kept on persisting, even though I kept telling him no. Most of the staff usually went to a nightclub after the hotel closed. At Kelly's insistence, I joined them one Saturday night instead of going home as I usually did.

Our group were sitting at the table when a man in his fifties joined us. Kelly and he huddled together deep in conversation, periodically glancing at me. When the music stopped, Kelly made the introductions. I instantly disliked Joe and his familiar manner towards me. I waited a discreet few minutes before excusing myself. As I was about to leave, Joe grabbed hold of my arm and said, "I hear you need quick cash."

Darting a suspicious look at Kelly, I said politely, "No, not really I'm fine, thank you."

"I can find you work that pays lots of money," he said, smiling.

I broke free of his grip and hurried towards the door, anxious to get away from Joe, upset by what I had been offered. Just as I was about to open the door, a hand grabbed me and pulled me backwards, I panicked, thinking Joe had hold of me again, and raised my hand ready to strike my captor.

"Hey hold on, calm down it's only me."

The light from the door shone on to the familiar face of my persistent suitor. Relieved to see him and not Joe, I relaxed a little and apologised.

"Can I buy you a drink?" he asked.

"No thanks, I'm leaving."

He followed me outside and down to the cabstand.

"What's your name?"

"Emma Calloway.'

He extended his hand as he said, "I'm Mark, Mark Hudson."

I was distracted and still thinking about the conversation with Joe and did not hear what Mark was saying.

"Can I drive you home?" he asked a second time. "Hey, where are you anyway? You seem miles away."

I felt horribly embarrassed when I suddenly realised that Mark was still holding my hand. I apologised for my vague behaviour.

"You can let me drive you home then," he said.

Hesitating for only a minute, I accepted his offer. "I'm too wound up to go home. I really need to relax and unwind. Can we go for a drive?" I said, looking into his warm, friendly, handsome face and thinking, 'Yes Mark, you seem like a very nice person. I would love to spend the evening with you.'

As we headed in the direction of the beach, I thought about my life up until that moment. 'What a mess I've made of things,' and I flinched at the idea of it all, I felt sad thinking about how I thought Matt was the light at the end of my tunnel. I trusted him enough to risk everything. What a fool I am, and now I'm spending time with a total stranger.' I gave Mark a quick sideward glance, 'a handsome stranger.'

He noticed me looking at him and smiled, "Nice night huh?" I nodded, looking out of the window. The moonlight lit up everything around us, creating a magnificent sight of mystical forms and shadows.

Mark parked the car then turned around and collected a blanket from the back seat. "Come on," he said getting out. I followed and hurried to his side. "Where are we going?" I asked playfully kicking sand.

He took my hand. "To sit on the blanket and look at the stars for a while. Take off your shoes and enjoy the feeling of walking barefoot in the sand."

"Heavens Mark," I exclaimed laughing, "it's been years since I've done that."

"Well, that's a good enough reason for doing it now."

Contact with the sand and salty air reminded me of my childhood Christmas holidays at Wollongong in NSW. 'They were good memories,' I mused. The night air was warm and tranquil as waves gently crept along the shoreline. Mark spread the blanket out on the sand and we both sat on it. I looked around with appreciation then gazed upward. Above us, huge stars blazed like millions of large diamonds. "Just look at how beautiful the stars are, Mark? They seem close enough to touch."

He playfully reached up then fell backwards on the blanket laughing, pulling me down with him teasing me. "You sound as if you haven't seen anything like this before. I see this all the time on the oil rig."

I poked a face at him then smiled demurely. We were quiet for a few moments, engrossed in our own thoughts, looking up at the stars.

Mark broke the silence with light conversation, then he mentioned his age.

"Twenty is so young," I murmured wistfully. "I feel so old."

He laughed. "Hey! So heavy for such a little girl," he teased.

"Not a little girl any more, but I wish I was, how about a woman of twenty three?"

"No! Really? You don't look any older than nineteen, tops."

Smiling ruefully, I said. "At times Mark, I feel so old that it's hard to imagine that I'm still young."

Mark looked puzzled but did not say anything. A comforting arm went around my shoulders, pulling me gently closer to him; I felt the strength in them when he held me. I could hear the sound of his heart pounding in his chest when I laid my head against him. Caution was thrown to the wind when I allowed myself to be swept deeper into his embrace.

Lovingly Mark caressed my body, bringing me into a self-awareness of being a desirable woman. Inhibitions had gone, leaving us to explore the depths of our desire, and rising to the height of pleasure beyond expectation. Time stood still when we came together as one. Nothing else mattered.

Sleep descended upon us without warning as we lay peacefully in each other's arms. We woke up at dawn and went for a quick swim. I was alive and full of energy after so little sleep, never imagining I could be as carefree or as daring as this.

Against my better judgment I agreed to see Mark the following week when he came in off the oil rig from Groote Island. He extracted that promise from me before taking me back to the flat.

"Okay, I promise, I promise, I will meet you next Saturday night," I said, laughing as I fell into his arms and kissed him goodbye.

Kelly and Joe were sitting at the kitchen table drinking coffee when I entered the flat. To avoid the previous night's conversation with Joe, I made a quick exit to my room, but stopped suddenly at the door when Kelly said, "I told Joe you needed help to get your kids away from your old man."

I spun around annoyed at her disloyalty and said firmly, "I can take care of things myself, and..."

"I have friends," Joe interrupted, "who can bring your kids to you within days."

Curiosity stirred me to ask, "And what do I have to do in return for this favour?" Leaning forward, Joe said enthusiastically, "Look sweetheart, you've got class. You can name your own price. I already have clients interested in meeting you. They are very important people. You just say the word."

I watched Joe closely as he spoke. His hands moved about to emphasise every point he made. A glow of greed and a threat of danger showed in his penetrating blue eyes and instinct warned me to tread carefully.

"Give me time to think this over," I responded, not realising that I was accepting his offer.

'There was no way I could bring my children here, that was for sure. But what could I do now? And how long could I evade Joe?' I wondered. My mind began to spin, knowing that I must be cautious.

The following day, Kelly and I were having lunch in the hotel dining room when a well-known local identity came in. Since I had arrived I had heard all sorts of wild stories regarding criminal activity and the man coming our way was rumoured to be in the thick of it. We sat in silence and watched him walk towards our table. He took the chair nearest to me and sat down without asking if we minded, waved a ten-dollar note at Kelly and told her to go and get the drinks. She quickly moved away, leaving me alone with him. The uninvited guest moved closer and cupped my face in his hand, drawing me closer to him. I looked intently into noticeably deep crevices that suggested a hard life. A scar visible near the right bushy brow gave him a sinister air. His voice however, contradicted his appearance. It was gentle and friendly and his eyes were warm and a soft brown. In his youth he would have been handsome. Still I was wary; I had heard about Rick Jenson's reputation. My heart pounded in my chest and my gut tightened. I dared not move and the tension in me mounted. I was utterly surprised when he said, "I know what you've been offered and I think you're a smart kid. Don't take it. I think you should leave and when you get home, don't tell your old man anything."

'He won't want to know,' I thought. 'He would not believe me, no one would.'

About the same time, unbeknown to me, my mother was calling the hotels and restaurants around the town, looking for me. I firmly believed that fate played a vital part in the events of the night when I overheard the bartender asking the manager if he knew anyone by the name of Emma Carter working at the hotel. Of course he did not, I was using Matt's name.

As soon as I finished work, I quickly slipped away without anyone noticing and went in search of a telephone box to call Sydney. My mother answered the late call.

"Oh Emma," she said anxiously sounding relieved to hear from me, "you have to come home, Les is beside himself."

She went on to tell me how the Carters took over the care of the children and she could not get near them. The longer I listened, the angrier I became. The money ran out but the line did not cut off. I suspected the operator was listening in on the conversation. My mother pleaded with me to ring Les, and I agreed to call him right away.

He began his sobbing the moment I said hello. I told him to pull himself together. "I hear you've given my baby away to your sister."

"Please come home, Bubby," he sniffled, ignoring my statement.

"Where is BJ, Les?" I demanded.

"With Bell. She wants to adopt him," he was still crying. "Please come home, I need you."

"Get my child back from your sister!" I ordered.

"Yes, Bubby," he said then asked. "Did you get my letters?"

"What letters? Where did you send them?"

"To the post office," he sniffed.

Through his tears Les managed to tell me that he had written a letter every week and sent it to the post office in hope that I would read them and come back home. "How could I, when I did not know you had written to me?" I said exasperated.

Once I reassured him that I would go to the post office and collect the letters, he sounded more coherent. The phone call ended with my promise to call that evening, "I want to speak to my babies when I call," I said.

The idea of speaking to my children gave me hope when I had thought there was none. Les was using them to entice me to return home; what irony that was. The letters were just as I had expected, full of empty promises not to hit me again, begging forgiveness and confessing his undying love for me. I read them with contempt, knowing that he was incapable of understanding anything short of violence. The phone call to the children that evening was more satisfying and I could not wait to see them.

I knew that my plans to leave Darwin had to be made and carried out in secrecy. I booked my plane ticket and then quickly packed my belongings and sent them to Sydney a few days prior to my leaving the flat, undetected. It was easily done, since Kelly was hardly ever home and I had mostly kept to myself.

On the Thursday evening, I went to work and acted as though nothing was wrong. Joe and a couple of well-dressed men were sitting at a table at the back of the room watching me. It was reasonable to assume that I was the topic of their conversation. I had to respond when Joe called me over to his table.

"Hello sweetheart," he grinned, "how about taking our orders?"

"Fine Joe," I replied nonchalantly, "what would you like?"

Thankfully, Joe did not bother me for the rest of the evening after I had brought them their drinks. At end of the shift however, he invited me to join him and his friends.

"Not tonight, Joe," I said. "I'm tired, I really don't feel that well. I would not be very good company."

He eyed me suspiciously saying, "I'll see you Saturday night, we will talk then."

The bells of impending danger rang loud and clear. I needed to work the next two nights to finance the return trip to Sydney but keeping out of sight was necessary too, and the rest of my belongings were still at the flat. I had to get them. My mind was racing, trying to work out what I should do. I knew Kelly would not be home, so after work I took a cab back to the flat and collected my things, then went to a motel and stayed there.

The following night was a long and tiring shift. I usually enjoyed my job, especially after I learned how to handle myself, but that night my tolerance was low. When a drunk became amorous with me, I stopped him touching me by pouring a jug of beer over his head. His mates roared and cheered with rowdy laughter and drew unwanted attention to me.

Kelly came over out of concern when she heard the ruckus, mostly out of curiosity. She whispered, "Where have you been, Em?"

"Shacked up with a guy I met last week," I said, and Kelly went back to her section smiling.

Later at the motel, I sat on the bed taking stock of my money and realised the added expense of the motel room had eaten into my finances. I did not have enough money to pay for the ticket. When I sent my things home, I had packed my bankbook in the trunk too, thinking that I would have enough with tips.

Saturday nights were always busy and boisterous. I was serving a table when Mark arrived. He waved from the door to get my attention. I looked at him with mixed emotions, wishing he had not come and yet pleased that he had. I noticed he carried himself in the manner of a mature man, confident and self-assured. I admired those qualities in him.

Instinct told me that, although there was much to be admired and like about Mark, it would be unwise to carry the friendship any further. I felt sad about having to let him down, believing that under different circumstances our friendship could have become something more.

Towards the end of the evening, Joe approached me with instructions to make myself available. "Just think of the three hundred dollars, sweetheart," were his parting words and I shuddered at the thought of some awful man touching me. Although I felt sick and was scared, the fact remained that I did not have enough money for the ticket and the motel. I did not want to involve my family in any way in my situation. I did not want to owe anyone anything either. My family was under the illusion that I was still with Matt. It was my business, not theirs. I'll deal with things my way, I declared to myself.

At closing time, I left the back way to avoid Mark. I saw him waiting out the front of the hotel talking to his mates, as my taxi drove past. I felt sad. He looked so handsome, dressed in dark slacks and a short-sleeved shirt. His black hair neatly combed into place when only minutes before, it had been unruly and falling onto his forehead. I lowered my head so he would not see me.

When the taxi pulled up in front of the nightclub, loud music from inside could be heard out in the street. I entered the dimly lit room with caution and waited a moment for my eyes to adjust to the haze. Kelly saw me standing at the door. She stood up and waved me over. I quickly glanced around the room, and then reluctantly headed for her table.

The drinks she ordered arrived at the same time as my dreaded nightmare joined us. Self-assured, Joe whispered to me, "Here's the address." He handed me a slip of paper. "Take a cab there, and then come back here with the money when you're finished."

I started to protest.

"It's all arranged, don't let me down," he said, throwing down the last of his drink before leaving. He left Kelly and me looking at each other. I suspected she was working for him, and thought it was the reason why she was hardly ever at the flat. "Make sure you come back here afterwards Em," she warned, "Joe doesn't like it if he's messed about."

The cab pulled up in front of an ordinary looking house. I checked the address to make sure it was correct. As a safeguard, I asked the driver to return in half an hour. "I'll wait for you at the end of the street," I said, then walked gingerly to the end of the pathway and knocked on the front door.

A man's voice from inside the house called out, "Come in!"

I timidly entered and found a couple of men, both about thirty, playing cards in the kitchen. Neither of them acknowledged me but the one facing me pointed to a door. Following his direction I opened the door and entered the room and closed the door behind me. The room was in darkness except for a streetlight filtering through open curtains. I stood petrified at the door, the sound of my heart pounding in my ears.

A kindly voice from the far end of the room said, "I'm not going to hurt you." I relaxed a little...

Instead of returning to the nightclub as Joe instructed, I went to the motel, where I showered and scrubbed myself, endeavouring to feel clean, utterly astonished at what I had done. The money on the side table told the story and yet it was still inconceivable. "Am I capable of anything?" I questioned. "No!" I told myself, "I had to do it to get home and get my children back."

That justification did little to ease my conscience but I knew I had to put it behind me. I cried tears of shame and loneliness. While still wrapped in a towel, I curled up in a foetal position and fell asleep. A figure standing beside the bed woke me with a start. I was about to scream when his hand covered my mouth.

"Shh, it's only me."

Indignantly, I pulled the sheet up to cover myself. "What are you doing in my room? How the hell did you get in?" I demanded sharply, angry at the invasion and forgetting who I was yelling at. Thankfully Rick did not take offence to the way I spoke to him. The point of his visit was to show me just how small the town was.

"I know where you have been tonight."

Interrupting him I said, "I've got a ticket booked on Monday's flight."

"Good! Joe's looking for you and wants the money. This isn't a good place for you to be. Go back to your old man and work things out with him and never tell him anything."

"Why do you keep saying that?" I asked puzzled.

"Because he won't understand, and some day he might try to use it against you to get even. Don't tell anyone anything."

It made me nervous that Rick had found me so easily. As soon as the stores opened I went into town, purchased a long, dark wig and dark glasses, and wore them in public until I boarded the plane. It gave me the freedom to get to the airport unnoticed.

The wait at the airport was a nightmare. The heat, along with the tension, was unbearable. I spent most of the time out of sight, hidden in the ladies room. Although I thought it was ridiculous I felt the need for caution, especially if Joe was looking for me to collect his share of the money.

During that time I thought about Matt and decided to call him at the Naval Base. His greeting was warm but he went quiet when I said, "I'm leaving Darwin, I'm going home." I felt sad and wished things had been different between us.

"When are you leaving?"

"In about a half an hour, Matt, I'm sorry."

"Me too Princess, I do love you, you know," he said.

I wiped my tears. "I know, and I love you, things just got in the way. I guess it was not the right time for us."

"You will always be my princess."

I laughed. "I really don't feel much like one at the moment. Bye Matt."

"Goodbye darling, I'm sorry,"

"Me too." 'More than you'll ever know', I thought, and knew that I would never forget him.

16

When the plane touched down at Sydney Airport, the thought of seeing Les again had my stomach doing back flips. I nervously waited until the other passengers had disembarked before I made any attempt to move. When I found courage to face whatever lay ahead, I removed the wig, brushed my hair into place, stood up, took a deep breath and then walked off the plane, confident that I was going to be in charge of my own life from then on.

From the tarmac, Les waved frantically to attract my attention. I ignored him and kept walking towards the gate. He continued to wave and I finally waved back. To my acute embarrassment, he then climbed over the high fence and ran crying and laughing towards me along the tarmac. People stopped walking and watched him. I looked at him with utter disbelief. I was shocked to a standstill, wishing the ground would open up and swallow me.

Les had lost weight dramatically in my absence. His looks had never appealed to me and now he appeared even less attractive. On the way home I mentioned the weight loss.

"I didn't want to eat anything, Bubby. I wanted to lose all the weight I could for you. I've been taking diet pills to help me," he happily confessed. I did not say anything.

Changing the subject, I asked who was minding the children.

"Your parents, they're waiting for you at the house."

"And BJ, is he there too?"

Les appeared uncomfortable and did not answer.

"Where is he, Les?" I asked, demanding an answer.

"Still at Bell's, she won't give him back." He was on the brink of tears.

"Oh yes she will. I'll take him. She can't stop me. He'll be home tonight. I can promise you that!"

When I entered the house the children welcomed me with open arms. It was astonishing just how much they all had grown while I was away. I gazed upon their dear little faces with fresh eyes, fully appreciating that those beautiful children were actually mine, while silently vowing never to leave them again.

I felt my parents' judgement upon me, but after experiencing my independence I was past caring what they or anyone else thought. Les hovered around me like an excited child but I was preoccupied with getting my baby home that evening. Fear engulfed him when I said I was ready to pick up BJ. He had led me to believe we would do just that after I had seen the children. His reluctance forced me to ring Bell to inform her that I was coming for BJ. Bell told me that I could not have him.

"Listen to me, Bell," I said, slowly and firmly, "You failed to hear me. I'm running this show now. I told you I am coming around to collect my son. I suggest you have him ready."

Will answered my knock at the door and Bell stood behind him holding my son.

"We don't want any trouble," I said, without fear of intimidation. "Just give me my child and I'll leave."

"This time," Bell said glaring at me, "look after him properly."

"Don't tell me how to look after my children," I snapped. "They were all in good health before I left." I stepped forward and took BJ from Bell, thanked her politely for taking care of him, then left.

Sitting in the car looking at BJ a few moments, I turned to Les and said venomously, "Don't you ever think about giving away any of my children, again."

Later I discovered just how badly neglected BJ was. Bell took over when Les could not cope any longer. BJ had lost weight and had an awful nappy rash that caused him great discomfort.

Since surviving the episode in Darwin and weathering the storm of my return, strength and courage had become my friend. I had changed and become my own person. I refused to be intimidated by anyone.

The money I earned was quickly absorbed into the household, with the exception of eighty dollars I put away for myself. When Les started asking a lot of questions, I remembered Rick's warning and was careful not to disclose too much. While watching my children playing together, the couple of months in Darwin seemed surreal. Did they really happen?

The change in me was inevitable and with that change came a desire to have more out of life. I had no idea how to fulfil the desires that stirred an irritating restlessness in me. But I was no longer content to accept life as it was. I wanted things to change.

Immeasurable dreams for the future haunted my thoughts. I believed that if one had a strong enough desire to succeed one could. My children became the driving forces behind me. I wanted a better life for them as well as for myself. Les however, did not hold the same views. He refused to dream or to plan any further ahead than the next day and even doing that much was quite ambitious for him. His lack of enthusiasm for life jaded and infuriated me. I felt frustrated living on time-payment and doing without.

When Mary and her boyfriend Tim announced their engagement, I splurged some of the money I had hidden away. I wanted a special outfit to wear to my sister's engagement and to buy them a nice gift. My wardrobe consisted of a couple of old maternity outfits due to be tossed away and a few pairs of jeans and tee shirts.

Perhaps the Norma Tullo black crepe pant-suit that I bought was expensive, but I looked and felt wonderful in it. The transformation when wearing the garment was amazing. The instant I put it on, I felt less like a dowdy housewife and more like an elegant, attractive woman. I just had to have it.

Les was outraged at the extravagant purchase, raving and ranting about how he worked his arse off while I wasted his hard-earned money. Enraged at his audacity, I reminded him that I too contributed to the running of the family and was entitled to a little something in return.

"I spent my money, not yours. Money I earned in Darwin!"

"Yeah and you ran off to Darwin with my pay and left us stranded!"

"What do you mean?" I was utterly shocked. "I did nothing of the sort. Diane can tell you that I left the money in the buffet drawer, I told her to tell you where it was. I knew that was all we had." I was crying, devastated at being accused of something so horrible.

"Yeah, well I didn't get it…"

The children were distressed at the sight of us fighting. Les yelled at them to shut up, only making the situation worse. In fury, he destroyed toys lying in his path. Brad watched his father demolish a favourite toy he had been given that Christmas, the destruction driving him to hysteria. Pandemonium ran rampant and the house was in turmoil. I was frantically trying to calm the children, to no avail. Les warned me if I did not shut them up he knew how to. I panicked and the children cried louder.

Les seized Brad by his arm and thrashed him. I tugged on Brad's free arm, screaming at Les to let go of him. Immediately after releasing Brad, he grabbed Cain ready to strike him too.

"Touch him and I'll kill you," I shrieked with venom. He let him go. "Get out! Get out!" I shouted and he left.

Brad, Celeste and Cain kept crying long after Les had gone. Utterly at a loss for a solution, I too sat on the floor and cried, slumped against the lounge with my legs outstretched. Celeste sat on one leg and Brad on the other, and Cain sat in between.

The commotion had woken BJ. I could hear him crying in his room. My mind was in turmoil and the children were not settling down because I was so upset. I pulled myself together, gently peeled clinging arms from around my neck and went to BJ. On my way to the bedroom I shuddered, realising that now my children were also in the firing line of Les' abusive outrage. Gut instinct told me that I had to do something before he hurt them.

When I opened the door and walked into semi-darkness BJ stopped grizzling and smiled at me. "Mom, mommm," he mumbled.

"Hello big boy," I cooed. BJ was jumping up and down, hanging on the side of the cot. He needed a nappy change. I pulled up the blind and opened the window. He blinked and turned away as sunlight flooded the room. After I had changed BJ. I gave the children a snack and thought about what I had to do. Looking around the clean, but sparsely-furnished dining room for the phone book, a sense of urgency came over me. Driven by fear and without a second thought to the consequences, I phoned Tom Hall, the child welfare officer, I had spoken to before going to Darwin. He lost no time in answering my plea for help. He could see that we were all visibly upset.

"So Emma," he said, "you now think your husband could be a threat to the children's safety?"

"That's why I called you. I need your help to protect them from him. I didn't think he would hurt them before, but now I'm not so sure," I was nervous and agitated, wiping my eyes.

He took me completely by surprise when he said, "I will take the children with me now. I have a place for them."

"Where? Where are they going?"

"I can't tell you. It's best that you don't know. It's for their safety that I can't tell you," he said.

"But... but I'm their mother. I should know. I didn't hurt them," I pleaded with him as he ushered my children out the door.

"Call my office tomorrow," he said. "I'll have details of the hearing date for you." Then he was gone to who knows where with Brad, Celeste and Cain. I was staggered, still holding BJ and staring at the opened door feeling heartsick, thinking that I may have acted impulsively. "Hell, what if I never see them again," I moaned. My head was thumping. It was as if a whirlwind had hit the house.

I imagined that I would have access to my children while they were in custody. That was why I called Tom Hall. I thought he was on my side and would help me. I feared that I had made a grave mistake calling him, but there was no other place to go, no safe place I could have gone with the children. I pulled myself together and packed a few of BJ's and my things and drove over to my parents' place.

Their house was small, certainly not large enough to accommodate my four children and me, especially since Tina and her young daughter, Kate had moved in after her short-lived marriage ended in divorce. Mary was also living there. BJ and I had to sleep in the lounge room.

I worried all afternoon. Even though Tom Hall had assured me the children were in good hands, still I wondered if I had done the right thing. I knew I had when Les arrived on my parents' doorstep that night. He was menacing and threatening, accusing me of getting rid of the children because I wanted to wear my new outfit to the engagement party. I stared at him in disbelief, realising that his ravings confirmed that he was dangerous. He was absolutely delusional, refusing to take any responsibility for his violent behaviour.

"You are insane, Les," I told him, shaking my head at his absurd statement, "You tried to hurt the children, that's why they were taken away. Come near me again with your threats and you'll never see them, ever again. They will stay in foster care as long as you are a threat to us."

He ignored what I had said and repeated his accusations, blaming me for the trouble.

"I won't give in Les, you've gone too far this time," I said with conviction. "I'll see you in court."

Remarkably, the atmosphere in my parents' home was less tense. Although no one knew the full extent of what had happened over the years between Les and I, it had become obvious to the family that the situation was very serious. A sombre atmosphere hung in the air when all should have been celebration and fun, in readiness for Mary and Tim's engagement party.

On the day of the hearing, I did not have any decent clothes of my own to wear other than the pant-suit, but that was evening wear and totally unsuitable. I had to borrow a dress from Tina that I did not really like. It was either that dress or a pair of worn jeans and an old tee shirt. The multi-coloured swirls on the dress looked like a psychedelic whirlwind, which was not my taste at all. I was more conservative, but that day the choice was not mine.

Feeling nervous and apprehensive about the unknown, and very self-conscious swathed in bright colours, I walked warily along the footpath leading to the courthouse. A sudden burst of false courage shot through me when I noticed Les standing at the top of the stairs glaring down at me. I boldly walked past him with my head held high, carrying BJ. As I entered the courthouse foyer I hoped I would see the children before court convened, but they were nowhere to be seen. Time seemed to stand still while I waited for what felt like an eternity. Tears of hopelessness filled my eyes and ran down my cheeks. I knew I had to pull myself together before Tom Hall arrived and misinterpreted my sombre mood. I felt relieved when I saw him walking towards me.

He was tall and slender with fair hair, and looked about thirty-something. Initially I had thought Tom seemed sympathetic and understanding about my situation, but that day he was more preoccupied with the papers he had in his hand than answering my barrage of questions. 'Perhaps,' I later thought, 'he did that to avoid answering me.'

As suddenly as he had appeared on the scene Tom disappeared, only to reappear again with the children and a female guardian, minutes before court was called to order. I only caught a glimpse of the children when they entered a room next to the courtroom. Tom Hall did not go in. He closed the door behind them and then hurried over to me, and ushered me into the courtroom to a seat at the front, then sat down beside me. I nervously scanned the room, looking for the children but could not see them. Just as I was about to ask where they were, the call for 'all stand' rang throughout the room. Court was in session.

Tom Hall stood up and read out my complaint. When he was finished, the magistrate looked at me and asked if I thought it was safe for my children to go home and be in the company of their father. I hesitated at the question, and before I could say anything, the magistrate raised the gavel he held and then slammed it forcefully down on the desk, announcing another hearing in two weeks from that day, dismissing me.

'What happened?' I thought, fighting the urge to scream, but I was too stunned to say or do anything other than tremble, clinging to BJ sitting on my lap. I was in shock and utterly bewildered. Then without any warning, Les ran from the courtroom like a lunatic when he saw the children being shepherded away. He grabbed hold of Celeste and tried to run off with her. She cried out to me in terror. I sprang to my feet and yelled at Les to let her go. Five duty officers tackled him. He fled the instant Celeste was freed.

I was given only a few minutes with my babies before they were taken away to who knows where. They clung to me in fear, uncertain of their destiny. Les' reckless action had frightened the wits out of Celeste but had given strength to my complaint, proving in front of so many witnesses that Les was indeed unstable. There was little consolation in that for me. My children were still in foster care when they should have come home that day.

Outside the courthouse in the parking lot, I sat in the car. BJ was beside me in his car seat. I had no idea what to do as I had expected the children to come home with me.

'Everything is wrong, it shouldn't be like this.' I felt sick to my stomach and pounded the steering wheel in frustration, crying. BJ gave me a puzzled look.

"You poor little guy," I said when I noticed him looking at me. "You don't have a clue what's going on, do you? Never mind mate, Mommy will look after you." He was only eight months old and so much had happened in his life already. "Thank God, you are such a good baby. You hardly ever cry. I thank God you're still with me." He smiled at me and I felt better.

Tina was sitting in the kitchen alone when we returned. Her concern for me was touching. She affectionately patted my arm and said, "Never mind, Emma, never mind. I'll make you a cup of tea." She jumped up from her chair and headed for the sink, then stopped. "Oh Emma," she said, holding her hand to her mouth, "look at the dress, it's covered in blood."

Thankfully, the blood was not easily detected because of the dazzling colourful swirls on the fabric. The shock of the day's events had prematurely brought on my period. I felt drained and prayed for the nightmare to end quickly. A shower and a fresh set of clothes lifted my mood and by the time the others had arrived home I was in higher spirits, ready to talk about what happened in court.

BJ kept me occupied the week that followed and I was grateful for the distraction. Preparations for the party were well on the way, the big event only days away. My parents encouraged me to go to the party, thinking that if Les came to the house in their absence and found me alone he might harm me.

I washed, set and dried my hair unenthusiastically, wondering why I was bothering at all, but as I dressed for the party a sense of excitement began to stir in me. While sitting on the side of the bed in the room I once shared with my sisters, applying my make-up, it occurred to me that I was doing the same preening ritual in the same place that I did when I was a teenager, in readiness for the Saturday night pictures, parties and dances. Vivid memories of those years flooded my mind. I imagined I could hear the sound of my old transistor radio, blaring out 'top forty' tunes that I used to dance to about the house, as I sang along with the pop artist while getting dressed. I love music and especially love to dance. When my favourite songs played on the radio, I would turn up the volume and sometimes dash to the other house radios and turn them on too. Music filled the house. The noise I created annoyed my parents, who were forever yelling at me to turn the music down or off, but I pretended not to hear them. My mother once admitted that the house died when I left home. The radio was hardly ever on after I moved away.

I slipped into the infamous black pant-suit, wishing I had something else to wear. As I did up the numerous tiny, sparkling, black buttons it crossed my mind that it must be the most expensive garment, in terms of heartache, that I have ever owned.

Catching a glimpse of my reflection in the mirror, I contemplated the image I saw and appreciated the remarkable transformation. I really did look different and felt elegant too. I liked the way my hair took on a new life. It fell smooth and sleek, turning under, just touching my shoulders. My eyes shone in disbelief, astonished at the difference the outfit had made in me. I walked slowly towards the mirror for a closer look and smiled, realising that I looked like someone I used to know. Me! Little did I know it then, but buying that outfit triggered a major turning point in my life.

At the party, I was talking to my aunty and uncle when Mary interrupted to say that Les was waiting in the front of the hall. "He wants to talk to you, Emma," she said with uncertainty. A knot in the pit of my stomach gripped my insides when Mary mentioned Les' name, but I hid what I was feeling and put on a brave face as I went outside to see what he wanted.

"I promise not to cause any trouble to wreck the party," Les said when he saw me approaching. "I just wanted to talk with you."

I stood a little distance from him and waited to hear why he had come.

"You look beautiful," he said.

"What do you want, Les?" I asked, half turning ready to leave.

"I'm leaving the country. I have a job with a company on Bougainville Island."

I was so surprised that I sat down on the fence.

"Where in the world is Bougainville Island?" I asked.

"In the Solomon Islands," he replied in monotone. "You can tell the magistrate I won't hurt you or the kids any more. I'm leaving the country. You can bring them back home now. Arrangements will be made for money to be sent to you. You won't have to worry about anything. I'll look after you and the kids."

Les left, promising to call me in a few days. After he had gone it took a while for me to digest what he had said. My head was in a spin. Finally my prayers had been answered, but I could not fathom why I felt so hollow.

The heaviness persisted, along with an unfathomable resentment towards Les for not being a better father. I felt hurt and betrayed because the children were not enough for him to build his dreams upon. Initially, I had been willing to give the marriage a go, but he betrayed me with my mother and refused to communicate with me, pushing me further away. And he blamed me for the trouble between us. Why didn't the children make a difference? It was true I didn't love him, but we could have worked together on a friendship to hold the marriage together for their sake, I reasoned. He would not even do that. Now things had come to this. My children were without a father because Les could not cope with the reality of life. 'He's a coward for hitting out at us the moment things get too tough for him to handle,' I thought. The bastard has no understanding of what love is all about. After I arrived home from Darwin, he confiscated and destroyed the letters he had sent to me. Getting rid of the evidence, I reasoned. Why the hell didn't he let us go long before all this heartache happened? Why didn't he? "Damn you, Les Carter! Damn you to hell!"

The magistrate awarded me custody of the children. I assured them when they came home that their father did not mean to frighten or to hurt them; that he was going away to work so we could have a good life and someday buy a nice home. They understood enough not to be afraid of him.

"Will Daddy come and say goodbye to us before he goes away?" Brad asked anxiously.

"He'll be here soon. This could be him now," I said answering the knock at the door.

The atmosphere in the room was sombre when Les apologised to the children. He looked at me with uncertainty. He stood in the middle of the room, opened his arms and beckoned me towards him. His demeanour reminded me of an over-grown child, unsure of what he had done wrong, knowing only that he was in trouble. Les looked so woeful and pathetic that it was difficult not to pity him. Hesitating for a moment, I stepped into his embrace. "Look after yourself," were my parting words.

Brad was the only one aware of his father's absence and kept asking when he was coming back home. The other children were content with their daily routine without him. Celeste, usually shy and softly spoken, was more out-going after Les left. She was a delightful, sweet and gentle child. I was always tripping over her as she shadowed me around the house wanting to help.

Cain on the other hand thundered throughout the house and bellowed like a bull calf when he was hurt in the slightest way. Although he was demanding, most times he willingly waited his turn for kisses and cuddles. The children were very affectionate towards me as I was with them. The moment I sat on the floor it would be a race to see who would get to my lap first. I would end up at the bottom of a pile of laughing and squealing bodies.

BJ's red-gold hair had initially caused me some concern. I expected him to have a volatile personality but fortunately my fears were groundless. His personality was to the contrary. BJ was the most patient of all my children. His approach to play reflected the attitude he would take throughout his later life. He would try for a short time to overcome or to master whatever it was he was trying to do, showing only a mild frustration when he failed, before moving on to something within his limits, and only challenged himself in areas that interested him. There was no way known BJ would be pushed into brilliance. He learnt everything in his own way, at times displaying independence and maturity beyond his years. BJ was certainly a free spirit.

The prospect of raising my children alone was not in the least bit daunting. I welcomed the challenge. All I needed from Les was his financial support. Tim, my soon to be brother-in-law, was a solicitor. He offered to help me work out a budgeting system I could easily follow. Les wanted an accurate account of every cent spent. He refused to put any trust in my ability because I was a female. His chauvinistic attitude annoyed me, but I realised that any man with his kind of attitude towards women was afraid of them. 'Discretion is the better part of valour,' I thought with amusement and agreed to whatever he wanted me to do. It was a game, his game at the moment, but some day things would change. It was only a matter of time.

A peaceful harmony had descended on our home. Each evening before going to bed, I crept into the children's room and watched them sleep. They looked like angels asleep. I smiled and wondered if they would ever know how much I loved them.

Shortly after Les had left for Bougainville Island, Luc called. He wanted to see me. A few months had passed since we had seen each other. He had phoned a few times but the calls were brief. I had been expecting him because of all the questions I knew he would have about me going to Darwin.

We talked for hours that night. I told him as much as I dared about Darwin and about my current situation. He sounded annoyed that I left Cain with Les and asked, "Why didn't you take him with you?"

"I would never choose one over the other Luc, even though Cain is your son and very special to me, I love them all equally. I couldn't take him and leave the others behind. It was hard enough leaving them as it was. Please try and understand," I pleaded. He said he did but I wondered if he really could.

Luc moved to embrace me but I turned away from him, not wanting to start anything I was not ready for.

"What's wrong?" He sounded concerned.

"Nothing's wrong, perhaps I'm just growing up."

"And what's that supposed to mean?" without waiting for an answer and sounding more irritated, he said. "Look, I know you've been through a lot, but I can't help you if I don't know what's going on. You and that damn pride of yours!" he said, raising his voice slightly. "Why won't you let me help you?"

"Don't yell at me. Nobody has that right. I won't stand for it," I said tearfully, and he quickly apologised.

"Tell me," I confronted him, "are you prepared to leave your wife and take me and my four children?"

He went silent and looked at the floor.

"No, I thought not," softening my voice I said, "I do understand that you have made a life without me and that's fine, really it is."

He looked at me.

"So what good would it have done for you to know the whole story? It's in the past now. I really believe things will change. I don't know how, but I can feel it."

"I hope you're right, Doll, for your sake."

"I am. I know I am. For the first time in my life I know what I want."

"And what's that?"

"Everything for the children; a nice home, clothes, private schools, the best of everything. They're my future and I'm determined that they'll have all that I can possibly give to them."

"How are you going to do all that?"

"I don't know yet. But, I will when the time comes."

Luc commented on how much I had changed and questioned whether I would have been satisfied with him if we had been together.

"We'll never know that, will we Luc?"

He appeared hurt by my sarcasm. Luc of all people should have known better than that. In spite of all that had happened, my feelings for him had not altered. They never would. After he left, I wondered what to do about our relationship. As much as I loved him I did not want to be in a nowhere situation. Perhaps a few months ago I would have, but things had changed and so had I.

I did not have to wait long before fate stepped in. Three months after Les left Australia for New Guinea, I received a letter from the real estate agent informing me the lease on our house had expired, and the current owners wanted to take possession of the house. We would have to vacate the premises as soon as possible.

When Les phoned that week I told him about the letter. He asked me to consider moving to Bougainville to start over. The thought of travelling overseas to live in another country sounded exciting.

From about nine months of age, eczema had plagued Cain's little body and progressively worsened. Weeping sores persisted in the folds of his skin around his neck, arms and groin, and in between his fingers and toes. I practically lived at the children's hospital, visiting doctors and trying all kinds of lotions and potions. "What can I do?" I asked the doctor in desperation, looking at Cain. "He's in agony. And if he cries, he scratches more. I don't know what else to do. I'm following your instructions but there's no improvement."

"The Solomon Islands would be the best place for Cain," the doctor said. "The climate would clear up the eczema."

At that time, the Solomon Islands were as remote to me as the moon.

Recalling what the doctor had said, I felt it was a sign and told Les we would come. My family thought I had lost my mind, but I was not to be dissuaded. My gut feeling was far too strong to ignore it.

I called Luc and told him. He said very little over the telephone but said, "Mind if I call around tonight?"

The children were still up when Luc arrived and they were thrilled to see him. The likeness between Cain and his father never ceased to amaze me. Luc obviously loved Cain and realised he would miss seeing him grow up.

The children settled down quickly without any fuss, which left the rest of the evening to us. I took a quick shower before joining Luc in the lounge room. When I entered the room wrapped in a towel he stood up and stepped towards me. He drew me closer and tightened his arms around me. Our bodies moulded together in an embrace.

"I'm going to miss you," he whispered.

I did not answer. He knew how I felt. 'He loves me, I'm certain. His love is shown with emotion, not with words.'

When I woke up the next morning, Luc was gone. He had stayed well past midnight, which surprised me, and I wondered what excuse he gave his wife. That thought lingered only a minute as I did not really care. I was far too happy to worry about anything, still marvelling in the pleasure of being with him the night before.

<u>Part Two</u>

Sassy and Unshackled

17

"Goodbye," Mary said, hugging me and then the children at the departure lounge. "Take care of yourself."

"I will," I replied, and smiled broadly. "Don't worry, we'll be fine." My words gave her little comfort. Her eyes were full of concern as we fell into line with the other passengers.

The children bubbled over with excitement as they climbed into their seats. It was their first taste of travelling. I went to pull Celeste's seat belt across her lap and she stopped me, saying, "I can do it, Mommy."

"Me too," echoed Brad and Cain from their seats in front.

I stood up and leaned forward to check on the boys. They tilted their heads backwards, gave me a cheeky look and grinned mischievously. Four-year-old Brad was quite the little man in a reserved way. He took his role as big brother very seriously and kept a vigilant eye on Cain and Celeste. Two-year-old Cain was bold and far from shy, his extrovert personality and good looks turning heads. Pert and pretty, three-year-old Celeste happily sat across the aisle from eleven-month-old BJ and me.

I exhaled long and deep once the children had settled down with colouring-in books and pencils. I sat back into my seat, contemplating how rapidly our lives had changed, while listening to the hum of the jet engines. My mind never seemed to stop, always thinking and analysing situations.

My family must have thought that I had lost my mind, leaving the country to live with Les in PNG. I knew I had made the right decision. My confidence was based solely on the predictions of the elderly hunchback, I was introduced to by an acquaintance shortly after returning from Darwin.

Les had found another position as diesel fitter just before BJ was born. He had been there only a few months when he came home from work and said, "I've invited Ray, a bloke from the workshop and his missus, over for dinner Saturday night, is that okay?"

I raised my eyebrows in surprise and nodded, welcoming the idea of seeing people other than my family and Les. "Why yes, of course. What are they like?"

He shrugged. "Don't know. Ray seems all right. He knows his job. Don't know what his missus is like, haven't met her."

Ray and Brenda Briggs were childless. Ray appeared to be about my age and Brenda perhaps a year or two older. They were trendy and wore the latest fashions. Both worked, and obviously made and spent a lot of money. They were into the party scene and had little in common with us.

During the meal Brenda talked about a weird man she and one of her friends went to see in the city.

"He was amazing!" she gushed. "He told me so many things. Some of them have already happened, haven't they love?" she said enthusiastically, nudging her husband.

"Yeah, the bloke's unreal."

Most of the evening was taken up with them talking about the numerologist. Les could not help himself and had to say, "Ah, that's all bullshit!" He left the table, bringing the evening to a close.

I could easily recall the old man's image, his small, crooked body and balding pate with stingy remnants of hair dangling around his collar, which gave him a Dickensian appearance, and his little dingy city office cluttered with books from floor to ceiling. I felt wary of him when I first saw him and wondered if coming to him was a mistake.

"What is your date of birth?" he asked holding his pen ready to write as I sat down. "Hmm, ah huh," he muttered as he scribbled on a note pad in front of him, when I told him.

My eyes involuntarily opened wide with interest when he began to tell me what my date of birth meant.

"You will travel over water and your life will change," he said, peering at the numbers. I waited patiently as he consulted several thick books lying on the desk beside him. When he spoke he described my children and what they would achieve in their lifetime.

"The child with red hair has a turn in his eye. Don't worry about it, the eye muscle will correct itself." My jaw fell open. I wondered how the hell he knew that and how he knew Celeste had a birthmark under her left arm.

"Your third child is different to your other children, he is darker. His father isn't the same as your other children." My eyes opened even wider. What other dark secrets would he reveal?

"Our paths are predestined," he said, as if reading my mind. "The children you have were no accident." He stopped writing and looked at me and asked, "Do you understand?" I nodded, although I did not have a clue what he meant then. "You'll have another child later in life."

All sorts of questions formed in my mind but I was too afraid to ask any of them, fearing the truth, since he had been so accurate with everything else.

"Yes," he said, scanning the chart he made, "you will go overseas. Everything will change for you when you do, but I warn you," he looked keenly at me again, "You must trust your instincts and you will be alright."

What he said puzzled me, but I sensed that it was all he was going to tell me when he handed me the chart. I took it, thanked him and went home thinking nothing more about the encounter until Les asked if the children and I would come to Bougainville.

When the aircraft landed at Port Moresby we received a rude shock, coming from Sydney's chilly winter into Papua New Guinea's stifling tropical heat.

'Had I known what to expect,' I thought, sighing heavily when the heat blasted me in the face the moment we left the air-conditioned cabin, 'I would have worn less underclothing.'

"Hell it's hot!" I groaned quietly, and glanced at the children. Their faces had turned bright pink and perspiration oozed from their pores within a few short minutes of disembarking.

The airport was no better than a huge open corrugated iron shed on concrete. It was congested with indigenous nationals. Rubbish and litter were everywhere and an awful stench hanging in the air assaulted my nostrils. Large groups of local people sat on the ground of the enclosure, black faces observing the children and me with keen interest. I felt weary from the heat and carrying BJ around on my back in the baby pack. I looked around for a vacant space to put him down. I needed to strip him to his nappy, and wipe him and the other children with a damp cloth to cool them down.

Cain had already taken off most of his clothes before I got to him. I told him to put his jeans back on. As much as he was an extrovert, he still liked to carry his empty baby bottle with him, as a comforter. He stood beside me all puffed up and grinning like a fool at the onlookers, hands on hips and his bottle tucked under his armpit. Shyness prevented Brad from removing more than his jumper and shirt.

The activity around Celeste caused her to feel a little overawed. She had never encountered people gawking curiously at her before, and I also was feeling uncertain of my surroundings. Cain and Brad were fascinated with everything. I had to caution both of them not to wander away, "Otherwise, you could get left behind and you wouldn't want that, would you?" I warned, bending down to look both boys in the eyes. "No Mommy!" Cain said, shaking his head. Brad silently shook his head too, looking worried.

The overpowering and unfamiliar stench made me feel queasy. It was coming from the curious sea of sweating bodies, sitting near the only place I found, where I could put

BJ down. The local people sitting nearby were friendly and smiled at us glazed eyed, revealing red-stained teeth. A few reached out to touch the children. Celeste's long blonde hair was a huge fascination to the women, enticing them to move in closer to touch it. She immediately cowered behind me when the black hands reached for her. "It's alright, sweetie," I said, gently easing her to the front of me "I won't let anyone hurt you. They only want to look at your pretty hair." Celeste relaxed a little but still clutched at my clothing, even though she knew she was safe. She smiled timidly as the mysterious shiny, black figures in bright tops, with colourful fabric wrapped around their full hips and tucked in at the waist, expressing their delight of feeling her silky locks, by giggling and babbling to one another.

I later learned that watching aircraft arrive and depart was a favourite pastime of the local people.

A sense of excitement and anticipation hung in the air when time came to board the plane for Bougainville Island. I gathered my children together and weaved through the human maze to reach the aircraft.

In a book called 'Bougainville, The Establishment of a Copper Mine,' I read, *'Bougainville Island is the principal island of the northern group of the Solomon Islands and is about 120 miles long and 30 miles wide. An island of great beauty, it features a steep mountain range in parts 8,500ft high, which can fall rapidly to the sea over a distance of 10 miles. It has active volcanoes, fast streams that rush along like rapids, native villages that clung to mountain ridges, plantations and elusive fish.'*

Bougainville was occupied by Germany before the First World War and then by Japan's armed forces during the Second World War. 'In peacetime,' the article said, 'the island has known little haste. The indigenes are Melanesians and are virtually jet black in colour and take pride in being the darkest in the Pacific area. They are easily distinguishable from the lighter skinned mainland natives.'

We must have looked a sight, straggling out of the aircraft one after the other, heat-exhausted and bedraggled-looking vagabonds, and not the neatly attired family Les knew. He did not appear to care and smiled broadly when he saw us.

As we greeted each other, I could not help but notice the number of locals loitering about the primitive airport and its shed terminal. Most of them were chewing on something and periodically spitting out red stuff on to the ground. When I asked Les what it was, he answered, "Betel nut", "It's some kind of drug." I looked shocked. "It's harmless, it's their culture," he said, trying to reassure me. "It keeps the darkies quiet."

As we drove away from the airport, Les told me our flat was not ready to move into, "We'll be staying at the Davara motel for a week." He said and glanced at me for my reaction.

"That's okay," I shrugged. "I don't really mind. It feels like we're on holidays. I guess it'll be a nice change to be waited on." He nodded, looking relieved.

The island was breathtakingly beautiful. I was captivated and thought, 'I've finally found my place on this earth,' the moment I placed my feet on the soil. Taking in my surroundings, I felt comforted by the sight of huge mountains looming up around me, as if straining to reach the sky. It intrigued me how green and lush the vegetation was.

We bounced along the pitted dirt road in the company Toyota, on our way the motel in Toniva. I gazed wide-eyed at the wonderland around us. The island was an artist's paradise. After the last downpour, clusters of raindrops lying on enormous fan-like leaves glistened in the sun like tiny diamonds; the afternoon sun shot streams of golden light through gaping holes in surrounding dense plant life, casting eerie, shadowy shapes across our path, travelling the road that coiled amid jungle, separated from the ocean by a few metres of undergrowth. Through coconut palms and village clearings, I could see blue ocean and white caps. Small groups of indigenous families dawdled alongside the boulder-infested road. When some of them waved at the passing Toyota, the children and I waved back.

The mystique of the island and its inhabitants more than intrigued me. The place was intoxicating and I had fallen under its spell. 'I love this place,' I thought, feeling totally at home, 'I never want to leave.'

The children chatted to Les. In their excitement they all tried to talk to him at once, eager to tell him their own experience of the trip. I sat back quietly and observed my husband closely. 'He appears to be interested in what they are saying,' I considered. 'Brad especially needs Les to pay attention to him. 'Dear God, I hope he will this time,' I prayed.

I arrived on the island with an aggressive determination to make a better life for the children as well as for myself, vowing to channel all my energies into creating a positive outcome. Irrespective of whether or not Les and I succeeded in our marriage, we were going to have some sort of meaningful existence. Although I felt nothing for Les, I intended to do whatever was necessary to hold my family together. Instinctively I sensed Les knew how I felt about him and believed he chose to ignore it. He made an effort to be attentive to the children and pleasant to me.

After an uneventful but pleasant stay at the Davara Motel, we moved into the flat provided by the company. It had only two bedrooms and was bare, apart from beds, a kitchen table and chairs.

"Not even curtains to cover the louvered windows facing the street. Lucky they are frosted," I groaned. I turned and looked at Les. "I thought you said the flat had three bedrooms and was furnished. You told me to pack only the essentials. I could have had our furniture sent with the other things already on the ship."

I was so disappointed. Although we did not own a lot, the furniture we did own was quality. A black leather lounge suite and a teak Parker dining room setting and matching buffet was left in the care of friends. "We could use that furniture now.

Les looked around the empty room bewildered, "I was told the flat would be furnished."

"Then where's the furniture and the other bedroom? Four children shouldn't be cramped into one room."

As soon as Les arrived at work for his afternoon shift, he went to see the general manager.

The following morning, an attractive, heavy-set stranger of average height was knocking at my back door.

"Hi!" he grinned. "I'm Chad Keel, the general manager of Ganmor Equipment. I hear you have a problem." We shook hands

"I'm glad to meet you, Mr Keel. Please come in. Coffee?"

"Sure, thank you kindly. Black please, and call me Chad. Mind if I look around?" he asked before sitting down to drink his coffee.

"Go for it," I said.

Chad apologised for the mix up and said, "The place we have for you guys over by the school isn't vacant yet. It should be ready in a few weeks. But I've made arrangements for a black leather lounge to be delivered this afternoon, if that helps."

I smiled wider and graciously thanked him, wishing he had included curtains as well. 'Well at least we'll have something to sit on.' I thought. The fact that the general manager had come to see me, sounding genuinely apologetic for the mix up, eased the problem a little. All I could do was to wait patiently for the other flat to become vacant.

Our new lifestyle certainly took a lot of getting used to. So many things were different on the island. Meat was always frozen and looked unappetising and many of the local vegetables were unfamiliar. Foreign canned milk replaced the four pints of fresh milk my young family had consumed daily in Sydney. Once the ship delivered its precious cargo to Burns Phillip and other trade stores, consumers paid exorbitant prices for the luxury of having them. Sometimes, I paid five dollars for a lettuce that I normally would have paid fifty cents for in Australia.

Nothing is perfect, not even in paradise, I reasoned, as my budget barely survived the pirate prices. Overlooking the shortcomings of life on Bougainville, I easily enjoyed the ambience of the island.

18

Bougainville was my ideal place. While living there I was able to avoid so many things - television, news of the Vietnam War and my past was left behind in Australia. I purposely avoided any news of the war. The atrocities happening over there caused me to worry about the friends I knew were there, especially Matt. I did not know for sure whether or not he was in Vietnam, but could only assume he was, since he was in the Navy. I could not do anything other than to pray that he would be okay.

The couple of weeks' wait for the three bed-roomed flat ran into a couple of months. My patience ran short when, one after the other, the children fell ill with measles, which was inevitable under the circumstances of having to share the same room. Adding fuel to the fire, I received an unexpected visit from the wife of a new employee.

Helen Watson was short, plump and lopsided. She was the first person I knew, other than my sister Tina, who was shorter than me. Ironically Helen bore a striking resemblance to my sister, with her dark hair pulled off her face and tied back with a headscarf, but Helen had calculating eyes and an air of superiority.

My visitor confidently introduced herself and her two pampered little girls. Katie, five, was the elder. When her mother said her name, Katie turned her pretty oval face towards me and smiled and her large blue eyes sparkled. Molly, two, was also pretty but looked sulky standing beside her mother with her fingers jammed in her mouth. I welcomed the thought of making new friends, and eagerly invited them in. I entertained my first guests, dressed in a cotton Meri dress, no make-up, my hair in plaits and rubber thongs on my feet.

Helen eyed me curiously, with an air of superiority, and watched me put the cups and saucers on the table. I felt her eyes on me and promptly said light-heartedly, feeling the need to explain my appearance, "I really love the casual life style of the island. I couldn't dress like this in Sydney."

She smiled and asked if I had any children.

"Yes," I said enthusiastically. "They're outside playing. They'll probably be in any minute asking for something to eat. You can bet your life on it."

"Where are you staying?" I asked, pouring the tea.

I almost spilt it everywhere when she said, "We're opposite the school. It's really lovely over there. Our flat overlooks the beach. I've turned the third bedroom into a playroom for the girls."

"Oh, really? We're waiting for a place over there," I said, suspecting Helen was in the flat promised to us.

"Are you?" Her voice rose in pitch.

"Yes. We...." The children came marching, one after the other, followed by a couple of the neighbour's children into the kitchen. They were all covered in dirt from head to toe.

Helen's eyes widened and her mouth gaped open, when I said proudly, "These are my children."

She asked, looking down her nose at them, recoiling in utter disgust at their grubbiness, "Are all these children yours?"

"Oh, no," I laughed. "I only have four."

"Four!" she shouted. "I've never met anyone with four children before," and practically ran from the flat, dragging her spotless daughters behind her. I was startled by her behaviour and was not sure whether to be offended or to laugh.

After my guest had gone, the children sat around the table eating sandwiches. I stood back and leaned against the sink, observing them. Brad sat up tall, chewing on his sandwich, quietly looking around at his brothers and Celeste.

'How he loves his food,' I thought. "Good, sweetie?" I asked looking at him.

Mouth full Brad, nodded, "Mmmm."

Cain sat opposite Brad swinging his feet, chomping into the bread, while Celeste on his left sorted through her sandwiches. BJ was to the right of Cain, sitting on the chair and elevated by a very thick cookbook, gulping milk from his blue plastic cup.

'It's amazing,' I thought shaking my head, 'only a few months ago Cain's skin was inflamed and red raw with eczema and now there isn't a trace of it. His skin is smooth and deeply tanned and also,' I laughed, 'his dark hair is sun bleached and almost white. He is so beautiful; I wish his father could see him.' Thinking about Luc made me feel sad. BJ spilled his milk as usual, quickly bringing me back to reality.

"Oh, you're a messy boy," I told him, wiping up the mess.

"More peas!" BJ said, holding up his plastic cup while jigging in the chair.

"Sit still, Bubby or you'll fall. Here," I said, and placed the cup in front of him, "try not to spill it again." He clapped his hands and knocked over the cup again, spilling the contents all over the floor.

"Mick!" I called, and our hous boi came running into the kitchen. I picked up my dripping wet toddler and handed him to Mick. "Wash him, please. BJ go sleep now."

Mick took him from me. "Aaah! You bighead true,' he said, walking away laughing while I mopped up the mess.

Celeste finished first. "May I leave the table, Mommy?"

"May I too?" the boys chorused. None of the children moved until I said they could.

I was firm but fair with the children. They were polite and well-mannered and I was proud of them. They could get as grubby as they liked playing outside, a bath would take care of the dirt. "Yep," I said in mock song to the tune playing on the cassette player, "I'd rather them be grubby kids having fun than sour looking clean brats!" I laughed, feeling a little silly and thought, 'anyone would think I'd lost my mind, if they saw me standing at the kitchen window watching my children, chasing each other around the yard while I sing a silly song.'

My smile faded for a moment, remembering what the doctor told me when I went to him before leaving Australia.

"I think you should seriously reconsider living in PNG, Emma."

"But why?"

"Have you forgotten that you don't have a spleen...? You could be risking your life going there. Chances are that your body won't be able to handle an attack of malaria. It can be fatal for a healthy person."

The doctor's warning did not worry me at first, but now that the children were growing up I thought about it a lot. 'Who would love and look after them the way I do?' I thought, realising that I might not see them grow into adults. 'Ah,' I told myself, shrugging off the morbid feeling, 'I'm being silly again. I'm not going to die yet. Only the good die young,' I laughed, 'and I'm as bad as they come, just ask my mother.'

When Les came home that afternoon I told him about the flat while I made him coffee. "Four children sleeping in one room isn't on, Les, especially when Helen is using the third bedroom as her children's playroom. Either you do something about it or I'll go to the company myself!"

Les became angry when he realised the foreman, who did not get on with Les, had given the Watsons our flat because they were his friends.

"Then please do something about it, Les." I asked. "Chad Keel promised that flat to us the first week we moved in here."

Our next door neighbours, Barry and Fran Barclay, were an older couple with a teenage son and daughter. They rarely spoke to us, other than a cordial nod when we first moved in. I felt the idea of four young children living next door, discouraged them from becoming too friendly with us. Fran spent most of her days either sleeping or reading. The times she did speak to me, she grumbled about the heat, the dust and the price of food.

Puzzled, I asked, "Then why do you stay if you dislike the island so much?"

Her shoulders slumped and she sighed heavily. "Oh, Barry's job holds us here. Besides that, the money is too good to leave."

I shook my head, looking at her, "I guess we are never satisfied are we."

Fran just shrugged and went indoors.

Molly Archer, the woman who lived in the flat above us, visited Fran nearly every day. I thought the women were similar in nature. Molly was an attractive newly-wed who always looked bored and sulky. I did not try to befriend her as I did not like her. I thought it odd that she had a hous boi when she did not have children and only lay around the house all day long complaining about the heat. Curiosity got the better of me one day and I asked Molly why she had a hous boi. Her initial reaction to the question seemed hostile, then suddenly she smirked, "It's just too hot for me to do any house work, Jacob is wonderful. He does everything for Russ and me."

I grinned and raised my eyebrows thinking, 'Yeah, I bet he does.'

Normally I would not have given Molly or her hous boi a second thought if I had not overheard the way she flirted with him. I thought Molly was asking for trouble and could not imagine why the woman would want to flirt with a kid.

A few days later, I was in the yard with the children when Fran staggered out of her flat, obviously just awake from her ritual afternoon nap.

"Hello Fran," I smiled. The older woman turned suddenly and looked over her shoulder.

"Oh, hello Emma, I didn't see you there. How are the children?"

"They're fine. I hope they aren't too noisy for you."

"Well no," she replied. "We all thought they would be. But no, we don't hear them after they go inside."

"They seem happy living here. I was worried that they might miss television and the life they were used to. Bougainville is so laid back and simple, it's an easy life to live."

Fran looked at me strangely for a second then said sharply, "Huh, you're not sophisticated."

I was startled by Fran's remark and thought, 'Why did she say that for heaven's sake? Mean bitch! What's up her nose? I could be sophisticated if I wanted to be.'

I was about to say so but stopped myself. "I didn't say I was," I replied sharply. "You know nothing of my life."

But Fran had already gone indoors.

I sulked for a few hours over Fran's mean comment, then hurried to my room and rummaged through my belongings, looking for my make-up, hot rollers, hair spray and something to wear other than the Meri dress I bought the first week we arrived.

After I turned the hot rollers on, I sat on the edge of the bed, assessing my features in the mirror before reaching for my liquid foundation. Dabbing a few dots on my face, I discovered the foundation was too light for my tanned skin. I rubbed it off with a tissue then lightly brushed my face with powder. Rummaging through my make-up bag again, I pulled out a light brown eyebrow pencil, black mascara and blush and placed them in a row on the bed. Working on my eyebrows first, I lightly pencilled them with feathered strokes for shape and definition, then unwound the mascara wand and slowly covered my thick blond lashes with black mascara, followed by a touch of blush on my cheeks. I rarely wore lipstick and did not bother with it. Appraising the finished results, I nodded with satisfaction, 'There, I look much better now.'

The rollers were very hot by the time I was ready to do my hair. "Ouch!" They burnt the tips of my fingers and I had to work fast to place them. 'What we women have to suffer,' I thought, winding the last roller.

Off went the Meri dress, to be banished forever. Standing in my panties and bra, I surveyed my image in the mirror before putting on a sleeveless top and snug fitting cotton shorts. I never thought of myself as pretty but I knew my figure was in good shape. 'Yep, and good legs too. Not bad! Not bad! You can hold your own against the best of them, sister,' I joked, removed the hot rollers and ran my fingers through a mass of curls, then surveyed my reflection again.

"Hmm, a bit over the top I think," I said, and quickly pulled the bunch of curls back into a ponytail, 'Unsophisticated my foot! I can be if I want to, but not today! I laughed, then slipped a Credence Clearwater Revival tape into the machine and danced to the music.

A few weeks later, Helen had recovered from the shock of meeting my four children. She whizzed her little car around to the back of the flats, pulled up right outside my kitchen door and tooted the horn.

"Hi!" I said coming outside, surprised to see her and her two daughters.

Helen popped her head through the open window, "I'm going in to Kieta to pick up a few things at BP's, want to come?"

"Be right with you. I'll get my bag. "Mick! Mick! Come!" I called, "Celeste! Brad! Cain!

When Mick came running, I said in Pidgin, "I'm going to Kieta, Mick. Watch the children, I won't be gone long."

"I want all of you to behave, do you hear?" I said firmly. "I'll bring back something nice for you, okay?" Then I kissed each of them on the cheek, stifling their grumbles about wanting to come too.

"Okay, Mick?" I looked at him, raising my eyebrows, confident that he would guard my babies with his life.

"Em missus, yes," he nodded. I climbed into the little car and waved to them as Helen drove away.

Mick was a thirty-something highlander. He walked in off the street one day and asked me for work. Initially I said no because I did not need any help. He returned the following day and asked again and I said no. He stubbornly refused to go away. He wanted to work for the missus who had children with white hair. He came every day for a week, and eventually I handed him the ironing when I saw him sitting on the ground outside our flat. Since neither Mick nor I could speak the other's language then, we communicated with signs.

Les was not happy to find a local in his house when he came home from work that afternoon. "What's that nigger doing here?" He glared at me.

I looked at him defiantly. "Shhh! Don't say that!" I was disgusted at his racial prejudice. "Mick is staying!" I said. "He can help me look after the children. Don't you be nasty to him," I warned.

Over time I taught Mick English and he taught me Pidgin English. Les ignored him for the first few months, even when Mick would say good morning and good night to him. Then one afternoon I heard Les asking Mick where he came from. I looked through the kitchen window at them and I thought, 'Guess he got tired of playing the Great White Bwana.'

Les finally came home with the news I had been waiting for. "Bubby," he called walking through the back door, "I got word today that we'll be exchanging flats with the Watson's." I hugged him as I thanked him.

The following day I started packing but in the middle of it, I felt unwell and a sharp pain stabbed at my abdomen. I thought I had caught some sort of bug and ended up tearing off to the bathroom with the urge to vomit. The pain worsened, forcing me to double over and take a hold of the hand basin to brace myself. Blood trickled down my legs. I removed my panties and suddenly a large clot splattered onto the floor. Horrified at the gory sight, I turned around and vomited into the toilet bowl, suspecting that I must have miscarried. 'But how can that be?' I thought, wiping my face with a damp cloth and stifling the urge to vomit again.

I cleaned the mess from the bathroom floor, showered, changed and took pain killers and then got on with packing, telling myself that when I had time I'd go to the doctor. I never mentioned what had happened that afternoon to anyone, not even to Les. There was no point since we rarely spoke about anything deeper than his job. Apart from my children, I was alone.

Later that day, I stopped what I was doing and ran to the back door when I heard Cain call to Mick, "Oooi! You come boy!"

"Cain!" I called waving him over. "I don't want you talking to Mick like that ever again."

He looked puzzled. "But Dad said he's my nigger."

"Don't you ever say that again!" I yelled at him and he almost jumped out of his skin. "Come inside!"

I left Cain crying in the kitchen and rushed outside to call Brad and Celeste in too. Mick was about to follow them but I put my hand up, "No Mick, mi tok savvy long pikinini. I want to talk to the children." He nodded and stopped in his tracks but looked puzzled as I marched the children inside. They sat in silence around the table, their eyes following me as I paced around the kitchen.

"Right," I said, glancing at them and wondering where to start. I grabbed the packet of cigarettes sitting on the bench, took one out of the packet and lit up. Cigarettes calmed my nerves.

"Now," I said, taking a deep draw and blowing smoke into the air, "let's get a few things straight around here. I don't give a damn what your father has said. There will be no calling anyone nigger in this house. I won't stand for it. I'm boss! You children will do as I say, understand?" Three heads nodded in unison, unsure of what had made me so angry.

"Never call black people nasty names. And never, never call them nigger, that's a bad word, black people are just the same as us only their skin is a different colour." While I had their attention I threw in, "And never, never ever make fun of handicapped people, because God might give you a child that is handicapped to teach you a lesson to be kind to them. Understand? And be kind to each other and always look after each other too."

Once I had calmed down, I explained why I was so upset. "It would break my heart if any of you were nasty and horrible to anyone for no reason. You are all better than that. Some people enjoy doing horrible things to other people but they're just cowards and bullies."

I looked at my sons questioningly, "You're not cowards or bullies are you?" They shook their heads. "Good! You can go and play now and behave."

"May I have something to eat, please Mom?" Brad asked.

"Yeah me too," Cain said enthusiastically, jumping up and down. I looked over at Celeste. She was still sitting at the table. "You too, sweetie?"

"Please Mommy," she nodded.

"Okay, but first, all of you go into the bathroom and wash your hands and faces and don't wake up BJ," I called as they tore off to the bathroom.

Later on I spoke to Mick, instructing him to come and tell me if the boys ever acted like bigheads towards him again.

'I intend to do everything in my power to counteract Les' stinking attitudes, with a vengeance' I thought, 'He's not going to poison my babies' minds.'

19

I did not blame Helen for our cramped living conditions. I was however, irritated with her for the begrudging attitude when they were told that they would have to exchange flats with us.

"You'll have to buy the curtains I bought then," was her sharp response, as we discussed details of the exchange.

"Well okay," I said, sounding as though I really did not have any other option, when I was actually thrilled to take them. I was with her the day she bought the fabric and would have bought some myself if she had not. Her attitude had ruffled me so much that I nearly told her off, but thought better of it, realising it would have been pointless.

Mick noticed Helen's attitude as well and insisted on helping her and her husband after he had helped me settle in.

"Missus, mi think lik lik missus cross with you. Mi go now. Mi go help her lik lik time."

I looked at him with surprise. "Thank you, Mick. You don't have to help the missus if you really don't want to. You've been working all day."

 "No! No! I go!" he said, shaking his head vigorously. "Mi make things good for you. Me go."

"Okay Mick," I shrugged, "it's your decision, go on then."

Mick's goodwill had impressed Helen. He had even led her to believe that I sent him. Later on I told her it was his idea, which surprised her. Helen's response caused me to feel that she had a low opinion of the local people. I also noticed that she watched her girls like a hawk. They were never allowed to stay and play with Celeste, and she made sure that Mick was not anywhere near her daughters.

Although Mick was certainly unattractive, I instinctively knew he was a good person and would never have harmed any of the children. It exasperated me the way Helen implied Mick might do something to her daughters. Also, it irritated me, knowing the way she felt about Mick, she did not seem concerned if my children were left in his care. My frustration with Helen spilled over on to my children. I found myself feeling agitated with them in her company and chastised them more frequently, hoping they would not misbehave and give her a chance to find fault with them.

Even though I was frustrated with my friendship with Helen, I took full advantage of it and accepted her invitations to go shopping. Les did not want to go. He became annoyed at having to get a company vehicle to take me. It was easier to go with Helen. I felt deeply sad when Celeste was not invited. Helen's car was small and could carry only four passengers at best. I felt even if the car had been larger, none of my children would have been welcomed. It was a sore point with me, as I waited impatiently for months for my car to arrive from Sydney.

On one of our weekly shopping trips, Helen and I were walking from the supermarket to the car when I suddenly felt uncomfortable. I looked around and saw several young local men grouped together, whispering and looking our way. I gave Helen a puzzled look. "What are they looking at?" I asked inclining my head towards the men.

"You," she said.

"What? Why?" I did not understand.

"It's your shorts and bare legs. It's a tease for them."

I was angry. "Why didn't you tell me? You've been in PNG longer than I have."

"I thought you knew."

I was seething. I knew nothing of the country's customs, but Helen did. She grew up in PNG. Her parents managed a plantation.

'I've had to pretend my whole life that I didn't mind, this or that. Well, I do bloody mind. And I'm fed up with all the bullshit I have to endure!' I thought. 'Her attitude towards my children is galling and hurtful. Why the hell does she act as if her girls are superior to my children? She even hinted that Celeste was chubby when she wasn't…what the hell's wrong with her?' 'Bitch!!"

As frustrated as I was with Helen, I always forgave her and thought, 'Hell would freeze over before anyone would convince me my children were not beautiful. They don't have to be perfect for me to love them.'

Helen's demands on her children, especially Katie, did not escape me. The poor child was forever getting a dressing down for one thing or other. I could never understand why. The child was nothing like her spoilt temperamental little sister. The girls were dressed up like dolls all the time. Their home was a mess due to Helen spending most of her time making clothes for the girls. All hell would break loose if either of them got dirty.

I offered to pay Helen to make a couple of dresses for Celeste. She declined, saying, "I'll teach you to sew instead." The sewing lessons never eventuated, but I watched her closely the times I saw her sewing; learning to sew opened another door for me.

Mick was truly a blessing to our family. He was devoted to us and the children were extremely fond of him. I was unaccustomed to having a servant so he became more like a family member than house help. I did feel however, that there were times when Mick was undermining my authority in the home, as well as with the children.

One evening when Les was at work, the children and I had an early dinner. When finished, I began tidying up. Mick came in as usual to wash the dishes. "No!" he cried, when he found me sweeping the floor, rushing over and snatching the broom out of my hand. "Mi sweep. You sit noting," he said firmly and ordered me to sit down. "Missus no sweep!"

I let his behaviour slide, feeling he only wanted to protect his job. Afraid that he would not be needed any more, like his friend, who had lost his job the day before. All the same, I was annoyed with him.

One time when I intended taking BJ into Kieta shopping, Mick stepped in and over-ruled me once again.

"Missus?" he called from the lounge-room, when I was dressing BJ.

"Yu laik wanem somting Mick? (What do you want Mick?") I asked.

"Pikanini em i go slip nau. (The baby must go to sleep now)," he instructed.

"No gat Mick, No Mick," I responded sharply. "Emi go long Kieta wantaim mi. (He is coming to Kieta with me)."

"Nogat! Nogat! (No! No!)," he replied impatiently, shaking his head. "Emi go slip nau. Dispella pikinini i got lik lik sik. (He must sleep. He is not well)."

I thought for a moment that perhaps he was right. BJ did seem a little off colour and an afternoon nap would be better than going out into the heat, so I agreed that BJ should stay home. I soon realised that my house boi, although right in his suggestion, was subtly bossing me around. I gave serious thought to the situation that day while driving into Kieta. 'Mick's getting far too bossy,' I told myself, then decided that perhaps he was just overly protective. But deep down I knew a day would come when I would have to take a firmer stand with him. Mick had been with us for two years. He was loyal and trustworthy. We were fortunate he had integrity. So many hous bois had robbed their employers.

Mick and I got along well. He listened with wide-eyed fascination whenever I spoke about 'Ples Bilong me' – my country. I told him about the animals at Taronga Park Zoo, Sydney Harbour Bridge and Sydney at night and how beautiful the city looked lit up... He wanted to know what my house and family were like and I asked him about his home and his childhood.

"Ples bilong mi, Mt Hargan," he said proudly, supported with a wide smile. "A long way, away," he said, stretching out his arms to emphasise the distance.

My knowledge of Pidgin English was relatively limited at that time, which made it difficult to competently decipher every word he uttered. We were laughing at each other as we tried to understand what the other was saying. The more he talked, the more excited he became, obviously having fond memories of his homeland. Never before had he appeared so joyful. Normally his broad unattractive features were serious, so it was delightful to watch the transformation in him as he laughed and giggled like a child. He clapped, hooted and almost did a dance when he said, "Em missus, Em missus," every time I spoke coherent Pidgin English.

Mick was short and chunky, with feet as wide as plates, which amazed me. I had never seen feet like his before coming to Bougainville. Feet like Mick's were common among the highlanders and I smiled whenever I sighted them. Mick might have been a mature man chronologically, but was as naive as a child. One day I plucked up the courage to ask him if he'd ever eaten human flesh. It was commonly known that some tribes in New Guinea practised cannibalism. A strong curiosity urged me to ask.

"Yu kai kai long pik Mick? (Have you eaten human Mick)?" I asked, and his laughter suddenly turned to embarrassment. He blushed and hung his head.

"Em Missus, yes," he whispered.

"Really Mick!" My wide-eyed surprise embarrassed him even further. Unable to contain my curiosity I quickly asked, "What did it taste like?"

"Abus Pik," Pig – he said.

20

One afternoon, prior to exchanging flats, I had visited Helen to talk over last minute details and was on my way to my car when I heard, "G'day." I looked around and saw a very tall man coming from the vacant flat below.

"Hello," I replied. "Are you moving into that flat?"

"Yeah, I'm Dan Wills. I hear you're moving in upstairs."

"That's right, but how do you know that?"

"I know Les."

"Oh, you're the new guy," I said feeling an instant dislike for him. His dark eyes lacked warmth and there was an ominous air about him. I challenged the penetrating stare he gave me until he eventually looked away.

"Yeah."

"Where's your family?"

"Joan and my two boys arrive next week."

Instinct told me he did not like me either, even though there was nothing in his manner to suggest it. He was friendly enough but his icy stare and body language told me what he was all about.

Joan on the other hand was a sweet and pretty woman, always impeccably dressed. We became instant friends. I recognised a little of myself in her nervousness and understood the cover up and secrecy about her life. I respected her need for privacy even though I could clearly hear what was happening downstairs.

I had skilfully disguised my intense dislike of Dan Wills until the night he came home drunk and beat Joan. The slapping sounds and cries for help became too much for me to ignore. Without a second thought of the consequences or for my safety, I marched downstairs and walked through the open door to their flat, demanding that he leave Joan alone. "Otherwise," I said, "I will report you to management."

My bizarre behaviour, when I stood fearlessly in his lounge room, clearly ready to do battle with him, sobered Dan.

"I'm not afraid of bullies like you," I said in a hard and deliberate manner. He was rendered utterly surprised and speechless as I went to Joan's aid.

"Are you okay?" I asked putting a comforting arm around her.

"Yes," she said tearfully and then began to sob. "He hit me for nothing. I don't understand why he does it. I try so hard to be a good wife. I'm so tired Em, will you help me to my room?"

We talked a little longer, but I could not advise my friend other than to encourage her to leave Dan before he ended up killing her. From that day on, Dan and I had a polite contempt for one other.

An influx of new employees had increased my circle of friends and some of their husbands were on the same shift as Les. Sometimes I invited the wives to my place in the evenings for drinks. Our little group get-togethers often generated a great deal of laughter and for some reason it aggravated Dan, who would bang on his roof, insisting we be quiet. I assumed that only he would be paranoid enough to believe that he was the source of our amusement.

Les worked an opposite shift to Dan and so was unaware for some time of the trouble between our neighbour and me. When I finally told him he ordered me to mind my own business.

"No!" I shouted. "I won't stand by and let that cowardly bastard beat up a defenceless woman. If I have to, I'll report him to the company."

The trouble downstairs persisted, so out of concern for Joan's safety I made a formal complaint to the service manager. His manner was off-handed even after I strongly suggested something serious could happen to her if the beatings were ignored.

"At least talk to him," I pleaded as we sat together on his front porch. "You're his boss, for heaven's sake. Surely he would take some notice of you. Warn him. Please don't ignore this. That bastard could seriously hurt Joan. She doesn't deserve it."

"Can't do a thing," the service manager said in a strong Southern American drawl. I had heard he held the belief that if a man can't manage his wife, then he can't manage anything. It would not have surprised me one bit if he beat his wife too. I had also heard rumours that he was a womaniser.

"Can't or won't," I challenged standing up about to leave. "Something awful will happen to Joan if you don't," I cautioned, then left.

Shortly after I made the complaint, Joan confided in me about the years of abuse she had suffered and the numerous trips to the hospital to repair broken bones.

"Why do you stay with him when he continually beats you so severely?" I asked, grateful that at least I had some bargaining power within my marriage.

"I love him," she sobbed, "I can't help it, I just do."

My heart went out to my friend, feeling that disaster was near, but warning Joan did little to persuade her to leave him.

"I know you're right Emma, but I don't want to. I live in hope that one day he will change."

She looked at me with sad eyes and smiled ruefully. "Please Emma, just be my friend."

A few months after that conversation, Joan and her family moved to Arawa when Dan secured a position with the copper mine. The idea of moving into a house and having a garden thrilled her. She firmly believed her life would change. It did, but not in the way she had imagined.

21

Bougainville was my birthplace in spirit. While living there, I did not feel tormented or in despair. The island's intoxicating beauty left no room for anything other than for me to enjoy my life. I wanted to shed the past and allow the future to bloom in the best possible way. Shrouded in the enchantment of the island, I dreamed of making a peaceful future possible. In my naivety I tried to persuade Les to look at the island through my eyes, in the hope that he would be open to its beauty as well. His response was to tell me that I was out of my mind and to get real. "I'm here to work," he said, sarcastically, "I live in the real world, and it's about time you did too."

While fiercely determined not to allow his pessimistic outlook to destroy my hopes, I discovered a new strength surfacing and as a result our roles reversed. Courage came to me from the seeds of Les' pessimism. I became the aggressor and he the submissive, at least that was how it appeared to the outside world. Temporary freedom from bondage gave birth to a devil-may-care attitude. I was sassy and outgoing and did not give a hoot what people thought of me.

A few times, in sheer frustration when people showed signs of feeling sorry for Les and chastised me for being too outrageous, I gave some account of the reality of my life but their eyes reflected disbelief. Apart from aloofness, Les did not show any signs of the monster he portrayed in Australia, and due to ignorance, sometimes sympathy went to him. No one understood my hunger for life and some even condemned me for neglecting my poor suffering, adoring husband.

The magic of the island caught the unsuspecting in its web, tempting them to lose sight of reality and give way to festivities and romance. Marriages fell apart, social drinkers became alcoholics and once responsible people developed irresponsible attitudes which eventually played havoc with them personally. There was no doubt the island had the ability to change people, some for the better and some for the worse. Parties were an accepted way of life and usually before noon of each Monday, news of the weekend's social events had already circulated around town.

At one of these social gatherings, I met a man two years my junior to whom I was attracted. Sam Rends was not particularly handsome or worldly but was fun to be with, his smile and boyish charm was captivating. It was refreshing be in the company of someone who enjoyed life and was interested in what I had to say.

When we went to a party Les would sit in a corner, unwilling to participate or to make any attempt to enjoy himself. From the other side of the room he would watch my every move and I did not conceal my flirtatious behaviour from him. The more fearless I was, the more withdrawn he became.

Sam worked at the same company as Les, which gave credence to our friendship, since employees often socialised together on weekends. Les hated parties, dancing and small talk. No matter how much I included him he refused to participate. I gave up trying and he stayed at home. Sam became my escort, friend and eventually my lover.

Our relationship started tongues wagging. Even my closest friends judged me behind my back while some of them conducted their affairs behind closed doors. I discovered Helen's indiscretion when I dropped into her place unannounced one morning and found her leaving her next door neighbour's flat, looking a mess. Her shocked expression said it all. She was frightened that I would give her away but I did not say a word to anyone. She was not so loyal to me.

Neither Sam nor I had any illusions about our relationship and although it was only for the moment, I adored him. At the peak of the affair, Les was offered a job away from the island for a week. Before he left Les went to Sam and asked him to move in with the children and me. He even went to the extent of telling Sam that he gave me breakfast in bed in the mornings. The so called breakfast was a cup of tea. The scenario was incredibly surreal.

While Les was away the company bus pulled up at the flats as usual, to collect Sam instead of Les, and also Ken Jonas, the new downstairs neighbour. When Sam boarded the bus, he took the stirring from his work mates with good humour. When Les returned to the island he could not cope with the gossip or heckling about Sam and me. It overwhelmed him.

Ken Jonas and his girlfriend Dolly Scot, who was 15 years his senior, had moved into Dan and Joan's flat after they left. Ken and Dolly's relationship blossomed when she first came to Bougainville Island for a short visit. She later returned to the island and set up house with Ken.

The flamboyant Dolly Scott had me intrigued. Everything about her was overstated. At first, her tales of rummaging through second-hand clothing stores searching for a dress and jewellery to wear to a ball had me enthralled.

"A dashingly handsome gentleman had invited me," she said in her deep gravelly voice. "Doug was so gorgeous and very handsome and on top of that darling, I was crowned Belle of the Ball." She sighed every time on cue.

Even though I felt Dolly's tales about her life, her lovers and her achievements were exaggerated, I did appreciate her gift for storytelling. She was thirty years my senior.

I had met Dolly while she was visiting her daughter and son-in-law. She knew of my affair with Sam. "Oh darling, it's so romantic," she purred in a deep Irish accent. "I understand, I really do. I was not in love with my first husband either..."

Tall but by no means beautiful, Dolly certainly had charm that beguiled many. She wore her one-of-a kind wardrobe and chunky plastic jewellery with unique style. Her bleached white hair and hairpiece was styled in barrel curls on top of her head.

Dolly was certainly belle of the ball on her first visit to the island, but things changed the second time around. Everyone had lives to live and they got on with it. The lack of adoring fans wounded her ego, mostly because she felt concern that public opinion was against her relationship with the much younger Ken. In truth, no one gave a hoot what she and Ken did.

Everywhere Dolly went she befriended anyone who crossed her path, including my former neighbour Molly Archer, the woman I caught flirting with her hous boi. Molly's Land Cruiser was often parked outside Dolly's place. One particular day when I saw the vehicle, I felt strangely curious and wanted to find out why she was there.

I went down the back stairs and popped my head in Dolly's door to say hello. I could only see Molly. She was slumped in a chair staring at the floor. When she looked up and saw me in the doorway, she waved me away.

'Hmm,' I thought backing away, 'I wonder what's wrong with her. She looks as if she was crying.' My curiosity was mounting.

The roar of the Land Cruiser told me Molly was leaving. Immediately she had gone, I tossed aside the book I was reading, bounded out of my chair and casually strolled down the back stairs again and headed for the washhouse.

Dolly called out to me on my way back, "Oh darling, did you hear what happened to poor Molly?"

I stopped dead in my tracks eager to find out. "No, what?"

"Oh dear, the poor darling was attacked by her hous boi. She is so upset. He's in jail."

"What!" My eyes widened in horror. "I don't believe that!" I exclaimed, about to tell Dolly what I knew. She became angry and cut me off mid-sentence.

"How can you say that? Molly's a lovely girl."

I walked away shaking my head in disgust. "Well, I don't believe her."

My apathy towards Molly did not win me favours with the women in the area; especially not after Molly had to leave the island. By the time I was given a chance to tell what I had seen happen between Molly and her hous boi the subject was old news, and no one really cared any more.

"In my heart," Dolly told me much later, "I really didn't believe that you could be so callous, darling."

'Yeah sure,' I thought indignantly, 'then why wouldn't you listen to me in the first place?'

The respect I once had for Dolly evaporated. Her repetitive repertoire of old tales of joy and woes and her sugar-coated words became tiresome. I saw Dolly as a crowd pleaser, lacking real substance. She told people what they wanted to hear because she was afraid she would be dislodged from her popularity pedestal if she had an opinion contrary to the populace.

Mick also was fast becoming frustrated with Dolly.

"Missus!" he called walking into the kitchen. I hurried from my bedroom to see why he was so upset.

"Lapun meri no got rausim doti wara na long dispella machine (The old woman did not empty the washing machine again.)," he said almost in tears, "Pamok! doti meri! (Whore! Dirty old woman!)."

"Mick no got!" I scolded. His complaint was becoming almost a weekly thing. He was so frustrated and angry that he refused to empty the dirty water out of the machine after Dolly had used it. "Samting bilong dispela lapun meri (It's the old woman's problem)."

When I spoke to Dolly about the water being left in the washing machine she accused Mick of leaving it in there, but I knew he had not as I knew his habits. When he cleaned the house he painstakingly removed everything room by room, placing the furniture on the veranda. He would turn the whole place upside down to make sure it was spotless. Before Dolly moved in the washing machine had sparkled. Mick took great pride in it and polished it every time he used it.

Dolly was furious with me for defending him.

"Mick wouldn't forget to empty the machine Dolly, he's far too proud and meticulous for that," I told her.

From her back door she stood and glared indignantly at me, hands on hips. Decked out with bleached hair and barrel curls, large white plastic earrings, bright red painted lips, and wearing the leopard print shorts and midriff top and white sandals she so often wore, she bellowed, "How dare you call me a liar!"

"What!" I recoiled as if she had slapped me. "I didn't. I just told you that Mick wouldn't leave dirty water in the machine that was all."

"Are you saying that I did?"

"No. But if you were the last person to use the machine then...well?"

"Oh," she said spinning around, "I don't have to listen to this," and stormed inside.

"Oh, why the hell don't you act like a grown woman," I snapped back, stomping up the stairs.

Dolly came running from her flat as if it was on fire. Waving her hand in the air she barked, "My little finger is more woman than you'll ever be."

I looked over my shoulder at her and laughed, thus starting a four-year feud.

At company functions, if Dolly was there, I ignored her. As far as I was concerned she did not exist. Her ego took a huge beating. When a friend told me that she heard through the grapevine that Dolly distorted her version of what had happened between us. All I said was, "Dolly who?"

22

My life's tide rolled casually along as I busily socialised with friends, taking care of my family in between juggling my accidental child-minding and hairdressing business. These business ventures eventuated when a neighbour asked me to mind her children for a few days. Word got around that I was minding children and I was asked to mind others.

Les viewed his earnings as his own and never as 'ours', so when the child minding opportunity arose, I seized it to gain financial independence, which inadvertently opened other doors for me.

One afternoon a mother of one of my charges confided in me about a problem she and her husband were having. I suggested she get her hair done and buy a new outfit to lift her spirits, unaware that the only hairdresser in Toniva had just left the island. In response, I volunteered to do the woman's hair and make-up for her. Her husband was impressed with the difference in his wife he took her to the local RSL for dinner that evening. The woman was my first regular hairdressing client and many followed her.

When my clients arrived and I was busy, I discovered that Mick impressed them while they waited by serving cups of tea and the cakes I had made for the children's lunches. His good service led to some of them trying to entice him to work for them with the promise of more money, but he said no. He so enjoyed the praise he received for his good service that I did not have the heart to burst his bubble. I allowed him to serve tea and cold drinks but insisted that he not serve cake.

As the weeks passed, Les could no longer deal with continually hearing the gossip about Sam and me, and threatened to hurt Sam in retaliation. Under the stress and worry of it all, my health deteriorated and I contracted malaria. I can only recall having a migraine the day I fell ill. As the migraine worsened, my body felt sore and chilled. I went to my bedroom to put on a jacket. Hours later Mick, finding me on the floor soaked in perspiration and shivering uncontrollably, immediately called an ambulance.

I spent several painful, delirious days in hospital, fighting monsters in my nightmares. When I finally recovered, I felt as if the stuffing had been knocked out of me. I had no idea that I was actually fighting Les and kept pushing him away whenever he tried to comfort me.

At home, Les angrily told me what I had said and done, "You only wanted that bastard," he snarled. "You wouldn't let me near you. He'll pay."

He ranted on but I had no recollection of anything other than distorted images. Those few days were a blur.

News of an accident ran through the town like wild fire and word soon reached me. "John Fergus was driving the van," a friend told me. My stomach did backflips when I hear the news and asked if he was badly hurt. "Don't know," the friend said, "but the smash looks serious."

John was Sam's closest mate. Naturally I was concerned for John, but was relieved to know Sam was not driving the company vehicle that day as he usually did.

Les came home in a strange mood that night. When I mentioned that John had been in an accident and asked if he had heard how he was, Les said, "It was meant for your boyfriend."

"What was?"

"The accident."

"You're not saying that you had anything to do with it!"

"Payback time, sweetheart."

I stared at Les in disbelief, and then suddenly thought about his confession about killing the aborigine years before. The sound of his voice shook me into sharp focus.

"The bastard deserved it. He made a fool of me, screwing my wife," he said angrily. "Everyone's laughing at me. I'm only sorry the wrong person got it."

He paused a moment then said. "Fergus is a bastard too. He needed fixing. He ripped us off clearing our car from customs. The bastard overcharged me, serves him right."

"You agreed to Sam being here. You invited him to stay with the children and me. Everyone knows you asked him to stay!" I screamed at him. "I'll tell everyone what you've done," I said, trying to comprehend the reality of it all. "You're a monster, Les! I'll tell everyone."

"Can't prove a thing, sweetness, I don't leave evidence," he said, unmoved by my threat. His smugness made me feel ill.

There was a whisper that Les might have tampered with the car but nothing was ever done about it and no one bothered to investigate the accident. John Fergus was medevac'd to Australia for further treatment to his broken jaw. He was fortunate not to have suffered a worse fate, while Sam left Bougainville a few weeks later when his contract finished.

As it does, life goes on. The evening I invited Helen and Billy Watson over for drinks, they arrived at the tail end of an argument Les and I were having over the new watch I had bought that day. The watch was not expensive but the sight of it had put Les in a bad mood. "Been squandering my money again, I see."

We had been at each other's throats since Les admitted to causing John's accident.

"I spent my own money. Money I earned," I hissed at him, emphasising 'I' and he grabbed my wrist. "Let go of my arm!" I said, gritting my teeth in pain.

We were standing at the breakfast bar across from the dining area. I managed to pull my arm free and Les backed away. He casually strolled over to the lounge area at the sound of footsteps on the sprawling, highly polished wooden floor of our spacious living room.

"G'day," Helen said cheerfully as Billy strolled in behind her. "Watcha doing?"

Les was sitting in one of the lounge chairs. Our guests sat down opposite him, facing the New Guinean artefacts hanging on the wall near the entrance. The blue floral drapes I had bought from Helen, covering the vast louver window walls in the lounge room and dining area, gently moved in rhythm with the warm evening breeze. Tall sapphire-blue lamps either side of the room provided soft lighting.

"Hi," I said, rubbing my wrist to ease the pain while trying to contain my temper. Glancing at my arm and seeing the watchband twisted and bruises forming, I became infuriated. 'That bastard is always destroying my things,' I thought, trying to hold in the mounting rage.

In the earlier stages of our marriage, whenever we argued, Les had a habit of picking up my things and asking me in a menacing way, "Do you like this?" When I nodded or pleaded with him to put it down he would smash it to the floor. He was not satisfied until he had destroyed something. It was as if he was destroying me. Remembering what he had done to my things in the past, the damaged watchband was the last straw. In a knee jerk reaction I swore at him.

Spoiling for a fight, Les leapt to his feet at lightning speed and seized me by the hair, then dragged me towards the kitchen wall and savagely slammed my head against it, leaving a hole in the wall.

Billy and Helen sat frozen in their seats, too dumbfounded to say anything. I can still recall the comical look on Helen's face, her eyes bulged in disbelief, utterly astounded. Her mouth moved but no sound came out. Everything happened so quickly. It was over before either of them realised what Les had done. Anger, hatred and pain from the blow to my head sent shock waves through my body. Once Les had exploded he'd calm down, but I was stewing and let fly, "You bastard!" I said, stamping my foot. I began pacing the floor nervously puffing on a cigarette, "You bastard! You bastard!" I muttered, pacing back and forth while Les and our guests watched in silence.

I was surprised that Les did not react. He remained in the chair smirking, but later I realised the presence of Helen and Billy was the only reason he did not. He let me make a fool of myself, knowing he could make good use of the scene later on, telling people that I was a nag, threw tantrums and gave him a hard time. Helen and Billy were witnesses to that. He could say that I pushed him too far.

Our guests did not stay long after the argument. I was amazed that they were so eager to leave, showing no concern at all for my safety. After they had gone Les grinned at me and said, "You put on a good show tonight, didn't you?"

"You're a bastard!" I snapped.

"Careful sweetness," he warned, waving his index finger at me before going to bed.

Although we were in constant battle with each other, Les had not taken his frustrations out on the children. Before leaving Australia I agreed to keep in contact with the Department of Welfare in Bankstown. Papua New Guinea was under Australian mandate then, which clearly meant the court ruling was still valid, granting the children protection under Australian law, should they need it. Les knew I would protect my children from him if I had to. He became more menacing to my safety with each passing day and I avoided him as much as possible. Most of the time I felt powerless and did not know how to handle his unpredictable mood swings. My greatest fear was that he would push me to my limits and I would end up killing him. I hated him that much.

Although I did not want to leave the island, we were due for annual leave and had made plans to return to Sydney for my sister's wedding. Mary had asked me to be her matron-of-honour. I was surprised and delighted that she had included me in the wedding party but really did not want to return to

Sydney. Thinking about the trip churned up all sorts of emotions that I did not want to deal with.

I felt apprehensive on the journey to Aropa Airport. Twelve months had passed and during that time I had virtually cut myself off from the world. 'Now I have to live in the real world. Les is forever telling me that I live in a dream world. I guess he's right,' I mused, looking out of the window at the road leading to the airport.

Screeching tyres from the aircraft hitting Australian soil brought good and bad memories flooding into my mind. Returning to Sydney had a profound effect on me. My self-assurance and confidence flew out the window, leaving me with only a shell of the identity reborn in Papua New Guinea.

In the company of family Les was attentive and affectionate but he was moody and aloof when we were alone, a skill he had perfected. He cunningly manipulated every confrontation between us and played the martyr husband. I could have participated in the facade but it was not my nature to play mind games. I simply called a spade a spade and Les knew it. I did not have the emotional strength to pretend for one second that I cared for him and I paid the consequences for that.

It seemed that my family showed sympathy towards Les, a clear indication that they believed me to be the villain. Their judgement showed me that they did not really know me at all or even care enough to find out. My absence had done nothing to improve my mother's attitude towards me either.

The fights with Les over my affair with Sam, and the severe malaria attack, had taken their toll. To make matters worse I had taken thinning scissors to my once long thick hair because Les would not allow me to cut it, telling me that he hated short hair. Upset about my appearance, my mother said, "For heaven's sake Emma, your hair was supposed to be long for the wedding, not stringy. Why did you go and do that to it, it looks awful." She exhaled loudly in exasperation.

I wanted to scream at her 'I'm a bloody adult. It's none of your business what I do with my hair...' but instead I said, "It's hot on Bougainville and I spend a lot of time at the beach..."

'Sydney's no longer my home,' I thought ruefully and reasoned that it never was. My melancholic mood convinced me that I did not fit into my family either. I was painfully aware that the bond I had with friends was stronger than my family ties. 'I do try, but it never seems to work for me. I always feel on the outer no matter what I do.'

My disappointment at feeling displaced went deep. Although I learned to live with my feelings of banishment I could not help but think, 'I wish I knew where I'm supposed to be. Where the hell is that anyway?'

Mary was a beautiful bride and the wedding was enjoyable. Everyone said the deep purple crepe dresses and cream; wide-brimmed straw hats the bridesmaids wore looked really lovely. Even though my dress hung loosely on me the colour was perfect and everyone liked the bob-style auburn wig I wore.

How I looked was insignificant to me because nothing could erase the sadness I felt. My spirit was not at the wedding and I longed to be anywhere other than Sydney. I yearned to see Luc, just to say hello, but dared not.

Mary and Tim had bought an investment house before they married and we stayed there while we were in Sydney. While making breakfast one morning I was pondering the hole in the wall incident, and without even thinking I said to Les, "I don't want to go back to PNG with you."

Returning to the island with him had lost its appeal. As much as I loved Bougainville and considered it home, living with someone I hated spoiled the illusion of paradise.

"What do you mean?" he said glaring at me. "Is this more of your bullshit?"

I looked at him, ready to explode, but remained calm, "No Les, my head still hurts. I want to stay here with the children."

"Oh no, you don't, the kids come with me," he said getting up from the table. Snatching the car keys from the shelf, he stormed out of the house and returned several hours later, but he was not alone.

I caught my breath at the smiling figure walking towards me. Les lingered in the background watching from the doorway, a trace of a smirk in his expression when Luc hugged me.

"What are you doing here?" I whispered, puzzled.

"I don't know," Luc shrugged. "Les came into work telling me that someone wanted to see me. I figured it had something to do with you."

I made coffee and Luc strolled into the lounge room adjacent to the kitchen and sat down. I watched him closely and thought he appeared at ease. We could see each other from where he sat. Then Les entered the room and sat in a chair out of view, making it awkward for me to communicate with Luc.

The children were sitting on the floor with their eyes glued to the television set. Luc was watching Cain interact with his brothers and sister. His mouth slowly creased into a smile and Les noticed. He leaned forward and lifted Cain up, placing him on his lap and saying, "Come here, mate, and give your old Dad a cuddle," adding, "You're Dad's boy, aren't you mate?" Cain nodded shyly and grinned awkwardly. Les rewarded him with a pat on the head before lowering him down beside his brothers and sister.

As I sat down beside Luc on the lounge, I placed my hand over his for a fleeting moment before handing him his coffee. He turned and winked at me, giving no indication that the taunting had bothered him. After an hour of small talk Luc left.

"What the hell was that all about, Les?" I asked, fuming. I was angry and heartsick for the way Les tried to humiliate Luc, so much so that I was not afraid of him.

"What?" Les responded irritated, acting as though he had done me a favour. "You're always going on about something. What's wrong with you now? Didn't you want to see your boyfriend?"

I spun around without answering and left the room. I was too angry to speak. In the solitude of the backyard I broke down and cried, wishing I was back on Bougainville. I was sad for Luc and wanted to yell from the rooftops for all to hear that Cain was Luc's son and not Les Carter's.

We niggled at each other for the rest of the holidays. By the time we were due to return to Bougainville, Les decided to allow me to stay behind. "The kids come back with me, though" he said the day of his departure. "That way I know you'll be back."

My resistance was too low to fight him. I did not have enough physical or emotional strength left in me. I knew Mick would take good care of the children; otherwise I would have gone with them. With a heavy heart I bade them goodbye at Sydney Airport, knowing that I would soon follow them and that Les knew it too.

23

Settling into a daily routine in Sydney was difficult because my thoughts were with the children and my presence at my parents' place was an obvious intrusion. I wanted to do something other than sit around the house all day long, so I went out and found a job in a city dress shop.

A few days into the job I was bored, relieved when it was five o'clock. Each day after work, I quickly gathered my belongings together and casually strolled out of the store, mingling with the bustling city crowd as I headed in the direction of the train station.

On the third afternoon a familiar figure hurried towards me. I stood transfixed in the middle of the footpath, unsure whether to laugh or to cry. Luc's handsome face was beaming from ear to ear as he provocatively said, "I've been waiting for you," wrapping his arms tightly around me. I smiled at the sound of his voice, the same voice I had heard over and over again in my thoughts and in my dreams. His intoxicating aftershave stirred vivid memories of the nights we spent together. Taking my hand in his he said, "Come on, let's go," and led me to his car parked nearby and opened the passenger door for me.

"Where are we going?"

"Nowhere. Just for a drive. I wanted to be with you. Is that okay?"

"What do you think?" I laughed mischievously, climbing inside.

"How did you know where I was working?" I asked, screwing my face up. "Better still, how the heck did you know I didn't go back to PNG?" I asked questions one after another but all Luc would say was, "I make it my business to know what you're doing, kiddo," kissing me on the tip of my nose.

Luc drove me home and parked down the street from my parents' place. We sat in the car and talked for hours, catching up on news about old friends. There was an easy silence between us as we listened to the car radio. Suddenly I blurted out, almost in tears, and hanging my head in shame, "I'm so sorry, sweetheart, for what happened at the house the other day. Les is a real bastard." I looked solemnly at him, vowing sincerely, "I promise you my darling, one day Cain will know who his father is and the person that you are."

"What good would that do?" he shrugged. "Will he really want to know?"

"Oh yes, yes he will," I said optimistically. "Of course he will. He should know. He must know how much we love him." But Luc was not convinced.

"How long do you plan to stay in Sydney?" he asked, changing the subject

"Not long," I said. "He has my babies."

"I'd like to see you while you're here," he said, kissing and nibbling my cheek.

"Every moment possible," I purred, thinking, 'He really is with me. This was not simply a figment of my imagination.'

"Well then, I'd better get you home otherwise your oldies will be upset."

"Hey, I'm a big girl now," I said, pulling away and looked at him with playful indignation. "I think I'm free to come and go as I please."

I could not have been more wrong. When I entered the house I was greeted with, "WHERE HAVE YOU BEEN?" I was taken by surprise and angry at my mother's attitude.

"Luc drove me home from work and we sat in the car talking for a while."

"Huh." She obviously thought I was lying. The idea of me seeing Luc sent shock waves of opposition through my parents' home and an awful argument erupted. Before I knew what was happening, I was yelling back at my mother, "I shouldn't have to explain anything, I'm an adult."

Hands on hips my mother spat back, "Adult! What a joke, married women don't sit in cars with men."

I glared at her, "WE-WERE-ONLY-TALKING! WHAT ABOUT YOU! YOU'RE A GOOD ONE TO TALK!" I should have reminded her of the affair she had when I was five years old.

"You have been a trouble-maker from the day you were born."

"Well," I snarled sarcastically, "I had a good teacher, didn't I?"

"Why you little bitch, after all I've done for you. You'd be dead now if it wasn't for me," my mother said, banging her chest with her hand as she usually did to make a point about herself.

"Yeah, yeah!" I replied, disinterested. "Can't you please sing another song; I've heard it all before."

"You think you are real smart, don't you?" There was venom in her tone.

"Well why not, Mom. I know your secret."

Mom reacted as if I had slapped her, then suddenly her features hardened. "YOU'RE A SLUT! And what about Cain?"

"What about him?" I challenged looking at her with indignation. "Well? I'm waiting."

My mother did not answer; she just stood glaring at me.

"If you think I am ashamed of my son, think again. I love my children." My tone changed saying, "it's funny how history repeats itself, isn't it?" I smirked.

Mom was wild and went to strike me. "Don't you dare," I said.

Our anger was unrelenting. I accused my mother of causing most of the trouble in our home and then Mom said smugly, "You think that you are lady muck travelling back and forth, don't you? Well, let me tell you something. You are not! For years, Les has been chasing after me!"

I thought at that moment that I had never hated anyone more in my life than my mother, not even Les. My mother made me feel physically ill and disgusted. I immediately gathered all my belongings together and fled from the house and went to stay with Peter and his wife for a couple of days while I made plans to return to Bougainville. Confused and distressed, I confided in my brother but he flatly refused to believe there was anything going on between Les and Mom. Mary felt the same when I told her on her return from her honeymoon but I knew better. Remembering the night in Port Macquarie, I knew that something had happened. Repelled and disgusted, I could not get away from Sydney fast enough.

The evening before I was due to leave for Bougainville, I telephoned Luc to let him know. He offered to take me to the hotel that night when I told him that I had booked a room in the city because of the early flight. We spent most of that night together but neither of us said very much. What was there to say anyway? We had no way of knowing if we would ever see each other again.

A deep sadness accompanied me all the way back to Bougainville, but the moment I set foot on the island it disappeared.

'I'm home,' I thought feeling good. 'I am home.'

As I had imagined, Mick had done a wonderful job of looking after the children. They were overjoyed to see me and welcomed me with cheers and chatter. When I confronted Les about his alleged liaison with my mother he denied everything, including the night in Port Macquarie.

"I don't believe you," I growled. "And don't you ever try to touch me again. I only came back because you have my babies."

Whenever Les made an attempt to become intimate or acted as though he was about to take what he believed were his rights as my husband, I would say, "Perhaps you should take a trip to Sydney, my mother seems to enjoy your company. Or maybe take a trip to Arkansas, to see that teenage hillbilly I saw you kissing in the water at Loloho Beach, the night of the company barbecue. I guess she stills fancies you."

* * *

Before Helen and her family left Bougainville to settle in Queensland, Helen took delight in telling me that seventeen-year-old Betsy, the daughter of an American who came to Bougainville on a short contract, was infatuated with Les. I had already known that and could not have cared less. I saw them together and thought it was amusing as the girl was only a teenager and very overweight.

At one of our 'girls' get together we were talking about who we thought were the sexiest men on the island. The conversation finally got around to our husbands. I did not think any of their husbands, not even my own, was worth a second glance and flippantly said, "If any of you want my husband, you're welcome to him. They laughed.

"Mind if I try?" a voice whispered.

Surprised, I looked at Helen and said, "Go for it. He's home right now."

She jumped up and practically ran down the stairs to her car. She had not been gone long when she returned grinning. Les never mentioned what had happened that night, but every time we quarrelled he told me Helen was not my friend. "All of your so-called friends use you," he would say, "just like Helen."

I kept Les at bay and still managed to keep the peace for many months by cleverly dodging his attempted embraces. The game of cat and mouse became a challenge that I began to enjoy. The satisfaction of succeeding another night was more gratifying than taking a lover, which Les accused me of doing. He told me that he did not care who I slept with, just as long as he did not miss out. When it was no longer possible to avoid him, I reluctantly gave in. My revenge was non-response. My heart had turned to stone where he was concerned.

I would have been a little more considerate if Les had continued to spend time with the children, as he did in the first few weeks of 1972. But his compassion as a father soon wore off, and the children quickly became an afterthought. I naively believed that if I shared the children's daily antics with him he would be encouraged to appreciate and enjoy them and want to be with them. Instead he showed little or no interest. His indifference towards the children frustrated me to the brink of tears.

By chance, during a shopping excursion, I discovered how Les exploited my daily commentary on the children's amusing antics for his own advantage. In the store I bumped into a man who worked on the same shift as Les. He told me how impressed he was with Les and how much Les loved his family.

"He talks non-stop about the kids and you," he said. The man was convinced that Les was a devoted father and husband and was ready to give him the father of the year award. Sadly, to my knowledge, not one person saw through the farce. Les had successfully fooled everyone. It was beyond my understanding why people could not see the kind of a person Les really was. I was ever mindful of the way Les treated our children and of my vow to never bear another child of his.

The visit to the doctor never eventuated after the miscarriage I'd had in the bathroom two years earlier. The loop the doctor put into my womb after BJ's birth had caused me a great deal of internal pain from the day it was inserted. I reasoned it was better to endure the pain than fall pregnant again. As time passed, the pain became too much to endure any longer, I had to deal with it.

The doctor's response was one of utter astonishment when I finally went to see him. After he had removed the loop he said, "I can't imagine how you tolerated the degree of pain you must have experienced with the contraption in the position it was."

"With great difficulty," I smiled ruefully. "But it was better than having another baby."

He observed me a moment then said, "I'd like to do a curette. It won't take long, just a couple of hours in hospital."

After the loop was removed I tried several different contraceptives, each with adverse effects. I had to stop taking them and the inevitable happened.

"It would be impossible to do it here," the doctor said seriously, when I went to see him a second time. He wrote down the name of a surgeon in Port Moresby on his note pad and handed it to me.

'Strategic planning is of the utmost importance,' I told myself, looking at the notepaper.

A week had passed by the time I had secretly arranged my flight to Port Moresby. A friend going overseas gave me a lift to the airport without Les knowing. The plan was that I would be over and back home before he arrived home that night.

While waiting my turn to see the Port Moresby doctor, what I was about to do felt more like a weird dream than reality. I was casually dressed in navy linen pants, white tee shirt and brown Indian sandals, and everything appeared normal. My long, recently-coloured auburn hair was twisted and tied in a knot and secured with a clip at the back of my head. I tried to act as naturally as possible but the uncertainty of my situation made me restless.

A woman close to my age sat opposite me. I smiled and we exchanged awkward glances until the nurse directed her into the surgery leaving me alone in the waiting room. My inquisitive mind began to work overtime, wondering why the woman seemed agitated. I turned and looked at the surgery door when it suddenly swung open. The woman came hurrying out with her head hung low, looking upset, but I had other things to think about when the nurse said, "The doctor will see you now, Emma. This way please."

The doctor was tall and spoke with an English accent. He was pale looking, too pale for living in Papua New Guinea, I thought. He raised his eyebrows when I told him my reason for coming to him. "There seems to an epidemic lately," he remarked, ushering me to the examining table. He said the same thing the doctor in Arawa had said.

"What am I to do now?" I asked him, feeling defeated.

"You'll have to go to Sydney."

I left the doctors surgery with another name and another telephone number. I took a cab to the Davara Hotel, where I saw the woman from the doctor's surgery sitting alone in the hotel lobby. She appeared deep in thought and looked worried.

"Hi! Fancy meeting you here," I said, strolling over to join her. She looked a little startled when she saw me.

"Looks like I'll be travelling to Sydney," I told her

"Hmm. Me too."

Without waiting to be invited, I sat in the chair opposite her.

"Look," I said introducing myself, "I think we have the same problem and are going in the same direction so how about we travel together."

Jane Burns was timid and very shy, but seemed to welcome my company. She lived in Moresby with her family.

"They think I'm visiting friends," she said. "I told them I might be away a few days. I hate having to lie, but it would be more terrible for them to know the truth," she said. She screwed up her face then drew back hard on her cigarette.

Once the hotel and flight bookings were made I rang Les and told him where I was going. He pleaded with me to come back.

"Please, Bubby, don't kill my baby," he sobbed. "Please come back. I'll do anything for you. Give you anything. I promise…"

'You sound so pathetic,'

"Huh, I've heard it all before, Les," I scoffed indignantly. "When I told you I don't want another child of yours, I meant it!"

Les was crying. I felt good for a split second and then my emotions turned to stone, recalling the day we brought BJ home from the hospital. He's not going to trick me into changing my mind this time. I'll never forget the way he treated BJ. It's not going to happen ever again. I'll never have another child of his. Never! 'I must be dreaming,' I thought, 'this is nightmarish and surreal. I'll do what I have to do.'

"How long will you be away?" he asked, once he realised that I was not coming back.

"Only a couple of days," I replied sharply. "I'll need my passport to get back into the country when I return to Moresby."

"I'll make sure it'll be waiting for you at the airport, I promise," he said, and ended the conversation with his usual, "I love you."

In Sydney, Jane and I checked into a hotel then took a cab to the surgery at Kings Cross. We hesitantly entered a dingy building and walked a short distance along a corridor that led to an empty waiting room. The room was stark and gloomy but clean. A cheery woman dressed in a white uniform greeted us warmly. She assured us that we were in good hands, she took our money and ushered us to a change room.

"You girls can undress in there," she said handing us gowns and pointing to a door. "I'll bring you both a sedative in a minute."

We changed and then returned to the room and sat in silence opposite each other, wrapped in the plain white gowns and our thoughts and fears. The nurse hurried in and gave both of us an injection, then hurried out. She returned for Jane, then a little later for me.

Everything around me seemed distorted while under the influence of the sedative. I was disorientated and, thinking I had given birth, asked the doctor what I had.

"Nothing," the masculine voice echoed, "you didn't have anything."

The doctor's voice sounded strange and reverberated around the room and in my head. Silent tears of regret slid down my cheeks as the woman in white assisted me to another room where I rested until the sedative wore off. Lying on the bed, alone in the bare room, I prayed for forgiveness and strength to put what I had done behind me. When there were no more tears left to cry my head cleared and my strength returned. I was ready to get on with my life.

Jane looked pale. Neither of us said a word in the taxi back to the hotel. We sat on opposite sides of the vehicle as if totally alone. From my window I saw the passing parade and wanted to become one of them. I was returning to Papua New Guinea the following morning and had no intention of dwelling on what had happened. I gladly welcomed the distraction of window shopping.

Once Jane was settled in, I left her to rest then headed for the city stores. My ability to carry on amazed me. Everything around me seemed so normal when only a few hours before I had had an abortion. 'Life's so bizarre,' I thought. 'Why don't I feel guilty or ashamed and not just relief and a little sadness? When I prayed for forgiveness, I certainly didn't expect to find peace with that prayer. It's remarkable that I didn't feel troubled.'

I had not notice the hours passing as I walked aimlessly around the city deep in thought. On my way back to the hotel I made a conscious decision to never mention or think about the incident again.

By the time I had reached the hotel, Jane was much better.

"Are you all right?" she sounded concerned, sighing with relief when I walked through the door. "Where have you been? I was so worried."

I looked at her propped up on the bed with pillows. "Been doing a lot of thinking," I said. "I'm never going to think or speak about what happened today ever again. I suggest that you do the same if you can."

Jane whole-heartedly agreed adding, "I can't believe that it really happened."

"Me neither," I replied sombrely.

The aircraft landed in Port Moresby late in the afternoon. I stood aside and waited for the crowd to thin out before I approached the immigration officer stationed at the gate. Another immigration officer came from behind and startled me when he said, "Can I help you?"

"Oh," I jumped, "Yes. My husband was supposed to have sent my passport over from Bougainville to this office. Can you please check to see if it's there? My name is Emma Carter."

He was gone for what felt an eternity but returned empty-handed, telling me he could not find the passport.

"But it must be there," I said anxiously. "Can you look again or call someone else please?" He did not move.

"Do you know anybody in Moresby?" he asked.

I shook my head. "My friends live on Bougainville, some of them work for Ansett and TAA," I then ran off a list of names.

"Well, it's obvious that you live on Bougainville. Come on," he said, cheerfully opening the gate. "Walk through, Madame." He made a sweeping motion with his hand, waving me through the gate, and bowed slightly in a playful gesture.

I followed the immigration officer's direction with a sense of relief and a touch of smugness at getting back into the country without my passport. 'Won't Les be surprised?' I laughed quietly to myself.

The immigration officer had also given me directions to a hotel close to the airport. Although I was exhausted after the long flight, sleep eluded me. My mind raced over the past twenty-four hours, dreading the idea of having to face Les when I returned home. 'I'm ready for him,' I murmured with clenched fists.

I was surprised to see my downstairs neighbours Ken and Dolly Jonas at the airport the following morning and tried to avoid them. They were on their way to Australia for their annual leave. Dolly called out to me and I responded out of curiosity. "Les is very angry with you," she said. The pleasure in her voice did not escape me either. "He's had enough of your antics," she smirked. "He's been telling everyone that he doesn't want you to come back…"

Typical of Les, and this old bitch.

"Well, I guess I'll wait and see what he has to say when I get back home," I said. "You know, Dolly," I laughed, "I got back into the country without my passport. It's not what you know, it's who you know. Enjoy your holiday!" I sauntered away, mumbling under my breath. "Hope you break your neck, you old hag."

The car pulled into the driveway and the children came running when they saw who it was. As I thanked my friends for the lift and waved them goodbye, the children gathered around me, full of excitement.

'Twenty-four hours feels like a lifetime,' I sighed. 'And so much has happened in that short space of time.'

I bent down and hugged them all together, then one at a time. I was thinking how remarkable it was that they all had grown so much. I watched and listened to them as they all eagerly talked over each other. Once again, it had hit home how really precious and innocent they were. 'These dear little people have put their trust in us as parents, to provide for them a happy and a secure home,' I thought, smiling at them. 'How could anyone not enjoy or love children, especially their own?' The joy of seeing me shone brightly in their eyes and it touched my heart. Suddenly I felt so unworthy.

The sound of the bus on the gravel driveway told me that Les was home. The children called excitedly from the balcony, "Dad, Mom's home."

The commotion prompted me to peep through the louver windows at what was going on downstairs. I stayed there long enough to see Les walk upstairs but darted away from the window moments before he entered the flat. He paused in the doorway a few moments, observing me before he spoke.

"You look different. You've changed," he said thoughtfully.

Normally I would have been trembling, but not this time. I was ready to confront him and deal with him if he attempted to lay a hand on me. I had nothing to say to him at that moment. Later on repeated what Dolly had said to me at Moresby Airport. I detected an element of surprise in his eyes.

"Aha, I don't know what you're on about," he spat and stormed out.

"Just what I'd expected you to say." I declared and then got on with my unpacking; fishing around for the gifts I had bought the children.

By now I was totally aware of Les' underhandedness but was not bothered by it. There was nothing I could do other than be alert to it. 'It's ironic,' I mused, 'although my life is full of deceit, mistrust and secrets, I'm surrounded by nature's beauty and I'm determined to enjoy it! Stuff Les!'

I enjoyed the evenings when the flat was quiet, the children safely tucked into their beds and sound asleep and Les on afternoon shift. I would sit on the veranda inhaling a cigarette and sipping wine, absorbing the magic of the moon's beauty as its rays danced upon the water, turning the bay into liquid silver. Mystical moon-swept shadows were mesmerising. Large palms silhouetted against the night sky. Their outstretched, long, feathery branches became haunting images, gracefully swaying to and fro in rhythm with the evening breeze. Rolling waves crept along the sand with the incoming tide; soft music playing in the background completed the picture.

Immersed in the ambience, I was able to travel back in time and spend time with either, Luc or Matt whenever I wanted to. As much as I tried, I could never erase either of them from my thoughts. I worried about Matt and wondered if he was alive. In my heart, I felt he was. The image I had of him was too strong in my mind, for him not to be. Not knowing for certainty, I had all sorts of what ifs and regrets running around my head. "I'll find out for sure one day," I told myself.

Alluring tropical evenings and cheerful sunny days overruled many negative forces in my life, while living on Bougainville. I drew strength from what was beautiful whenever my spirit was low, absorbing from such beauty, a hunger for life and a sense of adventure. The addiction was inescapable.

24

The days flew by. The children grew so fast that I felt a little overwrought when I enrolled Brad and Celeste in Toniva Primary School, concerned that Brad would have trouble settling into a classroom routine. While he lacked enthusiasm scholastically, he socialised with ease. Celeste on the other hand excelled scholastically, but found difficulty interacting with other students; she was so timid.

At the beginning of his first year, Brad came home with a torn shirt and a black eye. It was before my falling-out with Dolly Jonas, who presented him with twenty cents for his first black eye when she saw him that afternoon. "Oh darling," she cooed, "Are you alright?"

"Yeah, I'll get him next time," Brad said with false confidence.

Since Brad had obviously lost the fight, I thought it was time to teach him how to defend himself. During the lesson, I stressed that he should never start a fight, but finish it if he was set upon. That afternoon in our lounge room, I crouched down and held my hands in the position of a boxer and practised different swings with him until I was satisfied he knew the technique.

The very next day Brad came home with another torn shirt, but this time he had won the fight and made friends with his opponent. Although pleased with the outcome, I seriously cautioned him to avoid future fights.

Just as I was feeling content with life on the island, a series of break-ins around Toniva began. Initially, I was not concerned since crime and misconduct from the local community, in pre-independence, was neither alarming nor threatening to expatriates. As soon as anything happened, news circulated around the towns like wildfire, stirring up all sorts of speculation.

Early one morning, Celeste came in to my bedroom. She woke me to tell that a man had come into her bedroom during the night. I dismissed her story thinking she just had had a bad dream, but later that day, I noticed my basket missing from my room and went in search of it. I found it in Celeste's bedroom.

"What's my basket doing in your room, sweetie?" I asked.

Celeste looked up at me and said, "The man put it there, last night, Mommy." I studied her in disbelief.

"He did Mommy, but I pretended to be asleep," she pleaded. The fear in Celeste's voice validated her story. 'She's not prone to exaggeration,' I thought, trying to rationalise what had happened.

When I suddenly realised that something could have happened to my child, while I slept in the next room, I snapped, "You should have called me."

"I was too scared to Mommy, in case he hurt me," she said, about to cry

"It's okay sweetie, it's okay. You did the right thing. It's all right. You were very brave. I'm so sorry I didn't believe you. I thought you had a dream..."

Further investigation showed how the intruder gained entry to our home. The screen wire was cut and a kitchen, louver window was removed. The intruder simply reached in, opened the door and let himself in. According to Celeste, our unwelcome visitor walked through the flat looking in the bedrooms before going to the kitchen and helping himself to the contents of our refrigerator. Nothing other than food was missing. But the incident made me feel that we needed to be more cautious, before a tragedy happened. I saw the break-in as a warning. Security and the safety of my children became my first priority; a curfew was in place – the children had to be home before 5.00 pm.

Brad stretched my patience to the limit. Every time he failed to return home on time, I went searching for him, often failing to find him. I anxiously waited for him to return home.

After hours passed, the uncertainly of Brad's whereabouts and his safety would turn me into a screaming banshee the moment he walked through the door. There was certainly no gratification in punishing or yelling at him or his siblings. I was raising my young family the way I had been raised, with the exception that I explained why they were being punished. Sadly, Brad and I spent many of our days locked in conflict that drove a wedge between us.

Les continued to show little or no interest in the children, with the exception of Cain. He became aggravated whenever I complained to him about Brad's misdeeds. "Why the hell don't you pay attention to Brad, he needs a father," I roared at Les. His response was to tell me to shut my mouth.

I was the children's disciplinarian as well as their advocate. Raising four children solo was certainly a challenge. I had made many regrettable mistakes in the process. Eventually, I came to recognise that my worst fault was my acid tongue. Although I tried not to, I found myself using the same harsh tone and manner my mother used on me as a child. What I hated most about my mother surfaced in me, and I feared history was repeating itself.

So often I had apologised to my children for the way I had spoken to them. I hated myself the times I broke my self-imposed promises, not to be anything like my mother. To ease the guilt for my weakness and compensate for their father's indifference, I overindulged the children. Les echoed strong objections, accusing me of spoiling them. He believed they did not deserve anything at all. He complained bitterly, telling me that he did not have much as a child, so why should they? I felt it was all the more reason why he would want to give more to the children. Les' objections prompted me to become more defiant. I believed my children deserved a stable home and two parents who loved them, which they did not have, and consequently I was determined to give them all that I could.

I had a close relationship with my children, even Brad. They were all loving and affectionate towards me as I was towards them. The same could not be said about Les. Endeavouring to rectify that, I created a fictitious image of a father for them, which I later regretted doing.

"The reason Daddy can't spend much time with you," I told them, "is because he has a very important job. But he loves you all very much. He's working hard so we can have nice things. He asks about you all the time…"

Over the years I gave them the same excuse and consequently, Brad saw his father as a hero, which seemed harmless at the time. What did concern me though, was the way Brad absorbed his father's chauvinistic view that females were inferior to males. Dealing with Brad became increasingly difficult, especially when he began to show resentment of me playing a dual-parent role in his father's absence.

Brad's attitude raised its ugly head as early as seven years old. While he began to disrespect Celeste, he did not openly display defiance towards me. His contempt for females showed whenever he and his sister debated something. "Ah, you're just a girl, and girls aren't important anyway," he would say, dismissing Celeste. It was not what Brad said that bothered me. It was the hardness in his voice and the conviction of his belief, at such a young age, that did.

Brad was no match for Celeste, whose shyness ceased to exist at home. Celeste could easily handle Brad, confidently and eloquently, which left him frustrated and angry. "At least I have a brain," she would confidently say, "which is more than I can say for you."

Brad had to contend with having a sister who excelled in areas where he did not. His pride and ego took a huge beating. Perhaps, if Les had not expressed such negative views, his son's approach to life may have been different and possibly Brad would have suffered fewer defeats.

Saddened that any of my sons would hold such a contemptuous outlook, I took satisfaction in knowing that neither, Cain nor BJ followed their brother. They weren't as serious as Brad. They were cheerful children.

From the age of three years old, Cain could best be described as strong-minded and confidently assured of his direction in life. He had big plans for his future, success oozing from his pores. One of his dreams at that age was to be a garbage truck driver. Every Monday morning he ran out on to the veranda the moment he heard the garbage collectors coming down the street. With wide-eyed fascination he watched from the balcony, as the men emptied rubbish bins into the huge truck. Cain was mesmerised by the giant mechanical arm dragging debris into the compartment. The idea of rubbish being munched up as the truck moved slowly along the street, intrigued and thrilled him. He imagined that driving a truck like that was a very important thing to do. When friends asked what he wanted to be when he grew up, he proudly announced, "A garbage twuck dwiver."

There was never a doubt that Cain would succeed in the future, even though he had a slight speech impediment. His ambitious nature appeared in everything he tackled. Winning became his ultimate aim, relentlessly trying until he succeeded and to his credit, gaining rewards and praise for his achievements. I felt the attention he received from all quarters contributed to the moulding of his flamboyant personality.

When Cain and I stood on the veranda watching Brad and Celeste go off to school each morning, he declared almost in tears, "Mommy, I want to go to school too."

"You can when you're old enough," I promised, hugging him, but that statement never seemed to satisfy him and he repeatedly asked when. Without thinking I promised he could start school after Christmas.

Cain would have been five in May of the following year but he had to be five before the January to be able to go to school. When I told him that he could not go to school that year, he became angry and cried with disappointment and said, "But you pwomised."

Before Les' contract with Ganmor's expired, he was offered a position with the copper mine, as a leading hand in the truck section. It was common knowledge that employees of the copper mine enjoyed excellent living conditions, greatly subsidised by the company.

A furnished four-bedroom house in Arawa, a few miles inland from the east coast of the Island, was part of the job package. I encouraged Les to take the position.

With each move our financial position improved, allowing us to gain more assets and a better lifestyle in the process. I can recall the day during the first year on the island, when I wanted to purchase five acres of land at Ipswich in Queensland. Les refused to even consider it, saying, "I'm working my arse off for everyone else and getting nothing in return."

At the time we were struggling to clear debts in Sydney and saving very little money as a result. Nevertheless, I felt we should buy the land. Les refused to see any further than beyond the day he was living, but I did. The land as an investment for my family's future. When Les realised I was not about to give in, he saw a chance to negotiate a deal with me. He agreed to sign the papers only if I had sex with him. I recalled the episode in Darwin and thought why not, I was dead to him anyway, and it was a chance to gain a valuable asset.

A precedent was set that day, this being the last resort whenever I did not have the finances to cover whatever the children needed. But thankfully the need to negotiate was rare as I quickly became financially independent.

Although in my heart I knew the move to Arawa was in the right direction, the thought of moving away from the beach and the precious memories I indulged while there, left me feeling a little sad; I would be leaving a little of myself behind. The serenity of the beach at nights that I had so much enjoyed became an integral part of my escape, and my imaginary meeting place with Luc and Matt, would now become just a pleasant memory.

While standing on the balcony deep in thought, looking out at the beach with my hair and clothing ruffling in the wind, my mind reached back into the past two years. Sorting through my thoughts, Betty flashed into my mind. We did keep in touch, regardless of the awful and sometimes hazardous road conditions. The twelve-kilometre journey from Toniva to Arawa took longer than it really was, often taking several hours to complete because of the boulders, potholes and slush after heavy rain.

Tears filled my eyes as I remembered the tragedy that took place on the day of the opening of the new supermarket in Arawa.

Excitement stirred throughout the island and around the villages, as the grand opening of the new supermarket came closer. On opening day, just about everyone who lived on Bougainville, nationals and expatriates alike, crowded outside the store clamouring for a place in line. For us expatriates the new air-conditioned supermarket was a welcome bonus. We would no longer have to endure the excruciating heat, shopping in a tin shed, supermarket

Everywhere I looked I saw a sea of black smiling faces and wondered, 'What do these nationals really think about the supermarket?' It was highly unlikely that many would have seen anything like it before, and yet they appeared to passively accept progress on the island.

Crowds unnerved me, but out of curiosity I went to the Arawa supermarket opening with Helen. Among the hordes, I saw Betty with her youngest son struggling to move about the store aisles and waved to her. We pushed our way towards each other, but the lack of space and heavy flow of foot traffic prevented us from chatting any longer than a minute. The store was in chaos and the stench overpowering.

As we were about to make an effort to go our separate ways, promising to catch up later that day, Betty complained to me of a headache. Then suddenly she began to tremble, falling to the ground and convulsing at my feet. Shocked and unsure of what to do, I knelt down beside her and the crowd quickly engulfed us. I called Helen, who was a few metres away, looking at shoes. She pushed and jostled her way over to me, dragging Molly behind her.

"Please stay with Betty," I said urgently, "I'll go and get Dan."

A mercy dash to hospital found Betty in a serious condition. She did not recognise anyone when she was conscious, not even her husband. I felt a deep compassion for her when I saw the outline of her fragile body lying so still under a thin blanket. Her eyes seemed blank as they stared into space.

"Betty," I whispered, fighting the urge to cry. "Betty it's me, Emma." She slowly turned her head and looked at me and smiled. Without a word, she turned away and continued to stare into space.

Outside in the hospital grounds, the service manager from Ganmor's and his wife were waiting for news of Betty. They were talking among themselves, saying that it was a shame that something as awful as this should happen to a nice person like Betty.

Thinking about Betty lying almost lifeless in that bed, angered me enough to speak my mind to them.

"We all know who's to blame for this, don't we?" I snapped, "But no one would listen to me. Oh no." I looked directly at the Service Manager. "I warned you that something terrible would happen to Betty."

He said nothing. He would not even look at me.

A scar tissue that had formed around Betty's brain caused the seizure. It was the result of a fractured skull she sustained some years prior to coming to Bougainville. Everything changed for Betty after the seizure; she became a completely different person and seemed to age overnight. The incident had forced her to be flown back to Australia for treatment. I felt heart-broken for her, knowing that she never wanted to leave the island.

A few months later Betty returned to Bougainville, but she was only a shell of her former self. Eventually the whole family left Bougainville and returned to Australia. Although we lost contact, I never forgot her. 'Some people just stick in your mind,' I later wrote in my diary, Betty was one of those people.

As a passing thought, Mick came to mind. He had been my loyal hous boi until the day I decided to do a few things around my home myself. He took offence and complained that I was doing his job. We actually argued over a new broom, the incident finally bringing our association to an end when he tried to snatch the broom from my hand. Refusing to be dominated by him any longer, I ordered him out of the house

"No got," he said, making a stand with arms folded in defiance. "Me stay! Me work!" But I had had enough this time, after two years of his subtle controlling ways. His manner was intolerable. He had forgotten that it was me and not him, who ran the home.

In retaliation, Mick went to Les and told him his version of what had happened. When Les informed him that the missus was the boss, he told Les about Sam staying at the flat during his absence, unaware that Les already knew.

Mick's effort to be reinstated was in vain, but he and I did eventually part on good terms. I later learned that he had joined Mt Hargan Police Force.

"One might have imagined living in paradise would have been easy," I muttered to myself, "but for some it isn't."

Not everyone took pleasure in the vast greenery of the island and its beauty, or enjoyed tropical downpours the way I did. After a while boredom set in and a need for distractions to keep sane became a priority for many restless souls. There was always something going on somewhere on the island. I smiled, thinking about some of those things and about the plantation house and laughed softly, breaking my sombre mood while remembering Toburoi Plantation and the parties there.

A group of single guys rented a house on the plantation. In jest, someone renamed the plantation Falconhurst. All who visited there had a great time, parties, dancing and romance being the order of the day. It was all good clean fun and the wonderful memories of those days will always remain with me. Despite the tragedy of my marriage, I did enjoy life in Toniva with the people I knew. I remembered them fondly, grateful to have met them, but now it was time for me to say goodbye to all of that.

*****

The move to Arawa gave me the opportunity to make Cain's wish come true. No one knew us so I changed Cain's date of birth on my family's re-entry permit, and then submitted it to the Primary School as proof of his age. The document was accepted and Cain happily went off to school with his brother and sister, before his fifth birthday.

BJ on the other hand was quite a different story. He had no desire to attend school at all. From the day he could walk, no fence, gate or door could keep him from exploring his world. Wanderlust had captured his spirit and no matter how much I tried, I just could not keep him from roaming.

The little fellow did not really give me any trouble as such. He was not prone to tantrums like other children his age. BJ was actually very quiet when he was at home, but that was the problem, he was hardly ever at home. He began wandering away at two years of age. Under my instructions, Mick watched BJ like a hawk. After Mick left, I was run off my feet going in search of him. A gate was constructed on the veranda, but BJ easily climbed over it. In desperation, I put a baby harness on him and attached a long rope to it so that he could only wander in and out of the flat. Every few minutes I would call, "Bubby, what are you doing? Come here to Mommy." If he did not answer, I would drop what I was doing to check on him and often found him happily playing with his toys. I could not take anything for granted with BJ. Within a couple of hours of donning the harness, he had wormed his way out of it and escaped.

When we moved to Arawa I spent much of my time driving around the town searching for BJ. He would disappear for hours at a time. I was extremely anxious for his safety, to say the least.

During my search I discovered the local people knew BJ, just about everyone in the town knew BJ. Whenever I took him shopping someone would call out "Hey BJ!" or "Wan tok," to him. BJ would smile and casually wave back saying something to them in a language I did not know. Astonished I asked him, "What did you say to those boys?"

"Just asked them how they were going," he shrugged.

"What was the language?"

"Place talk."

"What?"

"Their village talk, Ma."

"Where did you learn that?"

"From my friends."

"Who are they?"

"Sitting over there, I see them when I go walkabout…"

BJ was a never-ending source of amazement. Hardly a day passed without him getting into some sort of mischief. I felt sure he did a whole lot more than I knew about. He was the proverbial Dennis the Menace and Huckleberry Finn rolled into one. His resemblance to these characters was uncanny. He was short and tanned, had a million freckles and sun-bleached hair, and rode everywhere on a little red tractor we had given him for Christmas.

He was notorious for his meandering. A woman had the audacity to accuse me of neglecting him. Anger boiled deep in me and I came close to slapping her but instead, I challenged the woman by saying, "If you think you can do a better job of raising my son, you're welcome to try."

Within my home environment I had to tolerate certain situations until I could change them. Outside that arena, I did not and would not tolerate anything that I found unjust, especially about my children. I was not about to be accused of neglecting any of my children. I could have told the woman that she should be more concerned about what her husband was up to rather than what BJ was doing, because he was having an affair with one of her friends. But I did not say a word, knowing that she would eventually find out by the gossip grapevine.

25

Now that Les was at the Mine and working three shifts, the children saw less and less of him. His mood swings and grumpiness became a bone of contention with me. My friends' husbands worked three shifts too, yet when they came home from work they always found time for their children. I made a point of telling him that, "So why the hell can't you?"

"Most of them bastards wouldn't work in an iron lung," he barked, as he usually did whenever I mentioned the subject. "That's why they can play with their kids. They're not stuffed like I am. I work all night. I don't go off and have little sleeps like most of them bludging bastards do."

"Oh," I said sarcastically, "and you run the mine all by yourself, do you?"

Disgusted with Les' usual reply, I walked away. He was too wrapped up in his own importance to give anyone the time of day unless they were on an executive level.

In the darkness of our bedroom, when Les thought I was asleep, he so often had whispered to me how much he loved me. I stiffened with loathing every time he uttered those meaningless words. I witnessed no acts of love from him. 'If you love me as much as you declare, why then don't you give the children the attention they need.' I thought, clenching my fists. 'My only demand on you was to be a good father. You have no clue about the concept of love. Your obsession with me is contemptible. What you feel isn't love, just a desire to own and to possess me. You only think of me and my babies as possessions.'

Because of his apathy towards the children, I told Les I was going to leave him. He just scoffed at my threat, knowing that I did not have the money. So I thought the next best thing would be to move into the spare bedroom. He soon got the message when days turned into weeks and weeks into months. Content with the arrangement, I viewed myself as just the housekeeper, separated from my husband. I even negotiated wages to seal the deal.

Separate rooms allowed me the freedom to sleep in peace at night without him groping to possess me at will. My new single status gave me a taste of what was possible in the future. Although I did not make my situation public, I did attend dances and parties without Les and people started talking.

Les began to protest, accusing me of having another boyfriend. "Go find a woman if you want sex, but leave me alone," I told him, and again reminded him of the teenage hillbilly and my mother. That would usually have him scurrying from the room while denying both allegations.

The idea of me giving myself to someone else while he fought for my favours irked Les. As I saw it, the sweetest revenge was to have an affair. There was something about the notorious womaniser and larrikin, Jack Ryan that I found appealing. I had seen him with his wife at company functions and parties we went to. At one of the parties Jack asked me to dance. He held me close as we moved in rhythm to the music. He did not say a word until the music had finished.

"Thank you, Mrs Carter, that was a pleasure," he said, then bowed and walked away.

I smiled, thinking, 'Now what was that all about?' He did exactly the same thing many times afterwards.

After that, Jack Ryan seemed to be everywhere I was. At times, I thought I caught him watching me. Even though I had heard all sorts of wild stories about his drinking and antics with other women that kept the gossip grapevine running hot, I acknowledged him with a quick wave when I saw him.

The thought of getting involved with Jack had crossed my mind. Then I scolded myself, 'Oh no you don't. This one could be trouble.

You could really fall for him. I'll just wait for the right man to come along, someone only to play with for a while.'

He was tall and dark and extremely attractive. His lean muscular body glowed with good health and vitality. I watched him with great interest as he strolled along the beach, my eyes following his every movement. I liked what I saw. His long dark wavy hair, blowing wildly in the wind, looked very attractive bouncing around his tan shoulders. He was gorgeous from head to toe and the sexiest man I had seen in ages, apart from Jack Ryan. I wanted to meet him.

The chance came a few weeks later at a dance. There was an instant attraction between us when a mutual friend introduced us. Before the end of the evening, Cody Burns asked me to meet him at the beach the following day. I raised my eyebrows, surprised to learn he knew I spent a lot of time there with my children.

"I've seen you with your kids at Loloho many times, but never with your old man. I take it you have a husband," he playfully mocked.

"Oh yes, I have one, if you can call him that," I mocked. "I take my babies to Loloho because he's always complaining about the noise they make. They're just being kids. It's easier to take them to the beach than to fight with him."

Loloho Beach became our meeting place, where we got to know each other better. Cody worked for one of the companies that subcontracted to the copper mine and had six months left before his contract finished. As we talked, I wondered why I had not noticed him before this. We knew the same people and had even been to the same parties. I reasoned that I did not notice him because I was not looking at the time.

I ran my home like clockwork, which gave me the time that I needed for myself without interfering with my family.

Visits to the beach were my daily ritual, Cody joining me on the days when he was not working. A month after our first meeting, I invited him home when Les worked the night shift.

That evening, the house was in darkness except for a street light shining through the lounge-room window. A gentle tapping at the door told me Cody had arrived. Nervous excitement filled the room as we stood in silence at the front door looking at each other. He took my hands in his and gently brushed his lips across my palms, sending a delightful sensation through my body. With one quick swoop he gathered me up into his arms and carried me across the room and gently put me down on the couch...

Cody's lean, firm body lay against me, stirring a desire to surrender to him. The pleasure became paramount as I basked in the sweetness of my revenge. My ecstasy became my husband's agony.

We enjoyed five wonderful months together, meeting at different places, until I became disenchanted and bored with Cody and my empty life. The relationship ended when I realised that in trying to punish Les, I was destroying myself in the process.

Dealing with my turmoil was a challenge. I felt alone. The women I spent time with were the only people I knew, but were not really close friends. I did not completely trust any of them. My real feelings were hidden. I hated my life. I hated Les to the pit of my soul, and yearned to be rid of him, but wondered how. Searching for ways to leave peacefully with my children proved fruitless.

Depression plagued me, shifting my mood from happy and carefree to angry and withdrawn in a matter of minutes. The nightmare of Cain's accident returned to haunt me again and again, every time I closed my eyes at night. In the nightmare Cain did not recover.

I would wake up startled, drenched in perspiration and in tears. The nightmare was so horribly real. The sound of my heart pounding in my ears frightened me. In silent hysteria I looked around the room, slowly emerging from the nightmare of an incident that happened eons ago. I bolted out of bed mumbling to myself, "I have to check on Cain to see if he is okay," even though I knew he was.

Rubbing sleep from my eyes and pulling my long hair aside, out of my eyes, I made my way to the bedroom where my three sons were. I watched them sleeping soundly, the room still except for their soft breathing. Looking at each of them I smiled - all brothers and not one alike. Leaning forward, I gently planted a kiss on each of their forehead, relieved to know they were safe.

I left the boys' room and crept into Celeste's bedroom. She was sleeping soundly too. How sweet and pretty she looked lying there, her long blonde hair falling across her face, covering it. She stirred when I gently brushed a golden strand away to kiss her cheek.

Lying in my bed, I knew that if anything ever happened to any of my children it would destroy me. I never considered being a mother or doing housework a chore. It was a role I enjoyed. Although I failed miserably as a wife, I was a competent mother and homemaker, ensuring our home was spotless and orderly. Over the years I had perfected my culinary and dressmaking skills. My children inspired me, as I envisaged them healthy and well dressed, idealising that all would be well despite their father's lack of interest in them.

The term 'just a housewife' irritated me immensely every time I heard someone say it. It sounded so demeaning. I did not view myself as 'just a housewife'. I considered looking after my family was a huge undertaking. Housewives should be ranked highly, especially with the responsibility that came with the job of managing a home and family. 'Managing Director of Home Affairs' was a title I wrote on forms, when an occupation was required. Many people, women included, thought the reference was laughable. But I stood my ground and refused to write housewife in the blank space.

While on our way to Sydney, a customs officer at Cairns Airport made an adverse comment about my occupation. He scribbled over what I had written and wrote housewife above it. He had infuriated me and I politely told him what my job entailed. He was not impressed when I went on and on, particularly as a queue was forming behind me. He quickly amended the form.

My views about certain issues were strong and I adamantly defended them, regardless of being laughed at or being called a stirrer. "They are my views and I have a right to have them," I have stated several times during my lifetime. "Raising a family is just as important as running the bloody country! Now, let's just say that we took each skill individually into account and were paid accordingly – private nursing, child-minding, chef, housekeeper, fashion designer, hairdresser and psychologist and so on. We would earn more than the Prime Minister of Australia."

As Managing Director of Home Affairs, I considered my family a business and my children products of that business. My job was to teach my children society's rules in the hope of them becoming good citizens. More importantly, as they were of a certain age, I had to review my own principles before I could conduct lessons on virtues.

Regardless of my adverse feelings towards Les, I felt the time had come for our situation to change. Endeavouring to acquire stability within the walls of our home. I surrendered my desire to flee from him, resigning myself to working towards buying a family home for the time that we would return to Australia. Les rebuffed my suggestion to buy a home. It had set him off on a tangent of accusations, from me using the children as a means of getting a home for myself, to having some devious plan to ruin him. In my defence, I candidly remarked, "Well then, what's the point of us being together? If you won't provide us with a home, then I'll have to." He did not respond.

The debate about the house became an issue of contention for months after, until I had had enough. In frustration I announced to Les that I was going to Australia to buy a house. His initial reaction was to laugh at me. "And how do you think you're going to do that?" he snickered sarcastically.

"I'll sell my car and use that money as a deposit," was my knee-jerk response.

"Huh, you'll never do it," he said confidently as he hurried from the house to go to work.

"Oh yes, I will. Watch me!" I called out to him as he scurried to get into the company ute and drive off.

A fierce determination spurred my plans into motion. The first thing I did was to sell my car. That surprised Les, even though he wore a poker face. I felt fortunate to have sold the vehicle for the same price for which I had bought it the year before. The sale was a blessing. Without that money, my chance of getting a deposit together quickly was very slim.

had to decide where to go, realising Sydney was out of the question because the Carters and my family lived there. I chose Mackay, Queensland. Helen and her family had moved there after they left Bougainville. The idea of taking the children to a city where I knew no one was a concern, and so Mackay it was.

In January 1975 Helen, Kate and Molly met my four children and me at Mackay Airport. After checking into a motel, Helen drove us to her place. She was surprised when I said that I was planning to buy a house in Mackay.

"Gee Emma," she said awkwardly, "I never thought you'd ever leave Bougainville..."

"Gotta get a home for my babies," I remarked, "since Les won't do it..."

Helen's reaction was puzzling, so was her hesitation to talk about our times on the island. I thought we were good enough friends, in spite of her uppity manner regarding my children.

After spending a pleasant evening together, Helen drove us back to the motel. The children were exhausted, quickly settling down and were soon sleeping soundly, leaving me alone with my thoughts. I noted in my diary over a cup of tea how circumstances and people change and that I should keep my distance from Helen. A few days later she came knocking on my door. She had come to apologise for her behaviour, explaining that her life was different to the one she lived on Bougainville and she wanted to keep it that way.

Helen's secrets were safe with me, but little did she know, a so-called friend of hers from Lae came to Bougainville after she had left. The friend told me about Helen and Billy's involvement in 'wife swapping' parties that went on in Lae. My mouth fell open in shock reaction. "Oh, yes," the friend stated, smirking, "our little Helen was a real devil." And the friend's husband confirmed the story. They both were also involved in the parties.

"Well," I laughed, "that just goes to show that you really can't judge a book by its cover." None of them were what you would call overly attractive people.

I hardly saw Helen but her husband did visit, making it very clear that if I needed 'anything' to call him.

I understood Helen's reasons for staying away and wanting her past kept secret from her family. None of that was important to me as I had more significant issues to attend to. The loan application I had submitted to the bank I had used for the past fifteen years was rejected. I was not one to be discouraged and went to a building society, after I found a house that I could afford. Once the loan was approved, I closed my account at the bank and joined the building society.

The high set three-bedroom house with a double garage on a huge block was nothing spectacular, except that it was brand new. At least it was a start, I told myself with modest pride. After I made persuasive promises, Les co-signed the application and the loan was approved.

The transaction went smoothly and so the children and I left the comfort of the motel to live in a new but empty house for a week or so, prior to the arrival of our furniture. The meagre budget I had, could no longer sustain the luxury of living in a motel, but did allow me to hire a television and a car for a few weeks.

The children took their circumstances in stride, without complaint - it all seemed a game to them. We sat on a blanket on the floor to eat meals and watch television. We even slept camp-style on the floor. It is extraordinary what children class as being fun.

I wrote to Les almost every day with stories of cute antics the children said and did, determined he would not lose touch with them. In turn I read his letters out loud when he replied, weekly at first, then fortnightly, gradually becoming monthly.

As the weeks turned into months a remarkable change took place in Celeste and Brad. Celeste seemed unhappy at school. At times she even refused to go, which was so unlike her when previously she had enjoyed school and excelled to a high level. Her grades were rapidly falling.

Brad's best friend's mother had several uncles and he asked if he could have an uncle too. When I told him no, Brad said, "Sam stayed with us when Dad went away. Why can't we have an uncle like Danny?"

None of the children actually said they missed their father or had asked after him. Nonetheless, there were tell-tale signs that all was not well with Celeste and Brad.

BJ settled in to his new environment without any hassles. During the day he wandered off to explore the countryside making new friends. He and Cain seemed happy enough but Brad and Celeste caused me a great deal of concern. I could see Brad getting into trouble, forming friendships with boys his age who were unsupervised. He expected the freedom his friends had.

My letters to Les were only of good news as I felt he did not care enough to want to know what was really happening. A distinct change in his letters angered me. The pages were filled with news about his new lifestyle. Tears of anger and frustration welled up. "He now has plenty of time to go fishing or to someone's place for dinner since we've left, but none for the kids while we were there," I ranted after reading it. My reply was full of sarcasm, "...we should have left sooner," I wrote, "it would seem we have been stifling you all these years..." I did not tell him friends had written expressing their surprise at seeing him out and about so much since my departure.

Les was due for annual leave and I was dreading the thought of him coming to Mackay, deeply troubled about seeing him. I had a dream in which Les was laughing, really laughing. He was extremely confident. His hair was shoulder length. 'Strange,' I thought, 'he's never worn it that length before.' I had no idea what the dream meant until the night I picked him up from the airport. I caught my breath when I saw him. He looked exactly as he had in the dream. I was guarded.

Curiosity got the better of me and I had to ask, "Why is your hair so long?"

"You're not there to cut it," he said.

"Okay," I nodded, "I'll do that first thing tomorrow."

From the moment I drove up to the house Les moaned, unimpressed and full of criticism. "It looks ordinary."

I bit my tongue so I would not yell something spiteful at him. "Of course it does," I said quietly in my defence. "What did you expect with such little money? At least we have a home, even if it is modest. It's better than nothing and it's more than you were willing to provide."

Les' arrogance offended my sense of accomplishment. In a few short seconds he had done his best to devalue my every effort, but I recalled the dream and refused to allow him to destroy my self-esteem. In spite of his arrogance and complaints I remained enthusiastic.

"With a little work, we can give this place some personality and have it looking great in no time at all."

By Les' expression, I gathered that he was not thrilled with that statement. His idea of fun was sitting around the house watching television, but he did begrudgingly agree to a few home improvements. Car tracks were definitely needed, a first priority, after that I wanted a couple of walls wallpapered.

Les' annual leave coincided with the children's September school holidays. They were so excited with the idea of helping him pour concrete for the car tracks, but he was not. Their enthusiasm drove him to distraction. It both amused and annoyed me to watch him lose patience. 'Wouldn't it be lovely if his hob-nob friends could see him now,' I thought, watching the episode from the veranda, 'and wouldn't they get a surprise to hear the abusive language he spat at the children?' Disgusted with the scene, I turned away and went inside to make lunch. Tears welled up as I thought about the way he treated my babies. I could not watch any longer and there was no point saying anything to him either, it would only make things worse. 'At least,' I thought, 'he hasn't hit them. I can't wait for the bastard to leave, I hate him.'

Wallpapering the lounge room wall was a memorable experience. Les was not interested in doing it at all but begrudgingly gave in. I doubled up with laughter when the paper would not stick to the wall and fell down on top of him. He looked hilarious wrestling with it. My laughter infuriated him and he threw the paper in a heap. When he had finally finished, red-faced and fuming, he swore and vowed never to paper another wall as long as he lived.

Despite his unwillingness, Les had done a competent job and eventually, much later, saw the funny side of things. I learnt a valuable lesson that day - never to ask Les to do anything around the house again, the trouble just was not worth it. I was relieved and pleased to see him leave and return to Bougainville.

Les' nine-week stay had been a nightmare for me as well as the children and it seemed that he did not enjoy his time with us either. The house did not interest him and he complained bitterly that he was on holidays whenever I mentioned additional improvements. I cannot explain why but his attitude surprised me.

Moments after Les' flight left the ground, I felt hurt and angry for the way he responded to everything I had done. 'Good riddance you bastard, I hope the plane crashes,' I thought, without any consideration for the other passengers. 'That bastard is an emotional vampire. I've supported and encouraged him throughout his career, regardless of our relationship. He called me every time he needed advice before making any major decision.' "You stinking creep, not one word of encouragement from you for me. Your behaviour justifies my hating you," I mumbled under my breath.

For a short time I wallowed in self-pity, letting it shroud me like a comforting blanket, recalling certain events I survived alone when I could have done with some support and encouragement. I knew there was none and never likely to be either.

The difficult times with Les were insignificant compared to the breast cancer scare. Although Les had sent me money each month, it was not enough. After the bills were paid there was very little left to buy groceries. When I asked him to send some more, he refused and said he was already giving me too much. Consequently I was forced to find a job cleaning houses.

The idea of cleaning someone else's home did not bother me as I enjoyed cleaning my own home. I heard someone say that we view the world by what we know. Well, I certainly got a rude shock with my first job.

My first client called and said, "...and I'll leave the key under the mat for you. Just do a general clean. Oh, and can you came back in the afternoon, I'll pay you then?"

I pulled up outside a large Queenslander in desperate need of paint. The yard was a mess. 'Heck,' I thought opening the squeaky rusted gate, 'what a dump. I hope it's better inside.' But it was not. Dirty dishes piled up in the sink, bits of food on the floor, breakfast cereal splattered on the walls and the kitchen table turned my insides upside down. The children's bedrooms were littered with dirty clothes and reeked of urine. Pornographic magazines were strewn around the main bedroom among dirty washing. The whole house was a pigsty.

I only stayed to transform the hovel into a liveable state because I needed the money. What amazed me most, the woman made no apology for the condition of the house when I arrived to collect my pay.

"I've never seen the place look so nice," was all she said. Two days later I returned to find the place in a worse mess. "Oh no," I sighed, "once is enough," closing the door behind me on my way out.

A few days later I was dressing to meet another client when I felt a small lump in my breast. For weeks I thought long and hard about consulting a doctor. The fear of having my breasts removed, leaving me with horrible scar tissue, stopped me. The possibility of leaving Les after my children were independent seemed unlikely and living with him in that condition an even worse fate. Accepting death seemed a perfectly natural thing for me to do. I was not about to give Les the satisfaction of holding the disfigurement over me for the rest of my life. I would rather die than let that happen.

Once I had made up my mind that if I was going to die it would be on my terms, I said, "I'll go in one piece!" resigning myself to it, and made an appointment to see a doctor at Mackay Base Hospital to confirm the worst.

The doctor noted the existence of the lump, but after I told him I had had Depo-Provera injections, a form of contraception that stops menstruation altogether, he was reluctant to rush into doing anything other than to observe the lump for a few months. During those three months, I lived with the uncertainty of my future. There was no one that I trusted enough to discuss my fears with. I felt totally alone and utterly frightened. I was actually preparing myself for death when a dream altered everything.

Nothing out of the ordinary happened that evening. I went to bed at my usual time, around ten o'clock, and fell asleep. Later I woke up and saw myself walking along a pathway beside a man dressed in a long brown robe. His hand was resting gently on my shoulder as we walked. When he spoke, I turned to look at him but could not see his face; the hood of his robe hid it from view. I could sense him smiling and hear the tenderness in his familiar voice. It was the same voice that had instructed me to return home when I was a teenager, and it was now reassuring me that I was not going to die. The voice was soothing and lulled me back into a peaceful slumber.

The weeks leading up to my next visit to the hospital were certainly less stressful. It was a foregone conclusion that I was not seriously ill and the doctor agreed and advised me against having any more Depo-Provera injections.

Shortly after recovering from that dilemma, I suddenly became seriously ill. One day I was perfectly fine and then the next I caught a cold that turned serious for no apparent reason. Anne Deacon insisted on taking me to the hospital, refusing to take no for an answer when I told her I would be fine.

I had met Anne when we first moved in to the district. From the day BJ had strolled into her yard, her daughter Bonny and BJ were inseparable. Consequently, Anne and I became friends too.

"All I need is rest," I said trying to convince her I was not ill.

"You look like you need more than that," Anne replied.

As we debated, my condition worsened. I finally agreed to go to the hospital. Anne took my children home with her that night after I was admitted into hospital. I had a severe dose of malaria and pneumonia. During the night my condition took a turn for the worse. Nurses came in at regular intervals and pounded my back to remove fluid from my congested lungs. Chills from the malaria and the constant pounding on my back left my body sore and sensitive to touch. In a weakened state, I felt the presence of death.

The following evening, after visiting hours, I drifted off to sleep only to be woken at a very late hour by 'whispering', telling me to go home. Weak and dazed, I slowly climbed out of bed and dressed, gathered my belongings together, walked out of the ward and into the bitterly cold night, undetected.

It was a struggle to walk with my small bundle of belongings weighting heavily in my arms. I thought I must have been hallucinating to leave the hospital and was about to turn around and go back when a taxi drove by. I waved to the driver to stop.

I climbed in the back and gave the driver the address: I also told him I did not have any money on me. "You look real sick sweetheart," he said concerned, "let's just get you home," and drove off in the direction of Anne's place when we arrived, the driver made a dash to get out and open the door for me.

"Please wait." I said, struggling to speak. "I'll get the money." The man climbed back in the cab and drove away, I never saw him again.

"What are you doing here? You should be in hospital!" Anne shouted, astonished when she opened the door and found me shivering on her doorstep. "Have you lost your mind, girl?"

I was too weak to explain why I had left the hospital, I really did not know why I did – I just knew I had to leave. Anne made up a folding bed for me in the lounge room and insisted I get into bed. Oddly enough, by morning I was much better and completely recovered within a couple of days. Normally it would have taken me several weeks just to get over an attack of malaria.

During moments of solitude I questioned what my purpose in life was. I began searching for answers in books about the supernatural. I had often sensed a presence too strong for me to ignore, it unnerved me not knowing who or what it was. Although I really wanted to learn more about the supernatural, I was actually afraid of what I would encounter if I delved too deeply. I gave up the search for the time being, promising myself that I would investigate it further, when I was ready.

Towards the end of the year, a letter arrived from Les with a request that sounded more like orders for the children and me to return to Bougainville. Regardless of how it sounded, I was actually relieved to receive it. I felt that whoever was looking after me was bringing us back to the island. Many nights I had lain awake worrying, wondering what to do about Brad and Celeste. The change in them was beginning to frighten me. I felt the island was the best place possible for them to be, and that returning to Bougainville was the most logical and sensible thing for me to do. Remarkably, everything just simply fell into place when time came for us to leave.

26

Bougainville was beautiful. Its magic still affected me in the same way as the first time I had come to the island. The children and I arrived in the middle of the festive season, just a couple of weeks before Christmas. The following day we went to the company Christmas party at Loloho Beach.

I felt ill at ease, not sure if I was imagining people watching me. Les seemed unnaturally cocky around his work colleagues. His behaviour seemed oddly out of character. I sat back puzzled and quietly observed the interaction between him and his co-workers.

While engrossed in the scene, a friend sat down beside me and inclining her head toward Les, whispered, "He is telling everyone you begged him to take you back."

I swung around to faced her. "And you believe that?" I asked horrified.

"Of course not!" she assured me. "I know you too well, Emma. Never mind," she smiled, "you still have a lot of friends here."

That statement did nothing to boost my confidence, especially with the uncertainty of what Les was trying to prove. One thing was certain; his manner towards management fiercely contradicts his mind-set regarding management.

"I know those bastards don't like me," Les had repeatedly told me during our times of truce, "But they have to be nice to me… because they need me to fix their trucks for them. If they're not nice, I'll stuff things up for good…"

By the end of the day I understood what was going on. The show was for my benefit. Les was telling me that he was a man of influence with important friends, and I quickly realised that I could possibly use this to my advantage at some stage.

To his credit, Les' position with the company had advanced in a short space of time, going from leading hand to workshop foreman and then to contracts coordinator. With the latter position he gained a certain amount of power, negotiating contracts between other companies outside the mine. He seemed to be telling me that he expected me to consider him important also. I found his ambition and self-importance amusing at first and humoured him by indulging his whims. His favourite food was served with a smile as I generally fussed over him. It was all a game.

A startling revelation came to light at a dinner party we attended. I learned that Les used the letters I wrote to him about the children to impress his friends. I almost choked on my food when the hostess cooed, "Les missed you and the children very much. The poor man, all he did was talk about you. And he ADORES the children," she said. I did not say a word to the contrary. On the surface, I remained calm and charming and went along with the farce, while seething underneath.

The new self-importance did little to improve Les' position as a father. He complained that Brad's low grades and poor behaviour were an embarrassment and annoyance to him. I suggested he spend some time with Brad but he refused.

Brad was becoming increasingly difficult to handle. Regardless of the punishment he received for his bad behaviour, there was no improvement or remorse. In frustration, and at my wits' end, I had at times used the belt on him. I thought it was the appropriate punishment at the time, but sadly his father whipped him with the jug cord and he used it with a vengeance.

One evening Les became enraged over another of Brad's bad report cards. Without warning, he rushed to the kitchen and picked up the jug cord then ran back to the boys' room where he unmercifully whipped Brad. He yelled and cursed at Brad with each stroke while my son screamed in pain, pleading with his father to stop.

In a desperate bid to stop Les, I threw myself on top of Brad and screamed at him, "Leave him alone! Brad doesn't deserve this. He only got a bad report card for Christ's sake."

"Get out of the way," Les bellowed at me in short breaths, "Or you'll get it too."

"No! You get out. Go on. Get out!"

He tried to drag me out of the way, but I refused to budge and clung to the bed and stayed put until he had left the room.

Cain and BJ huddled together in the corner close to the window, both crying softly, too afraid to move. Celeste stood sombrely in the doorway and jumped aside when Les stormed out of the room.

I whispered to the children, "Shhh," putting my finger to my mouth, "Quick, get into bed. Hurry."

They obeyed in tearful silence. I hugged them one after the other and made sure they were alright before I went to deal with Les. My heart went out to Brad. The savage beating Les gave him was not deserved and was inexcusable.

I walked calmly into the lounge room and stood in front of Les, hands on hips. He was reading a book as though nothing had happened. What I had learnt about his mood swings was that following an uncontrollable outburst he would become totally submissive.

"If I ever see you touch Brad or the other children again I will destroy you and your precious reputation. I will go with you to whatever functions you need me to go to and play your stupid game, but you'll leave the handling of the children to me. I'm moving back into the spare room. If you want me to cook and clean the house, you will pay me wages, because all I'm going to be to you is a housekeeper."

Surprisingly, Les agreed to my conditions. Out of the public eye, I treated him with utter contempt. I hated the man.

The power to hold Les accountable for the beating vanished with Papua New Guinea's independence. An Australian court order did not apply in PNG. I could not evacuate the children and myself again because I did not have enough money. Despite Les' treatment of them, I believed the children were better off staying where they felt secure and happy, in the only place they recognised as their home, Bougainville.

Years later, Celeste confirmed the story BJ told me about the time his father gave him a beating, when he was six years old, because he fell off the back of the truck when Les turned the corner. I felt heart sick and utterly speechless when I heard that, because I had no idea.

The children lived under the threat of more punishment from Les if they as much as hinted to me that he had hit them.

27

All of my children were at school, so I enrolled in a pottery class. Like most things I did, my way of moulding clay into worthwhile pieces was different to the other women in the class.

The first lesson covered the fundamental steps in hand-building clay. First the teacher demonstrated the technique of hand building a mug or bowl. That was enough as far as I was concerned. 'Now let's get into it,' I thought with mounting excitement. We were then instructed to do as the teacher had done.

"But I don't want to make a mug," I complained, yearning to do something else. My idea of coming to the classes was to be stimulated and to make creative art pieces, not mugs. When the teacher insisted that I follow the class and make a mug, my fire instantly fizzled for the day. I clearly lacked the discipline to conform to the ways of the teacher.

My best work was done in my makeshift studio in the storeroom under the house. The chunky, odd-shaped pieces I made were definitely different to the others, even down to the glazing. Ironically everyone used the same glaze. Although my style of pottery varied considerably from the others', my work had enough appeal to receive genuine praise from fellow potters, which I graciously accepted with enormous appreciation, feeling they were more talented.

Our group remained together after the course finished. We pooled our money, bought shares in a kiln and met once a week at designated homes. A local artist who expressed interest in displaying her work invited other artists and potters, including me, to contribute pieces to her exhibition.

On the evening of the exhibition I was astounded to be told that all of my pieces had sold within the first hour, never imagining that anyone would want them. When a friend whispered to me, 'If you took your work seriously Emma, you could make a good living doing this,' I thought he was joking.

That was part of my problem. Although opportunities were open to me, I did not have enough confidence in my ability. After a couple of years I lost interest in pottery and my attention turned to couture, more from necessity than desire.

The time I had spent watching Helen sew her daughters' dresses paid off. Child minding and hairdressing financed my new sewing machine. Curtains quilt covers and matching pillowcases were the first things I made. From there I advanced to dresses, shorts and tops for Celeste, shirts and shorts for the boys and even shirts for Les.

While I slept I dreamt about colours, fabric and designs, stirring in me a new excitement. Some of the garments I made created interest and I was often asked where I had bought my outfit. Learning to sew had opened another door for me.

Since I had been repeatedly asked to sew for someone, I thought I should take sewing lessons. I enrolled in a class at the Arawa Technical College. Jan Walker was the teacher. She taught indigenous students dress-making at the college. I found the lessons frustrating because Jan insisted everyone follow her instructions to the letter. She did more talking than anything else. Irritated by all the chit-chat, I mumbled under my breath, "I could have had this bloody thing cut out and ready for fitting by now."

Three lessons were all I could bear. Jan called me a non-conformist, as if I had some kind of disease, the day I went on ahead of the class. I was not interested in wasting time. I was interested only in learning to sew properly. Although I found the lessons frustrating, going there was a good thing inasmuch as I learned that I could already sew well. Besides that, I met and made friends with Barbara Moss, one of the women in the class.

Barbara intrigued me. There seemed to be something hidden behind her smile. On the surface she appeared humble, but I felt the contrary. Barbara was a little taller than me, very round and moved like a gazelle. She was partial to the local people, endearing herself to them like a pied piper. I found her easy to talk to and unloaded my many frustrations to her.

"You know, Babs," I said, "Success breeds enemies..."

"Hmm, I know what you mean," she said, and looked at as it were the first time. "Tell me about yourself, Emma."

"Gosh," I said, surprised, "where do I start? No one has ever asked me to do that before."

Over time we got to know each other and became each other's confidante, something I later regretted.

Les instantly disliked Barbara. "What are doing you with that nigger lover?" he demanded to know after she left. "I don't want her in my home!"

"Too bad, she's a friend of mine," I said, liking her all the more because Les did not. I suspected he disliked Barbara because she encouraged me to believe in myself more than anyone else had.

The praise I was receiving for my accomplishments frustrated Les, especially when he was introduced to my new friends for the first time. "Oh, it's nice to meet you, Les," they would say. "So you're Emma's husband. She is sooo clever, you must be proud of her!"

A sullen look would cloud his face and he would snap, "She's MY WIFE!"

When we arrived home, he would complain bitterly, "I'm sick of living in your shadow!"

Although I could not prove it, I felt that Les was assassinating my character behind my back. I knew there was nothing I could do about it. People will believe what they want to believe, whether true or not, I reasoned.

An accidental meeting with the wife of a colleague of Les' at the supermarket confirmed my suspicion. Right in the middle of our conversation, the woman interrupted me saying, "You're really nice, Emma. I've been told that you're a real bitch, but I really like you."

I knew her intentions were well meaning, but nevertheless was surprised by the candid remark. The woman did not seem to notice my reaction since I laughed it off so well, a skill I had mastered over the years.

"Gossiping is a common pastime for people who have little else to do with their time," I said when I was told by a friend that people were talking about me giving the teachers a hard time. "Everyone on the island seems to get torn apart at one time or another. Personally, I don't particularly care what anyone around here thinks about me. At least I'm not afraid to say what I feel…"

* * *

The incident that my friend was talking about was the day Cain arrived home with a report card that did not reflect his academic level. I saw the report card as a definite sign of a problem and possibly a clash of personalities between Cain and his teacher.

I entered the classroom just as Ms Wilton was about to leave. I asked if I could have a minute of her time. Ms Wilton nodded and placed her bag back down on her desk,

"What can I do for you, Mrs Carter?"

"This." I held the report card out to her and said, "You can take this back and give Cain the grade he deserves."

Ms Wilton stuttered and stammered, telling me she had given Cain the grades he deserved.

"So," I said with hands on hips, "what's the problem?"

"W-what do you mean?"

"Cain is passionate about school. He does his homework the minute he comes home from school. He's smart and is a straight A student. He has NEVER had any trouble at school until now. There must be a problem between you two. What is it?"

By her uppity attitude, I could clearly see that she did not like Cain.

"Look," I said leaning forward, "I know how boisterous he can be. I don't expect you to like Cain. I only expect you to grade him fairly."

I later learned that one of Cain's former teachers defended me, stating that Cain Carter was one of the brightest students she had ever taught.

A few days later I was back at the school, confronting BJ's teacher after he came home with a hand imprint across his cheek. I hurried into the classroom with BJ in tow.

"Oh," Mrs Jenkins said when she saw me, "I was just leaving."

"What's the meaning of this? " I said, pulling BJ to the front and pointing to the hand print.

'Oh, she really has a bad attitude,' I thought as I listened to her going into great details about how BJ talked all the time and needed to pay attention.

"Not a good enough reason to strike him," I responded with a penetrating stare. "I'm only a phone call away, Mrs Jenkins. If you're having trouble with BJ, all you have to do is phone me. Don't you ever strike my son again, do you understand me?" The teacher nodded.

BJ felt satisfaction, noticing the fear in Mrs Jenkins' eyes as we were about to leave. I immediately chastised him for misbehaving; discouraging him from thinking he could get away with anything. "You watch yourself too," I warned, "I don't like having to deal with this kind of rubbish..."

True to the vow I had made a lifetime ago, I refused to allow any of my children to experience unjust punishment from anybody. However, I was not the kind of mother who wore rose-coloured glasses where my children were concerned. I knew they were no angels.

28

Despite all the good things I had, namely a nice home, wonderful children, a husband with a secure job and interests that gave me an income, joy eluded me. My physical needs could be satisfied one way or another, but never my emotional ones. The image of Luc was ever present in my mind and in Cain. At times, I actually imagined Luc walking through the door instead of Les. I even greeted him warmly, only to pull away the instant I realised it was not Luc my arms held. The times I did that Les gave me an odd look, accusing me of being unbalanced, saying, "You need to be committed to the loony bin."

A deep sadness in me caused uncontrollable mood swings. One moment I was happy and carefree, the next moment melancholic and suicidal. During a particularly low period of my life a woman came to my home, wanting maternity dresses made. I found my visitor uplifting and instantly liked her. Observing the woman, I noticed her smile was actually genuine and asked what made her so happy. The woman surprised me by saying, "I have the joy of the Lord in my heart!"

I almost laughed but stopped myself out of respect for her sincerity. In the solitude of my home, the woman's words echoed in my mind long after she had left. Her joy motivated me to want to be happy. I could feel that the hatred I felt for Les was destroying me. I wanted to change my life but was reluctant to accept Judy Flank's invitation to the fellowship meetings. Later, I became curious and asked Judy if I could go with her in the event I decided to go to a meeting. If anyone saw my car parked outside the Women's Baptist Fellowship Group, I would definitely have been open to ridicule, something I neither needed nor wanted. The first meeting I attended was at Judy's place, only a short walking distance from my home. So many familiar faces were there that day, faces of women I had seen at the supermarket and when fetching my children from school. They welcomed me warmly but their over-friendly manner left me feeling ill-at-ease. I'm not tactile with strangers and don't like being hugged by them: I could only freely hug my children.

The fellowship opened with a prayer, followed by a number of songs. Judy led the singing and to my surprise she had a lovely voice. I scanned the faces of the group. By their expressions, the women were obviously singing from their hearts. The harmonies created a peaceful ambience within the room, something I had not felt in a very long time. It was that peaceful feeling and my love of music that enticed me to return.

Seeing myself as a candidate for the fellowship group seemed rather remote, and referring to myself as a Christian did not appeal to me. I naively thought of myself as unworthy, harbouring so much hatred in my heart. Nonetheless, I listened each week with quiet reserve as Scriptures were read at the fellowship and at church. The message was blazingly transparent, focusing on forgiveness and love. But I ignored it with an indignant belief that I was justified in not forgiving anyone.

My rigid view remained firm as the cancerous seed of hate riddled my being, dangerously becoming part of my nature. Change seemed impossible. But miraculously, a subtle change did occur, with many of my friends noticing a difference in me. I remained silent and told no one what was making the difference.

The weeks had run into months before I found the courage to support my commitment, parking my car for all to see outside the homes of women known around town as,

'Holy Rollers'. My car was soon spotted, with the expected adverse comments, but after a while the comments changed from hostile to friendly because I chose not to react.

Jack Ryan and some of his misfit friends gave me a difficult time when they saw me at social functions, so much so that I felt hurt, feeling Jack was a better man than that. He was a keen photographer and I was taken by surprise when Kate Ryan, Jack's wife, approached me and asked if I would model for Jack. I laughed, telling her I couldn't, thinking how I would do anything to avoid having my photograph taken. I changed my mind after Kate told me she would be assisting Jack.

For courage, I drank a glass of wine Kate offered when I arrived. After I had relaxed I found myself enjoying the shoot. Jack took his time, directing me to tilt my head one way then another, sending my waist length hair cascading around my shoulders and down my back before each shot, using up several rolls of film.

Sometime later, we were invited to a party at the Ryan's home. When we walked into the crowded entertainment area under the house, I was shocked to see dozens of photographs of me hanging up around the place. I stopped short at the entrance, embarrassed, and tried to act as though the photos were not there. But Jack's voice boomed across the room when he saw me and heads turned.

"Ahha, Mrs C, what do you think? Beautiful eh?" he said, pointing to his work. I did not know how to respond; I wanted to shrivel up and disappear.

"Hmm, good work Jack," I replied and forced myself to look at them properly. Never before had I seen myself in photographs or poses like the ones hanging on the walls. I was surprised they turned out so well and could not help but smile with appreciation.

"Come over here," Jack called to me. "Come, come. Come on I want to show you something." He held open the door to the dark room and waved me inside.

"What are we doing in here, Jack?" I asked.

"Tut, tut, all in good time, my dear," he said, and then set about developing another print of me. As he did I asked, "Why do you tease me so much about being a Christian, Jack? It's embarrassing and hurtful. I really thought you were better than that."

He turned and looked seriously at me. "I would never hurt you. I honestly respect you. It's just in fun that's all," he said, and hung the wet print on the wire above him.

He turned to faced me and then leaned forward and kissed me passionately. I was taken completely by surprise. Before I could protest, he had opened the door and stepped out of the dark room, inviting me to join him. Something had happened between us that day, but I wanted nothing to do with it, not because I did not like him, because I did. Jack was polite but aloof with me thereafter and his teasing ceased.

My worst adversary was Les. He was unrelenting in trying to undermine my belief but the strength I gained from going to church provided me with the ability to ignore his cruel taunts. By doing that I denied him the power to destroy my peace.

I blended into the church scene like the proverbial chameleon, attending the Sunday and weekly meetings. My children enjoyed Sunday school until Les displayed his totalitarian attitude, consistently voicing his displeasure of them 'God bothering', which resulted in Brad's loss of interest. Reluctantly, I allowed him to stay home on Sundays.

My efforts to impress upon Les that the children going to Sunday school was a good thing were pointless. "God bothering is rubbish," he rebuffed me. "I don't want my kids going to any of that churchy shit."

"Well," I said sharply, "they're old enough to make up their own minds about that. If they want to go to Sunday school, they can."

Celeste and Cain were more interested in going than BJ was. He found sitting still for two hours restricting and eventually stayed at home with Brad and his father. Cain enjoyed the stories and the refreshments served after the service, while Celeste enjoyed the activities and interaction with the other children.

One morning after the service Celeste seemed withdrawn and showed no sign of wanting to participate in the conversation between Cain and me. She usually talked about her morning on the way home. Her silence prompted me to glance in the rear vision mirror and ask if she was okay. She said she was but did not sound too convincing.

When we arrived home Celeste went to her room. Concerned, I followed her and asked a second time if she was okay. She burst into tears saying, "You don't love me." My eyes opened wide in astonishment. I took moment to regain my composure. "Where in the world did you get that idea?"

"Mrs Clare told us that parents smack their children because they love them. You hardly ever smack me," she cried. Putting a comforting arm around Celeste I explained, "The only reason you don't get smacked, sweetie, is because you're a good little girl. Only naughty children are smacked."

The following week Celeste acted totally out of character, doing everything she possibly could do to exhaust my patience. The end result was a smack - afterwards her behaviour returned to normal.

My association with the church had a profound effect upon situations I was dealing with at the time. I reviewed my attitudes and feelings rationally, with a view to fashioning my destiny. Exercising patience and tolerance towards Les and people I disliked absorbed a great deal of my emotional strength, but a vision of peace urged me forward.

Members of the church I attended were mostly born-again Christians. They were totally uninhibited in their praise and their worship. Some fell to the floor while others danced in the aisles. Exhibitionism was not my style and it was not long before I began to see that I did not fit in with the group. I did not know where in the world I fitted in - square peg in a round hole would have best described me.

Relating to Jesus the way they did, was difficult for me. At that time, my belief in God was every bit as strong as theirs. Regardless of what was going on around me in church, I contained a quiet reserve, shocked at the bizarre behaviour of some members. I knew I was being guided and protected by someone, of this I was certain. But as far as it being Jesus, I did not really know.

My reserve was noticed and I was encouraged to seek guidance through prayer and Bible study. I agreed to discuss what I was feeling with the minister. He was aghast to learn that I had a curiosity for the supernatural.

"The occult is evil!" he warned with aggression. "I will pray for your spirit to be released."

That statement had me thinking about a frightening experience I had had with a ouija board some time prior to joining the fellowship. Consulting the ouija board was something my friend Mandy and I did from time to time. One particular day Mandy wanted to know who was going to win the Melbourne Cup, so out came the board.

After Mandy was given answers to the question she had asked, I felt a threatening presence near me and wanted to run from the room.

"I have to leave, Mandy, there's something here and it's menacing me."

"No! Not yet, we have to close first," urged my friend.

"I can't stay any longer," I called out, running from the house.

My heart was racing at great speed. I could hardly breathe while running to my car. Never before had I experienced such fear or felt icy cold when my body was warm to touch.

"What is happening to me?" I was anxious and wondered when and if the horrible sensation would leave me. Fear of what I might see prevented me from looking into the rear vision mirror. My mind was like a vortex as I drove to the school grounds.

"Stay calm! Stay calm!" I told myself as I drove into the school car park. I glanced at the clock on the dashboard. The children will be coming out soon, I thought as I tried to comprehend what was happening to me. Unsure of what to do, I repeatedly murmured a prayer. Although the strange sensation persisted, it did not feel quite as threatening while I prayed.

Looking out of my window, I saw one of the mothers I often chatted to while waiting for the children, sitting in her car. I hurried over to her and asked her if I looked different in any way.

"No, love," she said give me a questioning look as she casually drew back on her cigarette. She blew the smoke into the air, "You look fine. Why what's wrong?"

Feeling awkward and silly I replied, "Oh, it's nothing really, just having a bad day. Got to go. See you later." I hurried back to my car when I saw the children heading my way.

I was nervous and agitated for days after the ouija board experience and dreaded being alone in the house. The following week I rang Mandy to tell her the thing that followed me home was still with me.

"I warned you," she scolded, "we must always close the circle before leaving. All you can do is keep praying."

Exhaustion led me to rest every chance I could. One afternoon I had fallen asleep but the sound of footsteps startled me. "Who's there?" I called out and listened for a response. Silence. 'Hang on,' I thought, 'no one can get in here, I've locked the door.' Realising the house was secured I relaxed and closed my eyes again.

Suddenly a heavy weight descended upon me. I felt as if I were suffocating. I was pinned down on the bed and could not move or make a sound. Panic seized me. I could not even open my eyes or call for help. Praying in my mind was all I could do. Tears of sheer terror slid silently down the side of my face. This was not a bad dream, it was real. "Please God, save me," I said over and over again in my mind until the pressure lifted from me.

The incident gave me the fright of my life. It took me years to recover from it. From that day to this I have never touched the ouija board. I allowed the pastor to place his hands upon my head and pray for me.

News of guest speakers coming to Bougainville usually sent ripples of excitement through the congregation. With a profound fascination I studied church members whenever a guest speaker presented his or her message. It intrigued me the way every eye appeared fixed on the speaker, as if every word he uttered was divine. Electric energy filled the room when voices praised the Lord in unison. I smiled at the sight, recalling Les' terminology; 'Holy Rollers and Gong Beaters'. How appropriate it seemed at that moment, I thought, with no disrespect to them.

The way the visitors were treated with such reverence had me bewildered. I viewed them as very ordinary people with very ordinary messages, but quickly learned to keep my counsel to avoid disapproval. The special guests often made little or no impact at all on me. Even before their departure their message was forgotten, with the exception of a man named Paul. I instantly liked him and his gentle manner. I found his honesty refreshing.

Paul spoke about his faults, his failures and his faith in God in a way that was believable. He made no effort to raise the roof from its foundations, or endeavour to attract attention with overstatements or animated rambling about the way the congregation should or should not live their lives. He shared the personal experiences he had had with God. The conviction of his words impressed me enough that I began to listen to what he had to say. Recalling something he said, during a conversation I had with him started me thinking.

"I find it very difficult to forgive some people," he confessed, which surprised me enormously. I had imagined him as being gracious to everyone.

I actually thought tolerance and patience were Paul's strongest virtues. I listened attentively when he explained, "Oh, I am very human," he grinned humbly. "I'm helpless without spiritual guidance, I ask the Father every day for help to overcome situations I find difficult in everyday matters. It would be impossible for many of us to like, and get along with everyone, but it's possible with God's help."

I had heard that said before, but coming from Paul it made sense. His words had me thinking about the way I felt about Les. Even with the support of my faith, moving back into 'our' bedroom, my response to him was still an irksome one. Try as I might, finding something to like about my husband proved futile. Praying, I developed a sympathetic tolerance of him but submission to a man whom I loathed was an awful ordeal. I could not do it. I prayed for a miracle to change my feelings towards him. In books I searched for enlightenment. God knows how much I longed for peace in my heart and within my home. It came to me in the most unusual way.

The evening I first heard a voice repeatedly whisper the name Bree, I thought I was dreaming. The whispering had woken me. I shot up in bed and looked around the room, thinking someone else other than Les, who was sleeping soundly beside me, was there. After several nights of the same thing happening I told Les about it, but he said he had not heard anything, even when I woke him the moment it started.

The whispering persisted long enough and often enough for me to believe that I was on the verge of an emotional breakdown. Only I heard it, and only I saw the vision of the little girl with blonde hair and brown eyes. Quite subtly a desire to have another child came, which seemed extraordinary to me. The image of the child was so clear that I said out loud, "I want a baby girl and I will call her Bree."

Not long after, I discovered I was three months pregnant. The pregnancy came as a huge shock but I sensed the baby was a gift to me.

Les was utterly shaken by the news. He collapsed into a chair nearby when I told him. He sat there in silence for a very long time. Then suddenly he began to cry. "I'll never be able to get near you," he sobbed hopelessly. "I'll be sixth in line. You give all your time to the kids as it is. There's never enough time for me now. If you have this baby you won't have any time for me at all. I only wanted you. I only wanted you," he whimpered and pulled me closer to him.

"Look Les," I interrupted him, endeavouring not to lose patience, gently prying my wrist from his tight grasp. "By all accounts I shouldn't be pregnant, but I am."

I knelt down beside him and spoke as tenderly as patience would allow. "Can't you see this baby is special? I believe she's been sent to give us a second chance. I know this baby is a girl. Even her name has been chosen. It is Bree. Remember the whispering?" I asked him gently touching his hand. "The name I kept hearing it in the middle of the night, then in the day as well. It was the baby's name. Remember?"

He slowly turned his wet face towards me and said, "Yes."

I spoke to him for a long time, like a mother reassuring a child that everything would be all right. The whole episode was draining and frustrating.

The news of the pregnancy shocked a lot of people, especially those close to me who were aware of how much I loathed Les.

"Have you taken leave of your senses? Having a baby at your age and feeling the way you do about your Les is crazy!" one friend said.

I was in my early thirties, fit and healthy, and I responded to negative comments with, "This baby is a gift. She will have blonde hair, brown eyes and her name is Bree." Rumours reached me, implying I had gone strange since being involved with the church, but I ignored those too.

Cain was the only one who seemed to welcome the news of a baby. The other three children did not say much when I told them although Brad was embarrassed at the thought of his mother having a big belly. Celeste just smiled and BJ could not have cared less one way or the other.

As the baby began to grow, the children, with the exception of Brad, showed an interest. I involved them as much as possible by encouraging them to touch my tummy and feel the baby moving. After all, she was to be special to the whole family.

29

In the seventh month of my pregnancy we moved from Arawa to Panguna. The town was situated 2,500 feet above sea level in the heart of Kawerong Valley. Bougainville Copper Mine, a project of the Conzinc Riotinto Australia and New Broken Hill Consolidated Limited, was destined to become one of the largest open-pit mines in the world. Forecast annual production was estimated at 150,000 tonnes of copper and 500,000 ounces of gold concentrate.

The sixteen miles of winding road leading up to Panguna, known as the port-mine access, was spectacular. I was told the construction crew endured rugged jungle-covered terrain, earthquake activity, and an annual rainfall of 200 inches, as well as landslides, to excavate 13 million cubic yards of earth at a cost of approximately $14 million.

Our house in Kokorei Street was in a secluded and secure area of Kawerong Valley, on the opposite side of Kupi Road. Break-ins had become a frequent occurrence in Arawa during the last year of our living in the town. Three times locals had broken in to our home. I felt more secure where we were in Panguna.

From our veranda and lounge room, we had a picturesque view of the valley and the bridge that crossed Kawerong River. The bridge was the only entry to and exit from our section.

I was enchanted with the scene and felt secure being surrounded by huge mountain walls covered in lush vegetation, especially the one that loomed up in front of our home on the other side of the river, where a group of company flats stood at the foot of the mountain. I especially enjoyed watching the river snaking its way downward along the valley floor. After heavy rainfall, the flow turned fierce, pounding huge boulders mercilessly causing a deafening roar as it tumbled down the valley.

Paguna's rainfall varied between 180 and 200 inches each year. A heavy downpour came almost without fail at the same time every afternoon. This climate was much more agreeable for my condition. I was grateful that I did not have to suffer Arawa's inferno.

In the distance, the murmuring of Euclid R105 dump trucks and P&H electric shovels working around the clock in the pit pulsated through the air; it took a little while to get used to the consistent heartbeat of the mine. At scheduled times: a whistle blew moments before ore was blasted from the mountainside – the whistle and blast could be heard for miles.

Although Panguna was much cooler than Arawa, Kawerong Valley was often overcast and dismal before the end of the day. Most mornings however, sunlight streamed through low-lying clouds: slender ribbons of light speared the asphalt and then sprang upwards and hit the leaves – the shard of light instantly made the million or so droplets sparkle like crystal. Surrounding foliage came alive to display a kaleidoscope of green. It was magical that well and truly made up for not having indigo skies and sunshine every day.

We quickly settled in. The children went to Panguna Primary School and joined the swimming club, where I met and made more friends.

My pregnancy soon became obvious and, although I had gained very little weight, my belly was huge. 'It's strange,' I thought, appraising my shape in the mirror, 'although I might look odd carrying this large lump around, I actually feel beautiful for the first time in my life.' My skin glowed and my long fair hair held its condition. I felt wonderful and thought I could remain pregnant forever, feeling the way I did.

My cumbersome size forced me to rest more than usual during the day. Just the thought of socialising exhausted me and I found sleeping at night almost impossible. Most evenings, while my family slept, I drank several pots of tea and reflected on the past and present.

While sipping tea, my mind was in turmoil thinking about my feelings for Les. I realised that no amount of prayer would enabled me to feel anything other than tolerance towards him, even though our relationship had reached polite civility since the pregnancy. 'The children are excited about the baby.' I smiled, 'I guess that's all that matters really. But I wish I could feel more for Les though. Lord knows I have tried!'

As I sat in the lounge room, admiring the view of the valley through the window, the Women's Fellowship sprung to mind. Going to the fellowship meetings and church never gave me the absolute peace I felt in these surroundings, here. "This is where the spirit of God is," I told myself. "It surrounds me in this glorious landscape." Church had become too complicated so I stopped going.

I smiled, recalling the words a woman from the fellowship had said, hinting that I shouldn't wear make-up. "We are all beautiful in God's eyes, Emma," she said sweetly. "Make-up is Satan's mask of deception. You don't need that."

I laughed and said, "Beautiful in God's eyes or not, I still need all the help I can get. If you prefer looking like a frump, then that's your choice, but it's not mine."

The next time the woman visited me she brought a friend with her. The subject of the magazines I read came under scrutiny. "They are evil and full of sex and perversion..."

"Damn it!" I said, jumping up from my chair and interrupting her. "The bloody evil isn't in the bloody magazine, it's in your bloody mind. Don't tell me what I can or can't read in my own bloody home. I buy these bloody books because of the fashions. I like fashion!"

Horrified, the women stood up together and scurried from the house, almost falling over each other in the process. I giggled, thinking how frightened they looked. 'I guess they imagined I was going to biff them. Aha!'

The valley looked eerier late at night, with streetlights glowing through heavy cloud cover. The chill in the air made me shiver. I looked around for my cream shawl and found it lying on the lounge. I picked it up and slipped it around my shoulders on my way to the kitchen to make another cup of tea. There was enough light coming in from the street to see, so I did not bother to turn on the kitchen lights.

"1979 is fast coming to an end," I muttered. "Bree will be here soon and Brad will be going to boarding school in the New Year, when I find a school to enrol him in. There's not much time left to do that," I shrugged. "I'm sure everything will fall into place. I know it will be okay," I told myself. And it was.

The neighbours across the street recommended a college at Campbelltown in New South Wales. At their suggestion, I contacted the college. But before enrolling Brad, I thought long and hard about being involved with my family and the Carters again. Brad would be in contact with both families, since the college was only a two-hour drive from Sydney, something I was not happy about. I knew however, that the time had come for him to be reunited with his entire family. For his sake, I put the past behind me and contacted my family to tell them about my pregnancy, and Brad was going to college. My mother's response surprised me. She actually approved of something that I had done for the first time in my life and sounded genuinely happy for me.

"Life is full of surprises," I said, shaking my head after the call.

I enjoyed my solitude at night. I was able to freely speak my thoughts out loud, as a sort of sounding board, and at times found solutions to my problems. Thinking about that made me smile, 'If anyone saw me talking to myself they would probably think I've lost my mind. So what's new?'

Speaking out loud gave clarity to my garbled thoughts. So many things ran through my mind. It never rested, jumping from one subject to another.

The night a major tremor hit the island flashed into my thoughts. It was seven on the Richter scale. The locals called tremors gurias.

The earth really moved that night, I grinned. For as long as I live, I'll never forget the terror of hearing rumbling deep in the earth, or feeling the house shaking and swaying the way it did that night. It really was nerve-racking, trying to stand in a house that literally swayed back and forth, sending valuables crashing to the floor. All of us huddled together in doorways. The boys thought it was fun that the house rocked about the way that it did. Kids! I was terrified they would be hurt and Les hardly said a word. In the morning we found fallen palm trees and coconuts scattered everywhere. What a mess. It was lucky there was no serious damage done and that no one was killed. A strange sense of uncertainty lingered in the air for weeks after, as if everyone anticipated the island opening up and swallowing us every time minor tremors were felt.

The baby moved. I rubbed my stomach and wriggled in the chair, trying to get comfortable. 'Christmas is only days away and Bree is due any day now. Dear God, please make sure she is born before Brad leaves for school.'

"Ouch," I said rubbing my back. "Take it easy in there kiddo, you're splitting me in two. How about keeping still for a few minutes so I can have a rest?"

My chatter seemed to stimulate the baby. I hoped that my time alone would be absorbed in reflection while I sat quietly with her. The baby was not quiet. She kicked and moved about, pressing on my spine and rib cage. "The last days are the longest," I complained to an empty room.

Brad consumed my thoughts while making another attempt to get comfortable. I gave up and went and stood by the window, staring wistfully down the valley.

"He's still not impressed with the idea of a baby in the home. I wish I knew why. If she doesn't come soon, he won't have much time with her before he leaves for school. It is so important for them all to welcome her together," I whispered to my reflection in the window.

My breath made mist on the glass and I drew a heart and wrote EC L LR and smiled.

I received a lot of attention from friends in the last days leading up to Bree's birth. One evening Les and I went to a Christmas party, I was surprised to be guided to a chair reserved for me with a sign overhead that read, "Mother Carter."

I always maintained my baby would be a girl. My belief never altered. But some of my church friends insisted I accept that I may have a son.

"But I don't have to, because I KNOW I'm having a girl," I stated.

It was difficult for some of them to understand the vision I had of my daughter. Some even imagined me to be unbalanced for being so adamant.

A little after midnight on January 10th, I woke Les. "It's time," I told him. "I'm spotting."

The drive down the mountain was glorious. Pakia Gap was usually engulfed in heavy cloud cover concealing magnificent coastline views from passing travellers. Not that time. The night sky was cloudless and full of the brightest and largest stars I had ever seen – even the moon was brighter than usual.

Mount Bagana, the island's active volcano, silhouetted in the moonlight, gloriously displaying her beauty. The majestic rise released white vapours that surrounded the rim of the volcano. The sight was never more beautiful than it was that evening. The mountain road was clear of cloud and fog all the way down to the valley.

'It couldn't be a more perfect night.' I smiled, feeling certain that someone was welcoming my daughter.

When we arrived at the hospital, the attending sister immediately prepped me for delivery. After examining me, she rushed out to telephone the doctor.

"What's wrong?" I called out, feeling a little uneasy.

The sister popped her head around the corner and said, "You can't have the baby yet. You certainly can't have it now. You need a caesarean section. Don't worry. Just relax." I smiled ruefully at her remark to relax but I was calm, because I knew everything would be fine.

Rumours were always flying around the town and one of those rumours reached us a week prior to my going into hospital. According to gossip, a local woman had died at the hospital after having a caesarean section. She was allegedly given the wrong blood.

My doctor arrived and confirmed the sister's diagnosis. Les was lingering in the background, watching what was going on. The doctor turned around when he noticed him there and offered his hand as he introduced himself. As they shook hands Les muttered stony faced, "Anything happens to her, something will happen to you."

Labour began just before the sister gave me a sedative. Foetal distress was the reason for the C-section. The cord was wrapped around Bree's hand...

"Emma! Emma!" the doctor called, stirring me to consciousness. "You have a daughter."

"I know," I slurred, then fell asleep.

Bree Carter arrived at 2.20am on January 10th, 1980. She weighed six pounds ten ounces.

A caesarean section was indeed an experience for which I was totally unprepared. Only a day or two after the delivery of my other four children, I was wearing my favourite pair of jeans and back in the swing of things. After Bree's birth, I woke up in the ward expecting to feel great, but instead, I felt lousy and very sore. The heat did nothing to improve things either. Although I was thrilled to have Bree, my mind was in battle trying to ward off an incredible sadness. I felt secretly fearful that I could be losing my mind. 'What's wrong with me?' I wanted to scream, 'I feel rotten. I've never felt like this after having my other children.'

My family was the first of a long stream of visitors. Although the effects of the anaesthetic had not fully worn off by the time they had arrived, I clearly remembered nine-year-old Cain standing by Bree's crib, looking down at her and smiling. He confidently scooped her up into his arms and announced proudly, "I have a baby sister."

Bree resembled Cain more than her other siblings, her eyes dark brown like his, with brown/blonde hair and olive complexion. Cain adored his little sister and subtly pushed his brothers and Celeste out of the way. All his young life, Cain had to contend with the stark difference between himself and his siblings. They were as fair as he was dark. I reasoned that Cain's resemblance to Bree gave him a sense of an identity.

The doctor later explained that Bree's olive complexion was due to her being jaundiced. She was immediately placed under an ultra-violet light, her condition monitored by daily blood tests. The jaundice was still at a high level when we left the hospital less than twenty-four hours later. My doctor advised me to leave to avoid the high risk of infection that was there.

At home, my melancholic mood persisted. Saying goodbye to Brad from my bed the day after I arrived home from hospital with Bree, and knowing that he was leaving without spending much time with his little sister, intensified my low spirit.

Apart from Annie Black, a nursing sister who came to the house to dress the incision from the C-section, the influx of visitors had overwhelmed me. Although I appreciated their kindness and well wishes, I desperately wanted to be alone. My intolerance at being sore, uncomfortable and immobile aggravated me to the point whereby, I struggled out of bed, holding a pillow to my stomach. The pressure on the wound eased the pain somewhat. I then precariously made my way along the hallway to the front door. When I reached the door, I closed and locked it, shutting out the world for a few hours.

Hobbling back down the hallway to the linen cupboard, I rummaged through it, turning my orderly cupboard upside-down until I found an old sheet. It took such a great effort to rip the sheet into wide strips, and wrap a couple firmly around myself to support the incision that felt as if it was about to burst open at any moment. I then headed for the bathroom, and eased myself down to the floor beside the bathtub and turned on the water. I swore out loud when I realised the shampoo and conditioner were on the shelf above me. Gingerly, I reached up and knocked them from the shelf onto the floor.

"Washing my hair has never been so damn difficult or as bloody painful as this is," I cried out in frustration, almost in tears.

Wrapping my hair in a towel, I carefully made my way to my room for the arduous task of dressing. With great care, I untied and removed the sheet strips, then my nightie and looked at my reflection in the mirror. My stomach was swollen and covered with a bandage. My hair and skin appeared dull and lifeless. The sight sent me into a fit of tears.

I cried a bucket load that day. It was also the day Brad left for boarding school.

'I wanted to say goodbye to him at the airport,' I sobbed, 'not from this bloody bed. What kind of a send-off is that and what kind of a mother am I...?'

For a moment, I actually resented my baby because she was the reason I could not go to the airport. And then I was immediately overcome with guilt, for feeling that way about my cherished child, I cried some more. By the time I had finished sobbing, oddly enough, I felt so much better, as though a burden had been lifted from my shoulders. I washed my face, re-wrapped myself in the sheet strips, dressed, dried my hair and then applied make-up. I looked and felt so much better. Then out came the vacuum cleaner... Thanks to Annie Black's excellent nursing care, I healed without any complications.

One would have thought that having already had four children, I would have been relaxed with the fifth, but that did not happen. During my pregnancy I had the luxury of time to read a multitude of literature about babies – the dangers, health and what to expect and so on. You name it, I read it. The information had not been readily available to me in previous years, and I would not have had the time to read it anyway. Being well informed only increased my concern for my baby's wellbeing, especially about cot death.

It is a custom of Papua New Guinea women to carry their babies in a Bilum bag. For the first few months, I adopted the same concept with Bree when I did housework. Not only did I feel Bree was safe, but the close contact strengthened our bond in a way that I was not able to do with my other children.

In her waking hours, Bree was content to lie in the sling as I moved about the house. I would usually speak to myself when I was alone and now I spoke to Bree. She would look up and fix her large brown eyes upon my face, at the sound of my voice. One set of brown eyes meeting the other. I adored her and the precious child responded to the love and attention I lavished on her.

She gradually changed into the image I saw in my dream - the same large brown eyes and blonde hair. Her name is Bree. I smiled smugly, "We showed them didn't we, Babe?"

The evenings however, were vastly different from daytime. I constantly woke up to check on my baby well into her second year, secretly fearful of losing her. I felt anything or anyone that I loved, was either destroyed or taken from me in some way. I did not want that to happen with Bree. She was most certainly the gift I proclaimed her to be. That child brought so much joy and fulfilment to my life.

Cain was besotted too. He consistently attended to her every whim whenever possible. His reward for such diligent devotion was her admiration and love. More often than not, she sought Cain's or my attention.

The other children initially displayed a mild degree of resentment at their brother's possessiveness but the resentment soon turned to indifference.

30

With the arrival of the Easter holidays, Brad came home from boarding school. I noticed that he seemed a little withdrawn when we met him at the airport. He had gained an enormous amount of weight, which caused me to worry. Obesity was evident in the Carter family. All, with the exception of Brad's grandfather and an uncle, had a serious weight problem. From birth, I had taken great care with the children's diet, endeavouring to eliminate the risk for them.

With one beaming smile from Bree, Brad's sullen mood disappeared. He took her in his arms and gave her a big hug. She responded with giggles, pleasing him. He kissed her cheek, hugged her firmly and buried his face into her chest. "I thought all babies smelled like pissy nappies," he said, astonished. "That's why I didn't want a baby in the house. I didn't think I could handle the stink, but Bree smells real sweet," he said with relief.

"That's it! That's what was bothering you all this time?" Brad nodded casually, his attention on Bree. "So you're okay about having a baby around now?" I asked.

"Yep," was his quick reply.

During the holidays Cain hovered around Bree like a mother hen, rarely going out. Brad gave up trying to get near her and decided to do the rounds to catch up with his mates instead. But they all eventually ended up back at our place, bringing the house to life on a full scale.

Celeste was on the verge of becoming a teenager. She filled her spare time reading. She had formed only one firm friendship. Neither she nor her friend Anna was interested in boys then, like other girls their age. They skipped rope, went skateboarding, swimming and to the movies. They seemed content enough doing that. Oblivious to her beauty, Celeste looked for esteem in academics, where she excelled and won awards.

BJ on the other hand rose early every morning of the school holidays to answer the call of the wild, disappearing all day and getting into all sorts of mischief. Reports of his misdeeds filtered back to us one way or another. He was reported as having been seen trying to start up a company tractor parked on the edge of a steep riverbank and begging for money outside the Panguna Supermarket. Les found BJ's behaviour embarrassing, totally ignoring him as a result, and often cringing at the mention of his name. I tried everything, in vain, to discourage BJ's nomadic ways and was glad to see the end of the holidays.

A welcome peace fell over the house once the children returned to school.

'At least I know where BJ is,' I thought, breathing easy, sipping my morning coffee, and noting a list of jobs to be done. Top priority was to restock the freezer. A couple of days cooking was an overall time saver since I worked long hours sewing the garments I designed. The sewing bug had bit once again and this time I turned my attention to children's designs. Selling them through a boutique in Kieta, as well as from home, had increased my income.

Enterprising and happy to work long hours at my small business, I maintained my home and family without disruption. The workload prevented me from being distracted from what I was doing and usually by the end of the day I was too tired to think about anything else.

As a perfectionist, I placed heavy demands upon myself so that everything at home would run to schedule. My mind and my thoughts were often in turmoil but I struggled through regardless, to at least accomplish the appearance of order on the surface.

Every project I embarked on had to be productive and worthwhile. My small business gave me financial freedom and Bree gave me joy and kept me sane. I loved the other children no less, but felt the tide of life pulling them farther away from me.

Soon they would all be going off to boarding school. I never wanted that for my children but circumstances dictated my family's lifestyle. What I feared most was having them grow up and moving away from me altogether. I wanted them to remain children so they would always need me. 'What will become of my children?' I had often asked myself. 'They're a mixed brew and so vastly different from one another.' Although I wanted all of them around me, I knew I could not control their destiny. I worried about them all the time.

Bree was a bright and content baby. She had short naps during the day and was happy to lie in the bouncer while I cut out fabric or sewed garments.

Music always filtered throughout the house and I often sang and danced to my favourite tune. Bree giggled and squealed with delight every time I picked her up and danced with her. She listened when I chatted to her and interacted with wide-eyed interest, appearing to understand what I said.

The money I earned was invested into my family and decorating our home. I ordered curtain fabric from Melbourne, household items and new clothes for the family as well as toys for Bree from America. Gradually, I transformed the house into a comfortable, unique home.

With gentle persuasion, I was able to convince Les to put two murals on the wall in the lounge room. One was a garden and the other a waterfall, and I entertained close friends in the tranquil setting of our indoor garden.

A mural of Snow White and the Seven Dwarfs, sitting in the woods with animals, dominated Bree's bedroom, which was full of colour. She spent a great deal of time playing in there. She particularly liked sitting on a large beanbag near the mural. When friends came to the house Bree would take them by the hand, inviting them to her room to play. It was not unusual to see adults sitting on the floor in her room surrounded by toys.

A large, white bookstand decorated with every colourful stuffed toy imaginable stood against the wall opposite the mural. More toys were placed around the room. Bree wanted for nothing. I gave her everything I had wanted to give my other children when they were babies, but could not afford.

The boys' bedroom was decked out in the latest Star Wars theme, while Celeste enjoyed the subtlety of Wedgwood blue, beige and dimity-print, patchwork bedspread with matching beige dimity-print curtains. Celeste chose the patchwork prints and colours and cushions for her bed and light shade.

The indulgence aroused disapproval from Les. He had convinced himself that I was spending his money and not my own. Every cent I had earned from hairdressing and my designs benefited the whole family. He complained about my spending to anyone who would listen, telling them, "The mother is spending all my money while I work my arse off..."

When his complaints reached me, I felt compelled to validate them during a holiday in Australia. I bought a china dinner set, silverware, crystal glasses and other items. I also added designer outfits to the list to fulfil my husband's prophecy.

The thought of another holiday with Les was like waking up in the middle of a nightmare, but I forgot all about that when David Collins and his new wife Yoko extended an invitation to us to visit them in Japan.

We met David through mutual friends. He was single and worked as an engineer for the copper mine. The children took an instant liking to him, and from the moment he set foot in our house, they demanded his attention. When Celeste was six she had a huge crush on David and declared that she would marry him when she grew up. As far as Celeste was concerned, David Collins was the most handsome, the most gentle and nicest man in the world. She treasured the fabric cat he gave her on her seventh birthday.

David married Yoko, his pretty Japanese sweetheart, on Bougainville. Later they left Bougainville to live in Japan. The opportunity to visit them came in 1982, when friends offered to move into our home and look after Celeste, Cain and BJ while we were away. The kids were keen for Jenny and Craig Masters to stay with them, so I booked and paid for a cabin with a bathroom and porthole on the Oriana.

* * *

In retrospect, the American holiday we had in 1978 should have been reason enough for me to not even consider going on the cruise, especially not with Les. Nine weeks travelling around the United States with him was abysmal. Brad and Celeste were three and two respectively when I promised them a trip to Disneyland, after watching the show on television week after week. The sole purpose of planning and saving for that trip was to take the children to Disneyland to fulfil the promise. I took in extra sewing; Les held a tight rein on the chequebook and between us we saved enough to travel for nine weeks around the West Coast of America, Mexico and Canada.

Driving along unfamiliar highways to unknown destinations, following unfamiliar road rules, was so horrendous that it cheated us out of a potentially great experience. As we motored along the Arizona highway, I shuffled through my thoughts, looking for a label that best described Les. 'A dream stealer! Yes, that's what he is, a dream stealer. He did everything in his power to spoil the holiday,' I thought, feeling content with that analogy as I sat beside him in the car, periodically sneaking a peek at him. He irritated me for making no effort at all to disguise his annoyance at travelling with the children. The persistent scowl upon his face said it all. Despite Les, I felt optimistic and convinced myself that we would all have a wonderful time. 'Who wouldn't have fun in Disneyland?' I thought as we set out for the park that day. 'Us, that's who,' I screamed in my mind later on, in the middle of having a hell of a day. Fun land! Huh!

Les complained about everything and refused to hold the camera or take photographs, "I don't want to look like a dickhead tourist," he moaned. It was horrible being with him and I was seething most of the time. The children missed out on many of the rides because Les refused to accompany them and I could not overcome my fear of heights.

Long distance road travel, with four children crammed in the back seat of a car, set off another element of discord. Adding to the mounting tension, I had to remain constantly alert in case Les ventured onto the wrong side of the road, as he had done several times, almost costing us our lives.

When the trip ended and we were all safely back on Bougainville, I vowed never to go anywhere with Les again, not even across the street. But time has an amazing way of dimming one's memory.

* * *

Signs that all would not go well on the cruise were apparent from the start of the journey, even before we boarded the ship. In my haste I left my new camera on the back seat of the cab that had taken us to the ship at Rabaul.

On board the Oriana, the cabin to which the porter directed us was not the one I had booked and paid for in advance. Naturally the inconvenience was annoying and very frustrating, particularly when we had specified our requirements and paid extra for the convenience.

Les went past being annoyed. I thought he was on the verge of starting a siege or something worse. His language and rage were obscene. I knew I could not let him handle the situation, so I took charge.

After insisting Les and Bree remain in the cabin, I fumbled my way around foreign corridors, trying to find my way to reception. Les' behaviour irritated me more than the inconvenience of not having a bathroom and I loathed the idea of communal facilities.

'Why does he always have to act like this whenever something goes wrong? And why does he always have to go to the extreme?'

I felt exhausted, my head was pounding and I wanted to retch. I found a vacant chair in a foyer and sat down to settle my stomach. I really wanted to cry but knew this was neither the place nor the time. Instead, I found some pleasure in echoing the same obscene language back to Les, screaming and shouting at him in my mind. Elderly passengers glanced at me as they passed by. I looked up at them and smiled.

Losing my way gave me time to compose myself and to think about how I should deal with the problem of the wrong cabin. As soon as I felt better I braced myself, stood up, and smiled at a passing passenger. I asked for directions to Reception and was guided to a lift.

I waited several minutes at the reception desk before anyone bothered to serve me. Even though the staff blatantly ignored me, I remained patient until a uniformed woman with a large nose and a bad attitude approached me. I told her what my problem was. In an off-handed manner she said that I had not paid for the facilities.

"I suggest you check your records," I said, starting to fume, "since I'm holding the receipt in my hand."

The woman's rude manner prompted me to say, "It's people like us who make it possible for people like YOU to travel the world. Where can I find the purser?"

When I found the purser he assured me the mix up with the cabin would be sorted out as soon as possible. He apologised for the inconvenience and the woman's behaviour.

By the time I returned to the cabin Les had calmed down but was close to tears. Bree was sitting on the bottom bunk playing with a toy. She looked up at me and beamed a welcoming smile when I came in.

Les was disappointed at having to wait a week for another cabin and began to rant again. He wanted a refund and to leave the ship after it had already set sail. In frustration I told him to shut up, "I'm not going anywhere."

At home, my days were full with a busy schedule and there were never enough hours in a day for all that I wanted to do. On board the Oriana the days were long and awfully boring, with intermittent gastronomic breaks that did nothing for anyone's waistline. Tasty delights skilfully displayed on large tables tempted even the strongest will. An abundance of decorated cakes, pastries and fruit that were served at the same hour every day seem to dominate the room. It was easy to tell what time of day it was since events usually ran according to schedule.

Devouring the delectable morsels soothed my yearning to go home and my desire to retreat from Les for a time. To avoid critical eyes he willingly indulged me whenever I asked him to fill my plate for a second or third time. One could possibly say that this was perhaps a rare special moment we shared together. Les playfully teased me about my lack of control with the sweets. I did not mind the teasing as there was no malice in his tone, but eventually lost interest in gorging myself on cakes.

We went in different directions during the day. I periodically strolled down to the playroom where, from the outer room of the nursery, I watched Bree interacting with the other children. She was having a great time. I could not resist the temptation to intrude and entered the playroom, assured that Bree would be overjoyed to see me. Seeing her enjoying herself gave me enormous pleasure. It was bad enough that I was ready to jump ship but if Bree had not been happy it would have been the last straw.

In hindsight, I could not blame my disenchantment about the cruise totally on one aspect because there were many contributing factors. One was the age of the other passengers, something we had overlooked. Ages ranged from sixty and upwards, all retirees. Sometime later, after meeting some of them, I learned it was unusual for our age group to take a long cruise. Thirty five day cruises were usually part of a retirement plan and the younger generation was still working towards that goal.

What amazed both Les and I about so many of the senior passengers was that they were extraordinarily bad-mannered. As a child I was raised to respect my elders, but that lesson demanded reconsideration after witnessing the behaviour of many elderly British women.

At the start of the cruise, passengers were allocated a seat at a table and a meal schedule valid for the duration of the voyage. It was beyond our understanding why a stampede occurred at mealtimes.

The first evening, the three of us leisurely strolled down to the dining room, Bree toddling between us and holding on to our hands. As we came closer to the dining area people began rushing past us, one elderly woman almost knocking Bree over in her haste. Les had to carry Bree to keep her from being hurt.

We entered the foyer outside the dining room and found a sea of blue-rinse and white heads, twisting and turning and noisily gabbling to one another. Collectively, hundreds of years of experience were gathered together, anxiously waiting for the dining room doors to open. Impatience to eat had turned these senior citizens, who only a few hours before were peacefully shuffling and ambling along the ship's decks and corridors, into forces to be reckoned with.

Over the murmur of chatter, a clicking sound of doors being unlocked was heard. Without warning, a surge of bodies slowly moulded into a wave, building up as the sound continued. The doors opened, and in an instant, Les and I were swept along with the swarm, coming to a halt at our designated table.

Amazed and horrified at what we had just witnessed, Les and I stood united on one issue; no more standing aside for our elders. It was everyone for themselves. The behaviour of these people warranted no respect from either of us.

David and Yoko met us at Yokohama when the ship docked. Before we set off for Toyama, we took our friends on a tour of the ship, ending up at one of the ship's lounges for drinks.

The weather was dismal, very cold and wet. I was hoping to see snow for the very first time in my life. David searched the sky in anticipation of my wish.

"Doesn't look like it's going to snow for a while yet," he said.

We travelled several miles, weaving through narrow streets before reaching our destination. When we arrived at David and Yoko's home, we followed Japanese custom and removed our shoes then selected a pair of slippers, provided for us, from the rack just outside their door and slipped them on before entering the house. I had no idea what to expect when I went inside. I was delightfully surprised to find a charming blend of European and Japanese decor. My understanding of Japanese traditions was limited and the most recent book I had read then was 'Shogun', a stark contrast from modern twentieth-century Japan.

I found it fascinating that in a country as foreign to me as Japan, television channels ran breakfast cereal commercials similar to the ones in Australia. Although I could not understand the language I could comprehend the message.

David and Yoko were wonderful hosts. They went to great lengths to make our stay memorable.

"We've made arrangements for you to spend a night in a Japanese inn," David told us.

"Will you and Yoko be joining us?" I asked.

"No, we've been there and done that," he smiled.

Yoko added, "And we've all been invited to dinner and a tea ceremony, Saturday night."

Our room at the inn was almost bare apart from a couple of kake jiku (wall hangings), a vase in the tokonoma (alcove) and two small wooden tables. The table in the middle of the room had cushions around it, where we sat cross-legged and sipped ocha (green tea.) The other table was against the wall below the other wall hanging. A tiny intricately carved urn sat in the middle of the table.

A Tatami (straw mat) covered a section of the floor in the centre of the room. It was customary to remove slippers before stepping on it. Neutral colours and the simplicity of the room enhanced the decor, inspiring a warm ambience. Before we retired for the night, the mistress of the inn, known as the Mamasan, came to our room and prepared it for sleeping. She lowered the central table level with the floor, took bedding from cupboards concealed in the walls, then rolled out futons and pillows and placed them side-by-side on the tatami. It took her no more than a few minutes to make up our huge bed. The sight of all that comfort had me fighting to keep my eyes open. David and Yoko said good night, but just as they were about to slide the door closed behind them, the Mamasan called to them and whispered something to David. He turned to us. "Oh I forgot," he grinned, "in Japan, we wash before getting into the bath. The Mamasan has prepared one for you. She has also brought you yukatas (robes) to sleep in. Change into them before going to the bathroom. Oh yes, and don't pull the plug and empty the tub because everyone in the inn shares the bath."

I looked at David, a little puzzled, but understood what he meant when I got to the bathroom. The ofuro (tub) was very deep and full to the brim with hot water. Beside it were a small wooden stool and hand-held shower. I lathered up Bree and myself and rinsed thoroughly, then climbed into the tub. Bree jumped into my arms, pretending it was a swimming pool. I sat chin deep, gently swirling her back and forth.

"Wow, this is wonderful," I said to Bree, "Got to have one of these, hey babe," I laughed, trying to imagine Les digging a huge hole for it.

"What are you laughing at, Mommy?" Bree asked rubbing her face.

"I was thinking how Daddy could dig a great big hole so we could have a tub like this one."

She put her hand over her mouth and giggled, "Oh no, not Daddy."

Back in the room, Bree crawled into bed and burrowed in deep underneath the quilt and fell fast asleep. Only the top of her head was showing. I slid in beside her and sighed, "What a wonderful end to an extraordinary day."

The morning brought a delightful discovery. Just outside our room, concealed behind rice paper sliding doors (shoji) was a miniature garden. I captured the lovely image on the camera I had bought at the duty-free shop.

There was a knock on our door. It was David and Yoko.

"Well, how was your night?" they asked.

"Fantastic!" I said with an excited ring in my voice, utterly thrilled with everything, and prattled on and on while Les nodded his appreciation.

"Are you ready for a tour of Tokyo?" David grinned when I finally settled down.

That week was absolutely amazing. We shopped, travelled on the train, visited famous temples and Korakuen gardens, and ate all sorts of different foods and sweets. Everywhere we went the streets were spotless; the city was beautiful. To add to my pleasure, we came across a blanket of snow after a light fall during the day, but a shower soon washed it away.

Before we arrived in Japan Yoko had bought herself an English designer suit. She wanted to wear it to the tea ceremony. For something different she offered me a traditional Japanese kimono to wear. It had been in her family for three generations. Yoko had also arranged for her sisters to help dress me.

Layer upon layer of silk undergarments were slid on and around me and neatly tied in place. I was surprised at the length of time and the skill it took to get ready to wear the traditional costume. A lot of giggling and chattering went on during the dressing and Yoko translated to include me in the conversation. For the outer garment, they dressed me in a long sleeved, royal blue kimono – embroidered with a spray of pink flowers and green foliage botu on the hem and left shoulder. They then wrapped a wide, red, orange and gold brocade silk sash, called an obi, around my waist – about 13 inches wide and 13 feet long, fastened at the back and kept in place by several girdles of the brocade silk. On my feet I wore white tabi, Japanese socks with one socket for the big toe, and a pair of Geta, wooden sandals.

I felt like a different person in the kimono and was very conscious that the garment was valuable. That evening was bizarre, with Yoko in an English designer suit and me in a Japanese kimono.

We dined in the home of Shimojo San, a prominent Japanese businessman who performed the tea ceremony in which Yin represents water and Yang fire. Shimojo San used a (fukusa) a fine silk cloth that represented his spirit to purify the chashaku (a slender bamboo tea scoop) before putting three scoops of tea into a tea bowl (chawan). A small amount of water was poured into the chawan then a bell rang several times and Shimojo San handed the chawan to me and motioned that I stir the tea into a paste and hand it back to him. Additional water was added to the paste and whisked into a thick liquid and was then given back to me. It was customary for me to bow before I accepted the chawan, raise it above my head and rotated it three times in my hand before taking a sip – the tea tasted bitter. I wiped the rim and then passed it to Les.

After we had all taken a sip from the bowl, it was returned to Shimojo San and he cleaned the ceremony utensils. When finished, he handed me the chashaku enclosed in a slender silk bag and said something in Japanese. David translated what Shimojo San said – the chashaku was a gift from him to me, and that it came from the root of a tree over four hundred years old. I found it remarkable how everything about Japanese culture was spiritual – everything had meaning, I really liked the idea of that.

After the tea ceremony we were directed to follow our host along a corridor. When he came to the shoji (sliding doors) he stopped in front of them, slid them apart and stepped aside for us. We entered a huge open room with more shoji on either side. The walls of the house seemed to open and close at every turn. I was fascinated with the idea of being able to add or subtract space so easily.

When Shimojo san spoke, David translated, "Please sit. Make yourselves comfortable," he said, pointing to the several small tables that ran parallel to each other in the centre of a tatami, identical to the one in our room at the inn. Behind the tables were zabuton (cushions) for us to sit on.

I looked around the room feeling as though I was in a dream, the décor, although sparse and simple was by no means ordinary, photographs hung on the wall above where Les, Bree and I sat, important-looking relatives staring down at us.

Our host clapped his hands and the meal was served. The menu seemed endless – small dishes of Tempura – a deep-fried fish with vegetables and meat. - Grilled brui-tuna, Sashimi, Sushi – raw fish on rice cakes. Bai – a shellfish like a snail found only in Toyama Bay. Shabu-Shabu – meat, steamed prawns, crabmeat and crab paste mustard, noodle stew came one after the other. It was all so fascinating. I had never eaten snail before and had only just learned how to use o-hashi (chopsticks). Bree and I were having the time of my lives sampling everything. I was astonished when we were told the seafood we were eating was caught especially for our meal and that the fish in a large bowl of sake, which was offered to us to drink from, was prepared only on special occasions. I have to admit a fish soaking in sake staring at me as I sipped from its bowl, was a little off-putting – I tried not to seem too awkward while drinking the sake.

During the courses Shimojo San played the Shamisen, an instrument introduced into Japan in the sixteenth century. It looks like a square banjo with a very long neck but sounds nothing like one at all. The echo box is covered with cat skin and it is played with bachi, a triangular plectrum.

As the evening came to a close we were given gifts as mementos of our visit. The whole experience was tremendous. I felt I was not just in another country but in another world. Everything about Japan was uniquely different to anything we had ever experienced before, heightening the pleasure of being there.

When the time came to leave, David and Yoko were not able to travel with us to Kobe where the ship was docked: we said our goodbyes at the bus station in Tokyo. Before leaving, David passed directions penned in Japanese to me, on the off chance that we should lose our way. Although we did not, I discovered that travelling in a foreign city totally ignorant of the language was definitely terrifying. The experience gave me some insight as to how migrants arriving in Australia for the first time, must feel.

31

Back on board the Oriana, the experience of Japan seemed only a dream. The photographs taken confirmed the extraordinary experience and with our departure from the country, the holiday became just a beautiful memory.

The routine of ship-life quickly returned to normal. Bree joined a couple of older children in the playroom. Even though she was the only toddler there, she was still eager to go.

In one way I dreaded the long journey ahead of us and longed to return to Bougainville, but in another felt excited at the prospect of visiting countries seen only in movies and read about only in books. I was missing the children. The thought of them lay heavily on my mind as I tried to imagine what they were doing at that moment and wondered whether they were missing me. 'Are they really okay?' I wondered, even after speaking to them briefly from Japan.

Organised games and get-togethers bored me and I ended up walking aimlessly the length and breadth of the ship, rummaging through remnants of my life, my thoughts poked around in old childhood memories that had me worrying more about the children when I remembered an occasion when I was five years old.

* * *

It must have been autumn or winter because Tina and I were wearing winter hats and overcoats on the day a lady came to our house and took us on a train ride. Vivid memories of a huge black steam-engine puffing loud bursts of steam at the station frightened me that day, but not enough to spoil the excitement of a train ride. I could recall the woman travelling with us being kind, giving us a bag of Minties and ever since then, just the sight of the sweet packet reminds me of that trip.

The rail journey seemed so long as we travelled a long and winding track from the city into the country. The engine chugged effortlessly along, spitting out a trail of white smoke. Restless and bored, I stood up and had to stretch to the tips of my toes to look out of the open window. All I could see was endless bushland. I climbed onto the seat and leaned out of the window for a better look and got a face full of coal chips for my trouble. I drew back quickly and spat fragments out of my mouth. At that moment I decided that I no longer liked steam engines.

The journey ended with Tina and me standing in the foyer of an unfamiliar building where a white statue dominated the entrance. Sounds of children playing outside filtered into the area where we waited. We had no idea where we were or why we were there or how long we would be staying.

A whooshing sound came rushing down the hall. I had heard that sound many times while in hospital. A woman dressed in a crisp white heavily-starched uniform entered the foyer and greeted us warmly.

"Hello," she said smiling down at us, "you must be Tina and Emma."

We nodded politely. "I'm Sister Mary, come this way," she said ushering us into her office where she applied a strong-smelling cream through our hair. I shuddered, thinking how awful the stuff smelled, and how greasy it made my clean hair feel. Our clothes were taken away and replaced with others that reeked of mothballs. 'Yuk!' I thought. I hate mothballs even to this day.

The underwear was stiff and uncomfortable from continuous washing. I wanted to wear my own clothes, but my request was always denied. I began to feel sad for the first time since leaving home.

Tina was three years older than me so we were separated and placed in age groups to go to the classrooms. It was my first experience of school. I can recall liking my classroom and feeling happy sitting at a little table, drawing on white paper during the day. But the nights were different.

Tina and I slept in the same dormitory with other girls. Our beds were very high off the floor. I had trouble climbing up on to mine. Bigger girls helped me when they saw me struggling to get into bed.

Every night I listened to Tina cry herself to sleep. I cried too at first, but stopped when I realised that months had passed and no one was coming to take us back home. I tried not to care about being away from home but Tina's tears made me feel that we were not wanted.

From recollection, we were treated well and I liked my new 'home' with the exception of the scratchy underwear and some of the food. If not for that I would have been happy to stay indefinitely.

The recreation room was a special place for me, especially when no one was about. It was a very large room with ceiling to floor windows on either side, and echoed when empty. The stage dominated the room and was visible through the glass doors at the entrance. On occasions, when no one was about I would sneak into the recreation room and boldly walk across the shiny floor, taking great delight in the sound of my footsteps echoing around the room as I walked towards the stage to sing silly tuneless songs I had made up.

In my backyard at home, I would often lay on the ground and gaze up at the clouds and watch them form shapes. If I stared long and hard enough I felt a part of the clouds. Playing in that room gave me the same feeling as losing myself in the clouds, until the day I was caught and punished for being in there without permission. A parcel my grandmother had sent was withheld from me. The parcel had significance. When I finally received it I discovered that I had turned six years old - no one had told me. Inside the parcel was a birthday card and sweets. I was astonished and hurt to discover that my birthday had come and gone without my knowing it, but losing the freedom to make tapping sounds on the polished floors and sing those silly songs disappointed me more.

In winter, the younger girls were given knee-high socks and the older girls stockings to wear. I liked the idea of wearing stockings and pleaded for weeks to Lucy, the lady in charge of the laundry, to have a pair, which eventually she gave me.

It was a sunny but very cold Sunday, when I first wore my stockings on our afternoon walk. Wearing them made me feel very special and all grown-up, just like the bigger girls. I was feeling very happy with myself as we set off down the scenic drive-way. Halfway, we were told to stop when a car pulled up alongside my group. I had not taken any notice as I was day-dreaming about my stockings. A voice from the car called my name and I turned to see who it was, flabbergasted to find familiar faces peering at me through the window. They were the last faces I expected to see, then or ever again. I was sort of pleased to see them.

"We've come to take you home," my father called from the car.

"Home?" I was not sure I really wanted to go home. I was resigned to staying where I was. I thought I was home.

"I don't know," I said.

I remember mumbling something stupid about my new stockings and how I had just got them that day after pleading for weeks to have a pair.

"We have a lovely surprise waiting for you at home," my mother said.

The car pulled into the driveway and I almost knocked the door off its hinges getting out in search of the lovely surprise. I boisterously charged into the house only to be told to be quiet.

"It's in my bedroom," my mother whispered, "now go quietly."

On the bed was a neatly wrapped gift. I opened it and found a multi-coloured xylophone in a box. When I lightly tapped the coloured strips, a strange noise came from the corner of the room. I looked up and saw a white cane basket under the window covered with a net.

"A baby!" When is it going back?" I said, not particularly thrilled to discover that this was my lovely surprise...

* * *

"There you are," said Les, interrupting my reverie, "I've been looking for you all over the ship."

"I've been thinking, Les. I want to call the kids today."

"Here we go again," he said impatiently, "What for? Can't you forget about them for five minutes? You just spoke to them from Japan."

"That was ages ago. I feel something is wrong. They could be missing us. I don't know. I just want to call them."

That afternoon I placed a call to Bougainville from the ship's phone. The moment the kids heard my voice, demands to hurry home came from Celeste, and BJ began to cry. I cried too and wanted to go home there and then, angering Les. He believed the children were playing up and refused to take any notice. All he was interested in was getting me into bed but I kept avoiding him. After that phone call I lost interest in the rest of the trip and was grateful when it was over.

Returning home felt good. Apart from the time spent in Japan, seeing the children again was the highlight of the whole trip for me. They were overjoyed to see us. Their faces lit up the moment we walked through the door.

Celeste promptly told me what had been going on in my absence. She was not impressed with her carers.

"They favoured Cain over BJ and me!" she said with her pretty face full of indignation. She then went into more details and after she had finished she said, "I'll run away if you ever leave me home again."

Cain was his usual cheeky charming self. He had the knack of twisting everyone around his little finger, just like his father always did. His likeness to Luc never failed to take my breath away, and being away from him for a month really emphasised it. Looking at Cain brought to mind the last time I saw Luc.

* * *

Bree was only weeks old when we flew down to Sydney to visit Brad in school and introduce her to the family. While we were there we caught up with old friends from Bougainville. I made the phone call to Luc from their home.

He was surprised and pleased to hear from me. "I guess you haven't heard," he said.

"Heard what?"

"I'm married again and have another son."

"Hey, congratulations...I'm happy for you. We'll have to catch up."

We arranged to meet the following day at our apartment. Luc looked handsome in his navy-blue suit, which complemented his olive complexion, cobalt eyes and black hair. He brought a photograph of his son, whom I was surprised to see was fair and looked nothing like him or Cain.

Conversation between us was casual and relaxed. Luc brought us up-to-date with news of old friends. Nothing in his or my manner suggested our feelings for one another were stronger than friendship.

After a friendly goodbye, I walked Luc to the door and closed it behind him, but I felt transfixed at the door. Quite impulsively I reopened it and stepped out into the hallway. Luc was standing at the top of the stairs looking in the direction of my door. We walked towards each other without speaking, our hands touching briefly before he turned and walked down the stairs. Cain was a constant reminder of a vulnerability and deep love I knew I would always feel for his father.

* * *

BJ's silence caught my attention. I was puzzled as to why he seemed so withdrawn. "What's wrong, mate?" I asked, brushing his forehead. "Are you okay?"

"Yeah Ma, I'm fine." But I felt that he wasn't.

Within a week of being back I received several disturbing telephone calls from friends, telling me what BJ was experiencing at school.

"Emma, you'll have to do something about it," a concerned friend said.

"What can I do? I've asked BJ several times if there's anything wrong and he has repeatedly told me everything is fine. I can't do a thing until he tells me what's going on. I suppose I'll just have to wait."

Screams from the boy's bedroom woke me in the middle of the night. BJ was having another nightmare. It had been going on for weeks. I was getting frustrated that obviously something was troubling him and yet he would not tell me what was wrong.

Many of my friends had said that BJ's teacher was treating him horribly in and out of class. "He's in tears most of the day at school," they said. But when I mentioned what I had been told to BJ, he appeared frightened and denied that anything was wrong.

Before he left for school one morning, I called to him in desperation, "BJ, if you get into trouble today you have my permission to leave the classroom and come home, okay?"

He managed a weak okay, but then hesitantly turned and asked, "What if she won't let me leave?"

"You have my permission to leave that bloody classroom!" I shouted.

Shortly before lunch that same day, BJ walked through the front door, the side of his face red. The whole sordid story unfolded as he told me the story of his victimisation.

"I was afraid to say anything, Mom," he cried. "She said you wouldn't believe me because you and her are friends. She called me names. She hit me and made fun of me in front of the class all the time. I hate going to school."

"I know, mate," I said, feeling relieved that he had finally told me the truth. "I couldn't do anything to help until you told me yourself. Why didn't you say something before this? Why did you wait for so long?"

"I thought she was your friend, Ma. You seemed to like her and I was afraid that you wouldn't believe me."

"BJ, friend or no friend, no one is more important to me than my children's welfare. Always remember that. Won't you?"

I hugged BJ, phoned the school in Arawa, and enrolled him there, then waited for the inevitable phone call. The phone rang shortly after I had hung up from calling the other school.

"BJ threw a temper tantrum and walked out of class this morning," said the indignant headmistress.

"Oh really," I was calm. "Why did he do that, Mary? I thought you said BJ was doing fine at school and there was no trouble with him, only with some of the other children."

Mary verbally ran BJ down. Fed up, I interrupted her and asked whether or not she had hit him. Her response was instant denial.

"Well Mary, BJ is standing right beside me and the red mark on the side of his face strongly resembles a hand print."

I took the opportunity to tell my former friend of the local gossip about her ill treatment of BJ. "As you know Mary, I don't usually listen to gossip. But this time, I'm glad I did. Otherwise, I'm not sure what would have happened to BJ."

She started to protest but I stopped her. "He's told me everything, Mary, and I believe him. I know what you have done to my son and he won't be returning to school. Goodbye!"

I turned to BJ and looked directly at him. "Don't you ever feel that you can't come to me for help. When you hurt, I hurt. Remember that."

Mary's husband had worked for Les in the mine until Les sacked him. Now it seemed BJ had become the catalyst of her revenge. He was not the only child to encounter her vindictiveness. Several other children soon joined BJ in Arawa.

Many parents complained among themselves about Mary Thornton's behaviour, but were reluctant to officially do anything about it. In order to hold her accountable for her ill treatment of BJ, I needed the support of the other parents but could not find anyone prepared to give that support.

Then one day, unexpectedly, I received a telephone call asking for my support in a legal suit against the headmistress. Other parents had declined, I was told. The case against Mary was heard at the courthouse in Kieta. I was willing to make my complaint but was unprepared for my reaction to the courtroom. Memories of my last encounter in a courtroom instantly became so vivid that I found it difficult to focus on the present issue. My mind was in the past, fighting for my children all over again, recalling the horror of looking for my children and not finding them. By the time my turn to give evidence came, I was emotionally charged.

In the witness box I had another flashback; Les was running from the courtroom holding Celeste. I felt panic, my thoughts were distracted and I fumbled with my answers to questions concerning the headmistress. I could not focus and the heat was unbearable.

During the questioning involuntary tears flowed and I felt powerless to contain them. My emotion surprised me as much as it did my friends. I felt their disappointment.

Although my friends lost the case, the headmistress' contract was not renewed.

32

Bree was now two years old. She adored Cain and followed him around the house like a puppy. The times he slipped away to go to his mate's place for a few hours, she would become distressed when she could not find him. But mostly he was happy to take her with him. "Come on," he would say squatting down, "Climb on." She would run up behind him, fall forward and grip him around his neck. He would then wrap his arms around her and spring to his feet saying, "Hold on tight, Babe."

On one such occasion during the holidays, Bree was with Cain and Brad at Max Hallam's place, just a couple of houses up the street from ours. There were several conflicting views about what had happened that day. But one fact was absolutely clear; the two teeth marks on Bree's cheek were very close to her eye.

The Hallam's dog was usually tied up when visitors came because she was unpredictable and dangerous. Ironically, we had given the Hallam's the animal when we first moved to Panguna. She was a pup from our dog's litter. Naturally I was upset about the incident, imagining the worst. Les had ordered the boys to capture the dog the next time it was on the loose.

Several weeks later, the dog was roaming around in our front yard and so the boys caught her, as Les instructed them to do. They secured her under the house and waited for him to come home. Bree was downstairs playing with Cain when he arrived. Les went crazy at the sight of the captured mutt and charged up the stairs calling out, "We've got that mongrel!" Celeste was sitting on the veranda engrossed in a book and I was in the kitchen preparing the evening meal with my thoughts elsewhere.

The thundering of Les' footsteps up and down the stairs suddenly attracted my attention. From the kitchen I could hear him shuffling through his toolbox and the muffled sounds of his strange laughter.

The order for nine-year-old BJ to, "Hold her!" filtered up stairs. The next order was to Cain and Brad, "Look you boys," he said, "this is how you teach this mongrel not to bite your little sister again."

Before my brain could fathom what was happening, several heart wrenching, piercing yelps rang in my ears, then silence except for heavy pounding on the ground. I dropped what I was doing and ran to see what was going on, but recoiled from the overpowering smell of warm blood. Covering my nose with my hand I peered over the railing of the veranda and saw blood everywhere. My brain registered that Bree was amongst the commotion.

"What are you thinking, Bree is down there! You didn't have to do that. You're a monster!" I shouted, running down the stairs. I quickly grabbed Bree, trying to ignore the grotesque sight, and dashed back upstairs. I felt awful because I was too late to save the dog or to shield my sons from that horror.

The piercing screams and blood excited Les. He seemed deranged, running upstairs and calling to Celeste. "Come on, come on, Celeste. Come and have a look at all the blood," he urged her.

"No!" she snapped and screamed at him, "You're disgusting. How could you do that to the dog and then want me to look at it? No! I don't want to. Go away." She turned away from him.

Les did not hear her. He ran down stairs, revelling in the horror, laughing like a fool, and threw the broken remains in the back of the company vehicle. Just as he was about to drive away, he noticed two of BJ's friends coming down the street heading for our house.

"Hurry up BJ," Les snapped, "get that shit cleaned up before those kids come snooping around here."

BJ was silent and glum, becoming frustrated because the water seemed to make the mess worse.

"Get out there and stop them from coming in here," Les barked. BJ dropped the hose and strolled over to his friends and spoke to them for a few minutes. When the boys left, he went back to his hosing. Les climbed into the company ute and said, "I want this shit cleaned up by the time I get back," then drove off.

I believed that if my sons had known the dog's intended fate, it would never have been caught.

* * *

While living in Arawa, I had been given a dog when the previous owners returned to Australia. Blackie was very timid, especially around Les, and would not go near him. He bitterly resented her trembling whenever she saw him and her refusal to come to him when he called her. She only came to the children or me. The dog's behaviour infuriated him.

"Treat her kindly and she'll like you," I said.

"What she needs is a good beating," he snarled.

"Don't you dare!" I warned. "Blackie is my dog."

"Not for long," he muttered, walking away and rocking his head from side to side.

Local rascals had hit our home during a series of break-ins around the town. A couple of days after the break-in, I arrived home about an hour after Les and found Blackie chained up and whimpering. I untied her. When I hugged her as I usually did, she winced in pain. Enraged, I stormed upstairs demanding to know what had happened to my dog. Les arrogantly confessed to flogging her with a chain.

"The mongrel should have chased the niggers away. She's a runner and we shoot runners," he bragged, "especially black runners."

Upset and distressed at the thought of the cruelty Les had inflicted on my defenceless pet, I screamed venom at him. But sadly, my reckless words would cost Blackie her life.

'It's beyond me how or why Les always manages to get away with so much,' I thought, utterly puzzled.

* * *

The incident with Hallam's dog was not discussed. On the surface, we acted as though nothing had happened. Shock would best describe our state of mind, I thought later on. It took ages for the animal's screams to stop ringing in my ears. Thinking about it made me physically ill. I could smell blood every time I heard the horrendous noise in my head. I could only imagine what impact the killing had on my sons and was too afraid to ask them.

When Hallam's dog's disappearance was noticed, rumours and speculation circulated as to what had happened to her. Les instructed the children not to say a word to anyone but Celeste told a few people and no one did anything. I felt that nobody wanted to get involved. 'Perhaps they were just too scared to tackle Les,' I considered. 'Who knows what's really going on in people's minds? Was their silence out of fear or wisdom?'

"I'm sick and tired of my life," I said aloud in frustration, strolling through the house and looking around me. "I'm a fake pretending everything's okay when it's not. On the surface, it appears that I can do almost anything, dinner parties, and themed lunches for my friends, design clothes, cordon bleu cooking, stylish home, great kids. Blah! Blah! Blah! But really I'm a failure. I'm married to a MONSTER and can't protect my kids from him. Please God, please don't let any of them be like him and please, please remove him from our lives, I don't care how you do it." But no matter how much I prayed or wished, nothing changed.

Cain was now of age to attend boarding school. I secretly worried about him going away and believed that he would fret for Bree and I, since the bond between us was so strong. He had practically raised Bree with me and gallantly responded to her every whim. In return she rewarded him by saying his name, which was one of her first clearly audible words. Mama was the other.

I loathed the idea of not having Cain around. It was difficult for me to come to terms with his departure. As long as I live, I'll never forget the day we drove Cain to the college to join Brad for the first time.

Bree had only just turned two. Cain was carrying her around on his hip, as he usually did, while Brad showed us around the college. Watching the two of them together made me smile. Cain moved Bree from his hip to his back when she became too heavy. With a quick bounce and a grunt, he slid her into place. It was a cute and comical sight, Cain's scrawny brown legs appearing to buckle under her weight as she clung to him like a baby koala clinging to its mother. Our neighbours had often said, laughing whenever they saw Cain piggy-backing Bree up the street, "Here comes Cain with the growth on his back."

Cain never seemed to mind carrying his little sister around but that day was especially difficult for both of them, when the time came for us to leave. Separating Bree from her beloved Cain was horribly heart wrenching. She clung to him with all her might and almost tore the shirt off his back, fearful that she would never see him again. I had to gently pry her free, as I did she pleaded with Cain to come with us. Tears spilled down her contorted face. Pitiful screams of desperation and outstretched arms reflected her agony and her deep affection for him. Cain looked on silently, utterly helpless, not knowing what to do. He could not ease her broken heart. All he could do was watch her fight, trying to get out of the car to run to him. As we drove down the driveway, I turned back to wave to Cain and Brad and saw Cain was crying.

Bree lay back in my arms and sobbed most of the way back to Sydney. Gazing down upon my distraught child, catching a glimpse of her lovely features and dark tear-soaked lashes, I could see the strong resemblance between her and Cain. For the first time, I also saw my own likeness in both of them.

It took a long time for Bree to settle down and to accept that Cain had to go away to school. Exhausted, she finally nestled into the contour of my body and fell asleep; letting out little whimpers every now and then in between her laboured breathing.

Looking at Bree, I was reminded of the times she said out of the blue, "I love Cain, Mommy."

An overwhelming sense of helplessness and sadness descended upon me when I realised that no matter how much I tried, I would never be able to completely shield my children from life experiences. That realisation frightened me.

I worried about my children constantly. Brad's progress at college was not encouraging. I had hoped that while there, he would acknowledge his inadequacies and in doing so discover and develop his own strength. Sadly that did not happen. He seemed totally withdrawn and refused to care whether he succeeded or failed.

Going to Mass and taking communion was an integral part of Catholic College life. Brad was required to go to church but was not allowed to take communion with his peers because he still was not baptised. I felt concerned that he may have felt alienated from his classmates because of that. I broached the subject with him during the holidays and tried to encourage him to make the commitment if he wanted to. I even anticipated making the necessary arrangements, offering to call the college on his behalf but Brad declined, saying that he did not care anymore. He once admitted to me that he wished he had been baptised at the same time as Cain and Celeste. I believe that Brad not being baptised had contributed to a large part of his apathy towards his school life and regretted that, years before, I had not fought harder to have him baptised. I also believe that Les could have helped Brad by putting his own prejudices aside and encouraging him to make his own choices without fear of ridicule.

I confided in some of my friends about my concern for Brad's regression at the college, hoping for a solution, and was told that the recently established correspondence school at Loloho was a huge success.

Parents who did not want their children going away to boarding school for one reason or another, had got together and organised a classroom situation down at Loloho Beach. The company provided three long prefabricated buildings called dongas for the classrooms, while professional teachers were employed to oversee the students' work.

A great deal of dedication and hard work had gone into organizing the correspondence school. The location had great ambience and tranquillity, a perfect place for students to learn. Tall palms, swaying gracefully in the breeze, lined the beach and surrounding areas of the school grounds. Crystal clear waters and a white sandy shore were only a short distance from the classroom, accessible to students who wanted to take advantage of the beach during recess.

The temptation to remove Brad from Campbelltown was strong but, I resisted bringing him home for a little while longer. While I had thought Cain's company would help Brad adjust, it actually made the situation worse.

Cain welcomed everything life offered with energetic enthusiasm and achieved highly. He even made his first Holy Communion. Cain was like Luc, not only in appearance but also in personality. He knew how to have fun and how to laugh at himself, enjoying life to full capacity.

Brad's moods reflected his father's; he was serious and sullen and rarely smiled. He appeared to view the world with gloom, and sadly lacked enthusiasm to succeed. But although he had Les' gloomy disposition, Brad's deep blue eyes and fine features were vastly different to Les. He was nothing like Les at all, more like my father. As a little boy, my son was gentle and kind toward his little sister, to me and our family pets. Unfortunately, in his craving for his father's attention over the years, Brad to replicated Les' personality in an attempt to gain his approval.

The contrast between the brothers was so startling that comments from students and teachers were unavoidable. Taking into account that Cain outshone Brad in just about everything, Brad showed no resentment towards Cain at all. He was actually very proud of his younger brother and I admired him for that quality. I was also aware that Brad felt overshadowed by Cain, but I was at a loss as to how to help him, other than to encourage him to try harder. Eventually his grades fell so low that I brought him home during mid-term to finish the rest of the year at the Correspondence School.

I had high hopes for Brad when he returned. I believed he would excel under my guidance and planned to help him any way I could. Unfortunately, I had not counted on his apathy and we fought constantly. Les became fed up with Brad and resented me spending time with him, telling me Brad was worthless. Les' negative attitude towards Brad only spurred me to become more determined not to give up on him. I just could not reach Brad in any way. His sour outlook concerned me deeply. Profound fears for his future plagued my thoughts constantly and I questioned what kind of adult he would become. Naturally I loved Brad, but I did not like the person he was. I knew he resented me and felt the reason for his resentment was that it was me helping him and always providing support, instead of Les. He did not want me. He wanted his father.

Brad sanctioned his father's wrongdoings in his need to be accepted by him. Inadvertently and progressively, over the years my son came to see me as the villain in the family, transferring all his hostility to me as a result. Although I understood Brad's need to gain his father's love and continually forgave him for the things that he did, my understanding of his needs did not automatically give me the wisdom and patience to cater to them. My patience where Brad was concerned was often stretched to its limits. I shed many tears of frustration for fear of losing my son' affection. Knowing that I could not help him almost drove me insane. Worry and concern churned my insides to the point that I became an emotional time bomb.

33

I was so grateful for my baby. Bree was the sunshine in my tortured days. We often sat on the carpet in her room, playing with teddy bears and dolls or just chatting about different things. We spent hours chatting to each other. One day I told her that she must be gentle with her teddies and dolls because they would get hurt if she threw them around the room, never dreaming she would actually believe me. I only said that to encourage her to look after her toys. Bree viewed her numerous teddies and dolls as her friends. Every night before bed she went through the ritual of saying goodnight to every one of them. Lovingly she hugged, kissed and patted them all. And if by chance she accidentally trod on one she would cry, "Oh sowwy. I'm so sowwy," kissing it better.

I had a good relationship with my children then. When I did the ironing, they would occasionally gather around the table and we would talk. At one particular time, when Brad and I were alone, he started talking about his time at boarding school. I was surprised to hear him say that he actually liked the College.

"When the baby was born," he said, "I felt that I didn't have a home here anymore. I felt that she took my place."

He was silent for ages as I continued ironing, shocked to learn he had felt that way. I waited for him to finish.

"And Nan told me she thought I wasn't Dad's son. She said she had judged you wrong, Mom."

He dropped his head and began to cry in a way I had never heard him cry before. I stopped ironing and went to his side and put my arms around him. He buried his head in my waist and sobbed.

In between his tears he asked pleadingly, "I am Dad's son, aren't I, Mom?"

"Yes Brad, you are. Yes, you are," I comforted him. Unfortunately you are, I thought and that was no comfort to me.

Brad's tears were tears of relief, I reasoned, and let him cry. His whole body shook with emotion and I hugged him tight, thinking how much I hated Maude. 'How dare that old bitch say things like that to my child? He's dwelt on this shit for two years. Her stupid comment almost stifled Brads' will to live.' I repeatedly cursed her under my breath. 'He's been holding on to all this crap and speaking to no one about it the whole time he was at boarding school. That old hag had no right to tell Brad that; she's caused him so much grief. BITCH!!!'

"Your father loves you, Brad. You're his first son and that makes you special to him. You're also the first grandson and that makes you very special to your grandparents as well," I said convincingly.

Brad knew I loved him but it was not my attention he wanted. It was his father's. With that burden lifted from his shoulders, he changed dramatically. He appeared more interested in things around him, and even smiled more frequently. Unfortunately, as months passed, Brad adopted his father's attitudes. Brad was attractive, bordering on handsome whenever his expression was not sullen. I feared he would be like Les, surly, overweight and aggressive. Thoughtlessly, I nagged him to stand up straight, to smile and to watch his weight, all the wrong things to do to any teenager at any time. I knew that but just could not help myself. Watching my son subconsciously imitate his father's ways was a nightmare for me.

The aesthetics of an individual were not necessarily important, I told myself, but judgements are often formed solely upon first impressions. Reference to Brad's similarity to his father was frequently commented on. These comments disturbed me because I knew Brad could be a better person than Les. And yet I still held grave concerns that he would become a wife-beating husband too, and there was nothing that I could do about it, other than pray that he would not.

Celeste also was finding life difficult in Tamworth. Her grades went from very high achievements to low achievements, which strongly suggested that something was seriously wrong. Like Cain, Celeste enjoyed the challenge of school. For her to receive low grades was unthinkable. She would not normally have allowed it to happen unless she had reason.

The telephone bill tripled with Celeste's calls, pleading to come home. This once well-behaved daughter of mine was fast becoming rebellious and demanding, and threatening to run away if she had to return to boarding school. She wanted me to enrol her at the Correspondence School with Brad. She was due to return home for the Christmas holidays and, during one of her numerous phone calls, I told her that I had arranged for a BMX bike for BJ to be sent on the same flight she was on. "Make sure it's on the plane and don't come home without it," I told her.

* * *

BJ was always getting into trouble for one reason or another but usually took his punishment without fuss. He never complained when life dealt him an unfair hand. But one day I was upstairs when I overheard a conversation between him and a couple of the neighbourhood boys. They had come to the house especially to show BJ their new bikes. When they started taunting and teasing him because he did not have one, I went to the window to see what was going on. It was not the first time I had seen those boys giving BJ a hard time. I did not interfere because I knew he could handle them. But this time was different. The boys were really cruel. After a while, BJ retaliated with a barrage of the strongest language I had ever heard him utter. I called out and told the boys to go home and for BJ to come upstairs. He was angry when he came inside.

"BJ," I called, "are you okay?"

"I'm fine, Ma," he said and went to his room.

* * *

Celeste knew how important it was to get the bike to Bougainville for Christmas, but when the time came to board the company's jet, she was told there was no room for a bike. She refused to board the craft and held up everything, understanding only that she was duty-bound to make sure the bike came with her, regardless of anything. As far as Celeste was concerned, I had instructed her to bring the bike back with her and that was that. Her refusal to board the plane frustrated the staff, because they could not leave without her. The passengers were annoyed because they had to suffer the bike crammed in between them for four hours. Seats in the company jet were not conventional, they were bench-seats that ran along either side of the plane and the passengers sat facing each other.

When we met Celeste at the airport she gave no indication that she had had any trouble at all. Several weeks later Babs told me what had happened on the flight. No one was more surprised than me when she said, "We were all annoyed at Celeste for holding up the flight, and she was very defiant about it. She absolutely refused to board the aircraft without that damn bike." Babs became annoyed when I smiled. "It's nothing to smile about, Emma," she said as if chastising a naughty child, "Celeste could have caused an accident."

"But she didn't," I said bursting with pride, imagining the scene of the annoyed passengers and Celeste, sitting opposite and glaring at each other. It took real courage for her to stand up to adults for the sake of her brother. I had to admire her for that.

BJ rode his new bike around the streets with pride, totally unaware of Celeste's battle to get it to him. Owning a bike did not stop the bullying, but at least he had a bike equal to those of the other boys, and that was all he cared about.

Both Brad and Celeste ended up going to the Correspondence School. As an interested parent I went to the AGM and eventually became a member of the board. As far as I knew, the school was running successfully under the guidance of Paula Jones. She was highly regarded by the students and Celeste had tremendous respect and admiration for her. Although firm with the students in general, she was extremely fair when it came to discipline and compassionate whenever students had problems.

At the time of my involvement with the board of management, changes within the school structure were about to take place, some of which I did not totally favour. One of the teachers, who had fiercely lobbied to have the Correspondence School changed into a high school with daily lessons as opposed to the correspondence material, had convincingly promoted himself and his ideas. Many were taken in with his plans of grandeur for the school. That is, all with the exception of Paula. The board voted in favour of change and Paula was replaced with the smooth talker.

As time passed dissatisfaction among the students became apparent. They signed a petition requesting the reinstatement of Paula as principal. I disapproved of Celeste's involvement and insisted she apologise to the new principal. Initially, he appeared to be a genuine man, deserving of respect, which by no means lessened Paula's credibility or esteem. Only time allowed the truth to be revealed, by then I had lost faith in the management of the school and went in search of another school outside the country.

The smooth talker was a huge disappointment. He became actively involved within the community, causing disruption everywhere he went. On occasions he and I had a heated exchange of words. As for the high school, another principal was appointed after the self-promoter left, while Paula was happy to remain a staff member.

Brad, Celeste and BJ were at a boarding school in Cairns. Placing them into a suitable boarding school without leaving the island was a huge challenge. I used the network system, relying on information from other parents' experience as a guide.

The Home School was recommended to me by an acquaintance. I knew nothing about it other than what I had been told. Although I felt uneasy about sending the three of them there, I had no alternative.

My opportunity to visit the school came when Bree needed urgent dental attention. She had reacted badly to fluoride tablets and without their protection, two of her back teeth had decayed. They needed to be extracted right away. The dentist told me that because Bree was so young, he recommended the procedure be done under anaesthetic. I booked a flight to Cairns for the treatment.

Bree and I stayed with Mandy Williams, the friend who liked to play with the ouija board, who was living in Cairns. The children spent some of their weekends with Mandy and her family.

The dentist's appointment was in the afternoon of our arrival. Bree was fine about visiting the dentist when I told her where we were going, but the moment we entered the surgery she had second thoughts about having her teeth out. It took two nurses and the dentist to hold her in the chair for the anaesthetist to sedate her. Watching my baby kick, scream, twist and squirm in an effort to get free was heart-wrenching. She fought like a tiger and I ended up in tears. The dentist lost patience when she locked her teeth around his finger and made it bleed. I protested about the way he was handling Bree and he ordered me out of the room. I walked no further than the doorway and remained there listening, ready for anything.

Moments later the door opened and I was invited back into the surgery. I found Bree lying like a limp rag-doll on the huge leather chair. Her face was drenched in sweat and tears. In a gruff manner the dentist said, "She's all right." I did not reply, only glared at him in disgust. In a few hours Bree was back to her cheerful self.

Later that afternoon we visited the Home School. On the surface everything appeared to be fine. Brad, Celeste and BJ were happy to see us and eagerly gave me a tour of the place, but I had an uneasy feeling which persisted even after meeting the principal. Without rhyme or reason, I went away convinced the children should not be there. Mandy assured me they were happy at the school but I wanted them out of there.

I saw very little of Mandy during the few days we were there since she was unable to get time off work. However, before Bree and I returned to Bougainville, Mandy took me to a tarot card reader. The reader told me that I loved one man deeply and would never love another in the same way; that I had wealth, comfort and the love and respect of my children. My husband would pass away on his forty-seventh birthday. "Never divorce him," she warned, "He will try to destroy you and steal your children if you do." Her parting words to me were, "Don't divorce your husband, he will destroy you!"

I thought long and hard about the warning. Divorce was on my mind again, but I decided to heed the warning and delayed doing it, with the hope that Les would pass away on his birthday as the card reader predicted.

When we returned to Bougainville I told Les how I felt about the school.

"I want them to come back home," I told him. "I feel there's trouble around them where they are."

Frustrated he said, "You can't keep pulling them in and out of school all the time every time you get one of your feelings, they can stay where they are."

Later on, incidents of students being involved in serious trouble circulated among the parents. But Les would not listen to my pleas to bring them back to the island. In desperation I told him I was going back to Australia.

Brad was sixteen and preparing to leave school and enter the work force and I wanted him to have a family to come home to. "I don't want him to be alone, Les. I'm going with or without you. I want all my children to be together. The island is changing, can't you see that? It's not the same as it was years ago. There's no work here for Brad."

Determined to convince him I said, "I'm leaving because I want my family together!"

Once I had spoken my thoughts out loud, as far as I was concerned, they were written in stone. I started telling friends that I was leaving but Les remained non-committal.

Three days a week I did hairdressing under the house, and it was I who actually told Les' boss we were leaving, the day he came for a haircut.

"Oh really,' he said, "Les hasn't said anything to me."

"He can stay here if he wants to, but Bree and I are leaving."

I told Les that Bree and I would leave the island when his contract finished. I figured by then it would give him time to adjust to the idea. The longer I thought about leaving, the more convinced I was that I had made the right decision.

34

Although my decision to leave Bougainville was final, I was still involved with the community. Dissatisfaction was brewing among the residents of Panguna because of the exorbitant prices at Panguna and Arawa's supermarkets. Expatriates, as well as local indigenous people, felt the financial strain.

An air of discontent arose, to such a degree that everywhere I went the subject of the supermarket usually came up. During a fundraising party for the school, the subject came up again. One comment led to another and, before I knew it, I was right in the middle of a plan to gather the community together to rectify the situation.

Along with many others, I had witnessed pilfering of goods from within the store and the warehouse by store employees, and we the consumers paid high prices to compensate for the loss. "Enough was enough!" people were saying.

Word quickly got around that a meeting about the supermarket's high prices was being held at the Panguna Cricket Club. Surprisingly, a large number of frustrated locals and expatriates turned up. A mixture of optimism, scepticism and a little hope filled the room that day. The community was obviously angry and fed up and everyone definitely wanted things to change. A committee was appointed to approach management.

The copper mine's general manager met with our committee in his office. He seemed disinterested and perhaps a little smug. A few of the staff from the company that supplied the supermarkets, sat on the sideline holding large black folders on their laps, ready to defend allegations of unfair pricing. The community was led to believe that the Wholesaler was an independent organisation, and not the company store, which we all knew was untrue.

After a lot of vacillating, the outcome of that meeting was a stalemate. Plans for further action were put into motion at a follow up community meeting. Avoiding the supermarkets was encouraged and alternative shopping arrangements were suggested. It took up a lot of time and energy arranging car pools to travel the long distance down the mountain to Arawa and purchase goods directly from the wholesaler, as well as going to the airport to collect cargo. The inconvenience was tolerated in hope of change. Purchasing goods from the local markets, co-op buying and even flying goods in, was cheaper than buying them through the supermarkets. In truth, the community was being robbed.

After several weeks of boycotting the supermarkets, the community's protest was heard loud and clear. The boycott had a huge effect on sales. As a result, subtle pressure to concentrate on the job and not the supermarket was applied to committee members working for the mine. Slowly the committee grew smaller in numbers, leaving only four to fiercely carry on. I was one of them.

Initially, Les could not have cared one way or the other what happened at the supermarket. He only showed interest when I told him what was happening to the committee. I asked him, "Will my involvement with this protest jeopardise your job in anyway?"

"Nah, I won't be fired. The bastards need me to fix their trucks. I'd fix them well and truly if they do."

He dismissed my concerns and confidently reassured me that his job was safe and secure. "I make the decisions for the little fat fellow, anyway," he said smirking. "He needs me. I do his job every day. Nah, I won't be fired."

As confident as Les was then, there was a time when he was not feeling so secure. A rumour that Papua New Guinea Government was considering investigating company employees' credentials and trade papers had sent him into a state of panic. "Anyone without them," he was told, "will have to leave the island."

Deeply troubled and fearful of the outcome for not having trade papers, he made a call to Australia to get a falsified indenture trade certificate. While I was in Sydney with BJ and Bree visiting Brad and Cain, I collected the papers on his behalf in exchange for four hundred dollars. Les' confidence was immediately restored once he had taken possession of the papers. Ironically, the rumour turned out to be just that, a rumour.

For weeks we diligently gathered prices from supermarkets throughout Papua New Guinea and Australia, for comparison with what we were paying at the company supermarket. The survey showed that in some cases we were paying a price difference between 30-85% above normal prices. At the meeting the wholesaler's figures showed considerably less. Anonymously, information was being passed on to me stating that the facts and figures we had were correct. "Stand your ground," I was advised, "you're on the right track."

A second meeting with the general manager was scheduled, but this time with startling results. Our small group was all geared up ready and armed to fight for a fair go. We even had proof of the company's connection to the store, along with a host of other information that confirmed our findings.

The general manager was wearing his familiar smirk when we entered his office. He was leaning back in his chair at an angle, with his feet up on the desk. After we were seated he unceremoniously swung around and gave us his full attention. Our spokesperson stood up and cleared his throat ready to address the CEO, confident he had the ammunition we needed to change the pricing structure. When he finished the CEO looked at all of us over the top of his silver-rimmed glasses. His light blue, eagle eyes did not miss a thing. "What I'm about to say," he said, is not to leave this room."

Everything we knew was confirmed off the record, with the promise of it being refuted if repeated outside the room. "It's all about politics..." he went on to say.

Needless to say, the wind was blown right out of our sails, and we left the office stunned. People were waiting for answers and we were not at liberty to give any. That made us co-conspirators to the cover up as well. Fortunately time dims memories. The episode became an event of the past and was soon forgotten.

I met up with the CEO at various functions from time to time, and his mocking of me was somewhat annoying. "Well Emma, what cause are you fighting today?" he would tease.

I was bitterly disappointed and totally disillusioned. I did not want to live on Bougainville any longer, everything around me was changing, but not for the better.

During his period of employment on the island Les seized every opportunity that came his way to gain recognition of some sort. I clearly recall an incident he had relayed to me when I returned to Bougainville from Mackay in 1975.

Ganmor, the company that initially employed Les, had organised a fishing trip for their visiting directors. Since Les was still largely involved with the company the general manager invited him to join them. During the outing one of the visitors misplaced his wallet full of cash and travellers' cheques. Les found it and promptly returned it to the visitor, who was very grateful and impressed with Les' honesty.

Les admitted to me that he could have pocketed the money without anyone knowing. "The stupid bastard," he muttered. "Everyone thought the wallet fell overboard. I knew I could've kept it, but that wouldn't have served my purpose. This way I look good and he owes me." Feeling very pleased with himself he stated, "I can get more mileage out of that than by keeping the money."

That was the way he operated, working under a mask of deception, pretending to like and respect his colleagues when in truth he despised them. He resented their position of authority and strongly believed that he should have had it instead of them. Over the years, I watched him masterfully disguise his contempt, waiting for the day he held a position of power.

With all that goodwill chalked up, I felt confident that a job offer would not be long in coming when it was known that Les was leaving the mine. Within certain circles he may not have been Mr Popularity, but he was respected as a specialist in his field. There was no denying that his expertise was often sought after.

Ganmor's were discussing a project in China, with Les in mind for the position. But he did not want to work for them after what had happened at the celebration of the Euclid170 Haul Truck's running 15,000 successful hours.

* * *

It was an evening of speeches and accolades for a job well done. Then the managing director of Ganmor presented a surprise plaque of recognition to Les, who was very proud and pleased to have been acknowledged for his work. That joy and pleasure quickly turned to outrage when it was pointed out to him that, although the inscription on the plaque was congratulating him for excellence, it was also suggesting he had gained all his experience and expertise while working for Ganmor. He felt they were taking credit for his knowledge and skill. Les was seething and never forgot the incident or forgave the company, even after an apology from management, with an explanation saying that it was all tongue-in-cheek.

The following Monday Les returned the plaque and asked for the inscription to be changed. It was quickly amended and returned to him with the intention of putting an end to a regrettable incident, but Les did not let it go. He viewed the inscription as insulting and deliberate, holding one man responsible and hating him for it. He vowed to get even some day.

* * *

Only a few days were left before we were due to depart the island. It was customary, before leaving, to throw a 'going finish' party and inviting everyone to come. The farewell party was a huge turnout and a great night. During the evening, I was asked by the man Les held responsible for the insulting plaque to convince Les to reconsider the position in China.

"We want him to work for us," were his parting words, "Hope you can change his mind."

After the party I mentioned the job offer to Les.

"It's a great offer Les, too great for you not to seriously consider. It'll probably be the only one you'll get. I'd take it if I were you."

The subject made him angry. He believed that by refusing the position he was making things difficult for his enemy and for the company, but I knew he would eventually take the job. He liked to make everyone sweat a while before giving in. It empowered him, doing things that way.

Part Three

Queensland

35

While I was involved with the church and women's fellowship, I had made peace with Dolly. The day I knocked on her door, I had only intended to apologise and leave, but she was moved that I actually come to see her and insisted I come in. Although our friendship was mended it was never quite the same, but Dolly and I did keep in touch after she and Ken left Bougainville to settle in Brisbane.

Once Dolly knew that we too planned to leave Bougainville and settle in Brisbane, in April 1984 she invited Les, Bree and I to stay with her for a week while Ken was overseas working. I accepted her invitation, with the idea that it would give us a chance to get our bearings and find a house before the other children joined us at the end of the first school term.

I was not looking forward to the tedious task of searching for a new home. In the first few days we had looked at so many houses, but none of them were suitable. The places that had some potential

did not have a swimming pool. The children had specifically asked for a swimming pool and I promised them they would have one.

While we were looking at the numerous photographs of houses through a real estate office window at Springwood, an agent joined us. He introduced himself and prattled on about how he could help find us our dream home. Les and I looked at each other and raised our eyebrows, indicating that neither of us liked the short, animated man in the fawn safari suit. His black hair matched an oversized, thick moustache that strangely resembled a butterfly struggling to escape his lip as he spoke in speedy tempo. The estate agent's dark eyes greedily peered through silver-rimmed glasses, scrutinising our every reaction. Tired and fed up with our futile searching, we agreed to tour the neighbourhood with him. We spent hours driving around and getting in and out of the car to wander through strangers' homes to look with a critical eye into every nook and cranny.

Les liked a house at Springwood. It had four bedrooms, but the rooms were cramped, and there was neither a pool nor a garage or additional room for either. However, we could have paid cash for the property.

My ideal choice was in semi-rural Waterford on a three-quarter acre block. The place was huge. It had five large bedrooms, two bathrooms, a walk-in robe, a huge family room, pool room, pool table and equipment and a swimming pool – perfect for our large family. But we would have to take out a small mortgage to cover the price difference, to which Les bitterly objected.

"Be reasonable Les, this house is perfect," I said. "The other one is way too small." I went on to explain that the children were young adults who needed space to move, a place where they could bring their friends home, as opposed to roaming the streets and getting into trouble.

Les viewed the situation differently and accused me of wanting grandeur to satisfy my ego. His allegations infuriated me. His refusal to communicate with me, other than with his unreasonable claims, had me almost succumbing to temptation to withdraw every cent we owned from the bank and leave the state, taking Bree with me. I went as far as filling out a withdrawal form, but instead I chose to stay and buy my children a decent home.

Later that evening during dinner, we were telling Dolly about the houses that we had seen. Les became angry when I told her about the house I liked. He said it was too expensive, then got up from the table and went to the bedroom. I followed him a little later and found him sitting on the edge of the bed, silent and sulking.

"Why can't you be reasonable? That house is perfect," I said, and he started crying.

Les' position working with the mine had him making huge decisions concerning heavy earth equipment involving millions of dollars, yet he was afraid to make a small one for the sake of his family for only a few thousand dollars.

To shock him back to reality I said, "What's the point in me hanging around if my family has to live in a box when we can provide better? We have to make a decision now or lose the house. The kids are due to arrive here in three days. If you want me to stay, then you had better phone Ganmor right away and tell them you will take that job in China. Why can't you understand, Les?"

I pleaded with him, "You need them as much as they need you. They will find someone else to replace you. You are not indispensable. The mine didn't fall apart when you left, did it?"

His tears disgusted me and I leant forward, closer to him, and spoke in a mean, low voice, "I'm the one who should be crying. You've given me enough to cry about over the years." I walked out of the room.

Dolly overheard our conversation and told me that I was cruel. She was probably right, I thought, but I did not care. In my defence I replied, "Sometimes you have to be cruel to one, to be kind to others. I did what I felt I had to do for the preservation of my family."

I felt Dolly's criticism was personal, rather than actually siding with Les, and therefore placed no value on her opinion. It was not my intention to be cruel to Les. I actually felt sick to my stomach every time I uttered an unkind word to him. In reality, I was not intentionally cruel or unkind to anyone, but simply reacted to the situation.

At the end of the week Les, Bree and I moved into a holiday apartment at Surfers Paradise, large enough to accommodate the whole family. While we were there, Les relented and made the call to Ganmor, and we bought the property best suited for the family.

The house I had bought in Mackay and the land in Ipswich turned out to be good investments. The house had more than doubled in value by the time of the sale and the land more than tripled. We sold both properties to buy the house.

Over the years, I had listened to Les bitching about how both properties were a waste of his money, but in fact they belonged to me. He allowed me to buy them in exchange for sex. So in reality it was I who provided my family with a home, not my husband.

The children's response to the house was what I expected. They were elated, in awe of everything about it. The excitement and pleasure in their voices and smiles on their faces were worth the battle to have it. And so we moved into the neighbourhood and began to live the farce of a happy family. I was very happy that Les would be away in China for months at a time.

The position in China took several weeks to come to fruition. Although the company paid Les a generous retainer while he waited, he still applied for positions with other mines throughout Australia. His failure to secure another position confirmed my prediction that nothing else would be available to him other than the job already offered. His ego took such an enormous beating when his applications were not accepted or just ignored that he became depressed. I had to encourage him to believe he still retained his expertise status.

"Be patient," I urged him. "I feel the job in China will lead to greater things." My predictions proved to be correct. Two days after my pep talk Les received a call to say he was needed in San Francisco immediately to discuss the China project.

Les departed to travel to the USA. That evening, I showered with my bathroom door open and slept naked in my bed. I would not have done that if he had been there. On several occasions I had caught him peeping through the ensuite door while I was taking a shower. As soon as I noticed, I slammed the door shut and locked it. Although the door would be locked, I could only relax when he was not around.

Our belongings from Bougainville arrived on the day after Les left for America. Les was eternally fortunate where packing and unpacking was concerned. In twenty years of marriage, he had never been around to lend a hand with either. But I really did not mind, he would only have been a nuisance

The removalists filled our formal lounge, dining room and garage to capacity with cartons. The tiny house Les wanted to buy would never have accommodated half of what we owned. I sighed with relief and gratitude that in this house we had room for everything. I was also grateful that I had had the foresight to clearly mark each carton, which made the job of unpacking so much easier.

While Cain helped me unpack Brad, Celeste and BJ found the cartons marked with their names and carried them to their rooms to begin unpacking also. Cain and I kept going long after the others were asleep, finishing around dawn. Fortunately for me, Cain shared my philosophy of staying on the job until it was finished, which saved me many hours of laboriously heavy work. Apart from one or two cartons left unopened, no one would have known we had just recently moved in.

It was amazing how quickly time passed after we settled in. Several months flew by with alarming speed. My older children were teenagers, sixteen, fifteen and fourteen respectively and were enrolled at the local, State High School. BJ, who went to the Primary School, turned thirteen mid-year. He looked no older and was not much taller than a ten-year-old, a fact that caused him some difficulty.

BJ had a lot to contend with during his adolescence. His lack of height, bullying from his father, teasing from his brothers and peers and persistent reminders from me to do the right thing. In retrospect, it would seem everyone was on his back at one time or another, resulting in the erosion of his easy-going nature. Being referred to as a short-arse, among other things, sent him into a rage of foul language and physical aggression. During one of his frenzies, I became so frustrated listening to his outbursts, that I grabbed him by the shirt and yelled into his face, "Look BJ, you ARE short and there's not a damn thing you or anyone else can do about it! That's the way things are. You can't go through life thumping people just because they call you names, just ignore them. You are short and that's that!"

His face was puffed and red with fury when I released him. I knew by the look on his face that what I said had hurt him. But soft words would not make him grow any taller. Later, when he had calmed down I playfully teased him, saying, "How's it going, short-stop? And, "Hi, shortie!" He would smile coyly and say, "Fine, Ma."

It took some time for BJ to adjust to his inadequacies but when he did he used them to his advantage. He may have been short in stature, but he developed a giant personality that attracted many pretty girls.

36

My first year in Brisbane was not an easy one. I would best describe the experience as a major learning period of my life. I discovered that living with four teenagers, each with vastly different and unique personalities and temperaments, demanded four separate solutions.

Although the changes I observed in the children's behaviour did not seem critical to me at the time, I did feel concerned about Brad's attitude. He appeared to think the world owed him a living and was apathetic about whether or not he had a job after leaving school. One of his teachers told him he could get the unemployment benefit, 'dole', if he could not find work. "It's okay, the government will look after me," was the message I received from him. I instantly overreacted to his deplorable viewpoint, leading to another argument, which was becoming the norm for us.

Celeste on the other hand remained quiet and reserved, maintaining her excellent grades. Although at times she appeared indifferent to her surroundings and seemed a mystery, I thought I knew her well. I actually thought I knew all of my children and naively viewed Celeste's silence and subtle withdrawal as a need for her to have her own space, which I respected.

As most teenagers do, Celeste gained weight, which played havoc with her self-esteem. She grumbled that she hated being fat. I responded by saying, "Well, do something about it, don't just complain," not realising how my innocent remark was interpreted, or that it contributed to her declining self-esteem, increasing her insecurity and feelings of neglect. I acknowledged Celeste's weight gain, but no one in the family ever condemned her for it, especially not me. As far as I was concerned, Celeste was beautiful and intelligent, and I was puzzled as to why she could not see it herself. I sincerely believed that I was doing everything I possibly could do for my children. They had trendy clothes, pocket money and the freedom to invite their friend's home...and I loved them.

There was no instruction manual on teenagers. I stumbled along blindly, trying not to repeat the same mistakes my parents had made with me. In addition to encouraging them following their dreams, I so dearly wanted them to have everything I did not have as a child.

Although I was invited to many birthday parties, I didn't had one until I was seventeen, so birthday parties for the children became my priority. Cain helped me make the parties memorable for his siblings and himself. He was always my willing helper for a price, anything from chocolates to a few dollars. His adolescence was the beginning of his enterprise-bargaining training.

Brad, BJ and sometimes Celeste found their assigned jobs laborious and often left them unfinished or undone, which got them into trouble. Cain was ever ready to offer his services for a small fee. Brad was the one who usually took up Cain's offer of paid help. And at times, Brad called on Cain for a loan as well, which he gave, expecting interest with the reimbursement. The tall, willowy, energetic, snappy dresser took his business dealings very seriously while the equally tall, heavy-set introvert did not, reflecting the differences in their personalities.

Cain was ambitious and dependable while laid-back Brad was mostly irresponsible. Brad's constant debt to Cain caused friction between the two boys, sending emotionally-charged currents through our home.

I was dealing with Celeste's withdrawal and mood swings, BJ's frustrations, Brad's negative attitude and Cain's determination to win at any cost. These additions to my frustration and helplessness

at not knowing how to solve everyone's problems combined with Les' inflated ego contributed to the breakdown of the family unit.

Amongst all that confusion and regular rollercoaster rides, laughter was no stranger to us. Cain provided most of the entertainment. He was as funny as he was frustrating and we all knew when he was around. My handsome teenager whooped and hollered and sang in the worst possible way at the top of his lungs. He was a top student, excelling in just about everything, but everyone certainly agreed that he had missed out when it came to singing. It was so awful that I had to bribe him to stop. He would oblige me only for a while, but his playful nature soon got the better of him, forcing his siblings and me to go running in search of pillows to either cover our ears or to thump him.

Cain's cunning mind was always working overtime, conjuring up ways to gain treats that he and Bree wanted. In doing that he instilled in me a keen shopping sense during our supermarket excursions. I was an indiscriminate shopper, buying whatever I needed without considering the cost of the items, rushing around the store as quickly as possible, eager to get out of the place and to get home. Cain on the other hand was happy to stroll the aisles, pushing the trolley cart and scrutinising the bargains as he went, advising me which items were the better buys and pointing out the savings. He figured that if I shopped economically and saved money, I would spend the savings on the items he and Bree liked.

When Cain wanted me to purchase something, a ritual hug and a sloppy kiss was usually planted on my cheek before pleas of, "Mommy, darling can I have..." started the process and he persisted until I gave in. The longer I resisted his pleas, the more shameless his grovelling became, endeavouring to embarrass me to give in to him. I only gave in because I allowed myself to be persuaded by his mischievous charm. I adored him and he made me laugh. He was as cheeky as his father and I would have given him the world if I could.

Les arrived home from China bearing gifts from his travels, expecting to be greeted like a lord returning home from the crusades. I bitterly resented having to indulge him. So what if he is treated as an honoured guest in China, he is still a low-life to me. He showed only a mild interest in being involved in the mundane happenings of our lives. Only when he had an audience did he portray the interested parent and adoring husband. I viewed his indifference with contempt and closed the line of communication between us, going about my business as though he were an unwelcome guest. Thankfully, Les' time at home between trips was short.

37

Living in Brisbane gave the Carter family easier access to us. The day Maude phoned and asked what the house was like, I told her, "Oh it's huge, just perfect for the kids. They love it. You'll have to come for a visit one day," never dreaming that Maude would actually come.

"I'd like to do that, love," she said. "I'd like to see Les before he returns to China."

Maude only intended to stay a week, but she stayed a month. "I'm really enjoying my holiday," she said. "I'd love to stay longer."

"So why don't you?" I heard myself say, surprised that I was actually enjoying my mother-in-law's company.

Maude was surprised to learn I was interested in antiques. So many things about me surprised her. She watched me manage my large home and family with keen interest.

"You're a good mother, love," she said one morning during breakfast. I smiled awkwardly at her and said, "Thanks, Mom."

A few days later, while on our way home from shopping Maude said, "I think I've misjudged you love, and I'm sorry."

I was silently humming along to a song on the car radio then suddenly stopped when Brad's image flashed into my mind. He was upset because he thought Les was not his father. My knuckles turned white as I gripped the wheel, remembering the pain my son had suffered unnecessarily because of her.

"I was wrong and I'm sorry," she repeated. "I can see that you've given Les so much, you've supported his career... I'm beginning to think that I was wrong about a lot of things. Maybe Marla's life would have been different if..."

"It's all in the past, Mom, water under the bridge."

I prevented Maude from saying anymore because I did not want to rake over old coals. The interaction she saw between Les and I was an act. But the interaction between the children and I was genuine. 'At least she acknowledges my support for Les' career as a major part of his success. I was grateful Maude gave me credit for something.'

In the New Year Les returned to China. Brad left school and become a recipient of unemployment benefits. I thought the army was the best place for him but he refused to listen to me, continuing to sleep throughout the day and play until the early morning. His behaviour was a great disappointment. People who did not want to work resided in other homes, not in mine. Brad's apathy prevailed and caused constant havoc. Beer, pot, and pornographic literature replaced orange juice and comic books. The realisation of this transition came as a great shock the day I entered his room and confronted reality.

I had delayed the intrusion to Brad's domain for as long as possible, but the ever-increasing mound of books and clothing growing in his cave offended my fastidious nature. A cleaning frenzy led to my discovery of what I considered the most disgusting magazines imaginable. At first glance I was stunned, not believing my eyes, and then shock set in. Tears of utter disappointment turned to rage and sickening disgust. My first reaction was to blame myself for failing as a mother. Then I convinced myself to rationalise the situation that the depravity derived from his father's personality. The uncertainty of what to do about the situation scared me.

I roamed through the house looking in each room, mystified as to why everything was going so wrong. "Why is this happening?" The sound of my voice broke an eerie silence. "I thought this house was a good place for the kids.

Why the hell is this happening? What am I doing wrong?" I yelled out.

The day the real estate agent showed us this house, I felt sure it was our rightful home. There was something familiar about the place; that was why I fought so hard to have it. The feeling was too powerful and too strong for me to ignore. Several months after moving in, the connection was confirmed in a dream I repeatedly had when I was a child.

In the dream I would be walking down a very long dark corridor. At the other end of the corridor was a brilliant light and, for some reason, I always woke up when I reached halfway.

****

Our new home had a hallway over twenty-two metres long and at the other end was my bedroom. The connection between the house and the dream came to me the evening, I walked from the family room into the dark hallway. Although I was standing in darkness, there was light coming from my bedroom at the far end. In contrast to the darkness the light seemed brilliant. Without turning on the light I headed for my bedroom and about halfway down the hall, I felt an incredible excitement in me, feeling as though I was walking down the same hallway as I did in my dream. I also realised that the brilliant light coming from my bedroom was the same one I had seen in the dream.

"I knew it! I knew it!" I jumped for joy in awe of the fabulous experience. "We're meant to have this house."

****

As I recalled that feeling while walking back to Brad's room, I said sombrely, "If that's true, then why is everything falling down around me?"

Tears of frustration and helplessness blurred my vision as I tidied up. Hours passed and I was no closer to solving the problem. Then to my horror, I suddenly realised that Bree could possibly be in danger. It is widely known that the lethal combination of booze, pot and pornographic material stimulates diminished responsibility. There was no room for second chances here, I thought, and I'm not about to tempt fate. Brad and his deadbeat mates are no longer welcome in our home.

When Brad walked through the door that afternoon, I felt rage and disgust resurface all over again. When I told him what I had found, he instantly reared up and bellowed at me, "Keep out of my room!"

His reaction turned me into a crazed banshee and I screamed my fears for Bree's safety at him over his thunderous spewing of obscenities. We verbally abused each for a long time, Brad's resentment at being under the authority of a woman was evident. He thought that he and not I should be the one in charge of the family in his father's absence.

A fine example you are, a pisspot, a junkie and a pervert," I mocked, every word reflecting my contempt and disgust. "Yeah mate the perfect person to be in authority. Get out of this house and find a hole to live in."

"No!" Brad trumpeted. "I won't! This is my home. I'll do what I like."

A replica of Les, swollen with arrogance, stood in front of me with the intention to intimidate. His large menacing frame loomed over me with arms folded aggressively, determined to rule.

A figure standing in the doorway caught my attention. I turned quickly and found BJ holding a knife in his hand ready to strike. I quietly asked him what he was doing with the knife.

"I'll use it if he hurts you, Ma," he replied.

Although my heart was pounding in my chest with alarm, I knew I had to remain composed. Any wrong move could suddenly send everything haywire.

"Give it to me, BJ," I said calmly reaching for the knife, "he's not worth getting into trouble for. I need you home with us."

Sombrely, BJ handed me the knife and then released his frustration with tears. As I hugged him I could honestly admit to hating Brad for the first time in my life. His arrogance so enraged me that suddenly I found the mammoth strength required to remove him from the house. He used his aggression to break the glass door, demanding to be allowed back in to the house. When I telephoned the police he left.

Too many times in the past, Brad had been reprieved for so many wrongdoings. I made excuse after excuse for him, lecturing him on the consequences of what he was doing wrong and hoping that he would listen to me. I overlooked the possibility that he needed professional counselling. Wrongly or rightly, I compensated for my parental shortfalls with material possessions, which he never seemed to appreciate the way his siblings had.

Brad's eighteenth birthday party, though elaborate, had ended up in disaster, with his friends dismantling the French doors that separated the billiard room from the family room. Most of the girls became heavily intoxicated early in the evening and were sick everywhere. His father's Akubra hat was stolen and a fight had broken out.

Brad asked me to buy him a car as a means of transport to prospective work opportunities. I purchased a cheap car for him with his solemn promise to reimburse me. The car was nothing fancy but a car nonetheless. The little red vehicle's life was short-lived as Brad and his mates systematically ran it into the ground. It never embraced the exterior of any establishment of potential employers. It served as a bush-basher and when it died under the thrashing it received, Brad informed me the car was a heap of shit and he was not going to pay for crap. The car issue was actually a test to see if he really should have one at all. I believed Brad had the car he deserved.

Brad returned a few days after I removed him from the house. Although his resentment toward me was apparent I apologised to him, with the intention of making peace and working towards a solution. He wanted to come back home but I said no, reminding him that he had already made so many promises to change his attitude and failed. I suggested he find his own unit and come home for meals a few nights a week.

I gave Brad furniture and curtains for his new home and for a while it looked as though he was actually making a change for the better. A couple of evenings a week he would join us for dinner and happily give an account of what he was doing. On the surface all appeared to be well. Brad assured me he was looking for work but without success. At least he is trying, I told myself, which was more than he had done when he lived at home. That thought made me feel more positive about his future.

Weeks turned into months with no prospect of work on the horizon. Once again I suggested Brad try the army and again my suggestion was rejected. I began to feel sorry for him when I saw his spirit declining. He moved back home, firmly promising to respect house rules. What a joke! Within a few short weeks he was back to lying around the house like a beached whale. I was so frustrated that I went to my diary and wrote, 'It is so easy to become an enemy to your children. Just ask them to do something they don't want to do and you immediately become the ogre, the reason their whole life, their hopes and their dreams, are crumbling around them...'

Brad took his frustrations out on me, accusing me of excluding him from the family because I had had a bedroom-cum-sitting room built for him under the house in Panguna. His insinuations hurt and frustrated me beyond belief. He had undermined every positive gesture I extended to him.

The separate room in Panguna had come about because Brad was at that age when a boy needed his own space. His large frame seemed to fill the limited area in the bedroom he and his brothers shared. I argued at great lengths with Les to have a room built for Brad, who had been excited at the prospect of finally having somewhere to relax with his mates without the intrusion of his younger brothers.

I hated the way Brad expected me to take responsibility for his failures, which I unwittingly had done, desperately searching for ways to solve his problems.

Every time I drove past the new shopping centre nearing completion a short distance from our home, the empty hot bread shop sign caught my eye. It gave me the idea to open that shop and start a family business. I hoped Brad could learn to manage the business and run it with me.

When the China project came to an end, Les took a management position with the same company in, New South Wales. He expected me to uproot the family and begin a new life with him down there.

"What – leave Queensland? I can't do that," I replied. "We've already settled in and the kids are doing well at school…"

I made it sound as if staying in Brisbane was a big sacrifice for me, when I was really hoping he would meet another woman in my absence. I was careful not to seem too excited about him having to live in another state, in case he forced the situation so that we had to move to there with him.

During the first few months Les came home every weekend. I was pleasant when he was with us and told him nothing that would upset him. When he did not seem interested in what we were doing I became cooler and more distant towards him. His indifference towards the children annoyed me beyond belief, especially when he only wanted to talk about how important he was in the town where he now lived. It was not long before the visits dwindled down to once a month. It was beyond me why Les bothered to come back at all since we were hardly speaking to each other.

The harsh reality of having to negotiate Les' support to get a loan to open the shop was that I had to change my tactics towards him and be sweet. I threw caution to the wind and telephoned him at work with an outline of my plan for Brad and the business.

Les mockingly laughed and said, "You've got to be joking." When I told him that I was very serious and wanted to do it for Brad as much as for the sake of having a family business, he sarcastically asked, "How much is your little brainstorm going to cost me?" When I told him he roared, "Forget it!" This was followed by his usual spiel of his life sacrifices and suffering in his quest to be a model husband and father to ingrates.

My need for Les' support outweighed my desire to angrily respond to his outburst of exaggerations. He was my only hope of creating employment for Brad, so I had more to gain by being silent. My life was devoid of any emotional fulfilment other than that of my children. They were everything to me; I remained sweet and totally charming throughout his ranting.

"This will cost you, you know," he warned smugly.

"Thank you," I said sweetly, hardly believing my luck. "You won't regret it…"

I hung up the phone and jumped for joy. 'Wow! He gave in. Heck, now I've got so much to do, where the hell do I start?'

I quit my part-time job with the city fashion store, which I had only just started, and focused my full attention on getting the new shop ready for opening. The way everything fell into place absolutely amazed me and I took it as a sign that the business would be successful.

I was in the middle of getting things ready to open the business when Luc's image began to haunt me. It had been four years since I had seen him. Although he was never far from my thoughts, I purposely did not contact him when we arrived in Brisbane. I felt he was happily married and I did not want to interfere in his life in any way. Regardless, the desire to contact him nagged at me and became overwhelming, until I eventually succumbed to the temptation to dial his number, only to find it had been changed. I rang directory assistance for the new number and was told it was silent. My heart sank to the pit of my stomach. Heartbroken, I tore the redundant number out of my diary and dropped it into the garbage bin, staring down at the useless piece of paper with a sense of loss. The emptiness I felt was beyond words.

Several weeks later the feeling to contact Luc returned. Although it had been several years since I had spoken to Helen Garret, I contacted her in hope of some news about Luc. I was not sure if Helen would even remember me but from the moment I said hello we chatted like long lost friends, which led to me to ask her about Luc.

"Haven't you heard?" she asked surprised.

"Heard what?" My heart almost stopped beating, by the tone of her voice, I sensed something ominous.

"Luc has cancer. He's been very ill. He's out of hospital and he's back at work now."

"Do you have his work number?" I said on impulse, and then hurried to end the call.

My hand trembled as I dialled Luc's number and a steady stream of tears forced me to replace the receiver in its cradle. I waited to regain my composure before dialling again.

"I thought you were running away from me," I teased, when Luc answered the phone.

"No, never, never," he quickly responded, assuring me the reason for the silent number was work related. "How are you?"

"How are YOU is the question? I got your number from Helen. She told me you've been very ill."

"It was nothing," he said. "I'm fine now."

I felt fate had led me back to Luc and this time I was never going to lose touch with him. We were in contact two or three times a week, with the exception of the days Luc was away. He explained his absence as business related, but I knew better, noticing the change in the sound of his voice. It was evident he was becoming weaker. I knew he was dying and believed he did too.

During that year we discussed many things, something Luc would not normally have done. He was a private person and did not easily share his feelings. He confided in me about his financial situation, explaining why he was unable to come to Brisbane to see me. "I can't afford to run up any debts," he said. "It wouldn't be fair to my family. I don't have any life insurance…"

The phone calls were the highlight of my day as we shared a small portion of our lives with each other. Luc was eager to know everything about Cain. I told him that Cain not only physically resembled him, but also had his same extrovert personality. He laughed when I told him of Cain's antics growing up. Sharing those moments brought us closer than ever before.

"I know you'd be so proud of him, honey. I wish you could see him."

After a pause he said sombrely, "I don't think I have time."

I fought back tears and quickly changed the subject. I told Luc about the bakery and my hopes for Brad. "If things work out with Brad managing the shop, maybe I could bring Cain to Sydney to meet you," I said enthusiastically. Luc liked the idea, but felt certain Cain would not want to know him.

Les finally returned home to claim his prize. I felt the loathing of it all and wondered whether my life was worth living, if this was the way it was going to be. The sight of Les simply spoiled my pleasure in everything. My tears of self-pity were shed in solitude. I desperately wanted to get away from him, whether in divorce or through my death. Either way I longed to be rid of him.

Luc's illness also had a profound impact upon me. I could not bring myself to imagine that one day soon he would not be there for me to talk to. Then suddenly I felt the impact of it and was utterly overwhelmed. The idea that Luc may not survive his illness made me feel empty as I could not imagine life without him. The sound of his voice made every awful thing in my life seem better. I wanted so much for him to recover. I needed him. I wanted to drop everything and go to Sydney to see him but I could not do that, it was too late to change my mind about opening the shop. I had already signed the lease.

The shop opened as a dry bakery and café but after a few months, pressure to bake bread on site came from the landlord. It meant the required expenditure would put the business under financial tension.

Brad was a huge disappointment and certainly an unsuitable candidate to manage a business. I was in trouble and had to find a way out of it some way. Instead of quitting like Brad when things became difficult, I struggled on and fell deeper into debt by adding the ovens. Perhaps I might not have been so determined if Les had not been on the sideline, persistently telling me that I was doomed to fail. He sneered and taunted me every opportunity, saying, "You think you're a big-shot business woman." He even refused to set foot in the place.

Cain came home from school one day and announced that he wanted to leave school and work in the shop to help me. His declaration stirred mixed feelings in me. I struggled with the idea of him not finishing school but delighted in the thought of us building a family business together. He was adamant about his decision so I agreed and gained an exceptional employee in the process. Cain worked like a Trojan for low wages without complaint. He was productive and deserving of my praise and admiration. We were a good team.

38

I canvassed for extra business and the shop began to prosper, wholesaling to other outlets. My likely success displeased Les and we argued. That argument was the catalyst that changed all of our lives.

Les was in a bad mood the afternoon he picked up Cain and I after closing. I ignored him and happily chatted about the day's takings. I was in high spirits, feeling confident the shop was going to succeed. While I was talking, and without provocation, Les struck me across the head, telling me that I was getting out of control. The blow took me by surprise. Looking at him and holding my head I snapped, "What's wrong with you?"

"Shut up!" he yelled, and punched me again and again as he drove the vehicle down the road. I crouched in the corner like a petrified animal, protecting my head. Cain, sitting in the back, was momentarily stunned and then called out, "Leave Mom alone!" Les ignored him.

When the vehicle came to a halt in our driveway, Les threw open his door and bounded to the passenger's side. He opened the door with force, grabbed handfuls of my hair, and pulled me into the house. Bree was in the hallway when we entered the house. She looked puzzled when she saw me crying.

"What's wrong, Mommy?"

"Please Les," I pleaded, "not in front of Bree."

He released me and I went to Bree. "Go to your room, pumpkin," I said and gently put a hand on her back her guiding into the bedroom, "I'll be in in a minute."

When Bree was out sight Les grabbed my arm, pushed me into the bedroom and closed the door. I glared defiantly at him as he removed his belt. "You're getting out of hand," he said again. I knew what was coming but was determined that this time I would not cry or beg him not to hit me.

"Turn around," he ordered, but I remained still and silent. Then suddenly he lunged at me and pushed me face-down on the bed and held me firmly by the neck, muffling my cries and almost suffocating me, as he laid into me with his belt. I tried so hard not to cry when the belt struck, but the pain was too much for me to bear.

"Do you want more?" Les asked, and I vigorously shook my head. "Are you going to be good now?" he asked, and I nodded. He released me and waved the belt in my face, threatening to give me more if I said a word or even looked sideways.

Humiliation and physical pain churned my insides. I was horribly embarrassed that my children knew what was happening. I wanted to hide in my room from them, but could not as I had to go back to the bakery and finish cleaning up. Cain came with me.

In the car he looked at me. "Why did you say anything to him?"

"I'm entitled to speak, Cain, he's not going to tell me what to do all the time. I'm running this bloody business. He should be pleased that we had a good day. We needed it."

I was shouting. I was angry that Les had hurt and humiliated me and I thought Cain was supporting Les. "I don't know why you are taking that bastard's side, Cain. He isn't even your father," I blurted out without thinking.

The moment I heard myself utter my thoughts, I wanted to rip out my tongue. I darted a sideways glance at Cain and saw Luc's and my son shrink away. By the look on his face he was devastated. I knew I had lost him. His jaw was clenched tight when he said, "You have just taken my life away from me."

In an effort to redeem myself, I told Cain about his father, but there was no response from him. In frustration I said, "Look Cain, your real father is a fine man. Les Carter is an animal. How can you possibly say that I've taken your life away from you?" He did not hear me.

It took months before Cain spoke to me in a civil manner. Our relationship as mother and son ceased that day and we became strangers. Because of my impulsive words, everything simply crumbled before my eyes and I could do absolutely nothing to stop it.

On the nights I could not sleep I drove to the bakery and stood in the shadows outside the shop, watching in horror at what was going on inside. Cain and his friends helped themselves to the drink machine and ran riot, throwing dough at each other, leaving deposits on the walls for me to clean up.

Cain was the baker's assistant and the two became close friends. I had given the baker permission to bake products for his food van with the understanding that he covered the cost of the ingredients he used. I later discovered that Cain told the baker that he did not have to pay for anything.

One by one my business lost wholesale customers. They complained that the orders Cain delivered were damaged. When I pleaded with him to be more careful, his response was to either swear at me, or to tell me to get someone else to do the deliveries if I did not like the way he did it, knowing full well that there was no one else. He acted even worse towards me when Stanley Carson, a work colleague of Les', came to the bakery or rang the shop.

I vowed that Les' vicious attack on me would be the last, so I took ill-afforded time off from the shop and travelled into the city to see a solicitor to start the divorce proceedings. I liked the solicitor I spoke to that day but the precious time lost travelling to and from the city forced me to exchange the city solicitor for one in the suburbs.

The suburban solicitor viewed me as pathetic when I told him that all I wanted was a divorce. Although I felt and looked tired and run down, I was determined. "I don't want anything from Les except my freedom."

I was afraid to tell the solicitor that Les had threatened to kill me if I ever tried to take any of his belongings or money from him. "You can have anything you want if you stay," Les told me the last time I mentioned divorce to him. "Leave and you'll get NOTHING from me. I'll kill you if you try. If I don't get you, I'll get your family. Someone will pay, sweetness, and it will be your fault."

Unlike the city solicitor, Paul Barry would not respect my wish to obtain only a divorce. He went into a mild frenzy, telling me it was not in my best interest to give up everything. I told him it was. "I'm too tired to fight for anything," I said. "He can have everything, I just want out of the marriage. All I want is to have peace."

Paul Barry looked at me as if I was out of my mind and then picked up the phone and asked, "What is your husband's number?" As I gave it to him I said, "What are you going to say to him?"

He held up his hand and said, "Shhh." I went quiet.

"Les Carter, please." Paul Barry introduced himself when Les came to the phone and suggested that he get a solicitor.

"I wish you hadn't done that," I said, feeling afraid as I thought, 'You don't know what you've just done.'

"My dear Mrs Carter, you are entitled to half of everything."

The war had begun.

My divorcing Les went beyond the beatings and humiliation. I was finally surrendering to my failed relationship with my older children as it was painfully obvious that none of them wanted me to be involved in their lives. 'So what is the purpose of me being in this nightmare of a marriage?' I asked myself. 'Absolutely none!' I replied, 'Absolutely none.'

39

One busy Saturday morning as I was serving customers, I looked up and saw a stranger, dressed in leather motorbike gear and helmet, enter the shop. He stood in the background facing me, with the helmet still on. I curiously watched the mysterious man in black from the corner of my eye, wondering what he was planning to do. When I looked again, he had removed the helmet and was sitting at a table in the corner, watching me and grinning. I thought he looked familiar but could not place him.

After the crowd had thinned out, he strolled over to the counter and said, "Business looks good."

"Oh Stanley, it's just you!" I exclaimed. "What are you doing in that get-up, I didn't recognise you. I thought I was about to be robbed," I said, and laughed with relief.

I had never really liked Stanley Carson, I felt he suffered with small man syndrome, was arrogant and full of himself. The few times we socialised with him on Bougainville, I had complained to Les that I did not like him. "Don't let me get stuck with that little dickhead tonight," I had protested bitterly, "all he ever does is talk about himself."

Stanley was a rep for a company that sold spare parts to the copper mine and Les was his main contact. It was common practice for company representatives to have a small function after a business deal. Every time Stanley was at a function, I somehow ended up sitting either next to or opposite him, and each occasion was dominated by the conversation about his travels.

"Do you have a family, Stanley?" I asked on one occasion, interrupting him in order to change the subject.

"Yes," he said, "a wife and two children. I'm off to Germ…"

"Girl and boy?"

"Yes," Stanley answered. "I'm off to Germany next…"

"How are they?"

"Who?"

"Your family."

"Oh they're fine," he said, and quickly finished his sentence before I could interrupt again. I listened politely but did not respond, then turned my attention to the person sitting on the other side of me.

When we arrived in Brisbane in 1984, Stanley met up with us while we were staying at the Gold Coast apartment, and then periodically kept in touch thereafter. It puzzled me why he wanted to keep in contact since neither Les nor I had anything in common with him.

Just before Les left for China, Stanley arrived on our doorstep one Sunday afternoon with his wife May, teenage son Jason, and daughter Sue. I could feel that May was uncomfortable, even though I went out of my way to be friendly. By the expression on the children's faces, they too wanted to be anywhere else but there. When May made an effort to make conversation, it was to complain about Stanley's unfinished home renovation. "He's never at home long enough to do anything about finishing anything; the bathroom's a mess," she said, glaring at him. For a brief moment he looked uncomfortable, but laughed it off and steered the topic to his next trip away. I actually felt sorry for May.

Stanley and May visited twice more but we did not form a close friendship. It was a few weeks before Christmas when Stanley phoned again. I was not interested in chatting to him, saying only that Les was in China and would be back in time for Christmas. "You can catch up with him when he returns.

Give our regards to your wife and family," I said, about to hang up.

"Oh, May died six weeks ago."

The casual announcement astounded me as I realised there was nothing in his voice to indicate sorrow or regret. I passed on my condolences and asked how his son and daughter were coping. I could not help but wonder whether or not he had ever cared for his wife. From the way he spoke, I would have thought he was speaking about an acquaintance rather than his wife.

May was only in her mid-forties when she died from a brain clot. The day it happened she was playing tennis with friends. The doctors had her on life support but Stanley chose to turn off it off immediately, saying he did not want to prolong the inevitable and incur huge medical costs in the process.

Although Stanley seemed different in leather gear, the idea of him handling a motorbike seemed almost comical. I had imagined him as a nerd. In the empty shop we drank coffee and talked about mutual friends. Whenever customers came in, he remained seated at the table while I served them. I expected him to leave after he had finished his coffee, but he lingered for several hours. He seemed different that day, not as annoying, and I could not figure out why. Later on, I realised the conversation was not about him or his travels. He actually seemed concerned that I was working long hours seven days a week without a break.

"You really need to take some time off," he said seriously.

"Easier said than done," I replied ruefully, "I don't know of anyone who would fill in for me. Besides that I really can't afford to employ anyone right now."

"What about Brad or Cain and..."

"So much has changed since I last saw you," I said solemnly, then took a deep breath, "I'm divorcing Les. Everything is a mess. I don't want to get into it right now."

We both went silent for a moment. Stanley moved in the chair and I hid the smile that tried to escape. Every time he moved his leather gear squeaked. I actually had to stifle the feeling to roar with laughter each time I heard him squeak.

'Poor Stanley,' I thought, 'you're trying to be cool, but you really are a nerd after all.'

When Stanley finally left, he sauntered over to his Honda parked out front, pulled on his helmet and gloves then straddled the bike with attitude, started the engine and drove away, faster than necessary. I sensed he knew I was watching him. Even with that motorbike he was still a nerd. The moment he was out of sight I roared with laughter. 'He makes me laugh,' I thought. 'It's been such a long time since I've done that. I guess poor old Stanley means well.'

Stanley, who was the same age as Les, represented everything I disliked in a man and his attitude about his wife disturbed me. But those concerns were lost in the midst of the tempest of my life and he seemed to be the only friendly face looking in my direction. Heavily burdened with the sadness of the destruction of my family and business, I reluctantly allowed him to become my friend.

The next time Stanley came to the shop he asked if Bree and I would like to join him and Sue when they visited mutual friends.

"Hmm, I'm not sure," I said. "Sounds good though, I'd love to see Ian and Gail but that's a three-hour drive. I... I don't know."

"Well anyway, think about it."

I only accepted the invitation because I felt the break would be good for Bree, as well as for me.

Celeste and Cain reluctantly covered for me in the shop that day. Precisely at 8.00am Stanley arrived at my place, just as he said he would. When I answered his knock at the door, he was grinning from ear to ear. My eyes widened in surprise as they travelled from his beard to his weather-beaten face and stopped at the top of his head. On top sat a mass of tiny curls. His hair was permed, not the whole head, only the top half. I bit hard on my lip to stop myself from laughing.

I tried desperately to ignore the perm, smiled sweetly and said, "Good morning." As an afterthought I said, "Oh, just a minute, Stanley, I forgot something," and hurried to my room. I ran into my dressing room, buried my face in the pillow I had snatched from the bed, and roared with laughter into it. Once I had gained my composure I joined Stanley outside. Bree was already in the car with Sue.

"Is everything alright? " Stanley asked, looking concerned.

"Hmm, everything is fine," I replied looking at the ground. I thought I would fall apart again if I looked at him.

Stanley opened the door for me. As I was about to climb in, I glanced into the back to say hello to Sue and was greeted with another shock, almost bumping my head. Sue had gone from a Pollyanna to a Gothic look. Her main form of communication was rolling eyes and lifting her eyebrows.

'Bloody hell,' I thought, wishing I hadn't said I'd go, 'What a day this is going to be - a nerd with a frizzed perm and a weird teenager in black.'

I found it torture not to laugh every time I looked at Stanley. The perm looked ridiculous on him but, by the way he was acting, he obviously thought he looked great. I noticed tattoos on his forearm and asked why he had them. He casually said, "Oh, I got them when I was in the navy."

"Really, when was that? I have a friend in the navy. I think he's still in the service. Where were you stationed?"

"Oh, I was in the navy reserve, we did weekend missions..."

I glanced sideways at Stanley and shook my head without him noticing. It certainly was a very long day.

The children, with the exception of Bree, resented Stanley's intrusion. Most of my time was consumed with the business, which left very little time for them. Excursions to the ballet with Celeste and Bree had ceased. Fresh pasta, rich meat sauces, delicious meals and desserts had become things of the past. Laughter soon vanished from our home, which was once warm and comforting and filled with the familiar aroma of cakes and biscuits baking in the oven, welcoming the children home from school.

I imagined the house seemed cold and empty without me being there to greet them. I was the heartbeat of the family; only heaven knows how much I wanted to be there for them and how much I truly loved my role as their mother. Unfortunately, no one could turn back the hands of time. All I could see was disaster and the hatred and anger in the eyes of my children. I felt heartsick when I realised that opening the business had unintentionally destroyed their home life.

BJ was running wild, Brad was boozing and smoking pot and Cain was doing his best to destroy the business while Bree, once a good student, was struggling at school. Celeste had left home in a fit of rage, accusing me of not having time for her, when she found out I had given Sue a driving lesson one afternoon.

Stanley had bought Sue a car but it sat idle in the driveway. I asked her why she was not driving the car.

"I know my kids would have it out and about with or without a licence. Why don't you at least have a go?"

"Everyone is too busy to teach me. Dad's always away."

I felt sorry for her. She seemed lonely and still grieving the loss of her mother, which prompted me to say, "I'll give you a lesson," thinking that an hour would make no difference.

Celeste was livid when I was not at the shop the afternoon she called. When I returned I called Celeste at home and was greeted with, "I'm your daughter, she's not. You should have given that time to me. You don't have time for me because of that stupid business; you don't care about me…"

I was deeply hurt by Celeste's insinuations and snapped back, "That's not true. All your bloody life you've demanded my attention and I've given it to you, to all of you. What's wrong with you, Celeste? That poor girl has just lost her mother."

"That's got nothing to do with me. You're MY mother!"

"I've tried to give you everything you've wanted. What about the car I hired for your birthday? I couldn't get the Porsche, but you got an RX7 instead…"

No matter what I said in my defence, Celeste was beyond reasoning, saying she was leaving home. In frustration I barked, "Well if that's what you want to do then go ahead. I'm too tired to deal with your crap…"

Celeste moved into the home of one of her school friends. She was beautiful and academic but often stubborn and childish. She allowed her head to rule when compassion was needed and her emotions ruled when common sense was needed. During her misguided judgemental teenage era, she also unjustly accused me of showing favour to both Cain and Bree over her. I had a strong conscience where my children were concerned, and giving more to one than another would not have sat comfortably with me. My heart and spirit were deeply wounded by Celeste's accusations because I unashamedly loved all five equally.

Sadly, Celeste had forgotten that she was the answer to my prayers when she was born. I had treasured and taken great delight in her, showering her with love and attention, fussing over her in the same way I fussed over Bree when she was a baby. The difference between my daughters was that Bree responded and Celeste did not. Hour upon hour I had spent designing and sewing pretty dresses and other clothes that I thought Celeste would enjoy wearing, only to be told years later that I had forced her to wear them.

In earlier times, Celeste would come every morning before school, comb and ribbon in hand, asking me to fix her hair. I would brush and plait or curl her lovely long blonde locks into different styles that she liked.

"You'll have to learn to do your own hair soon, sweetie," I once told Celeste, brushing a rebel wave into place.

"I like you doing it for me, Mommy," she replied.

Recalling those times, I wondered with a faint heart if Celeste also felt I had dominated her about her hair. I hoped not because it was a very special memory for me.

A few days after Celeste had left home I went to speak to her and was confronted by the father of Celeste's friend. He called me a bad mother.

"What do you mean?" I was horrified. I had never set eyes on the man before and he was calling me a bad mother. "My daughter has been given so much, perhaps too much. She has beautiful clothes, a lovely home, and pocket money. She attended good schools, she has been on trips overseas and has been loved and supported in everything she has done. What else do you expect me to do?"

"Did you ever ask her if she wanted the things that you've given her? Did you ever think that she might not have wanted those things?"

His attitude was arrogant as well as ignorant, which stirred me to anger.

"Yes, I did ask her what she wanted, all the time. And no, I didn't know that she didn't want the things that were given to her. I didn't hear her complaining at the time. All I noticed was that she had her hand out, just like her brothers. What business is it of yours anyway?" I asked indignantly. "How dare you accuse me of something you know nothing about?"

He had the audacity to debate Celeste's past eighteen years with me and, in frustration, I told him before I left, "If Celeste chooses to live in this dump as opposed to her own lovely home, then so be it."

The conversation with the man showed me that Celeste had told her friends' parents a coloured version of the facts. I could only assume that she had developed an outlook that she honestly believed. My daughter was a very pretty teenager but she was overweight and refused to deal with it. Whenever she was due to go somewhere special she would expect me to work miracles.

"Make me look beautiful, Mom," she would plead. "I wish I wasn't fat," she would moan.

"Well, don't eat rubbish and you won't be," I would casually reply, without malice.

"Why don't I have your genes instead of Dad's?"

When Celeste made comments like that, I responded by telling her, "I'm slim because I don't eat rubbish. Taking care of your appearance is a daily process Celeste, not an instant fix."

Unfortunately, my remarks were seen as criticism and not advice. Celeste accused me of calling her fat. I purposely avoided the word 'fat' due to what I had experienced from my own mother while growing up. I was indeed very mindful of my daughter's feelings.

When Celeste departed I was left with the bookwork for the business on top of everything else. Stanley suggested that Sue could give me a hand serving in the shop on weekends. Although I did not feel that Sue had the personality to deal with the public, I agreed, but as I suspected she was not suited for the job.

Everywhere I looked, all I could see was erosion. Little by little things were falling apart. Stanley was trying to take control and becoming all too annoyingly helpful, which almost drove me to distraction. He was more a hindrance than a help. He often commented that he had always wanted his own business and would love the opportunity to help out in the shop, just to get the feel of it. 'That would really send Cain off,' I thought, 'He couldn't even tolerate you calling here, let alone working in the place as if it was your own.' I shuddered, trying to imagine the scene.

40

One morning I was making up a job list for the casual to do while I went to the bank. Luc had called, and the effort it took for him to talk, and the weakness in his voice, sent a panic chill through my body.

"Are you okay?" I asked.

"I'm fine, just a little tired," he replied.

"You don't sound fine to me," I said, and suddenly unleashed what I was feeling. "I'm worried about you. Do you realise that I've loved you for so many years, that it's impossible for me to love any other man? Oh, I've tried, I can tell you. But you've dominated my thoughts. I have even fantasised that you were really with me, allowing my mind to see you. Can you believe that? I don't know what it is, but you have this power over me that I can't control. Tell me Luc, have I wasted my life loving you? Do you care for me, too? Or did I just imagine that you love me?"

"You didn't imagine it, Doll. I do love you. I always did. It's been difficult for me, too. I never knew exactly where you were and I wasn't sure how you felt. If this means anything," he whispered, "I've driven up your street many times just in case you were there. I've even parked outside your parents' home wondering if you were inside."

"Were you happy with your life, Luc?"

There was a pause before he answered, "Yeah, I guess so, under the circumstances."

"I'm glad to hear that, at least one of us was." There was a pause then I said, "Hey, listen to us." I laughed to stifle my tears. "Do you realise this is the first time we have actually said how we feel? That is so unlike you, Luc."

"Yeah, well, now we both know."

"It only took a lifetime to find out, and I regret so much of my life."

"No, don't," he pleaded with me. "Please don't. It's too late for us, and it's too late for regrets."

His goodbye was upsetting. His words 'It's too late' echoed in my head and I wondered how much time he actually had left. The thought had me in tears.

I left immediately the casual arrived, forgetting to give her instructions for that morning. All I wanted was to get away from everything and everyone. I had lost hope and ceased to care what happened to the shop. Tears engulfed me in the solitude of my car, despair of the inevitable weighing heavily upon my heart; I felt I was losing everything I loved and wanted. I wanted to go to sleep, never to wake up again, so I would not have to watch everything slowly dissolve before my eyes.

Instead of going to the bank, I went to the place that no longer gave me any consolation, because there was nowhere else to go – the house I had fought so hard to get for my family, a family I no longer have.

"What did I fight for?" I asked the emptiness, and then yelled into the vacuum of silence. "Nothing!" I have failed miserably at everything."

I felt I had wasted everyone's life by choosing to stay with Les, endeavouring to hold my family together. With the premonition of more trouble ahead I yelled, "I've had enough!"

Holding the pills in my hand gave me a sense of peace. I sincerely believed what I was about to do was for the good of everyone, especially for Cain. I had hurt him deeply and, although I was profoundly sorry, he would not forgive me.

In a letter expressing my regrets I gave Cain my life insurance policy and the business. He had earned it by working so hard beside me before I hurt him with the truth...

Mary was sitting by my hospital bed when I woke up.

"Oh good, you're finally awake," she sighed with relief when I opened my eyes. "You've been out of it for a few days."

I was disorientated and disappointed that I was still alive, as I had expected to sleep forever. I turned towards my sister when she spoke, surprised to see her.

"What are you doing here?"

"Don't you remember? You phoned asking me not to let Les take Bree. You sounded so strange, Emma. I was worried, so I decided to come up to Brisbane. Cain found you..."

I tried to focus on what Mary was saying but everything seemed hazy, like a nightmare. I could not remember calling her, but was very pleased to see her.

"How are you feeling?" Mary asked, concerned.

"Fine," I lied. My throat and stomach hurt. When I realised I would have to face everyone, I wished that I had not woken up at all. My strongest desire was to hide because of the shame I felt. Taking the pills had been on my mind for some time. Will I or won't I? I had asked myself that question so many times during the low stages of my life, but on the day I actually took them, I had acted more on impulse.

"Stanley wants to see you. He is very worried about you, Emma," Mary was saying. "Celeste phoned him at the conference in South Australia and he left immediately to come and see you."

"Oh no! Mary," I felt panic, "I don't want to see him now or ever. I don't think I could handle being with him any longer. Will you tell him I don't want to see him anymore?"

"The children want to come in tonight too," Mary said, changing the subject.

As much as I wanted to see the children, I did not want them to come to the hospital. I felt horribly humiliated. I disguised my discomfort behind smiles and dark humour and agreed to see them.

Later that day Celeste arrived with a school friend. The last time I had seen my daughter she was yelling at me, calling me a lousy mother. I observed Celeste closely from my hospital bed as we laughed and joked as naturally as we had done in the past, and thought how ironic life is.

Carla, Celeste's friend, told me she had brought her violin to play a tune to cheer me up. Quite innocently she said, as she prepared to play, "This is what I would've played at your funeral."

Her comment shocked me into really laughing for the first time in ages, and I actually felt better for it. The laughter faded to silence and Carla began a beautiful melody. The passion and skill with which she played was pleasantly surprising. I had no idea she was so talented. A number of people gathered around the doorway and burst into loud applause when she finished.

As Carla was leaving she promised to reserve the tune for me. "For a much later date," she said smiling.

"You're on," I called out as she disappeared around the corner.

Mary came back in the evening with Bree, BJ and Cain. The sight of Cain standing in the doorway stirred unfathomable shame in me. He stood in the background until I had greeted the others.

Bree's little face wore a look of concern. "Why are you here, Mommy?" she whispered as I hugged her tight. "Are you alright?"

"I'm fine baby, don't worry, I'll be home real soon."

Bree moved aside for BJ to come closer. "Hi Ma," he said, hugging me and then stepped back.

Cain edged his way forward, then suddenly reached out and hugged me tight.

"You left me," he said choking back tears.

"I'm so sorry, Cain." My remorse and emotion was profound. "I thought I was doing you a favour. I thought it was the best for everyone. I love you so much," I told him, wiping away tears. "I just couldn't stand all the trouble between us any longer. I left you the business," I offered as recompense sounding very child-like.

"I don't want it. You left me," he stated, firmly containing his emotion.

"I won't ever again." My promise was sincere.

Bree looked on, bewildered, with no idea of just how close her life had come to being drastically changed.

"Are you sick, Mommy?"

"No, baby, I'm fine."

My voice was light-hearted but my heart was heavy with dread. I knew I was not fine, and I certainly did not want to return home. The confines of the hospital walls shielded me from the outside world; they had become my safe place, a place I did not want to leave, especially since I did not have the courage to face the future.

Over the years Les had persistently accused me of being out of my mind. But although I rejected his taunts, in my brokenness I knew my actions gave credence to his statement. The deterioration of my spirit deprived me of the courage I once possessed. I had become a stranger to myself, ever fearful, without knowing exactly what it was that I feared. My senses, however, were alert enough to be terrified of returning to what I had run from.

The business was destroying me and I knew I did not have the emotional or physical strength to fight for it any longer. I had to find the courage to say so, even though the financial loss would be great. I knew Les would gloat over the fact that I had failed, but I had to close it.

The sanctuary of the hospital gave me time to come to terms with what I had to do without outside interference. A social worker made it easy for me to admit that it was okay if situations in my life were beyond my control. I did not have to be perfect. Once I had said, 'I'm going to let the business go,' a surge of relief came over me and made walking away from it much easier than I ever expected.

Stanley would not take no for an answer, insisting on coming to the hospital to drive me home. I was silently annoyed with him for not respecting my wishes, especially since I had told him that Mary and Tim were there and would drive me home.

Tim left his busy law practice in Sydney and came to Brisbane a few days after Mary. He had advised me regarding the legal ramifications of closing the shop. While we sat in the foyer of the hospital talking about what I should do, Mary went to get us coffee. Tim was talking and a thought flashed into my mind. I was recalling the phone call Les made to me after speaking to my solicitor. "Don't think you're getting the business," he snarled. "I'll make damn sure that you get nothing." I told Tim what Les had said and he shook his head.

"It's ironic," I said, "and now I'm heading for bankruptcy. He wanted me to fail and I have."

When Stanley arrived, I introduced him to Mary and Tim. They got acquainted while the social worker spoke to me.

"Here is the name of a psychiatrist," she said handing me a card. "I strongly recommend that you see him, Emma."

I took it and gave her a puzzled look.

"Oh, I'm not suggesting that there's anything mentally wrong with you, Emma," she hurried to say. "I believe Doctor Anderson can help you sort out whatever it is that's causing you concern."

"Thanks." Smiling, I slipped the card into the pocket of my jeans. "I'll think about it," I said, then joined the others.

"Right," Tim said, "got everything?" I nodded and we headed home.

The phone rang shortly after we arrived. It was Les. He had called to express his concern, assuring me not to worry about the shop. "Your health is far more important to me,

Bubby." The tone in his voice frightened and puzzled me because he spoke as though we were on good terms. My fear was heightened when he repeatedly told me that he was going to take care of everything. I began to panic. He also informed me that he was returning to Brisbane to discuss things with me. "Everything will be fine," he cooed and he told me that he loved me very much.

When I hung up Mary asked if anything was wrong.

"Les is coming home. He wants to talk to me," I said. "I don't want to talk to him."

The time had come for Mary to return to Sydney. Tim had already gone back. She had offered to stay longer, but I reassured her I would be okay. I really wanted her to stay but knew my sister had her own life and family to attend to.

Mary's concern for me came as a surprise. I really thought my family did not care about me at all. The crisis showed me that I was wrong. It had actually bonded us as real sisters as well as good friends.

The shop was officially closed and I avoided any further discussion of it. I remained in the house, hidden and out of sight of prying eyes, aware that many people had heard news of the incident.

The house felt strange as I wandered aimlessly through it, looking in each room, so many of them, all large and empty of the laughter that was once there. The house felt less like a home the longer I stayed there. I felt alone and vulnerable.

Les called every day, sometimes three or four times, confirming his promise to take care of everything, as well as me. He also led the children to believe that we had reconciled. I had a sense of dread when I heard it from Cain and insisted that we had not. It was beyond my understanding why my children could not see or understand my fear of Les.

In some ways it was fortunate for me that Stanley refused to go away. His response to my message that I did not want to see him anymore was that it was he who wanted me in his life. He insisted I see him, Heaven only knows why, as I had given him every reason to abandon me.

My relationship with my children appeared to be on the mend after I returned home from the hospital but a phone call from Les, telling me he was coming home that night, set another series of events into motion.

"I can't wait to see you again, Bubby. You won't have to worry about anything," he repeated for the umpteenth time. Each time he said it a chill ran up my spine.

"I'm okay, Les. You don't have to come to Brisbane. I'm fine, really," I endeavoured to assure him, but he ignored me.

"I want to," he said, growing impatient. "I'll be home later tonight. I want to talk to you." There was authority in his tone.

I was fearful at the possibility of Les touching me. No, I just couldn't stand that, 'I have to get away. I have to.' My mind was in turmoil.

I was trembling when I telephoned Stanley. Impatiently I tapped the handset while it rang several times. I sighed with relief at the sound of his voice and quickly told him what Les had said and of my fears for my safety.

"I really don't know what I should do, Stanley."

"I'll come and get you," he said.

"Don't go out, Mom, wait until Dad gets here. Please don't go," Cain said after I told him Stanley was coming over to pick me up.

"I'll be at Stanley's house. I have to get away, Cain. I don't want to be here when he arrives."

"Stay, Mom! Stay home." His pleas sounded more like a command. "Dad will get angry if you're not home."

"No, Cain. I have to go."

"Mom, don't go!" I heard him call out, as I closed the door behind me.

The whole scenario was confusing. I was frightened and unsure of what to do, but I knew I should not be there when Les arrived.

Stanley waited patiently for me in his car parked out the front of the house. He leant across and opened the door the instant he saw me approaching. I slid in beside him and we drove down the street in silence. The radio was on and John Farnham was belting out one of his latest hits. We spoke after the song finished.

During that brief silence, I thought how much I enjoyed hearing those songs. I had never been an avid fan of anyone's music with the exception of Elvis. However, John Farnham's music was poignant to me, especially the ballad, 'A Touch of Paradise.' I love that song. It was often playing over the radio at the times Luc called. I associated John Farnham's music with Luc, but Stanley thought I loved the tune because it was on the car radio the times we were together.

Stanley had driven the car only a short distance down the street when he stopped, parked on the shoulder of the road and proposed to me. I clearly surprised him with my speedy 'No' and he unsuccessfully concealed his disappointment at the rejection. I did not want to marry him or anyone for that matter. I was not yet divorced from Les. Marriage was the furthest thing from my mind. All I wanted at that moment was to be divorced, not married.

Exhausted and troubled, I sat in silence at the orange-top breakfast bar in Stanley's out-dated kitchen, while he made coffee for both of us. I observed him closely as he took the mugs from the pine veneer cupboard, wondering what I was doing there with him. His appearance had never really appealed to me. I disliked his beard but did not feel that I had the right to say so. How did all this happen? Did I panic? How stupid of me, running away like that. Was I wrong in doing that? My thoughts were shapeless. I was rummaging through them in an effort to make sense of everything, and ended up thinking about the few weeks prior to my suicide attempt. I was at a point of seriously questioning my association with Stanley, endeavouring to qualify why he was in my life at all.

Although Stanley had shown more than a casual interest in me, I had to admit I was not interested in him beyond a brief encounter. His attention did at least distract me from the horror of my life. He had entered my messy world uninvited, offering a helping hand at every turn. He even implied that my life was exciting. At times he was helpful, at others I found him controlling and stifling. On occasions we would sit for long hours discussing what we wanted out of life. In hindsight, I realised it was I who did all the talking and Stanley simply agreed with whatever I said. I was full of optimism and hope while sharing with him my dreams of a peaceful future. I was horrified to learn that at forty-five years of age he did not know what he wanted out of life. He confessed that he had been drifting along in life when he discovered me.

I knew my life goals, I just did not know how to go about achieving them. In Stanley's company I felt free to speak my heart's desire and he was a willing listener. No one else seemed to care what I felt or thought, and Stanley hanging onto my every word flattered my ego.

Stanley's job entailed a great deal of travelling. During one of his trips away I wrote him a letter asking what his intentions were regarding our relationship. In retrospect the letter was motivated by the need to find something positive within the chaos of my life, more than anything else.

I was jolted back to the present when Stanley placed a steaming cup of coffee in front of me but before I had time to drink it, the phone rang.

"Mom, come home quickly. Dad's here and he wants to see you." Cain sounded anxious so we left immediately.

On the way, a chilling feeling came over me. I envisaged Les hiding down the backyard with something in his hand, in readiness to strike at us the moment we arrived. I cautioned Stanley not to park the car at the back entrance. "Go round to the front gate," I instructed him.

"Why?" he questioned. "Les will be waiting there for you."

"No, he is waiting out the back."

"How do you know that?" he asked puzzled and ready to argue.

"A feeling I have, that's all. Please go to the front gate. I'll go in that way, it's safer." I was adamant.

Stanley let me out at the front gate, telling me to call him at his place if I needed him.

The moment I set foot in the house I was greeted with hostility from my children. They accused me of upsetting their father. When told I was not home, Les in a rage had destroyed the set of golf clubs Stanley had loaned to Cain. He was waiting at the back entrance, ready to strike me with the club, the same object I had envisaged him holding. He was infuriated at missing the chance to beat Stanley to a pulp.

When I came face to face with Les, he looked like a crazed man. I knew that look only too well and also knew that if I stayed in that house I would experience another beating, possibly one I would not survive. We argued and he demanded to know where Stanley was.

"Gone," I said, thoroughly shaken at the sight of him.

"Stay here," he bellowed, "I'll deal with you later."

Les left the house, threatening to kill Stanley when he found him. The moment his vehicle was out of sight I quickly phoned Stanley to warn him, and then frantically gathered together a few of Bree's and my belongings.

The children were yelling at me not to go but I ignored their pleas, knowing full well that if I stayed, Les might seriously harm or even kill me this time. They did not understand what he was really capable of but I did, and I was afraid for my life.

Les drove around the town looking for Stanley while I escaped unharmed with Bree. Stanley had gallantly come to my rescue again and the three of us went to a motel for a few days, not daring to go to his home until we were sure it was safe and Les had left the state.

41

The weeks that followed were a nightmare. Creditors came out of the woodwork, every piece of correspondence was a notice from a debt collector, and Les set about assassinating my character in every way possible.

On top of all that was going on around me, Christmas suddenly arrived. Stanley wanted to spend it in Sydney with my family, determined to meet them. Even though he knew I did not want to go, he made the arrangements anyway. Just the thought of having to face my mother's criticism drained me, but the possibility of seeing Luc again charged my spirits.

That Christmas was a tragically heartbreaking experience and was to be the first of many without all of my children. I missed them terribly, even though they had turned against me and collaborated with Les. No matter what they had done, they were still my children and I loved them. I had never measured my love for them by their behaviour. From the day they bellowed their entrance into this world, my life revolved around them. They were part of me. Separation from them could be compared to an amputation of my limbs, the adjustment to functioning without them as difficult as it would be for an amputee. Sometimes I imagined them still with me and planned meals for a family that was not coming home. The realisation of that stabbed at my heart time and time again.

Stanley did not understand the grieving for my lost children. He had admitted to me that he had not experienced a close bond with either his son or his daughter or even his late wife. He confessed he had not really wanted children and had given in to having them under pressure from his wife. I knew at that moment that Stanley and I were strangers thrown together due to adverse circumstances. I was astounded at his lack of empathy and he was amazed at the depth of my emotion.

This short man with the weather-beaten face was of the opinion that I should not be upset about anything. He had my situation neatly worked out. Once divorced from Les, he reasoned, I would receive half of the spoils, and he and I would live in comfort. But I knew differently. Les would do everything in his power to make sure I received nothing, not even the affection of my children. That rationale was difficult for Stanley to accept. He wanted me to fight for my share, which became a bone of contention between us and placed me under more pressure. My inner spirit was battered and emotionally scarred. My wounds were desperately trying to heal, but they could not under the constant antagonism. My exterior was not much better. Nervous tension ate away the kilograms and rendered me physically weak, with barely enough emotional strength to survive from day to day.

This man, who initially had claimed to be my friend and to understand me, really did not know me at all. How could he? His outlook on life was one dimensional, with no room for any grey areas.

The drive down to Sydney was uneventful. When we arrived the whole family was there. They greeted us as though nothing had happened, with no mention of recent events or criticism of me from my mother.

Getting away from the turmoil had shown me how much I needed a change of scenery and seeing Bree enjoying her time with her cousins allowed me to relax. I was secretly grateful that Stanley had insisted we make the trip, but he was not prepared for Mary and Tim's laid-back approach to the holidays. His energetic enthusiasm for early rising and going to great lengths to please, washing their cars and mowing the lawn in an effort to be accepted, had Mary and Tim raising their eyebrows. During the year they put in very long hours at the office and when the holidays arrived, they took a break from everything. If and when they wanted to go somewhere, it happened when they got around to it. Mary and Tim graciously grinned and tolerated Stanley. Somehow, despite the differences in personalities, we all had a great Christmas.

Stanley knew about Luc and how I felt about him. He did not object when I called him before we returned to Brisbane. I wanted to see him.

"I don't want you to see me like this," Luc said, explaining he did not look the same as I remembered him. While I was trying to reassure him that I did not care how he looked, I caught a glimpse of my own reflection in one of the glass doors separating the lounge room from the hallway, and noticed that I too did not look as he remembered me. Our insecurities outweighed our desire to see each other, both of us pretending to be in better spirits than we really were, Luc trying to sound in good health and I trying to sound happy. The familiarity of our voices gave us comfort, visualising each other the way we used to be, rather than the way we were. I promised to call him when I got back to Brisbane, but the process of arming myself against Les in court absorbed most of my energy and prevented me from calling him immediately. Luc would surely have felt my stress, I reasoned, and delayed the call until after the hearing.

The day I finally called Luc's office number another man answered.

"Haven't you heard?" he said when I asked to speak to him.

"Heard what?" I cautiously asked, dreading what I would hear.

"Luc passed away a week ago," he said, deeply apologetic.

The shock of his words hit me like a sledgehammer as I fought against the reality of that statement. Vibrations from my pitiful scream sent a crushing pain through my heart and my soul. I crumbled to the floor sobbing; wishing life's breath would leave me.

"My Luc has died. My Luc is gone," I repeated over and over again in utter disbelief. Nothing made sense. I did not know how to accept it.

The helplessness, emptiness and grief I felt was unimaginable, as my heartbreaking sobbing became unyielding in the regret of not calling sooner. I lay where I had fallen, too weary to care that I had been there the whole day.

Stanley came home and found me in a terrible state and asked what was wrong. My grief turned to anger as I looked at him and said, "Les should have died, not Luc. He was a good man, Les wasn't."

I was incoherently ranting, angry that everything around me was functioning as though nothing had happened. 'The tarot card reader was prophetic,' I mumbled. 'She told me Les would die around his forty-seventh year. It was not Les she was talking about, it was Luc. He died a few days before his forty-seventh birthday.'

Stanley tried in vain to comfort me, becoming frustrated and angry when I did not respond. He could not understand why I did not want to be touched or comforted, or why I wanted to be left alone to wallow in my grief. "I don't want to feel better or happy, don't you understand? Luc is dead..."

When Stanley told me that he knew how I felt, because he had lost his wife. I turned and glared at him. "Oh no, Stanley," my voice was harsh; "you don't know how I feel! You told me that you never loved your wife. You told me that you didn't even shed a tear for her when she passed away. You told me you felt only relief to be free. No Stanley, you of all people could never understand how I feel." He apologised and withdrew from me.

Resentment at having to keep living when I did not want to consumed my spirit. The responsibility of Bree felt so burdensome, but in my heart I knew God had sent her to me and somehow I had to take good care of her. In Les' care Bree would be tainted and spoiled. I was determined that he was not going to have an opportunity to spread his evil upon my child.

The sadness I felt was relentless. Getting out of bed day after day, pretending everything was fine, was such a struggle. A week after hearing about Luc's death, a most unusual and very extraordinary thing happened.

Friends had invited me to join them for lunch. I really did not want to go anywhere but they had insisted I come. I was in the shower, in the middle of rinsing the conditioner out of my hair, when the irrepressible sobbing began again. I was still crying as I turned off the taps, wrapping myself in a towel and then another around my head. The grief had me close to breaking point, but suddenly my tears ceased and my features broke into a smile. I leant forward and wiped the steam away to look into the mirror at my smiling reflection. I had the feeling that Luc was standing behind me and quickly turned around, fully expecting to see him. The feeling was so strong that the experience became my survival. I relived it many times over to erase my pain.

Having to deal with Les' solicitors and Paul Barry over the divorce, the custody of Bree, the property settlement and emotional pain of losing Luc rendered me sensitive and volatile. When Les came to collect Bree for his weekend access, he gave me his condolences saying, "I know how you felt about him..."

After all Les had done to keep us apart, the audacity of mentioning Luc's death to me, made me explode, incensed and deeply offended by his words. "It should have been you who died, not Luc. I hate you! It should have been you," I hissed at him. He quickly grabbed Bree by her hand and left.

Distraught and furious, I stood at the window and watched him drive away with my confused little daughter. Bree's first seven years were almost perfect. She was doted on and adored, everything around her seemed to be on solid ground, and then suddenly her whole world disintegrated.

I reacted badly to the thought of my daughter having a good relationship with Les during her first year of access visits with him. I had too high an expectation of my seven-year-old, not realising Bree did not have the foresight to know the expensive gifts Les gave her were to buy her affection.

When Bree visited Les during that time, he allowed her to do and eat almost anything she wanted, undermining every principle I had taught her. Bree would return home many kilograms overweight, infuriating me. She was full of stories about her time away and was eager to share them with me but the sight of her weight gain spoiled the moment. Try as I did, I could not listen, all I saw were the extra pounds. Thoughtlessly I would interrupt Bree, asking her what she ate while she was away.

"Oh I don't know," she shrugged.

"What do you mean, you don't know?" I'd snap. "I asked you not to eat junk food. Ask him for nourishing food, so you won't end up overweight, your clothes are too tight."

Bree ended up in her room in tears. I had successfully spoiled her holiday. After a moment of satisfaction I succumbed to guilt and then went to her and apologised. Peace would be restored once again, until the next time.

The same scenario was played out numerous times during the first year of shared access, causing a great deal of stress for both of us. I agonised over the thought of Les leaving the country with my child as he had threatened to do. Every time Bree went away I wondered if I would ever see her again. My life became a nightmare the moment she was out of my sight.

Les and his family refused me any contact with Bree whenever she was in their care during school holidays. Bree was oblivious to what was going on around her. She did not know Les and his family told me that she said she did not want to talk to me. When I asked her if that was true, she broke into tears, saying she did not know that I had called.

"I missed you a lot, Mommy," she said. "Everyone says nasty things about you. I know you're not like what they say you are."

Bree's reaction showed me just how much my hatred of Les was affecting her. I sat down with her and we talked about it. I explained that I had my reasons for disliking Les and one day she would understand, and added that her relationship with him had nothing to do with me. "I want you to enjoy your time with him without you worrying about me being unhappy about it."

It was amazing just how much pressure seemed to have lifted from her after that conversation. I felt secure in the knowledge that she would one day see Les for the person he really was and would make up her own mind about him.

A deep friendship and trust developed between us. I encouraged Bree to trust her instincts whenever in doubt about people or situations. As our bond strengthened, so did our respect for each other. Bree came home from her visits with many questions. When she asked about Cain, I explained everything to her in detail, choosing my words carefully when I spoke of my love for Luc. I was delightfully amazed at the compassion she expressed. "I wish I could have met him, Mom. He sounds like a really nice man. Cain is very lucky."

I looked at Bree and felt absolutely blessed. This child had given me so much comfort and strength. And to think I had almost destroyed it in a moment of despair!

42

Fighting for sole custody of Bree and trying to deal with Luc's death was unimaginably horrible. I could not get the words 'Luc passed away a few days ago,' out of my head. I wanted to ring Luc's office again, in hope that he would answer the phone instead of the man who had uttered those words. I felt as though I was on the brink of another breakdown, but knew I had to pull myself together and look my best for the meeting with my solicitor at the Family Law Court.

The off-white linen dress I took from my wardrobe was plain. I particularly liked its straight line because it made me look taller when I wore high heels. I went fossicking through drawers and found my Italian plum paisley scarf and matching clutch purse. I draped the scarf over one shoulder, clipped on bronze earrings and slipped on a matching bangle. After glancing in the mirror for a final check of my make-up and hair, I picked up my purse from the bed, my wallet and keys from the dresser and left. On my way into the city, I wondered if Les' claims that I had lost my mind had reached Paul Barry.

My solicitor was waiting for me at the coffee shop beside the law courts. I was puzzled why he had not acknowledged me, as I approached him.

"Good morning, Paul," I smiled.

"Good God!" he exclaimed. "I didn't recognise you. You look wonderful!"

"It's amazing what make-up and a nice outfit can do," I said, laughing.

He was smiling when he pulled out a chair for me. "Would you like a coffee? We have a few things to go over before we go inside."

The meeting with Les' solicitors was scheduled for ten o'clock. Although I could not be in the conference room, I would be waiting in the foyer for the outcome. Why Paul had asked me to meet him had me puzzled, as we could have covered everything we discussed over the phone. I could only assume he had heard from the opposition that I was a mental case and wanted to see for himself.

Time ticked away as people went in and out of the conference room. After what seemed like hours, Paul left the room too. He came and sat opposite me in the foyer. I was astonished to hear him say, "Your husband's solicitor, Marilyn Barker, was surprised that you are so attractive."

"I can imagine the ugly tales he has told her," I replied. "It's a reaction I often get when people meet me for the first time. Les must tell people he married a monster or something worse."

As the weeks passed, I was forever at the Family Law Court for one thing or another. So was Les, along with Brad and Cain. He remained in the background, silently mocking me and subtly manipulating my sons into battle as his storm troopers. Metaphorically speaking, he gave them the bullets and they fired them, but I did not fail to notice that they both enjoyed their tour of duty. Whenever I tried to make peace with either of them, or had to have contact with either or both of them, their hostility and barrage of insults and obscene language prevented me from saying anything. I was defenceless against the lies Les had told them. Neither Brad nor Cain would listen, nor would they allow me any explanation of the allegations Les made about me. Sadly, any association with my sons ended up with me in tears. They laughed and taunted me when I walked away devastated by their behaviour. Les would not simply give me a divorce and allow everyone to move on. He had declared war and vowed to destroy my allies and me.

I felt everyone around me was an enemy and trust was just a word. The very people I once trusted and loved became my enemies almost overnight. Even Paul Barry misinterpreted my frustration and disappointment over my sons' behaviour and began to believe that I was unstable. The more I tried to explain my bitterness, the less rational I appeared to him and the bond of trust between us was irrevocably broken. He too had become an adversary.

It seemed that when dealing with legal representatives, emotion was not tolerated or understood. My every word and actions came under close scrutiny from court officials. Les revelled in my frustration and used every opportunity to show my sons that I was indeed out of my mind. I reacted angrily to the lies he so convincingly told the court and was deeply hurt by the way he used my sons as his puppets, pulling the strings as they danced to his every tune.

The situation was sickening. My mind was in turmoil at the deceit I saw and heard. Feeling the effects of the treachery, I began to retreat within myself, and was closed off to everyone, with the exception of Bree.

Paul Barry, my solicitor, continued to treat me as though I was an idiot, which ultimately led me to sack him. He refused to listen to what I wanted and set about doing things his way without my consent, telling me that he was acting in my best interest, and running up an enormous bill in the process. On the day I had to meet him at the Family Law Court to discuss the custody hearing date, he was infuriated to discover that Stanley and I had married on the previous weekend without consulting him. I wore a bandage around my hand to conceal the wedding ring.

The marriage was revealed when a court counsellor, and also Paul Barry, commented about my bandaged hand, implying I had made another attempt on my life. Furious at the insinuation, I removed the bandage and showed them an engagement and wedding ring, saying, "I concealed the rings because I didn't want anyone to know that I had married, especially not my ex-husband. I wasn't ready to make any announcements."

Paul Barry was furious with me. He openly suggested to members of the court, and Les' lawyers present, that I was unstable, "I didn't know anything about this," he stammered, "she failed to notify me or take my advice about anything."

I responded by stating firmly, looking at everyone in the room, "Whom I marry, when and where I marry is my business...mine only."

When we were alone I turned to Paul Barry and said, "You're an idiot and a fool, among other things, to think that you can treat me the way you have and expect to get away with it. I came to you wanting only a divorce, nothing else. But you took it upon yourself to act contrary to my wishes and started a war. You caused all this trouble, you dickhead. Les thinks that I want his money, thanks to you."

He was clearly horrified at the way I spoke to him.

"No-one has ever spoken to me in such a manner," he said almost in tears.

"Well," I mocked him with hands firmly on my hips, "there's always a first time for everything, even for scumbags like you."

A few days later, an enormous account for a few weeks' work, and a letter arrived in the mail. The letter informed me that Paul Barry would no longer be representing me. The sight of the offensive correspondence stirred me to anger and ignited the fire in my belly.

"This account is way out of proportion," I protested over the phone. By the time I had finished yelling down the mouthpiece that I had already fired him for his incompetence, his suspicion that I was not of sound mind was totally confirmed. "You ran up this account making phone calls and writing letters without my instructions. I'm not going to pay for your stuff ups!" I shouted.

"I'll take you to court," he said firmly, but I only laughed sarcastically saying, "You'll have to get in line," before slamming the receiver down in his ear.

I felt alive for the first time in ages and was ready to take control of my life again. I had no idea what I was going to do about getting a legal representative to handle the custody hearing scheduled in a few days. Legal aid was out of the question because I was married. I was informed that I was my husband's responsibility. There was no way I would allow Stanley to spend one cent on my legal fees, this was my fight, not his. I chose to represent myself.

Stanley prepared the documents and the Family Law Court processed them. I represented myself on the grounds that I could not afford legal counsel. My decision to do that slowed down the proceedings and frustrated everyone, especially Les. He bitterly resented his lawyers having to brief me on procedures that he was not privy to prior to going into the courtroom. Having to stand aside out of hearing range while we huddled together annoyed him. The longer he had to wait, the more infuriated he became.

I was familiar with Les' habits, especially when he was annoyed. My attention was distracted from what the solicitor was saying by the sound of Les' familiar dry cough coming at intervals. I craned my neck a little to glance at him over the shoulder of the man instructing me and saw Les nervously playing with his car keys, looking tense and glaring at us. He fidgeted with the keys for a moment before using them to scratch his ear. His movements seemed involuntary as he contemplated his next move. I took enormous delight in his displeasure at being left out. To him, it looked as if I was gaining the upper hand. He certainly would not like that one little bit, I thought, grinning and feeling smug. My suspicions were confirmed as I watched his large bulky frame sway across the room and stop where we were huddled together. He interrupted the meeting with his usual gruff manner and dry cough, indignantly asking his legal representatives. "Who are you people working for, me or her?"

In the courtroom everyone took their places. The opposition sat to the left of me, a team of four plus Les. Looking at them I wondered how much Les actually paid for that small army. Cain and Brad were at the back of the courtroom. Stanley sat away from them.

The few moments after the court came to order were like a nightmare. The judge seemed to briefly and carelessly glance at my deposition. Then, just as offhandedly, he gave his ruling that Les and I would have joint custody of Bree.

"No! No! You can't do that," I called out.

"Shhh," came from my left. "Don't say anything. Just listen."

The judge ignored me and kept talking. "Many people spend their lives searching for their families, it is important for Bree to know her father..."

"No! No! You don't understand. How can you give him joint custody of MY daughter? Read the papers. Can't you see he's unfit?"

I was ordered to be quiet, but ignored the order and shouted at the judge that he did not know what he was doing, before running out of the courtroom. Stanley sprung from his chair and ran after me. When he caught up, he tried to embrace me, saying, "It will be all right, darling."

"Leave me. Don't touch me. It won't be all right. Bree is MY daughter. Les is trying to take her from me," I shouted, pulling away from him. "I want to be alone."

But Stanley would not leave me, he kept trying to hug me and I kept pushing him away. He was suffocating me when I wanted to think, but he would not let go as he led me to the car.

On the way home my mind spun like a top. I was devastated by the judge's decision and utterly helpless, as if sinking in quicksand.

'Bree is my child and there's no way to stop that bastard from taking her from me. He already has Cain, now he's taking Bree as well.' My thoughts were foggy. What could I do? Maybe everyone is right about my state of mind. All this was driving me crazy, going to and from the Family Law Court, and having to endure that creep grinning and mocking me every time he saw me.

The pressure pushed me further and further toward my limits. I went in search of a handgun, with the intention of shooting Les. 'That bastard,' I told myself, 'has done so much damage. I hate him to the depths of my soul for using my sons the way he has. He doesn't care about them; he's trying to get back at me. Now he's taking Bree away from me too. The scales of justice are unbalanced,' I thought, feeling frustrated. 'This awful creature has fooled everyone and succeeded at every turn. It isn't as though he's a good person.' I convinced myself that he deserves to die.

Searching numerous sporting goods stores looking for a weapon was exhausting. Handgun regulations prevented me from getting a gun that day. I had to apply for a licence before I could purchase one, which took time. I wanted a gun right away, not in a few weeks' time. I returned home empty-handed and told no one where I had been.

Shortly after that incident, Bree and I were sitting together in the kitchen talking about things in general while I made dinner, when she innocently said, "You know, Mom, I don't know what I'd do if anything happened to you, because you are the only person I want to live with. I worry about that a lot."

"Do you, Babe?" I asked surprised.

"Yep, a lot." Taking a deep breath Bree went on to say, "When I visit Dad, I wonder if I'll ever see you again. I even get scared that you won't be here when I come back home."

I had no idea until that day that my little daughter held such profound feelings and fears. Her comment was the lifeline I needed to justify my own existence.

"Well Babe, you don't ever have to worry about that, because I'll always be here to take care of you."

I reasoned that my love for Bree was far greater than my hatred for Les, and suddenly the need to want him dead vanished. I gasped with horror at the thought of what could have happened to Bree if I had actually shot and killed Les.

43

I finally got around to making an appointment to see the psychiatrist, a condition of my release from hospital. Refusing would have meant a report lodged with the police and a possible conviction. "It's against the law to try and kill yourself, Emma," Carolyn Parker, the social worker, had said.

I felt as if I was on a rollercoaster, living with Stanley. I was in the middle of the custody battle and I was still expected to visit a psychiatrist and appear normal. I would not have gone but knew I had to. My biggest fear was that the doctor would discover I was mentally unstable. It actually scared me just thinking about it.

"There it is, Stanley," I said pointing at the house, "number eighty six. See, there's Dr Anderson's sign on the gate."

Stanley pulled the car over to the curb and I quickly got out and closed the door. Stooping to peer through the window, I said, "See you in about an hour, honey."

"Sure you don't want me to come in with you?"

"I'll be fine. You go and do what you have to do and I'll see you later."

"Well okay," he said, sounding like a little boy who was not invited to the birthday party.

As I was about to make my way towards the gate, I turned just in time to see Stanley drive away slowly. I grinned, shaking my head, knowing he was probably watching me through the rear mirror in hope that I would call him back, and ask him to come inside with me.

'Poor old bugger, he hates to be left out of things.'

I inhaled deeply then slowly exhaled and walked through the gate.

"Good morning," I said, trying to sound cheerful, when I arrived at reception, "I have an appointment with Dr Anderson."

The receptionist smiled and asked me my name. When she had found it in the appointment book, she pointed to an empty chair, "You can wait over there. Dr Anderson won't be too long."

I looked over my shoulder and headed for a vacant chair beside a table piled up with magazines, picked up a magazine and sat down. While flipping through the magazine, I discreetly scanned the room, looking at the other patients and wondering what was wrong with them. Before I could give them a second thought, a tall thin man in an expensive suit called my name.

"Hello, Emma," he smiled, offering his hand and directing me into his unimpressive office. "I'm Dr Anderson. How are you? Carolyn Parker briefed me about your case."

"I'm fine," I replied, sitting on the couch opposite him, "but I feel embarrassed about what I did, or I should say, tried to do."

"Why do you feel embarrassed, Emma?" the doctor asked, leaning back in his large leather chair.

"Because it's another failure I have to live with. My whole life has been one failure after another."

"Tell me about your childhood, Emma."

I looked at him and laughed. "So psychiatrists really ask questions like, tell me about your childhood?"

He smiled, "Yes, Emma, I guess we do."

"Well," I said, "I began refereeing my parents' fights when I was six. My father is an alcoholic and my mother is a shrew. Our home was a battle field."

"You sound angry about that."

"I am. My parents acted more like selfish children than parents."

"Do you have any siblings?"

"An older sister, a brother and a younger sister."

"What is your relationship with them like?"

"Okay. I was closest to my brother growing up, but now I really don't know him or my sisters that well. I spent most of the time trying to leave home."

"What do you mean?"

"I was about five when I first left... I had another go at fifteen. I went to live at my friends' house, but my mother told her parents a heap of lies about me being a troublemaker. They told me they did not want any trouble and I should go back home."

"When did you eventually leave?"

"I was sixteen. I never really fitted into my family. I really don't know where I fit in."

Dr Anderson looked pensive for a moment then said, "Emma, how about you start from the beginning."

He did not have much to say after I told him how I survived my dysfunctional childhood. Never before had I spoken so freely about the resentment I had harboured against my parents, especially against my mother. To actually hear myself tell someone how much I hated my mother shocked me. The doctor did not react to anything I told him. I don't know why, but I did not feel at all guilty when I thought about it later on... surprising, since I was consumed with guilt for most of my life, feeling that way about her.

It seemed that I had only just arrived when the session ended; three quarters of an hour had slipped by in a flash. I thought that would be that, but when Dr Anderson said, "I'll see you the same time next week, Emma." I started to worry that perhaps Les was right, that I was loopy.

From the doorway of the surgery, I could see Stanley waiting for me in the car. He leaned across to open the door when he saw me.

"Well, how did it go, darling?" he asked as I climbed in beside him and closed the door.

"Fine, I guess. He wants to see me next week."

"Okay. What did you talk about? Did you mention me?" I turned quickly and just looked at him for a moment and then smiled, "Yes, hon, I told the doctor that you're a wonderful person." Stanley grinned broadly.

"The therapy is expensive darling, are you sure we can afford it?"

"I'll pay whatever it takes to get you better, darling. I don't want you worrying about things like that. We have medical insurance."

"That's good, sweetheart," I smiled, handing him the account. Stanley glanced at it quickly and said as his already lined brow deepened, "Okay darling, I'll take care of it."

I had several more sessions with Dr Anderson and during the third session he probed more deeply into my relationship with Les.

"I hate Les Carter, Dr Anderson," I said, looking at him with tears in my eyes. "I hate him with the essence of my soul. That man stole my children from me, not because I'm a bad mother but as payback for leaving him. He's robbed them of a mother. They don't have anything to do with me because of him... I'm their mother, they should be with me," I said, mopping my face. "I hate him for raping me, for killing my dogs. I hate him for so many things it would take forever to list them all." When I realised I was yelling, I went quiet and apologised and pulled myself together.

"I know harbouring all this hatred won't do me any good, but that's how I feel right now. I feel justified feeling the way I do. To be truthful, I'd like to shoot Les Carter dead, but I won't do it because I promised Bree I'd always take care of her. I can't take care of her if I am in jail. Bree is my world, my anchor. I'd be lost without her."

After I had calmed down Dr Anderson handed me a box of tissues.

"Boy," I laughed awkwardly, "I sure let loose today."

"Do you feel better?"

"Yes, I do."

He smiled. "Good, then I'll see you next week."

The following week, I entered Dr Anderson's office and sat in the seat opposite him, as I had done the previous weeks.

"Did you have a good week, Emma?" the doctor asked.

"Yes I did. But after the last session, I thought you would have had me committed."

"There's nothing wrong with you, Emma." My mouth fell open in surprise and he smiled.

"In my estimation, you're an intelligent and very strong woman. I believe you could be anything that you want to be."

I was about to interrupt, but he held up his hand and said, "It's my turn now, Emma. I've noticed that you don't give yourself any credit for what you've already achieved. Just look at what you've survived. I know a number of people who would have broken down much sooner than you did. The overdose was your breaking point, Emma, and that doesn't mean that you're a failure. A person can only endure so much..."

Dr Anderson's expression looked serious when he said, "I have patients who haven't endured as much as you and their lives are shattered... Not many people can protect themselves the way you have in an imaginary world and not lose touch with reality. Many go to a place and can't come back at all... I don't think you will try to hurt yourself again."

"Oh, I wasn't trying to hurt myself, Dr Anderson. I only wanted to sleep forever so I couldn't feel the pain of my life. I felt that I didn't have anything to live for, but I do, I have Bree and I'm okay."

He nodded and said, "You've led an interesting life, Emma. I suggest you write a book about it. You'll find that everything will come into perspective when you do."

"So what you're saying, Dr Anderson is that I'm sane."

He laughed, "Yes Emma, you're sane...the wrong person is sitting here."

"Can I have that in writing?"

"You also have a wonderful sense of humour." He chuckled as he stood up and walked to the door, "Come and see me only if you need to. Have a wonderful life, Emma, and write that book."

I left Dr Anderson's office in a daze, trying to digest all that he had said. 'I'm sane,' I thought, feeling good. 'Well, he would know, after all it's his job to know things like that. Write a book, eh. Don't know how the hell I'm going to do that. I was too scared to tell him I'm having trouble recognising simple words. I wonder, if he knew that, would he still believe I'm sane?'

44

Watching Bree leave every second weekend for her access visit with Les continued to tear me apart inside. Stanley could not see what my problem was now that everything was almost settled. He thought that I should accept the outcome and enjoy life with him. Perhaps I might have been able to do that if I had been in love with him, but the truth was, at times I did not even like him, let alone love him. I believe Stanley meant well in his naive way, and I was grateful to him for being there for me when I really needed someone. I might have lost Bree to Les if he had not offered to help me when he did.

When Bree and I went to live with Stanley, the interior of his house and decor was gloomy and very dated. He knew I was not comfortable living in his home.

"I've been thinking about selling this place and making a fresh start," he said, but he could not see that I really wanted to be in my own home, not his. I wanted to be with my family.

The estate agent who inspected Stanley's place gave a grim report, and confirmed my initial opinion about the house.

"You really need to do a lot of work to brighten the place up," he said. "It needs personality..."

Although Stanley lacked style and taste he was a whiz at carpentry. With my flare for decorating and design we made a good team when we worked on projects around the house. We had fun tearing down the brown brick bar in the lounge room. We also removed Stanley's former father-in-law's amateurish oil paintings that stifled the ambience of the house. Tired old carpet was replaced with new carpet, and the walls were painted in neutral colours. We hired a builder to enclose the back patio as we wanted to turn it into an open-plan kitchen and family room. A sewing room and small powder room was also included.

When the place was finally in order, Stanley stood back and patted himself on the back for a job well done. He was so full of himself that I just could not resist saying, "Yeah, hon, it sure is a job well done, you're the brawn and I'm the brains." That became my signature song whenever we did anything together.

I should have been happy but I was not. My heart ached for Luc. My mind refused to accept that he was gone. I could not cope with his death, so I simply brought him back into my life. When alone, I sat quietly and listened to John Farnham records and thought about Luc until he became real in my mind. I did it to keep sane. My world was surreal. Onlookers would have deemed me quite mad, talking to an empty space when I retreated into my imaginary world. At times I got carried away with myself and actually imagined Stanley was Luc. I knew he was not, but I wanted him to be.

The sadness and emptiness I felt was not just related to Luc. I was also grieving for my lost children. I worried about them all the time. I had no way of knowing whether they were really okay. I ached to see for myself, and the only way I could know for sure was to go to their house. I thought that by going there, it would help me understand how the boys really were.

No one was at home the first time I went there. Nerves churned my insides when I turned into the driveway, but the sight of Stella lying in the corner of the overgrown garden made me forget my fears. The sight of her, sad and alone with her spirit all but gone, brought me to the brink of tears. Our old Rottweiler sprang to life when she saw me get out of my car. She enthusiastically wagged her little knob, all that was left of her tail.

"Hello, old girl."

Stella whimpered and held out her paw. I squatted to hug her.

"I know, I miss you too." When I buried my face in her coat I recoiled, "Phew! Stell, you sure need a bath." She looked sad, obviously feeling the effects of the family's break-up too. "Never mind, you'll get all the attention you deserve soon."

Bree was ten months old when we got Stella. She was not just a dog; she was a member of our family. Even as a pup Stella was an amazing watchdog. "I didn't bring you all the way from Bougainville just to have you end up sad and alone old girl. I'm going to take you home, but not today. I'll have to make a deal with those little shits first. If I leave you here you'll die of a broken heart. I love you too much to let that happen to you. Where are the little buggers anyway? Is anyone home, Stel? Come on let's go see."

Stella stayed close by my side as I walked along the pathway and up to the glass doors that led to the billiard room. I had no idea what I was going to say to whoever answered my knock, but I did not have to worry about that as no one was home. The door was slightly ajar, so I slid it open a little wider, pulled back the heavy red velvet drapes, stuck my head in, and called out, "Anyone home?" I almost fainted at the condition of the room. The awful sight sent shivers down my spine. I walked through what was once my lovely home, which now resembled a squat.

Stella seemed concerned at my reaction to the revolting mess and pressed up against me. I bent down and patted her.

"How could they do this, Stel?" She almost knocked me off balance, offering her paw. "Look at that. What the hell is an ugly skeleton poster doing hanging on the family-room wall. It gives the place an ominous feeling. It's evil!"

I sat on the floor of the family room with Stella, contemplating the condition of the house, and came to the conclusion that it was symbolic of how the boys felt.

Everything they knew, that once was secure, was in tatters. The state of the house told me that they had absolutely no respect for anything that represented me, especially not this house. The realisation made me understand more fully how deeply my actions had hurt them and I began to cry. Stella whimpered and rubbed up against me, as if trying to console me. In the middle of my pity party, Monty and Molly strutted in and climbed all over me. Their purring was almost deafening. "Hello you two, want to come and live with me?" I said, wrapping my arms around them.

Leaving Stella behind left me with an awful feeling, especially since she sat in the middle of the driveway and whimpered as she watched me leave. I went back several more times just to spend time with her and the cats, but leaving them each time became more difficult to do. After discussing it with Stanley, I contacted the boys and went into lengthy negotiations to bring our pets' home with me.

Although Celeste lived with her brothers, she went back and forth between our home and the former family home, until she decided to move in with us. Before I was formally declared bankrupt I had given her my car and Cain the bakery van. Celeste's vehicle needed a little work to get it into perfect running order. Since she did not have the money to do it she asked her father but discovered there were strings attached. In return for his financial assistance, he expected Celeste to tell him what I was doing. She had not realised that I already suspected she must be giving Les information, whether innocently or otherwise, about my activities.

Celeste was home the morning I was going through legal papers and letters that were scattered over the table. She picked one of them up out of curiosity and read it. The look of sheer horror on her face spoke volumes.

"I didn't say that, Mom. He's twisted everything I said..."

"I know. Now you can see firsthand how your father works, Celeste. I've felt for some time that you were telling him what was going on here, but it doesn't matter anymore."

"But Mom, I didn't say…"

"It's okay, Celeste," I interrupted, "I don't care anymore. What's done is done."

That discovery was a valuable lesson for Celeste; she began to see things differently, and moved in with us.

Soon after, Cain telephoned out of the blue, sounding frustrated and fed up, wanting my help.

"Mom, I don't know what to do. I can't look after BJ any longer. He is uncontrollable. Can you take him?"

When Stanley came home that evening, I poured him his usual scotch and dry, then asked him if he would mind if BJ came to live with us too.

"If that's what you want darling, I don't mind," he responded enthusiastically.

"Even though Les won't be supporting him either, are you still okay with BJ living with us?"

I wanted to impress upon Stanley the expense he would incur in accepting BJ because he had a tendency to be tight with money. He assured me BJ was welcome, and BJ moved in. It was not long before I discovered that although Stanley agreed to support BJ and Bree, he felt he had been given licence to bully BJ, until I let him know that BJ had had enough bullying to last him two lifetimes. "He isn't going to experience anymore, not if I can help it."

For a few months it looked as if things were finally settling down. I loved having my children with me. It was one big happy family and I was back in the kitchen, baking again. The house was finally a home and the most amazing thing happened during that time. An unofficial truce developed between Brad, Cain and me and they started to visit us. I began to think the war just might be over; the dust was finally settling and even Les was quiet. That was until he found out Brad and Cain had visited me. He actually ordered them to stay away.

I knew Les had vowed to destroy me but did not realise it was going to be a slow torture of relentless incidents and lies that I would be compelled to defend at every turn, when I should have simply ignored him. But my wisdom only came with hindsight.

Fed up and frustrated with Les' persistent trouble making, Stanley seriously considered us migrating to Canada to get away from the constant upheaval. During that time Celeste came home and announced that she and a friend had decided to travel around Australia.

They packed up her car and left within a matter of days of telling us. I knew I would miss having Celeste around but was glad to see her leave with the hope that she would begin a new life, far away from the negative influences that surrounded her in Brisbane.

A few weeks after I married Stanley, I realised I had made a terrible mistake. Too ashamed to openly admit it, I pretended to be happy. After his initial proposal, Stanley had persistently asked again and again until eventually I said yes. He kept the marriage licence in the briefcase he always carried with him, "Just in case you change your mind," he teased. The reason behind his insistence, I believed in hindsight, was that he could not stand rejection and was determined to win me over at any cost. I became a challenge that he was determined to conquer.

Barbara Moss, the woman I had met in sewing classes on Bougainville several years before, encouraged me to accept Stanley's proposal. She and her husband Paul were spending their holidays up the north coast and had invited us to join them for the weekend. While Babs and I were shopping I told her about Stanley's pleas for me to marry him. She and Paul had previously met Stanley but had reserved their opinion of him. I felt they really did not like him, and did not miss the smirks upon their faces the times he tried to steal centre stage by talking about his bargain hunting. It was obvious that Stanley never made a saving on any of the purchases, especially when no one in the household liked the brands he bought. The ones he did not eat himself sat in the cupboard until the use-by date expired, then I would tossed them in the garbage without his knowledge. He was fast becoming a joke among some of my friends. Despite all of that, Babs believed Stanley had my best interests at heart and encouraged me to accept the proposal.

"But I'm not in love with him," I told her. "I can't get Luc out of my mind. I really don't want to."

"Emma," Babs said looking seriously at me. "It's time to move on and to look after yourself and Bree..."

In the end she convinced me that I could possibly have a good life with Stanley and protect Bree as well.

When we returned from shopping Babs and I joined Stanley and Paul on the balcony where they were leisurely enjoying a beer. I looked at Stanley and said, "Do you still want me to marry you?" He was lost for words and looked awkward for a moment, then smiled and nodded. "What are you doing next weekend?" I asked and Stanley grinned like a cat that had eaten the cream. "I have two stipulations, buy me a large diamond engagement ring and lose the beard."

The ceremony took place in the gardens of the holiday units. Celeste, Bree and Babs made up the wedding party. Paul was Stanley's best man and Babs my maid-of-honour. They were the only people present.

Celeste tried to talk me out of the marriage, aware that I did not love Stanley. Although I knew Celeste was right, I went ahead in the hope that it would work. More than anything I wanted to prevent Les from getting custody of Bree and marrying Stanley would achieve that.

A few days before the ceremony I mentioned to Stanley that I wanted to keep my own name. He seemed offended so I relented, but secretly resented losing my identity a second time.

Sadly, the longer I spent in the company of my new husband the less appealing he became. His persistent nagging about petty issues annoyed me to distraction. I would playfully tease him back into good humour, thinking his attitude was out of character and was only due to having a bad day at work. But I soon discovered that Stanley was really being himself.

Sue enlightened me further, telling me that her father liked to watch porno movies. "Dad really has a bad temper and usually swears, but not in front of you," she said sarcastically. "He's playing Mr Goodie-two-shoes around you. Look," Sue said, "here are a couple of videos."

I loathed pornographic material of any kind and knowing that Stanley indulged in that garbage sent me cold.

In the turmoil of the previous months, I had never bothered to really look at Stanley, but when I finally did, I realised that I did not find him attractive at all. I also felt that I could not trust him either. When I asked him about the videos he told me that they belonged to his neighbour and he was holding on to them so his wife would not find them. At that moment I realised I had been stupid, marrying for the wrong reason again, especially to a man almost identical type to my ex-husband.

'Well,' I thought, 'I'll have to make the best of it.'

I was grateful to Stanley for his support in my time of need and for all that he had done for Bree, BJ and me, but our incompatibility lessened the possibility of the marriage ever surviving long term. Initially, we shared some pleasant moments but all too quickly the pleasant moments became less frequent. Small incidents evolved into large issues, fanning my spark of frustration into a towering inferno.

Six months into the marriage I was ready to quit. I was unwilling to spend my remaining years in constant conflict with Stanley. Clearly we were not an ideal couple, but Stanley refused to acknowledge that. I confronted him with the situation and suggested we separate but he objected, insisting all we needed to do was to discuss our problems more and work through them one at a time.

"Well, let's talk about it now," I insisted. "My problem is that I don't want to be married to you any longer. I want to leave."

He argued with me for hours, telling me that I had not given us enough time.

"Can't you see, Stanley, I don't want to be with you? I've had enough rubbish in my life to last two lifetimes and I refuse to take on any more. You nag worse than I ever did. Men don't nag, at least none that I know of, with the exception of you that is. Your pettiness and meanness angers me. I hate being in a constant state of anger."

I started to walk away from him but stopped and turned to him, pleading in an effort to make him understand, "I want to love my husband, not hate him. I don't love you and I don't want to fight with you either. I didn't want to fight with Les but I did - all the time, because we weren't right for each other. You and Les have the knack of bringing out the worst in me. We're wrong for each other can't you see that?"

"No, I can't," he shouted.

I looked into his weather-beaten face and saw stubbornness, and realised that he would never understand because he did not want to. Even after we had debated for hours on end, he still refused to accept our incompatibility.

"I'll change," he promised. "I'll do anything you want me to do, but, give us a chance."

"It's not you Stanley, who is wrong. It's us!"

He had no idea what I was talking about and that set the precedent for the duration of our three-year marriage.

The first time I actually left Stanley, he demanded that I return the engagement ring before leaving the house. The ring had no value for me so I did not feel that I was losing anything of great importance by returning it. I left with Bree, having to return a short while later as we had nowhere else to go. I explained to Bree that it was unfair of us to take our troubles to our friends' home. I also thought that if news of my marriage break up reached Les, he would file for full custody of Bree.

Stanley was relieved when we walked through the door. He immediately apologised for taking the ring and asked me to wear it again. He held my hand trying to slip it on my finger.

"No!" I said pulling my hand away. "I don't want it again, now or ever."

He looked shocked and could not understand why I did not want to wear such a beautiful ring. He was determined I should wear it and I was just as determined not to. The engagement ring was beautiful but I honestly did not want it. Taking it from me was a despicable act and its beauty faded after he did that. Weeks later, the subject of the ring came up again. He wanted me to wear it but still I would not accept it. Stanley took hold of my hand and slid the ring on my finger.

"I'll never return this to you ever again," I said looking at the large pear-shaped diamond on the third finger of my left hand, thinking that the sparkle in the diamond was the only sparkle in our marriage.

45

BJ found living under Stanley's tyrannical rule impossible. He chose to move in with his brothers when they rented a unit, after the sale of the house had been finalised. Fifteen year old BJ had become an enigma to everyone. No one knew what he was up to with his comings and goings. He telephoned me regularly but did not volunteer any information about what he was doing, and was evasive when I asked. I waited anxiously for the ominous phone call to inform me BJ was in serious trouble or even worse. When it finally came I was shocked to learn the trouble was firearms and not drugs.

In a restless moment BJ had been target shooting from his bedroom window into a neighbour's backyard.

"I didn't mean any harm, Ma," he told me. "I was just bored."

Thankfully no harm was done. I attended the hearing with him and the outcome was that he had to have counselling.

On the drive back to the unit after the first session, BJ started talking.

"I like her, Ma," he casually remarked about his counsellor.

"That's good, mate. Perhaps she can help you, if you let her."

Then suddenly he began to sob.

"Hey, what's wrong, mate?"

"I saw what he did to you, Ma, but I couldn't help you."

"Saw what, BJ? What are you taking about?"

"Dad. I saw him beat you up. I saw him drag you into the bedroom and tie you up. I tried to stop him but I couldn't help you. It's my fault," he said almost hysterical. "I couldn't help you."

I was so shaken by what BJ was saying that I pulled over to the side of the road. I had no idea he had seen anything as a child. He would have been about four or five years old at the time, I thought, recalling the incident.

"It's my fault that Dad raped you," I heard BJ say, interrupting my thoughts.

"What are you talking about, BJ?" I asked wiping my tears.

"I heard you call Dad a rapist, and I'm the result of him doing that to you. I was born because of it."

"Yes you were, BJ, and I'm glad you were. I've never regretted having you BJ, only what your father did to me. You're one of the good things in my life. And as far as you not being able to help me all those years ago, tell me how a small child could fight a large grown man?"

"I couldn't help you, Ma, I couldn't help you."

"Nothing was your fault, BJ. It's the way things were then. You have to put it behind you. I want you to have a good life. I love you so very much and I'm very glad you were born. I'm glad you're my son. Don't ever forget that. Please don't let your father or anyone ruin your life. Rise above what happened. Show him and everybody that you can make it. Life is difficult at times I know, but we can make it, mate."

I knew BJ had a long way to go and the road ahead of him was going to be bumpy. There was a lot he had to sort through before he would find peace. I shuddered at the number of times I thought he would call it quits. Thankfully, he had the strength to stay in the race. I understood his struggle only too well, and I admired him for his tenacity to survive one day at a time.

A few weeks after Stanley put his house on the market, a slump in real estate occurred. He was fast becoming frustrated because we were eager to move and find another place. Endeavouring to move things along, the real estate agent convinced Stanley an auction would get him a quick sale. When I suggested that we should wait, he made it quite clear that it was his house and therefore his decision to make. The property sold at auction, but at a loss of ten thousand dollars below market value. I advised him not to let the house go.

"Wait a few days," I urged, "you'll get a better price." But Stanley was adamant he knew what he was doing and accepted the sale. Just as I had predicted, an offer nearer to his asking price came two days later.

We had thirty days to find another home once the sale was official. I was fortunate to find a two-bedroom cedar homestead-style house that had everything we wanted, large bedrooms, open modern kitchen, wide verandas, high ceilings and most importantly, a shed for Stanley to potter around in. Initially, I thought we would live there for many years to come, but within a few months of us moving in, and although we were busy settling into our new home and designing gardens, I felt we would leave soon.

The house had a wonderful ambience. I felt very much at home living there, comfortable enough to sit quietly and meditate. Sometimes during the meditation I would see things in my mind as if watching a movie.

* * *

One afternoon before we were married, Stanley dropped by my home with another man.

"Hi!" I said a little puzzled, when I answered the knock at the door, "What are you doing here?"

"Thought you might need a hand with somethink," Stanley smiled, and I automatically thought 'thing, it's thing, not think.'

"This is me father, Clive Carson. Dad, Emma."

"Nice to meet you, Clive," I smiled and shook hands. "I'm making coffee, would you like a cup, Stanley? Clive?"

"Thanks," they said, and followed me into the kitchen via the formal lounge and dining room.

Stanley settled himself at the breakfast bar, as did his father.

"What do you think of the house, Dad?"

The older version of Stanley looked around the kitchen and over his shoulder into the family room. "Big."

"Kids need lots of room," I said, looking at Clive. "They've been in boarding school the last few years. It takes time to adjust to being a family again."

"How many do you have?" he asked.

"Five."

"Five?" he said and raised his eyebrows looking at Stanley.

"I've just recently had the kitchen renovated to make more room. Had the wall knocked out where you're sitting," I said, drawing a picture in the air with my index finger, "and added this bench and heaps of rosewood cupboards and drawers, as you can see. Enlarged the window over the sink and laid new tiles, Italian. I designed the kitchen.' Clive nodded. "I love it. I can be with the kids and cook dinner at the same time. We're very close. More coffee?"

"No, I'm fine."

"Stanley?"

By Clive's expression, I wondered if he was thinking that Stanley could have easily put his kitchen, lounge room and laundry into my kitchen and family room.

From our first meeting I had felt Stanley's parents' disapproval of me. No one actually said anything to my face, I just felt it. Stanley laughed when I told him what I was feeling.

"Don't be silly, darling," he said, trying to sound convincing, "my parents like you. It's your imagination working overtime, that's all."

I let the subject slide because I had nothing other than a feeling to go by, but I would never forget the evening his parents came to dinner a few months after we were married. The idea was to win them over with my culinary skills and table presentation, but all I succeeded in doing was to alienate them further.

"There," I said putting flowers in the centre of the table, "all finished."

"Everything's wonderful, darling. It looks very flash," said Stanley, beaming with pride.

"I hope your parents approve."

"I'm sure they will," he said, and hugged me.

"Hello, anybody home?"

"They're here." I whispered to Stanley.

It was the first time Stanley's parents had seen the changes in the house, and they scanned the place with a silent critical eye.

"Not bad," Clive said nodding, "but it's posh with all these matching colours, wouldn't you say son?" Then he saw the dining table. "Struth, didn't know we were comin' to the Ritz."

Although we laughed, I didn't miss the sarcasm.

As soon as they were seated I served the entrée.

"I hope you like this," I said placing a small crystal dish full of king prawns, draped over crushed ice, topped with sauce in front of them. "Stanley said you like prawns."

Daphne looked at the prawns and Clive laughed. "Yeah we like prawns, but never had 'em out of crystal before. Hope we don't get a bill after we're finished, we couldn't afford it."

We laughed again and started eating.

During the meal Stanley and Clive talked about the renovations and his father said, "Ya did a fine job, son."

Before Stanley could take all the credit, I patted Stanley's arm and, smiling sweetly, said, "Yes Clive, we are pleased with the results. Stanley and I make a good team. I'm the brains and he's the brawn."

Clive seemed annoyed and responded, "Not so long ago, Stanley built the ensuite in the main bedroom on his own."

"Yes, I know, May told me."

Not once during the conversation did Stanley mention that I designed the layout or that I had any input at all.

I watched my frail mother-in-law pick at her food and asked if anything was wrong.

"The meal is lovely dear, but it's too rich for my taste."

Clive unappreciatively devoured everything I put in front of him. He sawed into tender fowl as though it were leather and thoughtlessly clanged silver cutlery against fine bone china. I was seething. He had no respect.

Pouring coffee I said, "Well Clive, perhaps you may never dine at the Ritz, but at least, now you know how the other half lives. Ground glass or arsenic?" I asked smiling and handed him the cup and saucer.

A few days later Stanley told me his father called him at work. "How is he, darling?" I casually asked.

"He doesn't know how to take you."

"Poor old bugger," I shrugged, "he can dish it out but can't take it."

Stanley looked puzzled. "I tried so hard to be nice to your parents on Saturday night. I went out of my way to please them but all they did was mock me. I was willing to accept them the way they are, but my style seems to offend them. Well then, fuck them!" I said stamping my foot. "I'm having nothing more to do with them."

"B...but darling, they didn't mean anything to..."

"Bullshit! Your father knew exactly what he was doing. They're your parents, you can visit them without me. I don't intend to suffer your family the way I had to suffer the Carters. Les never protected me from his family and I don't believe that you'll protect me from yours either, that's why I'll never have anything more to do with them."

"If you won't come with me, then I won't visit them without you."

"That's a stupid thing to say. If you don't go, you can bet your last penny they will blame me and think that I'm stopping you. Oh no Stanley, you'll visit them, but without me."

Stanley vowed that he would distance himself from his family in support of me, but I knew he was lying.

I discovered Stanley's deceit one day when, during my time of meditation, I picked up a conversation which took place between Stanley and his parents before we married. In my mind's eye I saw Stanley with his parents at their home. They lived about a half an hour drive from our place. Clive was telling Stanley he should reconsider his involvement with me.

"Are you sure you know what you're getting yourself into son? She's in a lot of trouble from what you've told us."

I was annoyed at Stanley's betrayal. When he arrived home that afternoon, I mentioned what I'd seen and heard. Even though he was surprised, he denied speaking to his parents and being at their home that day.

"You've just lied to me Stanley, even though I can't prove it," I said looking him in the eyes. "I know your father told you he disapproves of me." I paused, he was about to speak but I interrupted him.

"They have no right to judge me when they don't even know my situation. Let them voice their concerns to my face, not behind my back," I challenged. "All they know about me is what you have told them and I can just imagine what you've told them." Stanley protested his innocence and implied I had imagined everything.

A few weeks after moving into our new home, I was alone one day when I had another vision. Stanley was on his way to work. I saw him turn his vehicle off the freeway and head for his parents' house and pull up outside their home. I was utterly amazed and called his parents and asked to speak to Stanley. I wanted to tell him what I had just experienced.

Clive hesitated before saying Stanley was not there, but I knew he was. When I hung up, I rang his office, but there was no answer. I tried the office again an hour later. "So you've finally arrived. I called to tell you..."

"Is that right?" Stanley said in his usual condescending manner.

"You were there, weren't you?"

"No," he laughed, "it's your imagination again."

This time there was no denying it; I knew what I'd seen was real and that Stanley was lying again. "Well, he's not getting away with it this time," I mumbled.

When he arrived home that evening, Stanley appeared confident that I'd forgotten the subject. But I confronted him after dinner, telling him, "I don't care whether you visit your parents or not, that's up to you. But I refuse to live with a man I can't trust and I don't trust you, Stanley. You've deliberately lied to me more than once without any reason. I would be a fool to trust you."

We argued for hours as he endeavoured to convince me I was imagining everything

"No! Oh no, you don't! You're not going to try that on me. Les used to do that. He would say that I was crazy. I know what I saw and know what I heard. You're lying to me. I can feel it."

Eventually he admitted to the truth, and I responded by telling him, "I'll never trust you again. You tried to insinuate that I was out of my mind because you thought I wouldn't like what you were doing. I'll tell you something, Stanley. I don't care what you do. You and your family can go get fucked!" He looked as if I had slapped him in the face. "What's wrong with you?" I said sarcastically. "I've wanted to say that for a long time and it feels good."

"You don't use language like that," he said stunned.

"I've been told that YOU swear and also have a very bad temper."

"I don't," he snapped. "Who told you that?"
"Oh, a little bird."

Stanley's pettiness became so intolerable that I made a habit of swearing at him. It riled him so much that it gave me a thrill to see him all het up. He was so petty and picky that I suspected he might be gay. To ease my mind I called Ronny, a customer from the shop with whom I had become friends.
"Hello." The voice was female.
"Are you wearing a dress today, Ronny?"
"Oh," he giggled, "how did you know, Em?"
"Come on Ronny, you sound like a woman... I need your help."
Lowering his voice he said, "Do you need rescuing again?" He sounded excited.

* * *

Ronny was referring to the time up he had come to the shop one evening as I was about to close, dressed as a woman, wearing a dress, wig and full make-up including false eyelashes. My baker turned up drunk and menacing. Ronny whispered in a male voice, "Don't do anything, Emma, I'll be back as fast as I can," and then dashed out of the shop. He returned fresh faced, in jeans and tee shirt, approached the baker and introduced himself as Ron. He whispered something to him and the baker left without causing any trouble.
"What did you say to him?" I asked, amazed at the transformation in Ron or Ronny. I was so confused that I did not know who he was that day.
"Can't tell you, Em, it's a trade secret. In my line of work I deal with difficult guys all the time."
I was shocked. "Are you a... a working girl?" I asked, and he smiled.

* * *

"I want you come to my place and meet Stanley and tell me if he's gay."

On a Saturday evening Ronny and some of his flamboyant friends turned up at our place on their way to a fancy dress party. I was expecting Stanley to be uncomfortable surrounded with a bunch of gay guys, but he wasn't.

I pulled Ronny aside. "Well, is he?"

"No," he said, vigorously shaking his head.

"How do you know?"

"We have little antennas," he whispered.

I laughed and whispered back. "Stanley IS gay because he's got a little antenna too."

"Emma!" Ronny grinned, "You can be such a bitch. Your husband is NOT gay, he's too unattractive."

"Crap! I've seen ugly poofs!"

"Not in my circle of friends." He glared at me for a moment then said, "Darling, your husband isn't gay, he has a personality disorder. He thinks he's better than he really is..."

As far as I was concerned, it was only a matter of time before Stanley and I would separate, but he was under the illusion that he was the best thing that had ever happened to me.

"No one could or would ever love you more than I do; and no one has done more for you than I have or ever will," he told me numerous times during our marriage. Stanley had actually convinced himself of that, almost driving me to the brink of insanity with his persistent statement, "Darling, you would not be able to survive without me."

Stanley also became all too consuming. My interests became our interest, while his interests remained his own as he subtly robbed me of mine. Everything concerning me became 'we'. Whenever I discussed antiques or art and so on with any of my friends, while we entertained, Stanley implied he knew more about it than I did, even though he had never picked up a book on the subject. Consequently, I pretended to lose interest in everything and shared very little with him.

When he asked, "How was your day darling?" I replied, "Okay, didn't do much, just housework."

When that became my signature song, he realised I was shutting him out. Frustrated with the thought that he could be missing out on something, he insisted on knowing why I was doing that to him, and persisted in questioning me until I exploded.

"You want to know why I don't tell you anything anymore," I yelled. "Well Stanley, I'll tell you. I'm tired of you stealing my life, my ideas, my thoughts and my identity, that's why."

"I don't know what you are talking about," he said innocently.

"How about this Stanley, we are not interested in antiques, I am. We are not interested in interior decorating and art. I am. Anything that I do, you talk about it as if you discovered it."

"I'm sorry, darling," he said. "I'm just proud of your achievements and abilities and admire you for them. I want to be a part of it too."

"But you are stealing the joy I once had for everything. There'll be times when it can't be 'we'. Sometimes, it's just you or just me. I don't invade your hobbies so please, don't invade mine."

Stanley played golf most weekends and a few times a week with some of his work colleagues, before work. One weekend, at his insistence, I joined him on the golf course for a game. When I became bored I mischievously used the golf club as a weeder, and playfully teased him about his handicap, telling him that my handicap was better than his, because mine was a much higher number, way higher. In his eyes, I had committed the greatest sin of all - I did not take the game seriously. We agreed that I should not play golf with him again.

In a quiet moment, I began to contemplate what my life was all about. There must be a reason for all that's happened,

I thought while scanning over the past for answers. I actually made a conscious effort to look into the reason why my life had taken the direction it had. The answer was out there somewhere, I was sure of that.

In my frustration of dealing with a second pointless marriage, I really began to question why I was in the mess I was in.

46

A few months after settling in Brisbane in 1984, I met Maggie Foster in a little café at Woodridge. She read cards and predicted my divorce and second marriage two years before it actually happened. When Maggie finished the reading, she handed me a piece of paper with her telephone number on it and whispered, "I don't usually do this, but I feel we'll be friends. You can call me if you need to."

We were good friends for fifteen years. Before I made any major decisions I sought advice through Maggie's cards. I even followed the advice against my own judgement in a desperate attempt to find solutions to my problems.

From my first reading, my life spiralled downwards very quickly. The readings were as often inaccurate as they were accurate. In retrospect I think I would have been better off sticking to trusting my own intuition, saving myself a heap of heartache.

In my quest to understand the purpose of my life, and trying to satisfy my spiritual needs, I have travelled many different paths, looking for the reason why I was attracting so much negative energy. The answer was out there somewhere, I was sure of it. I just had to find it and the only way I could do that was to delve into all kinds of spiritual aspects.

Being raised a Catholic only instilled fear in me. For many years I actually believed my first marriage was God's punishment for missing Mass on Sundays. I can still hear the priest yelling at the class, "It's a mortal sin to miss Sunday Mass. God will punish you. You'll BURN IN HELL!" Every time I said or did anything wrong, I was scared that I would be struck down.

While growing up, I was terrified of the Catholic Church. I was well into my twenties before I realised that I shouldn't be. The very fact that the Catholic Church is perhaps the richest establishment on earth, and millions of people in the world are still dying of starvation, is obscene to me, especially when it need not be that way at all.

These days I'm an absolute sceptic. I need to discern fact from fiction, delving and probing to unlock the mystery of what I have been encouraged to believe. I cannot simply accept anything as fact any more. I now have to know how, why, when and where before I embrace anything.

Life is without a doubt full of mysteries and contradictions. I have experienced some of those mysteries, and this has opened my mind to the possibilities of there being more to the essence of spirituality. That is why I continued my search for answers until I was able to find the ones that helped me understand what it was that I needed to learn to change my chaotic life.

Amongst the chaos I saw Bree as my sanity. If it was not for her I don't know where I would be today. Amazingly, she adapted quickly to the changes in her life, never once causing any trouble. Her ever-present smile made me feel good. It was little wonder that I felt empty when she was away visiting Les.

Several months before we moved to our new home, I noticed that Bree seemed unwell. "What's wrong, Babe?" I asked, feeling her forehead. "You don't seem yourself. Where's that beautiful smile?" I teased.

Bree smiled half-heartedly. "I don't feel like smiling, Mommy. I'm very tired and my tummy is sore..." And so began a series of visits to the doctor.

"I think you pamper that child too much," Stanley complained. "She's having too many days off school; all she wants is attention."

Stanley's remark annoyed me, and he knew it when I narrowed my eyes. "You're so insensitive, Stanley, Bree isn't well."

"What's wrong with her?"

"The doctor can't find anything."

"Then send her to school."

Bree was never a noisy or outgoing child. She was always very polite and well behaved. When I think about it, Bree was shy. At first I thought the mystery illness was a delayed reaction to the upheaval of our lives but I had a nagging feeling that something was not right. My only option was to consult another doctor, and I made an appointment two weeks before we moved.

The doctor who saw Bree at the medical centre seemed awfully young but I saw this as an advantage, feeling he would be more flexible than his senior colleague. During the consultation I quickly ran through Bree's medical history as best as I could remember.

"Well," he said leaning back in the chair, "looking at Bree right now she seems fine."

"I know that," I said irritated, "that's what the doctors said to my mother about me when I was a child, and I was dying. That's why I want you to do a blood test to see if she has Hereditary Spherocytosis. I was born with it."

"Oh, I don't think that'll be necessary, I really don't think she would have that. She looks too healthy."

His self-assurance was beginning to annoy me. "Regardless," I told him firmly sitting upright in my chair, "I would like the test to be done."

"I guess there's no harm in elimination," he muttered.

A few days after settling into the new house I had a nagging feeling to contact the surgery, and when I did my call was immediately transferred through to the doctor's office.

"Oh, I'm so glad you called, Mrs Carson, I've been trying to reach you," Dr Ferguson's voice was full of concern. Although I knew the results, I waited for him to tell me.

"You were right and I have to admit I was surprised," he said apologetically. "Bree has Hereditary Spherocytosis and she needs to see a specialist right away. Her blood count is so low, it's a wonder she has the strength to walk."

Although I did not want to, I thought I had better let Les know what was happening with Bree. When I phoned him, he bellowed through the earpiece, "No quack is going to put a knife to Bree. I won't allow you to do this to her just to make yourself look important."

"Bree needs this operation to save her life, you idiot!" I bellowed back. "She will have it, with or without your consent!" and I slammed the receiver down.

I had tried to do the right thing but all my call did was to stir up another hornet's nest. Les telephoned everyone he could think of, telling them that I had invented Bree's illness as a form of seeking attention for myself. Les was beyond my understanding. He knew I was a good mother, regardless of what he told everyone else. Had he finally convinced himself of his own lies?

During the visit with the specialist I mentioned Les' response to Bree having the operation.

"This matter is out of your ex-husband's hands, Emma," Mr Walton smiled. "The operation is very serious, it is a matter of life and death. I will simply get a court order if I have to. There's no need for either you or Bree to worry, I'll take care of it."

He looked at Bree, smiled, and asked if she had any questions or concerns. She smiled back and shook her head, "No, I want to have the operation so I won't feel so tired all the time."

Before anything could be done, Bree needed three inoculations over a period of a few weeks. The vaccine would protect her against infection and boost her immune system. The spleen, the offending organ, had to be removed because it was killing off Bree's red blood cells. Her blood cells, like mine, are round instead of oval. The spleen acts as a filter for the blood and because our blood cells are round, the spleen was destroying them. If the condition were left untreated, Bree would have died.

Bree's only worry about the operation was that it would not take place. "What if Dad does something and I can't have the operation?" she asked, as we made our way home.

"I'll protect you from him, Babe," I said with conviction, "and the doctors will help me. They're on our side and so is the law this time."

Ever since Bree could understand, I have told her that she was special. "God sent you to me because he knew that I would look after you. There's nothing for you to ever fear because you have an angel with you all the time, just like I have. You're so special, Babe, that God showed me what you looked like before you were even born."

Bree nodded. "I remember Dad telling me the story and how you used to hear my name being whispered to you. He thought you were crazy." We both had a laugh about that. "We're all a little crazy at times, sweetie, it keeps some of us sane," I said, laughing.

At the same time Bree's illness came to light, Stanley was made redundant, which forced the wheels of change back into motion. Within weeks of him leaving his former position he was offered similar employment in Victoria. Bree's operation was transferred from Brisbane to the Royal Children's Hospital in Melbourne.

We found tenants for the house and re-housed Stella with Babs and Paul Moss, who had been living at the Sunshine Coast since the war on Bougainville forced them to return to Australia. The Victorian weather would have been too harsh on an old dog unaccustomed to extreme cold conditions. Stella preferred a warmer climate. She was also well acquainted with Babs and Paul and they were happy to have her. The cats came with us to Victoria. They were more adaptable and spent most of their time sleeping on our beds.

47

We rented a house in Werribee, Victoria. After making several telephone calls to the various schools in the area, I found a vacancy for Bree at a Christian College within a short driving distance from our home.

I discussed the idea of attending a Christian College with her before going to the interview with the principal. Before the divorce, Bree's world as she knew it was safe and secure and almost perfect. In her own words, "I had a dream childhood." She was doted on, fussed over, loved and protected. Then one day I was running in fear from the man she called Daddy.

When it came to major decisions concerning Bree, she and I would discuss the situations first to alleviate any concerns she might have. From the day we left our home, every decision I made affected her as much as it did me, and I felt Bree should have peace of mind knowing that she also had a say in the decision making, especially when it involved her.

Since she was able to talk, Bree and I were always having in-depth chats about things from cloud formation to religious beliefs and spiritualism. I loved the way she craved information. If I did not have the answers to her questions I would do a little research. She stirred a curiosity in me to learn more, but I fell short whenever the subject came around to her siblings. I could not reassure my daughter that all would be well in the future regarding us being friends with them again. Although I wanted that more than anything, in my heart I did not believe it would be possible, not as long as

Les was alive. But I encouraged Bree to always have hope that it would one day happen, because it was glaringly evident to me that she was missing her brothers and sister as much as I was.

Moving to Victoria gave us a chance to start a new life. Bree and I had agreed to try and separate ourselves from the troubles of the family while we lived in Victoria. She chose to use Stanley's surname instead of her own. Her decision made things easier for us since Les had refused to support her financially. Stanley took on the expense of her private education and medical insurance.

I would not have chosen a Christian College for Bree. I was concerned that the school would place too much emphasis on religion and not enough on the curriculum, but as it was the only school in the area that had a vacancy, I had no other alternative but to enrol her. Before I did so, I promised that if she was not happy there I would look for another school.

"But for now, Babe," I said, "let's see what the college has to offer you."

I was surprised how quickly Bree fitted into her new environment and how well she made friends. When I remarked about it Bree said, "You know Mom, there are a lot of kids at school who have stepfathers just like me, and I'm really glad I changed my name."

I gave her a quizzical look, "Why, sweetie?"

"Because some of the kids talk about how unhappy they are that their father's not living with them," she said. "I'm glad that I don't have to talk about anything like that, because no one knows that I have a stepfather. I feel sad for them because they seem so unhappy. I know how they feel, but I'm not unhappy."

"Are you really happy?"

"Yep," she answered quickly. "I love being with you, Mom. But I miss the boys and Celeste. I feel sad about that sometimes, but I am happy."

"What about Les? Have you ever thought about living with him?"

"No Mom! Why? Don't you want me to live with you anymore?" she asked, sounding concerned.

"Oh no, no, it's nothing like that. I only asked just to make sure that living with me is what you want."

"I don't want to ever live with him," Bree said adamantly.

Stanley liked his new position as Service Manager with a leading Coach Company. Bree was happy at school, but I felt lost and lonely – something that I had not expected. I missed my friends. Apart from Bree and Stanley, I did not know a soul in Victoria.

When I began writing letters to some friends in Brisbane, I discovered that at times I still could not remember how to spell simple words. When it happened I felt panicky, wondering what was going on. It had occurred too frequently for me not to feel concern. Initially, when the problem started, I thought I was just tired and still recovering from the effects of the breakdown, because there were days I could read and write without struggling, but they were fast becoming few and far between. I was seriously worried when I found it increasingly difficult to recognise once-familiar words, and comprehending text in magazines and books was fast becoming a challenge. I chose to ignore the problem because I could not face the possibility that Dr Anderson was wrong, that I was really losing my mind. Les and Stanley had repeatedly insinuated that I was unbalanced. Although I did not accept their analysis of my personality, they had subsequently planted the seed of doubt in my mind. I knew that I could not discuss my concern with Stanley, and also that I had to do something about it.

The loneliness and living in a strange place stirred me to feel deeper regrets about the past. When I felt that way I would sit quietly. My diary became my confidant and companion, and for many years I poured profound emotion onto the empty pages. The journal had become my sounding board. I wrote with acid honesty, which sometimes frightened me.

When I was unable to write my private thoughts in my journal, I was left feeling depressed and vulnerable. My words resembled jumbled hieroglyphics. It was a frightening experience. My journal was the only place where I was free to express how I really felt, without retribution. 'Let's face it,' I wrote in better times, 'people in general are liars. They spend a lifetime hiding the darker side of their personalities from the world and especially from those closest to them. People are afraid to be honest. They fear rejection. They are cowards. The truth is difficult to accept, especially if one doesn't want to hear it. My truth is that I HATE my life and regret everything about it. Luc told me not to have regrets, but I do. My whole life is about, 'What if this or what if that'.

Luc had been the one I wanted to marry. HE was my choice, damn it!!! I hadn't wanted to marry anyone else, especially not Les. It would never have happened if I had not fallen pregnant. I feel like a broken urn with all of its pieces glued back together - no matter how one looks at me, I will always be broken. I shouldn't have married Stanley, I didn't love him, and I didn't even like him. He is a FUCKING IDIOT!!!! And a lousy lover...poor bastard. Perhaps he would have been a better person with someone who likes him and, is willing to put up with his pettiness and meanness. What is wrong with me? Apart from my children I don't love anyone – I wonder where Matt is. What port did he sail into? Amazing how he's never left my thoughts. Luc and Matt are my dear hearts. I loved one and was in love with the other. I hope Matt is happy with the choices he has made. We shared something really special and I want him to be happy. I'll have to find out for myself one day. Things must change or I will go insane.

The days ahead dragged, each one seeming the same as the one before, empty and endless. Weekends gave little consolation and Monday came only too quickly.

Stanley drove Bree to school on his way to work and I cleared away the breakfast dishes as soon as they left. But one particular morning I didn't. Instead of showering and dressing, I made a fresh cup of tea and curled up in the lounge chair nearest to the window, the one that caught the morning sun.

It was bitterly cold in the Victorian winter. I felt empathy for Bree, having to venture out in the frosty weather each morning. It did not affect Stanley at all. He seemed to thrive in the colder climate. "No sense no feeling," I smiled cynically, thinking about him, then shook my head and frowned, reprimanding myself for being so bitchy towards him.

Sipping hot tea, I relaxed, listening to the radio playing softly in the background and embracing the peaceful ambience of the room. I whispered a prayer.

"I feel so lost. Tell me what to do," I murmured. "I know I need help. Am I losing my mind? Where do I go?"

I fell asleep and woke up about an hour later, feeling more refreshed than I had in ages. I showered and dressed, then drove to the shopping centre for no particular reason other than to have a change of scenery. I only purchased a magazine which I did not read until several days later.

I cannot recall what diverted my attention from cleaning the lounge room to the magazine lying on the coffee table that day. I was not in the habit of deviating from any task in hand; my meticulous and fastidious nature just would not allow it.

I felt drawn to the magazine, enough to stop what I was doing to pick it up and browse through it. As I flipped over the pages I came across an advertisement promoting 'The Year of Literacy' with an 1800 number that almost jumped out at me. Out of curiosity I dialled the free national number and asked for more information. The telephone call led me to the Community Centre in Werribee.

"Thank you, I'll see you then," I said calmly, but inwardly my nerves were churning as I thought about how much courage it took for me to make that phone call. 'I hope I don't get found out. What if? No, no, it will be okay;' I debated with myself. 'I'll just have to be careful, that's all. I've never done anything like this before. But I can't keep on living a lie any longer. I'm going. I have to. Not only my future but my life depends on this.'

A week later I was sorting through my wardrobe looking for something suitable to wear to the meeting. Clothes were strewn all over the bed and I was getting frustrated, "What should I wear? I don't know what to wear," I moaned, feeling panicky. 'I won't go. I can't do it. I feel stupid.'

'But you have to,' my inner voice said, 'you have to', and I began to dress. Finally I settled for a black and cream, striped mohair jumper and ankle-length tomato red, silk and wool, box-pleated skirt and black leather boots.

A few hours later, I gingerly entered the humble community cottage, nestled among large gum trees on the outskirts of town. As I entered, a woman in her thirties came from an inner office. "Hello," she said, smiling and extending her hand, "you must be Emma Carson. I've been expecting you. I'm Debra Parker." She directed me to follow her into the front room. "We can talk in here."

Several chairs were placed around four white tables. Near the entrance, a large whiteboard was secured to a pale green wall and sunlight filtered through bay windows opposite. Worn emerald green carpet covered the floor.

Although my stomach was jumping with nerves and I wished that I had worn something casual, I was comfortable in Debra's company. She spoke softly and had an air of sincerity about her. During the interview she encouraged me to enrol in an English class, after assessing my problem as lack of self-confidence. She made it sound so simple, an extreme lack of confidence due to trauma, she said. I was amazed when she told me. I had agonised for the past three years about this, thinking that I was losing my mind.

On the first morning I was introduced to several people of different nationalities. I enjoyed their company and found them interesting. Later I enrolled in other courses and developed a hunger for learning that surprised me. My mind felt less fragmented and my thoughts were clearer. I had formed new friendships and was making a fresh start. I discovered that I enjoyed the challenge of learning, joined a local art group and discovered another talent of mine.

Re-education gave me an opportunity to put many things into perspective and my secret was safe. Stanley had no idea where I went twice a week, nor did he have to know. I was accepted into the class on face value. Although initially apprehensive, I quickly settled in with the other mature students from various ethnic backgrounds. My association with them gave me new insight and respect for other cultures, with the interchange of information about one another's culture and cuisine. The exercise united the group as contemporaries.

Ben Matheson, an energetic young man with a crop of thick, blonde, unruly hair that persistently fell into his eyes, was the co-ordinator at the cottage. He eagerly organised a creative writing group to celebrate The Year of Literacy, a Government-funded community program.

The cottage had a certain charm about it, appearing warm and cosy even on the coldest Victorian night. The room where we gathered resembled a lounge more than a classroom. Faded cracked cream walls gave the room character. Comfortable-looking old chairs, covered in well-worn floral fabric, were placed casually around the room. A pile of books, stacked neatly upon a sturdy maple table, looked inconspicuous standing in a corner adjacent to the window. Near the books stood a quaint old jade vase, full of dried bush flowers that were supposed to hide the chips and fine cracks. A telephone sat alone at the far end of the table.

I joined the group to write my story. The initial meeting was organised to gauge whether or not there was any interest in the course. Ten women, including me, were enthusiastic about meeting once a week.

With eager hearts we pulled our chairs into a circle, light-heartedly joking about our future as budding novelists. The lecturer, Joanne Mills, was an encouraging young woman in her late twenties. Her bright, bubbly personality was infectious. She had enormous faith in our ability. Eventually her enthusiasm had us believing in ourselves and we all began to produce some good material.

Ben was very passionate about the literacy project, passionate enough to apply for and receive funding for the stories and poems we had written to be published and distributed throughout Victoria's Community Centres. Although he had mentioned the possibility of our work being published, none of us took him seriously, never dreaming our writing would be good enough.

Several months later, scanning the pages of the little book that held the words we had written, our confidence soared. That book was symbolic. It showed us what we could achieve by simply having a go.

The classes had also distracted me from having to deal with my marriage. There was no time to dwell on it. My mind was occupied with studying and writing short stories. I also found a common interest with three women in the group.

Beth Cartwright, Willy Simms and Sylvia Kerr were strong women, each with a different point of view and outlook on life. A bond of trust quickly developed between us. Our friendship evoked empathy for one another's experiences with ex-husbands.

While each of the three struggled to make ends meet on their social security pensions, I lived comfortably in a villa unit.

Even so, I felt a twinge of envy, mixed with admiration, for their independence and ability to survive against the odds. Their courage had me questioning my capacity to cope with day-to-day stresses as a future single parent. I worried if I could survive the struggles of caring for my daughter, the way they cared for their families.

As I dissected my past and shared confidential details with my new friends, I found a certain amount of humour among the debris. It was refreshing no longer having to pretend that my life was not a shambles. Confiding in them gave me insight into my second failed marriage, as well as the self-assurance I needed to end it.

Stanley was the only reminder of my vulnerability. He made me feel inadequate in the same way Les had. The difference between the two men was that Les was intelligent and cunning and had the ability to hide his hideous personality. Stanley, on the other hand, thought that he was intelligent, when he was actually arrogant, petty and mean spirited. Many of my friends thought so too but were too polite to tell me at first.

48

Once I had regained my confidence I casually mentioned to Stanley, over breakfast, that I was interested in furthering my education with the intention of finding employment. His reaction was what I had expected. Another income would mean that he could afford a better set of golf clubs, afford another holiday, and so on. His thoughts were never far from his wallet or his own comforts.

When Stanley saw that I was enjoying the classes he became disgruntled, saying, "I've always wanted to get a better education and improve myself too."

I could not help but laugh when he said that. I reminded him of the times I tried to encourage him to read, to watch documentaries and current affairs to broaden his mind instead of watching sport, and how he would moan and reject my suggestions, saying "I'm not really interested in reading. I just can't seem to concentrate long enough to finish a book these days. Anyway, I have you to let me know what's going on in the world."

That day I wrote in my journal, "I sure am enjoying my class and I don't feel the least bit guilty about it either... stuff Stanley."

I had invited Stanley to some of my student functions, but he did not fit in. My friends did not like him. One woman actually asked me why I had married a man like him.

"Emma, your husband doesn't suit you at all," she blurted out. "He's not the kind of man I'd expected you to be with."

"Oh, and what kind of man is that, Jill?" I smiled anticipating her reply.

"Someone attractive and charming, someone you'd be happy with, it's obvious that you're not happy with Stanley. He's dull and boring. You change when you're with him, Emma. We just feel that you deserve better, that's all."

Jill later apologised, but I was not offended by her remark. What she had said had been echoed many times before by other friends in Queensland. I actually appreciated her candour, since my decision to leave Stanley was on my mind. His pettiness and tit-for-tat attitude really irritated me so much that I retaliated by going to great lengths to annoy him.

Poor old Stanley detested being late for anything. I was usually the same, but due to my loss of interest in going anywhere with him, I would deliberately procrastinate while getting ready. The more he told me to hurry, the more I dragged my feet. I enjoyed his frustration and took pleasure in his discomfort. The way I reacted to Stanley and his peculiarity was not really the way I would normally behave. I knew that I had to leave him, because I could not restrain myself, and my actions were depriving my character of merit.

Resentment towards Stanley really set in the day of Bree's operation. Although the operation was a success, Bree had a bad reaction to the morphine, but we did not know that at the time. I wanted to stay at the hospital just in case she needed me, but Stanley insisted that I go home with him, saying, "There's nothing you can do here. The nurses will take care of her. You'll only get in their way. Don't worry, she'll be fine."

Against my better judgement, I reluctantly went with him. On the way home I thought about Stanley's attitude and it angered me. He was saying, "You fuss over Bree too much."

I did not reply, but I thought a lot about what I wanted to say to him. I should not have listened to Stanley. He was so selfish that he would not even let his son beat him in a game of golf. Every time they played a game, Stanley would come home gloating that he had beaten Jason again. The boy looked so disappointed that I felt sorry for him.

"Why don't you let Jason win just one game?"

Stanley gave me a look of horror. "Why should I?"

"Because he's your SON, that's why, Stanley." But he only laughed at me.

I worried about Bree all night. If we had not lived so far from the hospital, I would have gone back. When I arrived at the hospital the next morning, Bree was vomiting and was distressed.

"Hey, Babe," I cooed wiping her pale face, "how are you feeling?"

"Rotten," she moaned. "I'm so sore. I've been sick all night, I was crying for you and you weren't there."

"Don't worry, Babe, I'm here now and I'm not going anywhere."

When Stanley came to pick me up, I told him that I would be staying at the hospital.

"For how long?" he asked, clearly lacking compassion for Bree.

"I don't know," I shrugged, "perhaps a few days."

While Stanley was coming to terms with my decision to stay with Bree, a group of her classmates came to visit her, which surprised me. I had no idea she had made so many friends in the space of a few weeks.

Later on, Bree was voted class captain. The position was supposed to be for only six months, but she was voted in twice in the same year. I was so proud and pleased for her when she told me, but Stanley's half-hearted reaction made me suspect that he was jealous of her.

When Celeste wrote, her newsy and often humorous letters encouraged me to hide my feelings about Stanley from her. She sounded so happy. I did not want to spoil that and have her worrying about me. Her letters perked me up and I found myself laughing at her witty remarks.

She had met someone. "You'll love Terry, he's just gorgeous, Mom. I want to have his baby....."

Now that was a big statement, especially coming from a girl who said she would NEVER have any children.

"I want Terry to meet you, Mom."

Telling Celeste that my life was a mess and my second marriage was in tatters would have been unfair to her, especially since she had strived to convince me not to marry Stanley. Besides that, I had not yet thought the whole thing through properly. I had no idea what I should do. Thinking about leaving was about as far as I got.

Bree's access visits with Les highlighted the incompatibility between Stanley and me. On our way home from the airport, after putting Bree on the plane for yet another time to visit Singleton, I said to Stanley, "I think I'll drive up to the Sunshine Coast and spend Christmas with Babs and Paul."

"What!" he replied, looking at me horrified. "What about me? I can't get time off work."

"I know. I don't want to spend Christmas with you. I don't want to be with you at all. I've had enough, Stanley." I said calmly.

"Huh, you could not survive without me. I'm your meal ticket."

His nasty tone made me angry, but I remained calm and said slowly and deliberately, "That's why I don't want to be with you. You make me feel like an emotional cripple. I don't know who I am, Stanley. I intend to get a job when I'm in Queensland. I don't want anything from you."

He began shouting, "I won't give you anything and then we'll see how you get on. You need me."

"We'll see won't we, arsehole," I shouted back.

"Why are you doing this?" he shouted repeatedly, thumping the steering wheel when we stopped at the lights. "I love you. You're MY wife. You're ruining my life."

I looked on in utter disbelief as bits of broken wheel flew about the front compartment, and roared with laughter when Stanley, crimson-faced, veins bulging and splattered with saliva, ended up with the steering wheel on his lap.

"Now look what you have done, dickhead. And you want me to stay with you. You're a madman."

"It's your fault, you bitch. You did this to me."

"All the more reason why we shouldn't be together, I'm going to Queensland."

The argument continued at home. "You're stupid to even consider driving all that distance alone," he shouted at me. "You won't be able to do it on your own."

When I actually thought about it, I realised that driving to Queensland was rather daring for me. Street directories were a mystery to me - I had often read them upside down, then ended up lost the moment I turned a corner.

"But," I told myself, "it's time to conquer my fear. I need to take control of my life."

I looked at Stanley defiantly. "I don't care. I'm going all the same. I need a break from you and I don't think I'll come back."

"What do mean, you don't think you'll came back," he squealed like a stuck pig as I packed up the car. "You couldn't survive without me."

"Just watch me," I said, ever so sweetly, and then drove away.

This past year has certainly been eventful, I thought, filling up the tank. We had all settled into new environments. Bree had her operation and was on the way to recovery. I had made new friends, I am seriously considering university in the New Year and now I'm about to leave my second husband.

Yes, I'd say it certainly has been an eventful year. I smiled and started humming, "I'm a Travellin' Man……," as I replaced the pump after filling up with petrol.

49

The Sunshine Coast is picturesque and tranquil, a place where I thought I could take time out from life's turmoils. But that was not possible with Stanley calling me at Babs' home several times a day, apologising for the breakdown of our marriage and promising to change in his quest for another chance to prove himself. Every time he called, I endeavoured to convey to him that our marriage did not fail because of him. "It was many things," I said. "The main one being that I don't love you."

He interrupted me whining, "But I love you and need you in my life."

"That's what this is all about, isn't it Stanley? You. Always you and what you want. Well, I want out! And I am going to do what's good for me from now on. Goodbye!"

If he was not telephoning me, he was writing letters or sending cards. He was completely irrational and made me wonder about his stability. The letters and cards came one after another. After the second one I did not even bother to read them any more since it was blatantly obvious that they were all the same. There was no point - I had been through it with him so many times before.

In an effort to stop Stanley from persistently calling, I asked him to give me six months to consider my options to decide whether I wanted to remain married or not, when I really wanted to scream, 'Get out of my life, arsehole!' But I knew if I said anything like that, it would only set him off and would prove non-productive.

The non-stop telephone calls, cards and letters were embarrassing. The way Stanley acted, the general consensus was that he was a fool and a nuisance. Frustrated, Babs spoke to him after he had telephoned six times in one day, in the hope of reasoning with him, saying that I needed time to decide what I wanted to do. Her advice fell on deaf ears.

In one way, I was pleased that Stanley acted the way he did; it had given credence to what I had said about him. His behaviour showed my friends what he was really like. To say they were surprised at the extent of his obsession would have been an understatement.

For all Stanley's declarations of undying love, I could not bring myself to believe him. He was competitive and loathed the idea of losing, and like Les, wanted something he could not have. It would seem that I was more desirable as a challenge and Stanley was determined to win me over, even going as far as humiliating himself to achieve it.

"What are going to do?" Babs asked, as we lounged in patio chairs overlooking her rainforest garden and waterfall.

"Not what I would like to do," I grinned mischievously.

"Well, I won't ask what that would be," she said, and then changed the subject to their evacuation from Bougainville.

Tears always formed in Babs' eyes at any mention of the last days on Bougainville. I had wondered why she continually talked about it when it was so obviously painful. Among other things, Babs mourned the loss of her material possessions but as far as I could see, her new home was overflowing with the same furniture and New Guinea artefacts she had in her home on Bougainville.

Whenever the subject came up, I could not help thinking that there were so many conflicting stories regarding the war on Bougainville Island. All factions involved blamed the other party for the upheaval. Who really was the enemy? I wondered. No one really knew for sure. Everyone involved had an agenda. My personal view of the war was that it was generated from greed and lust for power. But sadly, innocent bystanders always suffer, and that's where my empathy lay.

As Babs reminisced, my thoughts slipped back to the evening my children saw the television news footage of the devastation of their childhood home. The look of shock and utter disbelief in their eyes revealed their feelings. The places that they knew as children had been blown to smithereens. BJ had mournfully mumbled something about returning 'home' someday, but now there was no point. There was nothing left to see.

My nomadic thoughts snapped back at the sound of Babs' voice, "Feel like another cup of tea?"

I smiled my thanks and watched her walk through the sliding door from the patio and go into the kitchen. I could see her moving about from where I lay and thought that although I had known Barbara almost thirty years, she was still a mystery to me. She was far from beautiful but managed to beguile people with her flamboyant way, presenting herself as an astute businesswoman. I could never work out what it was she actually did. Her office was tastefully decorated in expensive décor, but nothing much seemed to happen there. It would also seem that at every opportunity she gave advice about anything and everything, while failing to heed it herself.

"What a complex person she is," I mused, trying to work her out.

For whatever reason Babs was motivated to extend generosity and open her home freely to anyone, I was grateful to be one of her recipients. But as life experiences have taught me, nothing is ever free.

I had some serious options to consider while I lounged on the patio chair and one of them was employment.

"I have to find a job, Babs," I said, feeling a sense of urgency. "Where's the local paper?"

After a futile search through the employment section, Babs offered me a position as receptionist with her company in exchange for room and board. She told me that her business was not capital-flush and could not pay wages. I took the offer as an opportunity to learn to handle the computer. I was beginning to feel that doors were finally opening for me; that I could manage on my own merit and look after Bree as well.

The office work was not demanding. There was not much for me to do other than to practise learning the computer. Most calls were from Stanley. When he discovered that I was already working, he told me that he was seriously thinking of quitting his job and coming back to Queensland to be with me. He had me convinced that he would do just that and my heart sank to the core of my stomach. If he came, leaving Victoria would have defeated my purpose. Beaten, I ended up telling Stanley that I would return to Melbourne after the holidays.

50

The festive season brought frequent visitors to Babs' and Paul's home. The telephone rang as refreshments were being served. I answered the phone, since I was the closest to it.

"Merry Christmas, Ma!"

"Hi BJ! How are you?"

"When are you coming down to Brisbane, Ma?"

"Are you okay, mate? Is something wrong? I can come tomorrow if you need me."

"I don't feel so good, Ma, I've been vomiting blood. I've been to the doctor and he gave me a blood test. I have to wait a few days for the results…"

"What did the doctor say? How do you feel now…?" I was firing questions at him one after the other, even before he could answer them.

"It's cool, Ma, I'm okay. Don't worry."

"But I am worried BJ."

We talked a little longer and before I said goodbye I insisted that he call me the moment he had the results of his tests.

The following day Brad called. "I rushed BJ to hospital last night," he said, "he's in a bad way, Mom. You'd better come quickly."

"What is wrong with BJ, Brad?"

"No one seems to know, but he's already had three blood transfusions. His blood count was critically low and he needed the transfusions immediately. The doctors aren't sure what's wrong with him, Mom. You'd better come down."

My arrival at the hospital was timely and I was able to shed light on the mystery illness. The effects of the Hereditary Spherocytosis were severe enough to warrant BJ having six transfusions. Once the problem was confirmed, BJ was rushed into surgery to remove his enlarged spleen.

I decided to stay in Brisbane for whatever length of time was necessary, insisting that I was not going anywhere until BJ was out of danger, and well on the way to recovery. Knowing that I did not have a place to stay other than a motel, Brad offered me BJ's room at the unit, fully aware that his father would strongly object to my being anywhere near the place. Brad told me that Cain was living with his girlfriend and her family and would not be there.

Brad's act of kindness surprised me, but I graciously accepted it in the hope of healing old wounds.

At the unit Brad was hospitable and seemed relaxed in my company. Then without any warning, Cain walked through the door and darted up the stairs. About halfway he turned to acknowledge Brad and was surprised to see me sitting on the couch drinking coffee. He did not say anything, only giving me a nod. Brad silently cursed when Cain entered, realising that he would tell Les I was there.

Later that evening the telephone rang and Brad answered it.

"Nah, she's not staying here. She's at the hospital. Yeah okay, I know..."

When he returned to his chair Brad did not say that it was his father who had called, but I knew by the irritation in his voice. I later learned that Brad had been ordered not to let me near the unit again, as Les reminded him that he was the one who paid the rent. Feeling Brad's discomfort, I told him I would go to a motel. "Nah, it's okay, Mom, you can stay here," he said.

At the hospital, a couple of BJ's mates kept me company while we waited for BJ to be brought back to the ward after the surgery. When the orderly wheeled him into the ward, he was semiconscious.

"Ma, I love you," he mumbled. "I love my mom," he murmured again and everyone chuckled. It warmed my heart knowing BJ was genuine. He was not in the least embarrassed when his friends later told him what he had said under the influence of the anaesthetic.

"Well," he announced proudly to everyone present, "I do love my mother."

The following morning I heard Brad vomiting violently in the bathroom. When he called me he sounded distressed, "I think something's wrong with my kidneys, Mom. I've turned an awful yellow."

"Oh, I don't think so, Brad." I said. "It's Spherocytosis.'

"Ah, crap!" he yelled back irritated.

"Well then, let's get you to the hospital and find out."

Brad's girlfriend arrived in the middle of our debate and she assisted Brad to her car while I followed them in mine.

Driving along the freeway, my thoughts were on Brad and how quickly he had changed towards me. I could hardly believe that he was the same person who only twenty-four hours before had been so warm and friendly. Within a short space of time his friendliness was replaced with hostility. "What a disagreeable and aggressive young man he can be," I said out loud, "A perfect copy of his father. Nonetheless, I'm still his mother and I'll be there for him if he needs me."

I felt a deep regret at the knowledge that my presence calmed one son and caused disharmony in the other. 'I love both of them,' I thought. 'I don't know why the universe allowed me to have only three and not all five of my children in my life.'

Coming to terms with my loss was very difficult. Losing my son's affection left a huge gaping hole in my heart that I felt would never heal. But I was determined that I would not let it get to me this time. I patted my eyes dry, turned up the car radio and sang along with the tune.

At the hospital, the debate about Brad's condition carried on in the outpatient's room. He refused to accept that I could be right. When the doctor arrived to examine Brad, he asked him what was wrong. Brad moaned in discomfort, "I think it's my kidneys, Doc."

I was standing close by the cubicle and overheard what he had said and quickly stepped inside and introduced myself, then politely suggested to the doctor that he consider Hereditary Spherocytosis.

"Why?" he asked, looking at me.

The doctor returned a couple of hours later with the results I had expected and informed us that it was highly unusual for so many in one family to have the disease. "It normally skips a generation or two before showing up again," he said. At that moment I thought, just about everything about my life was unusual, so why not this too.

Brad was admitted into hospital, under instructions not to even walk around due to the high risk of suffering a heart attack. He was under observation but surgery was inevitable. Ironically Brad was allocated a bed not only in the same ward as BJ but right next to him.

My sons were as unlike each other in personality as in stature. What BJ lacked in height, he made up for in personality. He possessed a kind and forgiving nature and was well liked and held in high esteem by his peers. The influx of visitors confirmed that, all having something nice to say to me about him. I felt a certain pride in knowing that he was successful simply by being a caring human being.

BJ was almost eighteen. A surfing lifestyle had captured his interest in a huge way and he indulged in all that was attached to a free-living environment. Material trappings had never interested BJ as his nomadic lifestyle had no room for 'things'. His long, thick strawberry-blonde, sun-bleached, unkempt curls gave him a bohemian appearance. As he lay clad in a hospital gown, I thought his style fitted perfectly with his free spirit. 'My beautiful wild child,' I thought, smiling. I knew that BJ's playful nature and smile hid the pain that lay deep in his soul, and prayed that one day soon he would find his place and be happy in the way he deserved to be.

Brad was vastly different to BJ. His large physique filled the hospital bed but his good looks were spoiled by a sullen abrasive attitude. How sad, I thought, standing back and observing him from the other side of the room. His lack of compassion and patience were tendencies inherited from his father. Watching him, I felt sad when I noticed that his smile did not reach his deep blue eyes. I thought he looked unhappy, but knew that I could not ease his burden. I could only hope that he too would eventually have peace in his life.

While I was silently contemplating the difference in personalities between BJ and Brad, Cain walked in with his fiancée Cindy. He greeted me coolly. I was surprised how stern and hard his features had become. Even while he interacted with BJ's friends, his expression did not soften. I saw no joy in him, only bitterness, especially in his eyes. Physically, Cain resembled Luc, but Les' cruel and vindictive nature had rubbed off on him over the years.

I ignored Cain's apparent contempt for me, hoping that one day he would forgive me. Cindy did not even acknowledge me. Her attitude triggered a memory of something Les had told me in a moment of truce. Cindy had confessed to him that she was jealous of anyone who came near Cain. But I knew that Cindy's dislike of me went further than that.

Cain became involved with Cindy shortly after I had left the family home. She was fifteen and he seventeen. I had suspected that she was the girl I had seen in a compromising situation with Cain, one morning when I came to the house thinking no one was at home. BJ's friends told me that she and her girlfriends had a reputation, but since I had not met her, I could not form any opinion.

My initial impression of Cindy was surprise. She was not like any of Cain's previous girlfriends. They were generally far more attractive.

Whenever Cain came to Stanley's home to pick up Bree for the weekend, Cindy was with him. Since she was not old enough to drive, Cain drove the car her parents gave her for her sixteenth birthday.

I thought Cindy looked uncomfortable in my company. Her narrow, elongated face wore a forced smile and her hair, although fashionably permed and coloured was pulled back into a ponytail. A frizzy fringe that sat above her brow line accentuated the length of her face. The light coloured jeans and snug-fitting singlet top she wore emphasised her curves, and did little to disguise her large bottom.

I neither liked nor disliked Cindy but was surprised that she lacked style, because her parents were wealthy. Irrespective of her reaction to meeting me, or my opinion of her, I failed in my attempt to put her at ease by trying to make small talk. She was not like Cain's other girlfriends, who had always been warm and eager to become my friend. Cindy acted as though she did not want to know me at all and actually supported Les' disapproval of Cain visiting me. I sensed her pulling him away from me. When I told Cain during a phone conversation that I felt Cindy's family was grooming him for marriage to her, his response to that was, "Ah, bullshit! You don't know what you're talking about."

"You think so? Well, let me tell you something mate, you will be married to that girl within two years." He slammed the receiver down in my ear.

Cain had it good living with Cindy and her family. Her parents showered him with lavish gifts. A gold watch was an impressive temptation to a young lad whose world had just fallen apart. He went from his broken home to Cindy's, where he found a family.

Almost a year after my prediction, I was in the middle of a conversation with a friend, when a vision of Cain and Cindy's engagement flashed into my mind. The suddenness of the vision shocked me enough to mention it to my friend.

"You seem worried, Emma. Don't you like the girl?"

"It's not about the girl, it's about Cain being too young and I'm not sure if he's getting married for the right reasons."

Brad officially announced the news of the engagement to me with an impromptu phone call. I quickly let him know that I already knew, taking him completely by surprise. Although I had had a heavy heart about the whole thing, I bought an engagement card, intending to send them my best wishes, but could not bring myself to send it. Instead, I wrote a letter to Cain telling him that I would normally have seen his engagement as an occasion to celebrate, but I could not celebrate when I was not sure if his reasons for the engagement were the right ones. I told him I felt it was motivated by the need to be part of a family more than being in love with Cindy, and stressed the importance of love in a relationship; without it life could be unbearable.

Cain's immaturity inhibited honest interpretation of the letter and my words were misconstrued and twisted. Cindy viewed it as a personal attack on her, which was not my intention. If either of them had given the letter a second thought, they might have seen that my own experiences were reason enough to urge Cain to assess his motives before marrying at such a young age. The infamous letter had sealed my fate to be permanently banished from Cain's life.

Cain and Cindy were married shortly after the hospital visit, just as I had predicted, and Cindy's family gave them everything they needed to ensure an easy start to their future, but their marriage ended in divorce some years later.

'How amazing it is,' I considered, standing beside BJ's bed, 'even after all this time the tension they brought with them could be cut with a knife. But I certainly did not feel ill-at-ease. I enjoyed seeing Cain.' I smiled with gratitude because it had been ages since I had seen him.

I actually found myself enjoying Cindy's challenge. Although I had never been hostile towards her before, I found her attitude towards me particularly provocative that day and did not let it slide. BJ's friends knew of the rift and waited in great expectation of a scene.

I can't recall the remark Cindy made to me that incited me to retaliate, by asking Cain if he had seen Kate lately. I was fully aware that Cindy knew Cain's old girlfriend was still interested in him and that I was very fond of Kate, who was my choice as a daughter-in-law. Cindy's sullen silence told me that I had successfully hit a nerve.

After they had left, BJ gently scolded me, "Now, Ma, you shouldn't have said that. Cain is going to get his arse kicked," and everyone chuckled because they knew he was right.

When BJ was discharged from hospital, it was time for me to leave Brisbane. My presence only seemed to aggravate Brad. Since BJ was fine and Brad's girlfriend would take care of him, I returned to the north coast.

51

When I returned to Barbara's place, I had to brace myself for Stanley's arrival. Even though I felt awkward having to face him, given that my respect for him was totally diminished, I knew I had to resolve the situation one way or another. There was no way of avoiding it.

When Barbara had introduced me to Eric Thompson, an associate of hers, the first week I had arrived, I knew that my marriage to Stanley was over. Eric and I were instantly attracted to each other. He was a fine artist; I admired and even envied the ease with which he executed his craft.

The scene was set for romance the evening Eric asked me to join him for dinner. We dined on seafood and drank white wine *alfresco* before a stroll along the deserted beach. In an illuminating moonlight, our silhouettes cast elongated shadows across the sand as we walked along the shore's edge.

"You're so lucky to be surrounded with all this beauty, Eric," I said, brushing my hair away from my face.

"You could enjoy all this too if you stayed," he replied, sitting down in the sand. I stood looking down at him, thinking that his cheesecloth shirt, cotton shorts and sandals were a stark contrast to Stanley's clothes.

"Hmm, I'd like to, but I don't know," I said, shivering in the cool breeze, "Stanley's being a real pain, as you know. He's calling me all the time and now he's talking about coming up here."

I plonked down beside Eric. As I made myself comfortable tucking my long cotton skirt around my legs, he moved closer and put his arm around me.

"Cold?"

"Mmm, a bit," I replied, looking at the water. It sparkled like millions of tiny diamonds.

That evening was pleasant. I knew it was only an interlude, and that being with Eric was wrong. I could take up drinking, I thought, trying to convince myself that having a fling with him was okay because I was not in love with Stanley and never was.

In the light of day, my analytical mind became my conscience, and I began to question what kind of person I had become. I noted in my journal, 'Perhaps I really am a bad person, driven by revenge, but I'll worry about that later on.'

When Stanley finally arrived, he was so happy to see me that he almost smothered me, declaring that he had changed and everything would be different. He greeted Barbara and Paul as if they were close friends, talking about his trip as if they cared. They smiled awkwardly and seemed embarrassed for him, but Stanley did not notice.

A few days later we left the coast, collecting Bree from Brisbane on our way to Victoria. Once we had settled back into our routines, I decided to visit a Spiritualist Church in hope of discovering why I cheat on my husbands.

The church I wanted to visit was close to the city, but I was not sure how to find it. Reluctantly, I asked Stanley to drive me there. True to form, he wanted to know the whys and wherefores of my visit.

"Why do you have to know everything all the time?" I asked, exasperated. "Can't I simply talk to a minister without having to tell you why? It's my business. I bet you don't tell me everything you do."

After I had spoken, Stanley's questioning look said, 'Well, why are you going?' That look forced me to lie to him.

Since the appointment was for me, Stanley was not invited to join us in the church and had to wait for me in the foyer.

"Who's the man with you?" the minister asked, "Your husband?" I nodded.

"He's not good for you." His frankness surprised me. Then after a pause the minister said casually. "But don't worry about that, you won't be with him for much longer."

The church looked ancient and in disrepair. Wooden pews lined both sides of the church and the minister's huge frame took up a large portion of the seat. The dark blue batik-print caftan he wore expanded under the pressure of him flicking his white ponytail aside. I thought he was interesting and liked the way his weathered features appeared youthful when he smiled.

We talked at great length and I expressed concerns regarding my affairs.

"Oh, don't worry about that," he said, almost laughing, "none of that will happen when you meet the right man. We are funny creatures," he said thoughtfully, "we can act out of the ordinary when wrongly placed. You're not in harmony with your husband," he said then paused, "but you already know that."

I was really surprised that the minister dismissed the matter as trivial, expecting a lecture on morality. I left the church feeling much better and could actually see a brighter future ahead of me. Driving home, I told Stanley I wanted to go to the meditation circle held at the church. He did not understand what I was looking for, but did not object to my joining the group.

The first evening a woman talked about the technique of psychometry, holding an object in her hand and visualising the person who owned it.

'I've done that,' I thought, but had no idea I was doing psychometry.

Going to the group was a great learning experience. What I learned was invaluable and I used it whenever I needed to make major decisions. I kept going until the evening I heard my inner voice tell me not to go any more. Even though I was halfway there, I turned the car around and went home and never went back.

I came back from the Sunshine Coast with the intention of trying to mend my marriage, and even went house hunting with Stanley. We moved from the rented house into a lovely villa-unit Stanley bought, with the promise that my name would be added to the property deed the day I was discharged from bankruptcy. As I had expected, the promise was broken but I did not pursue the matter. I just waited, hoping that he would surprise me, even though, in my heart I knew he lacked integrity.

Stanley's persistent nagging and bullying of Bree over petty issues became a bone of contention with me. I saw little purpose being in a marriage with a man who made it very clear that everything belonged to him, and insisted that his way of doing things was the right way.

Whenever Bree asked me for assistance with her homework, Stanley would butt in and take over. His method of helping was to bully her, which would lead to an argument. It was maddening the way he managed to turn a simple situation into a nightmare. I felt concerned and worried that he would strike Bree in my absence, when she started to talk back to him.

The close friendship Bree and Stanley once had, had quickly dissolved, due to his attitude. His competitive personality challenged her every accomplishment, as opposed to giving her praise.

Bree's forte was horse-back riding. She had displayed a keen interest in the sport from the early age of four years and dreamt of one day owning her own horse. I promised that she would when she turned fifteen. Her first riding lesson showed that she had great potential, but instead of encouraging Bree,

Stanley found fault and fancied himself an expert horseman. He had led us to believe that he was experienced at handling livestock. We did not know at the time that his only experience with horses was as a child, when his father owned four acres of land and had a few horses agisted on the property.

Bree had taken Stanley's criticism of her riding ability to heart. While I had no prior knowledge of horses or the art of riding them, I believed in her potential and encouraged her to believe in her ability, realising that Stanley was actually jealous of her.

Each morning I would wave them goodbye from the front door then go and clear away the breakfast dishes. One morning I went to the window instead and was surprised to find the car still stationary in the driveway. I craned my neck to see what was going on. Stanley was waving his finger in Bree's face and appeared to be yelling at her. I could only see the top of her head and did not know whether or not she was crying. By the time I had reached the door, Stanley had driven out of the driveway and down the street.

That afternoon when I collected Bree from school, I noticed that she seemed a little subdued. I mentioned what I had seen through the window that morning and saw fear in her expression.

"Is there anything I should know, Babe?" I asked and she shook her head, wanting to know if I was going to say anything to Stanley.

"Is there any reason why I shouldn't?"

"He told me not to say anything to you about getting into trouble. He said I'd be in worse trouble if I did."

"Well sweetie, you won't have to worry about that much longer."

"What are you going to do, Mom?"

"Leave him. I've had enough. Okay?"

"Okay," Bree sighed, and a smile crept across her face as she relaxed in the seat.

After dinner that evening, I looked at Stanley and said cheerfully, "Guess what?"

"What?" he responded enthusiastically.

"I've been discharged from bankruptcy for over three months. Are you going to add my name to the property deed like you promised?" As I had expected he said, "No."

"Well then, I'm leaving," I said, and told him what furniture I wanted as I gathered a few of my belongings from our bedroom and headed for the spare bedroom.

"What are you doing?"

"What's it look like? I'll stay in the spare room until I leave in a few days."

He followed me from room to room, telling me I was ruining his and Bree's life by breaking up the family. "You can't take anything, I won't let you," he screeched

"Fine," I said calmly, "we'll do without. We don't need anything from you. I'll just take what belongs to me."

He stood in the doorway of my room ranting for hours on end about how I could not take care of Bree or myself without him, while I tried to block out his voice and sleep.

"I'm your meal ticket," he scoffed.

When I did not respond in the way he had expected, he promised to have the deed changed the next day.

"What you fail to understand," I sprung up from my bed and hissed at him, livid with fury after hours of listening to him whingeing and depriving me of sleep, "is that I hate you. I wouldn't stay with you a minute longer than I have to. Even if you gave me this bloody place, I wouldn't take it. I don't want it. I don't want anything from you other than a divorce. All I want is to be free of you! Get out! Get out and let me go to sleep!"

Stanley ignored what I said and continued to whine. I lay still listening to him go on and on, saying the same things Les had said to me years before. I wondered if there was a losers' manual circulating about somewhere, because of the similarity in the dialogue. As the hours passed I hated Stanley that little bit more, remembering his imperfections, some of which were so silly that they were funny.

He had a habit of posing naked, admiring his image in the bathroom mirror. Propped up in bed engrossed in a book I heard, "Well, pretty good huh?" he said, challenging me to admit that he was right. I looked up and found him posing in the doorway of our en suite. Bright lighting behind him illuminated his every imperfection, which was unflattering to the point of being hilarious. I lost my composure and began to laugh hysterically, not only at the unattractive rectangular torso and shapeless legs, but at the longest scrotum I had ever seen, when all he could see was perfection.

"What's so funny?" he asked with uncertainty while still in the pose.

"And women worry about their breasts drooping," I roared. "Perhaps men should take a really good look at themselves too. Now I know the reason your jocks seem so full. Your balls are jammed inside them."

I laughed so much that he ended up laughing too. If he was not so conceited, he would not have missed my insult.

"You need me," I heard him screech. "I've done so much for you."

"And what have I done for you?" I spat back, sitting up to face him. "It was I who introduced you to a cultured lifestyle and encouraged and showed you how to improve yourself when you asked me to. Then suddenly you became an expert and took credit for everything I had shown you. On top of that, you tried to steal my life and my identity and left me almost a shell of myself. I'm becoming as nasty as you, is that your legacy to me for helping you – your personality? I can't bear the sight of you. You're a conceited little man. You didn't even know much about sex, I had to teach you that too! And you believed yourself to be God's gift to women. Huh, you may hold a chance with someone else now that you know how."

"I don't want to be with anyone else!" His face became taut and crimson, choking out the sentence.

"Why not? I don't want you! You're a small man with a small mind and a small dick."

"I haven't got a small dick!!"

Stanley refused to believe that I meant all the cruel things I had said to him. He believed I loved him, apologising once again for his weaknesses, pleading with me to stay, saying that he needed me in his life to help him to become a better person.

"Stanley," my words were firm and deliberate, "if you don't go away from me, I'll end up killing you."

He finally withdrew, the wisest move he had made that night, and I went to sleep. I had murder in my heart. I felt heavily weighed down. Stanley held me responsible for ruining his life and the failed marriage, just as Les had done years before.

I felt tortured about the destruction of my family. For years I had wrestled with the guilt, believing that it was my fault, but not this time. I was not having any of Stanley's crap. It was his life and he was responsible for it. The following evening he came home and told me that he had seen a lawyer.

"A settlement will be ready for you by the end of the week," he said, "you can take whatever furniture you want."

When I told him that I did not want anything other than Bree's and my belongings, he pleaded with me to take what I had initially asked for. To shut him up I reluctantly accepted his offer, expecting him to break his agreement when I moved. Surprisingly, he not only kept his word, he helped me move into my new home in the next suburb.

52

Living in a peaceful environment and having the freedom to visit my friends did not feel natural. I kept looking over my shoulder, expecting to see Stanley pop up and ask, "Where are you going?" Things were too perfect, I thought, life has never before given me what I really wanted, so why would it happen this time. Just as I was beginning to relax, Stanley telephoned, wanting to know how I was coping without him.

"Great," I said enthusiastically. Time away from him had eased my grievances against him and I saw no reason why I should not tell him what I was doing. "I'm waiting for notification from the university. I want to get my Associate Diploma in Social Science."

"That's good," he said mournfully, "you can use my computer whenever you need to. I'm not doing anything. I can't concentrate on anything. I just go home after work and stay there. I miss you so much. Life isn't the same without you." He sounded so pathetic that it took me all my strength not to laugh.

The first telephone call was easy to dismiss. Then Stanley called several more times and started sending cards and letters asking me to forgive him and give him another chance. He sounded so sincere that I ended up feeling sorry for him. In one of his letters, he asked me to have dinner with him on our wedding anniversary; I accepted the invitation out of pity.

Surprisingly, that evening went well, and I accepted other invitations, not realising that I was misleading Stanley. He was angry when he discovered I had changed my name, and exploded, "You're still officially MY wife."

"I'm not yours or anyone's anything any longer," I said calmly; "I belong to me."

After the first fight Stanley rang, accusing me of ruining his life, and I slammed the receiver down in his ear. He called back immediately and kept the phone ringing until I answered it. It went on like that for several weeks. In frustration and livid with fury I would violently snatch the receiver from the wall and scream obscenities into it then slam it down again. I had to take the phone off the hook to prevent him from calling me, but he would start calling again when I hung up. He almost drove me insane. I knew the way we both acted was ridiculous and childish, but I felt powerless to control myself.

When Stanley finally tired of calling, an eerie silence hung in the room and I felt exhausted. Silence allowed me time to analyse his accusations. I sat quietly thinking. The more I thought about what he accused me of, the more my stomach churned with anger that carried over to the following day. I would respond to his lies by leaving a message on his answering machine, knowing he would have already left for work. Then in a moment of extreme regret, I would call back and leave an apology message, telling him that I did not like what my association with him was doing to my character, and that there was something about him that irritated me so much that it triggered off a negative response in me that I couldn't control. "It is in our best interest," I said, "if we don't have anything more to do with each other."

It would have been easy for anyone who listened to those messages, without having any prior knowledge of what had provoked them, to assume I had lost all sense of reasoning. During one of our telephone battles, Stanley let it slip that he had kept the recordings. "I have evidence that you're unbalanced," he said spitefully, endeavouring to prove his point.

"What are you talking about, arsehole?"

"I've kept the messages you left on my machine, all of them. You really sound unbalanced."

"Of course I'm unbalanced, who wouldn't be after living with you. You know what Stanley? You are a mean-spirited little man with a little mind, and you're a liar too. You told me that you were lonely. You were not lonely at all. You were having the time of your life going to clubs, playing tennis and playing golf."

"I can go out if I want to."

"Yes, you can," I said, then mimicked his mournful moan. "But you were so lonely without me and you didn't want to do anything. I found out about your imaginary loneliness the day you asked Bree and I to that social club trail ride. We only went because I had ridden a horse only once before, and was eager to ride again, and Bree loves riding," I said sarcastically.

"While we were selecting our horses," I rambled on quickly so he could not respond to anything I said, "Bree and I overheard your office cronies discussing the tennis and golf games they recently had, and YOUR riding ability. We had a good laugh about that when we heard it. Riding ability my foot. The trail boss really showed you up when he handed you an endurance champion to ride after he overheard the conversation too. From the moment you plonked your butt in the saddle, the horse jigged and jogged about because you held a tight grip on the reins, locking up the horse. Bree and I were on the brink of laughter."

Stanley butted in and yelled at me, but my mind was on the rest of that day. It all came flooding back and the scene played in my brain like a movie.....a white pony had been saddled and ready for Bree but she walked past it and mounted a black thoroughbred standing nearby. The trail boss called out, "That mare might be a bit much for ya little girl, it's only been off the racetrack a few months."

"May I try?" Bree asked politely.

The trail boss nodded, then said, "Well hmm, okay, walk 'er round the yard a bit," and watched her check everything before mounting up. She eased the horse forward and walked around the yard.

"Yeah," he grinned, nodding, "you'll be right."

"How long's your daughter been ridin'?" The trail boss asked, coming up alongside me an hour into the ride.

"About a year."

"Guess she's a natural, like 'er mom."

"This is only my second time on a horse," I laughed, thinking he was joking

"Well, ya could'a fooled me," he shouted, galloping off.

I grinned with pride and sat taller in the saddle because I knew Stanley overheard him.

"You tried to make me look stupid," I heard Stanley say, breaking into my thoughts.

"What! I did not. You were pissed off because of the trail boss' response to us. You obviously couldn't control your horse, dickhead. You made yourself look stupid. And then you gave us an earful on the way home because we had unintentionally stolen your thunder. You're full of shit, Stanley. I only went out with you because you made me feel sorry for you. Arsehole! Little dick!" I snapped, angry with myself more than with Stanley, for not seeing through his lies. Just before I slammed the phone down, I heard him screech "I haven't got a …" and I roared laughing, '… a small dick,' I imagined he wanted to say.

The phone rang again but I resisted answering this time. It kept ringing until well after midnight and started again around five the next morning. I tried to ignore it but after a while it began to grate on my nerves. Seething, I snatched up the receiver, waited for him to speak and then let fly with a barrage of profanities that would make a drunken sailor blush.

I heard my voice, but could not fathom that it was me who was saying those dreadful words. Realisation of what I was doing shocked me into shrieking, "Look what you're doing to me! You're dragging me down to your level. I don't know myself any more. I never used to swear, but listen to me now.

I am one of the best. I hate you so much and I hate myself for what I've become since I've been with you."

Out of the corner of my eye, I noticed a movement in the doorway. I quickly turned, while in the middle of an ear-splitting sentence, and found Bree standing there open-mouthed and wide-eyed. I put my hand over the mouthpiece, while Stanley was screaming back at me and whispered pathetically, "It's all right, Babe. I'm so sorry that you had to hear this rubbish. I know what I'm doing is wrong but I can't help it."

I turned back to the telephone and listened for a moment to Stanley's ranting, before quietly placing the receiver on the hook. He rang back again but I let the phone ring out. It went on for almost an hour. When it rang for the umpteenth time, I took the receiver off the hook and let it dangle by the cord. Bree and I could hear him squealing for me to pick up the phone. We silently giggled as we ate breakfast. 'And he has the hide to accuse me of being unbalanced,' I thought.

Although Bree and I were laughing that morning, it was by no means a laughing matter, but indeed a very serious situation. The way Stanley and I behaved affected me greatly. It was dehumanising. When Bree left to spend time with Les shortly afterwards, I fell into a deep depression.

In the silence of my unit, all the horrible words Stanley and I spewed at each other echoed in my mind. I thought about how both husbands blamed me for destroying their lives and both said I was insane and caused them a great deal of heartache. Living in a steady breeding ground of torment was dragging me down. I felt worthless and once again wrestled with the decision to exit my miserable existence.

I sat at the antique dining table Stanley and had I bought just after we were married, staring at the glass of water and small bottle of sleeping pills in front of me, awaiting my decision. My mouth felt dry. I took a sip from the glass then placed it back on the table. I picked up the pills and removed the lid and poured them into my palm. At that moment I had a clear image of Bree and, just as suddenly as her image appeared, it vanished. I sobbed with shame, then took the pills and flushed them down the toilet.

The following week, I arrived at the airport to pick up Bree. She rushed towards me when she saw me and hugged me tight. "Are you okay, Mom?" she asked, as if she knew what I had intended to do. "I've been so worried about you. I'd die if anything happened to you."

"I'm okay, Babe, nothing is going to happen to me. I've got you."

* * *

Visiting the Community Centre twelve months before was one of the best steps I had ever taken. Going to classes kept me balanced. I met not only Beth, Sylvia and Willy, but also a couple of young ambitious teachers, who were preparing to open a private tutoring school and needed a receptionist. They offered me the position. My response was one of surprise and I declined, confessing that I did not have any experience other than limited computer skills.

"We'll teach you," they said. "We can't pay you until we are established, but we'll assist you with your uni assignments."

"I haven't been accepted yet, "I laughed.

"But you will be," Michelle Larson and Marko Spiro chorused, beaming encouraging smiles at me. "Think about it and let us know."

Since I had financial security I took the job, for the experience as well as a distraction, to prevent me from dwelling on the battle I was having with Stanley.

Several weeks after I started at the tutoring centre, I received a letter from the university telling me that I was not accepted. I was so disappointed that I called the university to ask the coordinator why.

"Your number didn't come up," she said.

"That's it? My number didn't come up."

"Yes."

"Well," I said, "I need a career because I have a daughter to look after. I'm going to call back in two weeks' time because I know there will be dropouts and then there will be a place that I can fill."

"This is unusual, but I see no harm in you calling me then."

I did call back, several times in fact. On the last call I was given an enrolment schedule.

My days were full with work at the office, night classes, study and taking care of Bree. When Les found out that my marriage to Stanley was over, he declared his intention. Bree arrived home with a gift for me from him, a book on Renoir with a note enclosed that said, "I love you, I can't help myself. I always will, Les."

My heart sank with dread, sensing that Les would not be easily dissuaded. On Bree's birthday he sent me a dozen long-stem red roses thanking me for our beautiful daughter. What the hell is he doing? I thought, what's he up to? I tore up the note and was about to dramatically toss the roses in the garbage just like they did in movies, but I could not do that, they were too beautiful.

The evening Les called to speak to Bree, I was polite and made no mention of either the book or the roses. "Hope you like the book," he said just before I called Bree to the phone, "I remembered that you love art. I also hear you're pretty good at painting."

I was not sure how to respond as being civil to each other seemed unnatural. Before he could say another word I blurted out, "Thank you for the book, I'm giving it my best shot, the roses are lovely. Bree is waiting," and handed her the phone.

Summer and winter passed quickly and in the freshness of spring I considered returning to Queensland. On the surface everything appeared to be running smoothly when it really was not.

The tutoring centre was a disappointment. A surprising discovery about the integrity of my employers was highlighted within the first few weeks, when I was asked to unpack and stack several boxes of books on the shelves. I came across books I knew belonged to the community centre and went to the office to tell them I thought that there must be a mistake, because so many of the books had the community centre mark on them.

"Oh just black that out," Michelle said looking coyly at Marko.

"But they have obviously been stolen," I said, feeling concerned and uncomfortable.

"It's okay, Emma," Marko said getting up out of his chair to put a reassuring arm around my shoulder and guiding me out of the room. "It's okay, Emma," he repeated. "We know. We need them for our library. The community centre doesn't need them, we do."

I carried on with unpacking while Marko and Michelle split their sides laughing behind closed doors. The office was close to where I was and the walls were paper-thin.

"Shit!" I heard Marko whisper. "Do you think she'll say anything?" "Don't worry, Marko," Michelle replied, "Emma's on our team."

I was up until then, but the longer I stayed the more I saw what kind of people they were and decided that I did not want to work for them. The promised tutoring never eventuated. They were too busy, which was a blessing in disguise because I was forced into realising my own ability.

What I needed most from my employers was the use of their computer to type up my assignments. While I worked full time for Marko and Michelle, minding the office five, sometimes six days a week without pay, the computer was at my disposal until I mentioned that I intended returning to Queensland in December of that year.

On my birthday I was invited to join Marko and Michelle as their guest at an expensive restaurant. They gave me an expensive gift and a cheque for the sum I needed to buy the coat I mentioned that I had on lay-by. During the meal my importance to the business was mentioned more than once. I was puzzled as to why they were showering me with so much attention. Their behaviour made me question why they could not pay me even a small wage. Lord knows I had earned it.

"Really?" I said puzzled. "Am I that good?"

"We appreciate all that you've done for us, Emma, and the students love you."

"That's good. I'm hoping you'll give me a reference before I leave."

"But Emma, we're hoping that you will stay with us, we need you," Michelle said, glancing at Marko, who nodded.

"But I want to go back to Queensland. I feel that I must go back and soon. I want to get away from Stanley." I felt uneasy because they did not understand that I had to leave Victoria.

"So you're leaving?" Michelle asked and I nodded feeling guilty. "Yes I am."

I had no idea that the look on Marko and Michelle's faces indicated a gloomy portent.

"Look Emma," Marko said, leaning forward, "don't make any decisions just yet. Seriously think it over before you decide." I agreed to do that and give them my answer in a few weeks. I took their advice, seriously considered my alternatives and came to the conclusion that Brisbane was my best option. Celeste and her family were living there and so was BJ. I wanted to see them and there was no reason for Bree and i to be in Victoria now that Stanley and I had parted. My family was not there.

"Bree and I are moving to Brisbane in December. I have to get away from Stanley, otherwise I'll go insane," I announced one morning.

"Yes we know how difficult it's been for you Emma," Michelle said in a way that sounded condescending, "your work has suffered and the students are complaining about the way you're treating them."

"What?" I said, startled. "What a turnaround from a few weeks ago. I was so important to the business and the students loved me then." I stood up and glared at both of them. "I see what you're doing. Well, since my work isn't so good, it's a good thing I've decided to go back to Brisbane,' I said and marched out of the room.

I went to finish off my assignment that was due the next day and found that, mysteriously, the computer was out of order. I marched right back into the office without bothering to knock and blurted out, "What's wrong with the computer?" They glanced slyly at each other.

Smirking, Michelle said, "Oh I forgot to tell you, Emma, it's been playing up for a while, we will have to buy another one."

"It was okay yesterday," I snapped, and they grinned.

"Oh I get it. Well, that's it then," I said, marching back to my desk to grab my belongings and walked out.

I was seething all the way home. 'Shit! Shit! Shit! What the hell am I going to do now? I don't know of anyone else who has a computer and the campus is too far away. I was yelling in the privacy of my car, "What the hell can I do?" Then I remembered Stanley had a computer. I was feeling more hopeful when I dialled his number, only to discover that it had been changed.

"Dickhead," I muttered. "It was I who was trying to get away from you, not the other way round."

I called Stanley's office.

"Hi! It's me," I said casually. "Is that offer to use your computer still valid? The one I was using crashed before I could finish the last couple of pages of my assignment. It's due tomorrow."

He hesitated, "Well, I..."

"We don't have to see each other, I'll come to the office and pick up the key and put it under the mat when I leave," I broke in. "I'll go to your place this afternoon, finish the assignment and leave, I shouldn't be very long. I'll be finished well before you leave work."

Just as I had finished typing my assignments, my attention was distracted when audio tapes flashed into my mind's eye. I realised what the images meant, and left the computer and went into Stanley's bedroom. I looked over at the wardrobe. The door was slightly ajar. On the top shelf near the door was a small stack of audio tapes. I reached up and took one from the pile, slid it into the machine and pressed play. I was shocked at hearing the sound of my angry voice. One by one, I erased the ugliness, then without rhyme or reason telephoned Stanley and told him what I had just done. He was incensed at the confession and threatened to get me for doing it.

I hurried to finish up and leave, but was shocked to find Stanley on the doorstep when I opened the front door.

"I'll get you for this, you fucking bitch!" he spat as he lunged forward to block my pathway. The armful of books I was carrying prevented me from blocking a blow to the side of my face. He grabbed both of my arms. I told him to get away from me and shook myself free. He caught me again and threw me up against the wall and pinned me there. His face was taut with rage and he raised his clenched fist ready to strike at full force bellowing into my face, "If it's good enough for Les, then it's good enough for me! You ripped me off, taking my money, my furniture, and everything else!"

I struggled with all of my might, throwing him off balance. I broke free, frantically struggling with the door until it opened and I was able to run to the safety of my car. That outburst was not his first but it certainly was going to be the last. I went to the police and filed a Domestic Violence Protection Order against him.

On the day of the hearing, I was sitting on a bench outside the courthouse when Stanley approached me. He sat down beside me uninvited.

"Please drop the charges and I promise never to come near you again."

I looked at him and said, "You're in breach of the order, so move away from me." But he ignored what I had said and pleaded again.

"You beat me up, Stanley. You acted as if you had the right to do that. You also believe that I ripped you off when you had insisted that I take the furniture. You offered those things to me. I did not ask you for anything, only what I owned prior to marrying you. What you have done is enough to convince me to feel that you're a danger to me. Now go away before I call someone and have you arrested for breaching the order."

He moved away quickly without uttering another word.

In the courtroom I gave my account of what had happened. My statement was straightforward and to the point, concluding with me saying, "I no longer feel safe in my husband's company and wish to have a protection order against him."

When Stanley took the stand he was full of accusations. Notebook in hand, he gave distorted accounts of events unrelated to the issue. Everything he said was exaggerated and petty. I silently wept at his lies, recalling my previous court battles with Les. Stanley also told the magistrate that I had violated his privacy.

The magistrate looked up from his papers when he mentioned the privacy violation

"In what way did your wife violate your privacy, Mr Carson?"

"She went through all my things,"

"And how do you know that, Mr Carson?"

"She found my lolly jar."

The courtroom went still and everyone stared at him, some people grinned and others shook their heads. I dried my eyes and quietly laughed, recalling that when I ran from the unit that day, I had made a mean comment to Stanley about his weight, "Got your face in the lolly jar again, have we?" From that remark he assumed I had gone through his possessions.

The magistrate looked directly at Stanley. "Mr Carson, I feel that you still have very strong feelings for your wife." Stanley smiled and nodded in agreement and said, "Yes I have," but the smile quickly evaporated when the magistrate continued, "And therefore, I am granting the order for twelve months. I feel you need this time to realise that your marriage to your wife is over."

Stanley interrupted him, "What about her? She has to stay away from me too."

The magistrate looked my way, instructing me not to telephone Stanley or to go anywhere near him in the future. I nodded in agreement.

That was the last time I saw Stanley.

I had not discussed the idea of returning to Brisbane with Bree in detail, prior to mentioning it to Michelle and Marko. I had little doubt that she was missing her siblings and would be enthusiastic when I told her.

"Well, Babe, what do you think we should do? Stay here or go back to Brisbane?"

"Wow Mom, you really mean it, we're going back?"

"If that's what you want to do."

"You bet. When can we leave?"

"At the end of the year, we'll make a fresh start in Queensland at Christmas, okay?"

"Okay."

Although I was making plans to leave Victoria, I felt uneasy knowing that Les was lurking in the background, hoping for reconciliation. I'll never forget the frightful experience I had with him the previous Christmas.

53

It was 1990. I had just separated from Stanley and was free to make plans to spend Christmas with Mary and her family. Instead of driving up to Sydney, I had decided to book a flight, expecting Mary to meet us at the airport when we arrived. To my utter horror, Les was waiting for us instead. The sight of him walking towards us sent chills through my body.

Les hugged Bree then turned to me and did the same, as natural as an everyday occurrence. Noticing my discomfort he said, "It's alright, I won't hurt you."

I was not sure what was happening.

"Come on," he said, "the others are waiting for you."

Puzzled, I automatically fell in line beside Les to collect our luggage.

"Where's Mary?" I asked, hoping my voice sounded steady.

"At her house with the others." He saw my puzzled glance and said, "I called Mary and offered to come to the airport, because I wanted to talk to you."

I fell silent. I felt sick to the pit of my stomach. I did not want to have to face him again or listen to what he had to say. 'No please,' my thoughts were racing, 'not now, not him.'

Les led us to his car and packed the luggage into the boot. He opened the front passenger's door as I was about to climb in the back of the vehicle. "No! I want you to sit in the front beside me, Bubby," he said. I hesitated, and then reluctantly obeyed his command.

During the journey, I did my best to sound casual and relaxed and prattled on about minor things, keeping my face turned toward the window and deliberately steering the conversation to the demographics of the suburbs we travelled through, until we arrived at my sister's home.

The house was a welcoming sight when the car finally came to a halt outside the front gate. Les' confidence surprised me. He fetched the luggage from the car and carried it into the house, clearly having no fear that he may not be welcome.

'What's going on?' I thought, utterly dumbfounded. 'Have I overlooked something here?'

When I went inside everything seemed normal. The family greeted us warmly, except for mother, who adopted her usual mode of disapproval.

"Oh, you look so thin, Emma. I prefer your hair short." Never, 'Hello, it's good to see you after all this time.' Always criticism from her the moment she set eyes on me.

Les came to my rescue and said, "I think she's beautiful just the way she is." Then Tim chipped in, "Yeah, I think she looks great for an old chook."

"Hey, who are you calling old? May I remind you that we are the same age," I teased and we all laughed.

Everything seemed surreal. I could not understand why Les was there. I was so confused, wondering if they had forgotten that they once had a security check on Mom and Dad's phone because of his threats to harm them. I was shocked but said nothing when Mary invited Les to dinner after my mother left. While Mary was in the kitchen preparing the meal, I had a chance to ask why she did not come to the airport. "Well," she sighed and shrugged, "I didn't see any harm in Les going instead when he phoned to ask if he could pick up you and Bree. Why, is there something wrong?"

I wanted to scream, 'Why didn't you say no to Les and come to the airport yourself, when you knew that I loathe him,' but instead I said, "No, not really, I just don't feel comfortable around him. He wants us to get back together again and I don't want that."

"Surely he's all right now," she said in an off-handed, naive way. "Maybe you're worrying about nothing. He seems fine. Don't worry."

Les came into the kitchen and interrupted our conversation. Looking at me he asked, "Do you have a minute?" and went outside. I followed him to the garden seat under the tree and sat down beside him. I felt uncomfortable being anywhere near him. The horror of what he had done became fresh in my mind, when I wanted to forget.

"I'm sorry I hurt you, Bubby."

I looked at Les in surprise. He was looking at the ground.

"I didn't mean to. I still love you very much. I can't help myself. I guess I always will." He lifted his head and looked at me, then reached out and took my hand. I could not bring myself to look at him even though he seemed remorseful of the past, asking me to forgive him. I was thinking, 'He's said and done this so many times before,' but I listened anyway.

The scene was strange. I had wanted to have harmony between us for so long and there I was sitting beside Les on a garden seat while he held my hand, pleading with me to forgive him. His words gave me no comfort or peace. I felt uneasy and awkwardly afraid of him. His hold on my hand made me squirm and I tried to gently ease my hand from his grip.

"I won't hurt you," he frowned, and clasped tighter. "I want to touch you. I need to touch you. I promise I won't hurt you."

Fear churned inside me but I knew not to overreact, feeling it would set Les off. I thought of him as a time bomb slowly ticking away, likely to explode with any wrong movement. Patiently I sat on the bench seat and listened to him talk.

"Bubby, I need to know two things." I did not want to look at him. My gaze was set to the side of his head.

"You told me Bree wasn't my daughter. I need to know the truth."

"And what else do you need to know," I asked, playing for time. So much had to be considered. What I would have gladly given to watch his face fall if I told him that Bree was not his daughter was anyone's guess, but that was not on my agenda. I was not about to harm my child.

"Was I really a bad lover?" In a kneejerk response I looked directly at him for the first time in years.

"I'm afraid to be with anyone because of what you said. Please, Bubby, I need to know."

I had no idea that I had made such an impact. I felt pity for Les because he was a disturbed man, greatly in need of help. Stanley on the other hand was a nasty little man. Les certainly needed to be pitied. I told him what he *wanted* to hear, hoping that he would move on with his life and leave me alone. I also told him as gently as possible that I could offer him nothing more than friendship, which he seemed to accept.

While we were in the garden, Les invited me to drive up to Brisbane with him and Bree to see Celeste and my granddaughter Liza Jane. I wanted to see them so badly, but did not feel comfortable going with him. When I mentioned the trip to Mary she said, "At least you'll get to see the baby and you never know when you'll get another chance to do that." So I reluctantly agreed to go.

The evening was pleasant enough and everyone, with the exception of me, was relaxed. Mary and Tim did not see what I felt and I did not blame them for their lack of insight as they had no idea of what Les was capable of. They did not know the whole story or that he could be in any way a threat to me. I had often thought my family felt I had exaggerated the few facts of which they were already aware. My gut feeling told me that I should not take the trip but I dearly wanted to see Celeste and the baby

It was late when Les finally said, "Well, I'd better be going." I could feel myself beginning to relax, and then every nerve in my body tensed up when he asked me to walk with him to the car.

Under the streetlight, we stood awkwardly beside the car. I stared blankly into space while he gazed longingly at me. "Well, I guess I'll see you in a few days," I piped up, about to turn and jog back inside.

"Wait a minute," Les grabbed my arm. "I want you to take this."

He placed a wad of rolled up notes in my hand. "There's seven hundred dollars. I wanted to give you a thousand, but that was all I could get out today. I want you to buy yourself chocolates or something."

"I can't take this," I said, snatching my hand away, "I don't want it." I offered it back but he refused to take the money.

"Please take it, Bubby, I want you to have it. I want you to buy yourself something, please. You can get Bree the VCR she wants."

I took the money. Any gift Les had given me always came with strings and conditions attached to it, so every cent went on gifts for everyone else other than me. He left satisfied when I had taken the money. I felt he thought that he finally had me hooked.

While Mary and I were talking about what we should take to our parents' place for Christmas Day, she expressed a desire to have Christmas dinner at her house that year. "We've lived in this house for over seventeen years and not once have we had Christmas dinner here."

"If that's your wish, then I'll phone Mom and tell her," I said.

My enthusiastic call to my mother was not received well, but I ignored the lukewarm response with the best of intentions. "Every year, you've worked so hard preparing the Christmas meal, Mom. Now it's your turn to relax. We'll take care of everything."

The first visible sign of our parents' displeasure with the change was when they arrived well over an hour late. They had obviously been fighting and their foul mood put everyone on edge. My father, who usually overindulged himself, ate sparingly. He sat silent and withdrawn in his chair, refusing to interact or to communicate with anyone, while my mother found fault with everything although Mary and Tim had greatly exerted themselves in an effort to please them. My good humour faded into an uneasy silence. Gradually my anger was aroused at their continuous childish behaviour and lack of appreciation of the hospitality extended to both of them.

Mary and Tim left the house for a couple of hours to visit Tim's family, leaving the rest of the tense group to contend with our parents. In an endeavour to uplift the mood, I made light of things in general and for reasons known only to my father, he made nasty obscene comment towards me. Then he felt obliged to tell me that I had become a know-all smartarse since attending university. The unwarranted remark was the last straw and I lost control.

"How dare you! Why can't you at least be proud of me for doing something positive instead of putting me down? Not once can I remember you ever giving any of us praise for anything."

My mother interrupted me. "Don't you speak to your father like that."

"What? What do you mean, don't speak to my father like that? You heard what he said to me."

Her face turned cold and hard as she verbally attacked me.

The years of hurt and anger I felt had surfaced, spewed out and shaken the foundations of the house. My brother

Peter, Bree, nieces and nephews were all shocked to a standstill when they heard me tell my parents they were selfish. I went on to tell them how they had never appreciated any of us, never showing any love or warmth towards us, that they had no appreciation for Mary's and Tim's efforts in serving a delicious meal. "While you two went out of your way to find fault with everything, they went out of their way to make this a special day!"

Tears of frustration fell and I violently wiped them away. "This was their first Christmas in their home, and you two did your best to spoil it for them."

"What do you mean?" my mother spat back. "I've done everything for you, you selfish little bitch, and all you have ever done is cause trouble in this family. You're a troublemaker. Who took you to the doctor when you needed medical attention?"

"Shut up about that!" My voice was hard with contempt. "I owe you nothing. I did the same for my children, and I didn't hold them in debt to me. I looked after them because I love them. They owe me nothing and I owe you nothing." I took a deep breath in order not to totally lose control.

"You made me pay all my life for that. Well, I'm not paying for it any longer. We were never good enough for you, were we?" I challenged my mother, as she glared hatred at me. I knew that look only too well.

"Neither of you have ever said that you love us. We love you," I said lowering my voice, "but you don't love us. I don't think you know how."

I paused for a moment, waiting for my mother to say something but she didn't. Her face was set as hard as a rock.

"I've had it with you," I responded in disgust, "I don't plan to try and please you any longer. You're not worth it. You're not good enough to be my parents." My voice was cold and very deliberate.

My mother lunged forward to strike me but stopped dead in her tracks when I said. "That's about it, isn't it? You hit me," I warned, "and you'll regret it."

"Come on, Bill," she ordered, "We're going home." He struggled to get up and scurry away.

"Yeah, run away, that's right. Just run!" I shouted as they disappeared through the door. "Cowards!"

Neither my father nor my mother understood the pain I felt. They both selfishly wore their armour of pity, clutching it close as protection against the world. In their indulgence they heard only their own cries of misery.

When they had left, I turned to my speechless brother still sitting at the table and said, "We are their children; they are supposed to be our parents. Doesn't it matter to them whether or not their children are hurting? Why couldn't they see that I needed to hear them tell me they were sorry for the past? That's all, and why is it always everyone else's fault and not theirs? Why can't they share some of the responsibility too? The trouble in the family wasn't my fault."

Peter remained silent and let me rant.

"Well, am I right with what I told them?"

"Yes, but they are old," he answered ruefully.

"That's no excuse, Peter. They weren't old when we were young. I know so many people their age that aren't mean spirited. Most of the people I've met throughout my life have been warm, loving, caring, kind and very encouraging towards me. My friends are nothing like them," I said. "My friends know me well and accept me the way I am. I don't have to continually prove myself to be accepted by them. Have they ever told you that they love you?"

He shook his head.

I looked at Peter and asked, "Why can't they love us? Is that so hard? I love my children and I've told them that I do. Not every day, mind you, but I have told them. At least they know that I love them. Those two have never ever said it at all or even given us a spontaneous hug. I hugged my children all the time when they were little. I couldn't imagine not hugging Bree or not telling her that I love her."

"I must admit," Peter confessed, "I haven't told my kids that I love them."

"Well you'd better start. They need to hear it."

"Yeah, I guess you're right."

Mary and Tim came home shortly after the tornado had passed and cheerfully asked how the afternoon had been. I told them what had happened and Tim quipped, "Well, we certainly won't forget this Christmas in a hurry, will we? Coffee anyone?"

My mother refused to make peace with me when I saw her the following day. Instead of being sad, I was fed up. I shrugged her off and decided that I would get on with my own life. I believed I could handle any situation, just as long as I knew what it was I was dealing with.

Les arrived early on Boxing Day morning to pick up us. I felt troubled about driving that long distance to Brisbane with him, but was excited at the idea of seeing Celeste and her baby. I had last seen my granddaughter when she was only a week old.

As we pulled away from the kerb the early morning sun shone through the windscreen. I reached up and adjusted the sun-visor. I wore the diamond engagement ring Stanley had given me as a dress ring. Sunlight caught it and sent a prism of colour dancing around the car's interior, attracting Les' attention. He kept glancing at my hand, his sullen look telling me he was not happy that I was still wearing my engagement ring. He relaxed when I moved, discreetly keeping the ring out of view.

We hit a bump and a number of cassettes that had been sitting on the dash fell on the floor near my feet. I picked them up and looked at them. Les was watching me and said, "Look in the glove compartment, there's more."

I found the compartment full of my favourite country music. I was actually surprised that we had a common interest. While I listened to the music Les began talking. My mind was lost in the melody and his voice sounded far away. "Did you hear me?" he said. "I've made a will."

"Oh have you?" I replied, wondering why he was telling me.

"Marla is the executor. I'm leaving what I have to you."

"What?" I said and sat up. "What about the kids? What about Cain?"

"Why would I leave Cain anything, he's Romano's bastard."

I was horrified at his remark and felt hatred rise up in my gut.

"I don't want your money, Les, give it to the kids."

He looked sideways at me and said slowly, "I want to give it to you."

I did not respond. I looked out of the window stifling the urge to scream at him. "All I've ever wanted was my children, and all you have done is to use them as pawns.'

"I want to stop at my place on the way," he said, breaking the silence, "I want you to meet Sue and Eric Wilson, they're good friends of mine. They're expecting us."

I glanced at him quickly. 'How ironic — now he wants to introduce me to the people he has spent years convincing that I was a class bitch, hoping that we will all become friends. Well it won't happen!'

I was reluctant to get out of the car when we pulled up in front of the Wilson's house. But Sue Wilson hurried out of the house when she saw us and invited me inside.

"It's so good to finally meet you, Emma," she said, hugging me. Her openness surprised me and my defences fell away in response to her friendly manner. "Bree talks about you all the time when she visits us. We all love her." Then she whispered, "He talks about you all the time, he adores you, Emma." Her remark astounded me as I realised that Les had tricked them into believing he was a deserted, broken hearted ex-husband and they pitied him.

"I don't know the full story, Emma, but I encouraged Les to call you. He only told me that he had made mistakes and was sorry. He's been good to us. We owe him a lot."

'But why can't you see through him and see him for who he really is?' I wanted to say. Instead I smiled awkwardly and asked how long her family had lived in Singleton, genuinely interested in hearing about their lifestyle.

"It's really pretty here," I said.

The Wilsons were lovely people, but it turned my stomach listening to Sue trying to convince me that Les was a good man and that I should give him another chance. I wanted to leave. The trip was about visiting Celeste and my granddaughter, not about Les.

I found it interesting, the way Les had made every effort to make our trip pleasurable when in the past he had gone out of his way to do the complete opposite. His enthusiastic hospitality was draining. As we continued towards Brisbane I feared a backlash at my persistent refusal to stop for coffee and to look around the little towns we passed along the way.

I tilted my seat backwards slightly and laid quietly in thought, half-listening to the mournful music playing in the background. Les had expected me to think that he had changed because the Wilsons thought highly of him, but he had not fooled me. I told myself I was living a hell on earth and when I died, God would take pity on me and let me into heaven right away, and I wouldn't have to fear anything or anyone in heaven. Then I realised how silly that sounded and shrugged the thought away – God doesn't exist.

By the time we arrived at Celeste's place in Brisbane, I was exhausted. Her eyes widened in surprise when I walked through the door with her father. She looked concerned and annoyed at the idea of me being in his company.

"I wanted to see you and Liza Jane," I said, hugging and reassuring her that everything was all right.

Bree and I stayed with Celeste and Terry while Les drove over to Cain and Cindy's place.

"The kids will be over in the morning," he told me before he left.

"Cain too?" I asked, wishing that it was already tomorrow. It had been over five years since we had all been together. The way things had happened, it looked as if Les had given his consent for Cain and Brad to be respectful towards me, which made me think that he thought reconciliation was possible.

It was awkward for us all to be together after everything that had happened. In the hope of lightening the mood, I cheerfully passed around the gifts I had bought for everyone with the money Les had given me. Although everyone began to feel festive I remained wary, feeling Celeste's strong disapproval because I was in her father's company.

Although I loved and respected Celeste, our relationship was often strained. Like Les, Celeste lacked tact and compassion, which lessened her ability to comprehend my need to be on good terms with all of my children. She deemed her brothers unworthy of my attention and believed that I should forget them and get on with my own life.

"You're too emotional, Mom," she would say, as if I had some sort of disease.

What Celeste could not appreciate was that my emotion and passion had given her and her siblings the things they all enjoyed throughout their childhood, the very things her father believed that none of them deserved.

Celeste had often puzzled me. She would be intolerant and frustrated with me one minute, then the next deeply concerned for my safety. 'Perhaps now that she's a mother herself she'll be empathetic to my plight and support me,' I thought, but my assumption only annoyed her and strained our relationship further.

"Why do you bother with them?" she asked about her brothers, sounding exasperated. "All they've ever done is beat you up emotionally. Why do you bother?"

"Because they're my children and I love them. I would do everything in my power to mend things with you, if you and I weren't talking. Why can't you understand how I feel?"

"Well, I just don't!" she said indignantly. "You're allowing them to hurt you. I don't think that's right."

I had to make a conscious effort to hide my feelings from her, sensing that she felt helpless at watching me long for something that was beyond my reach. Once my emotions were in check, I had her attention, and we were back on a comfortable footing again. The visit went well regardless, but it was all too short.

We spent three days in Brisbane, and the morning we were to return to Sydney, I learned from Celeste that BJ was due to be in court that day. I felt horribly torn, leaving him to go alone. Because I was due back in Sydney, I made the excuse to myself that perhaps it was time for BJ to start taking responsibility for his actions, but that was no consolation and I regretted not being there to support him. I felt concerned about BJ and ruefully said to Les as we approached Armidale, "I wish I could have stayed longer in Brisbane. Perhaps I should have gone to court with BJ."

He turned and looked at me and said, "He wouldn't be in trouble if you hadn't broken up his home."

"I wouldn't have had to if you hadn't kept beating me up," I spat back, thinking that he could have gone with BJ. He was on holidays. If he really had cared about BJ he would have bought Bree and I an airline ticket home, instead of driving us back. The only thing he did was to blame me.

Bree was sitting in the back seat listening to her Walkman through headphones, oblivious to the shouting going on in the front of the vehicle. In the middle of the uproar my ring caught the sun again and Les went crazy.

"Stanley stole my wife," he screamed, thumping the steering wheel, "I'm going to beat him and beat him until blood comes pouring out of his head and his eyes. I'm going to kill him. I hate him! I hate him!"

"He didn't steal your wife!" I screamed back. "I was never your wife. You had to rape and beat me to make me submit to you. No Les, I was never your wife. I never loved you. I loved Luc, only Luc."

Les punched me across the head and I screamed. I crouched in the corner like a trapped animal while he savagely drove his fist into me again and again. He steered the car with one hand and punched me with the other. I felt him unbuckling my seat belt and the car slowing down. He then stretched across me, opened the door and savagely pushed me out of the moving vehicle and then sped off like a madman. I rolled onto the roadside. When I stopped I managed to look up and through the rear window saw Bree's contorted face, looking terrified. I screamed out to her, petrified that I would never see her again.

Cars drove past without stopping. No one seemed to notice or care that I was left crying by the roadside. I struggled to stand up and thought I must be badly injured because of the pain I felt in my shoulder and legs. It was a wonder that I had only minor abrasions and severe bruising. While walking in the direction Les had driven, my mind was trying to focus on what had happened and what to do next.

"Bree, he has Bree," I screamed, half out of my mind with terror. 'What if he hurts her as a payback,' I thought, "Oh God no! Please no," I cried. I fell in a heap to the ground and buried my head in my hands.

Something made me look up. I saw Les' car speeding towards me. I struggled to stand up, ready to run and nervously looking around for somewhere to hide, but I was frozen with fear and could not move. I assumed he had come back to finish me. My heart was beating so hard and fast in my chest that my whole body rocked back and forth. Everything happened in slow motion.

The car skidded to a halt close to where I stood dazed. Les violently pushed the vehicle door open and charged towards me. I closed my eyes, bracing myself for the final blow.

For a few brief seconds I felt no fear. I had surrendered to what I thought was the inevitable end. But instead of delivering the final blow, Les almost suffocated me in an embrace. He was crying and pleading for me to forgive him.

"I can't help it, Bubby," he sobbed, "I can't face the truth. I don't want to hear the truth. I'm sorry. I love you. I just go crazy when I hear it."

I stood still, petrified, silently weeping from relief that Les had not killed me, but sickened by his touch. I was too afraid to push him away. With his arm still around me, he guided me back to the car and we continued our journey back to Sydney.

I laid on the back seat and wept silently. When we arrived in Sydney, Les left Bree and me at my sister's front gate and then drove away. The seriousness of what had happened to me that day did not penetrate anyone's mind, but the discomfort from a fractured shoulder was a constant reminder of that day. I did not call the police, fearing retaliation from Brad and Cain as well as from Les. I was just glad to get away from him.

That day, I vowed I would never marry again and noted in my diary, 'My destiny will never be determined by anyone other than myself.'

The incident at Christmas had reinforced my fear of Les but I still considered the move to Queensland appealing, even though I knew he visited Brisbane several times a year to see Cain and Brad. Although at times a burst of temporary courage would see me through times of adversity, I had often imagined that I would one day make the six o'clock news, 'Crazed man kills ex-wife.'

Tired of being afraid, I reasoned that if Les thought that he could get away with it, he could easily harm me wherever I lived in Australia.

54

Now that Bree and I had unanimously agreed to return to Brisbane, I quickly made the arrangements. A difficult part of relocating to another state was leaving treasured friends behind. To ease Bree's sadness I shared with her a philosophy of mine. "Distance never separates real friends," I told her. "Once a bond has forged between friends it binds them together forever. Even though years might pass before paths cross again, because of that bond, the possibility of meeting again is always there."

Bree accepted what I had told her and moved forward with her life. I marvelled at her maturity and ability to adjust to situations she encountered. She was never prone to tantrums and never displayed a disagreeable attitude towards anything regarding the changing tide of our lives.

The trip to Brisbane with Les had opened Bree's eyes to the kind of person he really was, and I noticed that the excitement of her holidays with him slowly faded. I was waiting for her to ask, "Do I have to go, Mom?" When she finally asked that question, I told her that once she turned thirteen she was legally free to decide for herself.

Over the years I have mixed with diverse groups of friends. When one of them saw my struggle in handling the frustration of dealing with Les, he told me that he could permanently remove Les from my life once and for all, but I declined. Many times afterwards I had seriously considered my friend's offer, especially after the last episode with him. Although I did not give in to the temptation to be rid of Les, I did however feel safer in the knowledge that help was just a telephone call away.

Sometimes my thirst for revenge had me indulging in imagining Les suffering. In my fantasy I issued orders to have him brought before me bound and gagged. In my hand I held the same jug cord with which he had unmercifully whipped me. I taunted him with it until he broke down and pleaded with me not to hurt him. I visualised him distressed and on the brink of hysteria, before I casually ordered him released with a wave of my hand. The moment I thought that he felt safe I shouted, "Seize him! Tie him up in a spread-eagle position," to several menacing men standing nearby. I ordered them to touch and taunt him and threaten to rape him. But I was kinder to Les in my fantasy than he had been to me in reality; he was never physically harmed, just tormented.

I knew the hatred I felt for Les was unhealthy. The promise I had made to Bree a few years before, to take care of myself, prevented me from making my fantasy a reality. Perhaps my daydreaming could have become dangerous. I craved gratification somehow, and it would be this way until I had a change of heart. I jotted a note in my diary, 'I don't entertain this kind of trash often, but when I do it feels wonderful.'

Before leaving Victoria I had one last get together with Beth, Sylvia and Willy. That day Beth surprised me with a poem that she had written. It was called, 'A Woman of Substance' and went like this:

'She came into my life one day so unexpectedly.
I've known her for one whole year or is it two or three?
She has a way of making you desire to be your best.
Always there encouraging, to be better than the rest.
She makes you laugh;
she makes you cry when she tells you of her life.
The joy, the pain, the suffering, challenges and strife.
You walk along the street with her, the men all stop and stare.

They know she has a quality that's deeply hidden there.
No one before has made me think that I could do so much.
She really has an eye for flare, a distinctive woman's touch.
She's leaving soon, moving away, pursuing other goals.
Taking up another life, touching other souls.'
It was signed, *Friendship and best wishes, Beth - Praying for you always.*

I was deeply moved and humbled by Beth's poem. I treasured it. Beth's words were the substitute validation that I wanted but never received from my mother.

Two days later Bree and I left our dear friends in Victoria and headed north. When we arrived in Brisbane, Bree and I stayed for a few days with Celeste and Terry before we moved into the two-bedroom unit Celeste found for us in Holland Park. They gave me a hand to settle in but I was speechless when Terry said, as he greedily caressed my antique furniture, "Look Celeste, we'll inherit all this."

Celeste and Terry came by often, but they would usually make some kind of excuse to leave Liza Jane with me, saying that they would not be long but disappearing for hours. Initially I did not mind, I loved spending time with my granddaughter. But when I realised I was being used as a babysitter I was hurt, but did not say anything because of the trouble it might cause.

At the beginning of the New Year, the only school I thought suitable for enrolling Bree was another Christian College. I really did not like the idea of doing that after the difficultly I had with the principal of the Christian College Bree had attended in Victoria.

* * *

The principal was an overzealous, portly, bearded gentleman who sauntered around the college grounds with his Bible tucked under his arm. Although a kind man at heart, he believed that he was acting in the best interest of the college, enforcing idealistic rules. A comment he made during religious instruction caused Bree to voice her disapproval.

I had taught her that although we may not agree with some people's lifestyles, we should at least respect their right to live their lives in the way they prefer. "It isn't our place to judge anyone," I told her. I had also encouraged Bree not to be afraid to express her opinion regarding social issues if she felt strongly enough about them, affirming that if she wanted to make a point, "Remain cool-headed, be sure of your facts, and look your opponent directly in the eyes."

When the principal addressed the class during religious instruction with the subject of homosexuals on his agenda, and implied that such people were unclean and should be destroyed, she promptly and fearlessly stood up and told him that he had no right to judge anyone. "Only God can do that."

That comment led to me engaging the principal in a very lengthy telephone debate. I told him that I supported Bree one hundred per cent and did not intend to reprimand her in any way whatsoever.

"I've raised my daughter to care about and to respect people in general," I said as pleasantly as possible, "and not to accept or to tolerate prejudice against anyone." The telephone call ended with us agreeing to disagree.

Following that incident, the issue of students hugging each other hello and goodbye was viewed as being unacceptable by the principal. Hugging was banned and many television programs were frowned upon, along with certain children's books.

"Things are getting way out of control," I said to other parents when the subject came up.

Although discontent stirred the parents, no one seemed willing to do anything about it. I decided to withdraw Bree from the college but before I did, I wrote a letter to the president of the board, expressing my concerns for the future of the college and that of the students.

The letter stated the reasons for Bree's withdrawal, *'Negative atmosphere accompanied by a dictatorial attitude towards the students. They are not allowed to watch a number of television programs, they were told not to hug their friends, not to read certain teen magazines and so on.' I wrote, 'I do agree that many programs can be harmful to some teenagers if their viewing is excessive. However, not all children/teenagers are so impressionable. This is a good opportunity to turn a negative into a positive. These programs could be used in discussion groups or to discuss problems that some students are going through. Students need to feel supported not only academically but also emotionally within the school. This is not the case with most students at this college. What the administration must not lose sight of is that, to enable the younger generation to develop into responsible adults, they need contrast to see and to experience the difference between right and wrong.'*

On the issue of hugging friends being unacceptable I wrote –

'Hugging is a concept that I am led to believe is not encouraged at this college. A constant bombardment of negative attitudes or beliefs will only succeed in alienating the students. Young people today enjoy showing friends affection, and that is all that it is – affection. I would rather see affection displayed between friends in the schoolyard than hostility. I often wonder what is going through the minds of those who oppose the students showing affection towards each other.

This negative attitude has been reflected more than once. Although I feel sure that the intentions of the administrators of the college are well meaning, such intentions without flexibility can cause emotional damage, frustration, and low self-esteem, which can reflect on the students' grades. This is why I am withdrawing Bree from the college.

Bree's first eighteen months at the college were happy. She has formed close friendships with her classmates and has a good relationship with her teachers. I sent Bree to this college with the intention that she would be in contact with Christian values, but so far all I can see is negative, judgemental, dictatorial, and critical attitudes. The standard is just not good enough. Cultural relativism is fine for a culture that lives for one belief and idea, when the whole society agrees totally to the concept. In a non-denominational school, these attitudes are not appreciated.

I suggest that if the board is really interested in the students' and the parents' opinions and feelings about their dissatisfactions, they should circulate a questionnaire among the families and omit names allowing the parents to freely express their dissatisfaction. This would help the board amend the situation and enable the college to move forward in a positive direction.'

I ended my letter by thanking the teachers who had shown a positive approach towards the students and thanked the board for allowing me to voice my concerns.

To my delight and utter surprise, I received an encouraging response within the week. The board informed me that other parents had also expressed their concerns and that a subcommittee has been appointed to prepare the questionnaire as I had suggested.

With the previous incident in mind, I felt compelled to stress to the principal of Bree's new college that I was also interviewing her, to assess whether the college had to offer what I as a parent wanted for Bree, and asked her a couple of direct questions:

"Does the college respect the students' point of view? Do their opinions matter? If they don't, then this college isn't for Bree."

The woman sitting opposite quickly assured me that I did not have to be concerned about any of those things.

"The students are my primary concern," she cooed, but I was uneasy with the way her lips were pursed. I observed her closely as she made her point and thought that she was every bit a principal, which should have been warning enough. I estimated her age to be late fifties. It was really hard to judge since her stern features and small mouth had stolen any potential youth from her. I knew the woman sensed that I was not a meek and mild parent and that I would not go out of my way to impress and gain her approval.

Choosing a school for Bree was serious business, I thought, especially since she would be spending long hours in that environment. Ideally I wanted Bree to enjoy her time in class as much as possible. I expressed that point during the interview. I also stressed that Les Carter was not to be notified about anything concerning Bree. "He has been extremely unpleasant in the past; neither Bree nor I want him involved in any way." I was frank but pleasant in my appeal. She gave me her word that all matters concerning Bree would be referred only to me. "I'll always act in Bree's best interest," she promised. I gave her the benefit of the doubt and enrolled Bree.

55

The next few months seemed perfect. Then one afternoon while I was babysitting, Terry arrived home with a couple of his friends. They were drinking and smoking pot. A discussion about a rock icon of the sixties began. "It would have been cool growing up back then," Terry said taking a swig of his beer.

"It wasn't that terrific," I innocently replied.

"Ah, how would you know?" he said sarcastically. "Celeste told me you were a goodie-two-shoes."

"And she would know."

"Yeah well, you told me yourself you never smoke weed."

"That's right. But that doesn't mean I didn't have a life. For me the late sixties and seventies were shit. I hated the change. So many kids my age were off their face on drugs. The change was too radical for me, that's all. But I agree the music was great." I paused then said, "I have no idea why you're telling me about the sixties, you weren't even born..."

"You think I'm an idiot, don't you, Emma?"

"Well, you said it mate, smoking weed in front of your daughter and teaching her to swear isn't very smart."

Shortly before the discussion about the sixties started, Liza Jane came toddling into the lounge room holding a toy. When she dropped it, Terry roared, "Say fuck it, Lizzy! Say fuck it!" She did and Terry yelled, "Naughty girl, Lizzy! Naughty girl! Granny will smack you!"

I gave Terry a scathing look, got up from my chair and scooped up my granddaughter into my arms, kissed her on the cheek and said, "Granny won't smack you, sweetie."

The following day Celeste called and flayed me, not even asking for my side of the story. "How dare you tell the father of my child he's an idiot?"

"I didn't say that."

"But you think it. You also think that he's not good enough for me, don't you?"

"Where the hell has all this come from, Celeste?"

"You're a snob, Mom."

"What? Well, Celeste," I said, "If that's the way you feel then perhaps I should keep my distance from you. I guess Terry's tale of what happened is all you need to hear. Never mind that there are two sides to every story, you're just interested in one," I said sarcastically. She interrupted me to tell me that I should remain in my ivory tower.

"Look Celeste," I snapped, "since Terry is the man you've chosen to spend the rest of your life with, I suggest the two of you just go and do your own thing and I'll do mine. My argument isn't with you, it's with Terry."

"Well then, you can't see Liza Jane."

"If that's the way it has to be then so be it," I said, thinking everything would settle down in a few days. Celeste knew how much Liza Jane meant to me. It was pointless to try and explain anything to Celeste. All her life she has avoided hearing the things that were unpleasant. I reasoned that she just could not accept that Terry could possibly be wrong. That would make her wrong too.

Several weeks later, Terry apologised to me when I phoned and asked to speak to Celeste.

"She won't talk to you, Emma," he said apologetically. "I don't know why she won't. I'm sorry for the way I treated you. I was wrong and I regret the trouble it's caused."

"Can I see Liza Jane?"

"Celeste doesn't want you anywhere near her."

"Why not?" I almost shouted, holding back tears.

"I don't know why she won't, Emma."

I kept my distance from Celeste and her family, hoping time would soften her towards me. I became involved with the women's craft group at Bree's college as a means of making friends.

Sitting around a table a few days a week gossiping was not really my style, but it was something different to my daily routine and something I came to enjoy, especially since the characters were so amusing. The concept of the group was to make craft to sell at the annual fete.

Marion Timms headed the group. She seemed to take great pleasure in holding the weekly meetings at her home. I imagined Marion had encouraged the group to her home because of her cumbersome stature and inability to get about on her own. Considering she rarely ventured far from her home, she was well informed about folk and matters concerning the college. It intrigued me the way she freely shared that information with us.

My impression of Marion Timms was that of a grand queen presiding over her subjects, taking enormous delight in colouring events as she shamelessly told stories. Her manner was bold, her high-pitched laughter coming at intervals. Although most of her comical comments were cruel, she had a talent for making gossip sound harmless and entertaining. Once a rapport had formed between us, my telephone rang daily with newsy bulletins about the college. I was in constant amazement at what she knew.

When I first met the grand lady, her bubbly personality and striking features impressed me. But as I began to see the person she really was, her beauty faded and her personality seemed spiteful.

Each Wednesday, I drove thirty minutes to Manly to spend the day with Marion and her subjects. I had to admit those days were certainly social occasions. Each of us brought delectable dishes and the lunch resembled a banquet.

It intrigued me the way Marion placed herself in a prominent position, discreetly looking for any misdemeanour to later dissect when alone with her favourite partisans. She took great delight in drawing attention to the amount of food consumed by certain women who were there, even though she greedily devoured as much as she could herself. Her audacity in cruelly criticising the women shocked me, but I could not help but feel an overwhelming pity for her. Instead of abandoning Marion I remained her friend, because I genuinely liked her.

We all worked well as a team. I found Marion fascinating and watched her closely, and noticed that she would encourage a friendship with women who had knowledge of a particular craft that she wanted to learn, and then subtly withdraw from them once she had learned the skill. Sometimes she would even go as far as to ostracise a woman from the group all together, claim the newly acquired talent as her own and happily teach the skill to new members of the group.

The craft stall's intake at the annual fete that year had largely contributed to the fete's success. We were overjoyed and agreed to keep the group going for the following year.

Most of our social activities were in the Manly area so it seemed logical that Bree and I move there. Within a week of making that decision we had relocated. I marvelled at the quaintness of Manly village close by. It was so pretty, reminiscent of bygone years. I also took great delight in introducing my friends to the area, finding the place calming while walking along the foreshore. Seagulls hovered in mid-air and some swooped to scavenge food from the blanket of grass around the marina below. Loud screams could be heard in the distance as the birds cried in unison, fighting in scandalous manner over a morsel of food.

Rows of expensive boats of various shapes and sizes gently rocked beside their moorings, creating a marvellous backdrop to the picture-perfect scene. Some of those beautiful vessels seemed to be permanent fixtures and I assumed that their owners were probably too busy working to play with them. The marina suggested an affluent district.

In the tranquil setting of my new surroundings, the idea of writing my book came to mind. I felt that if Dr Anderson thought it was worthwhile then I should do it. My limited knowledge of computers left me vulnerable and a so-called trusted friend had talked me into buying her out-dated computer. When the machine crashed I lost all fifty pages of the manuscript I had written. The frustration of losing my painstaking work and the friend's irresponsible attitude infuriated me. I had trusted her judgement and outlaid an exorbitant fee for a worthless object. I insisted she pay for the repairs. Once she agreed the matter was put to rest, but I never had faith in anything she said or did from then onwards. That awful issue settled, I began all over again the arduous task of writing my story. My many shabby diaries were dragged out of an old suitcase and translated into readable text, which was to be the beginning of my slow and very difficult healing.

My life was full – busy with Bree, painting in oils, contributing time to the craft group and trying to become familiar with strange technology. Bree was finally given the opportunity to ride a horse again. While in Victoria she had had weekly riding instruction. Although the subject of riding lessons frequently came up, I postponed them until I had the time to look for a good instructor. Bree was familiar with my way of doing things and was not in the habit of challenging or making demands. Whenever I said she would have to wait for the right time for something to happen, she was patient, meanwhile she entertained herself, making new friends at school.

She made friends with fun loving Troy Burton, who was in her class. The mischievous twinkle in his sparkling blues eyes instantly caught her attention and the bond they formed was similar to siblings. Troy, an only child, eagerly embraced Bree as his sister and the two were almost inseparable for the duration of their school days, remaining close friends.

Troy's mother Cassie knew of Bree's profound passion for horses and told me that a friend of hers could not exercise her horse due to ill health. The horse was agisted at their property and had not been ridden for some time.

Cara was an ex-racer with wins to her credit. Although she was a nice-looking bay her condition was poor, which probably contributed to her sour disposition. But the moment Bree climbed into the saddle she confidently won the challenges the mare declared. That was, until one afternoon Cara threw Bree, and instilled in her a fear that almost robbed her of her confidence.

Bree's reluctance to return to the paddock after the fall concerned me enough that I broached the subject when she recovered from the shock. She denied that there was anything wrong but hinted to me that she wanted her own horse.

"If you're still interested in riding, how come you haven't wanted to go to the paddock?"

"I have lots of homework, that's all."

I laughed and Bree frowned at me in disgust. "What happened to all your dreams?" I said and waited for a response, but she sat in silence, head hung low.

"You'll never ride at the Olympics being afraid, Babe." I tried not to sound condemning and waited for her to say something.

Bree finally broke her silence, lifted her head to look at me and said, "I'm not afraid."

I was not convinced and endeavoured to impress upon her that she must face her fears the moment they occurred. "Otherwise they will become a handicap in the future," I said gently, determined not to allow the situation to gain life. "It's okay to admit that you're afraid, Babe, I'd be scared too. But what you must realise is that falling off the mare is part of the test, to see if you are brave enough to get back on. Anyone can fall off a horse and stay off, but it takes real courage to climb back on again."

I watched her closely when I spoke. "What you do now will determine how you face things in your future. I believe that you can ride Cara and take complete control of her. She won't ever throw you again."

Bree lifted her head again and looked at me wide eyed, asking, "How come?"

"The moment that you decide to ride her, Babe, it will be you and not Cara who will be in charge because YOU'VE decided to be. There's nothing to fear when you get back on that horse again, because you won't be alone. You'll have your angel with you who will always take care of you. Once you overcome this, it will be much easier for you to overcome other hurdles in your life. But you must first ride Cara. I believe that fate has chosen a special horse for you, and it's waiting for you to prove yourself worthy. Once you do that the horse will be released to you. But you won't ever know whether what I'm telling you is true or not if you run from this fall. I cannot see the point of me getting you your own horse when you're already afraid of this one."

That evening, we were both deeply immersed in our own thoughts as we went about our routine. I had to trust that Bree would understand the significance of my words, and left her to choose her own path while ready to support her in whatever decision she made. The hours that followed were a little tense, but Bree relieved the tension at breakfast the next morning when she asked me to drive her to the paddock after school.

Dressed in riding attire and looking every bit the part, Bree nervously climbed onto her mount. I tightened the girth and said, "Remember, Babe, you're not alone. Your angel is with you. Just show Cara who's the boss, be firm." I stepped backwards as she moved the mare forward.

The bay was ready for action and immediately began to misbehave. Bree took a deep breath and sat tall in the saddle commanding Cara to move forward again for the second time. This time the horse reluctantly obeyed and fell into submission. Bree worked her for an hour and whenever Cara looked like playing up, Bree confidently rode her through it.

It was indeed a proud moment for both of us that day. My brave twelve-year-old displayed courage, maturity and determination beyond her years. Bree's beautiful smile lit up her whole face when she rode towards me.

"I was so scared, Mom," she breathlessly confessed as she dismounted. "But I knew I had to do it, otherwise I'd never ride again. I remembered what you said about not being alone. I'm not afraid anymore," she said, hugging me.

My smile almost split my face in half, I was so proud. "Well then, I think you're ready to have your own horse."

"You really mean it?" Bree could barely contain her joy.

"Yes I do. You certainly have earned it." Then suddenly I became serious. "You know, Babe, if you hadn't faced that fear, I wouldn't be considering looking for your horse. I hope you will never forget that rewards come from the challenges you overcome."

56

It was a fresh Saturday morning and Bree was still asleep. I went to the kitchen, turned on the radio, cooked toast and made a pot of tea. The weatherman was saying, "It's nice right now, but it's going to be a scorcher of a day."

I carried the breakfast on a tray into our spacious dining room.

"That smells good, Mom," Bree said as she came to the table. "I was going to have a sleep in but the smell of food made me hungry."

"I knew it would," I grinned. "You've only got a couple of hours before your lesson with Pam."

"I can't wait 'til I have my own horse, I'll ride all day, every day," she said enthusiastically. "Want juice, Mom?" she asked and I nodded.

"It will happen, Babe, you just have to be patient until the right horse comes along."

"Hmm. I know," she said wistfully, coming to the table and putting one glass in front of me and the other in her place, "but I wish I had her now. Hey, Mom," Bree said with excitement as she plonked down in her chair and reached across the table for the toast, "I almost forgot. I had a weird dream last night."

"Did you? What was it about?" I said with keen interest, hoping to interpret its message.

"I was surrounded by ugly monsters and scared out of my wits," she said, wide eyed. "Then a beautiful black horse came charging out of the darkness and chased the monsters away. The mare came and stood beside me until the ugly things disappeared completely. It was so real, Mom. I can still see her, she's so beautiful."

I felt the dream had confirmed that Bree's horse would be significant to her life, but I was looking for something else in the dream, looking to discover whether or not Bree was really happy. The fact that she had pretended she was happy for my sake during my marriage to Stanley worried me. I could not help but wonder if she was doing that again when she really wished her family would be reconciled; that seemed to be her only real concern.

Even though we laughed and joked and had fun together, and Bree would tell me without any encouragement that she loved me and was proud that I was her mom, I listened intently to whatever she said. I listened to the inflections in her voice and watched how broad her smile was, searching for any sign that she might be unhappy. I could not bear it if she was. I felt so guilty that the war between Les and I had separated her from her siblings, but when I searched her face and listened to the sound of her voice, I did not see or hear any despair.

It was my heart's desire for Bree to have her dream fulfilled. I asked Pam Cartwright, Bree's riding instructor, to help me find that special horse. The search took us to the property of a local trainer. I told Bree that Pam had called to tell me she was checking out a chestnut gelding for another client and asked us if we wanted to come with her.

I watched Bree closely and saw she was not interested in the gelding, only giving him a gentle rub. We were about to leave when a ruggedly good-looking young man, dressed in jeans and denim shirt with his weather-beaten hat pulled down to shade his eyes from the morning sun, came riding our way on a black filly. Bree saw them at the same time as I had and whispered to me, "Mom, that's the horse in my dream."

I replied without taking my eyes from the horse, "Well then, I guess we've found your horse."

The young man slowly dismounted. The sound of gravel crackling from the pressure of his leather boots could be heard as he walked over to where we were. I asked if the horse was for sale. With outstretched hand Jake Watson introduced himself and said in a friendly but adamant manner. "Nah, this one's too special to sell to just anyone. I want to make sure she goes to the right person. If and when I decide to sell her that is."

Bree's eyes were transfixed on the filly. "May I pat your horse, Jake?" she asked. He nodded. I watched Bree walk over to horse. She was a beautiful creature and I was completely captivated.

'The eyes have it,' I thought, 'they look gentle as well as intelligent.'

I could not take my eyes from Bree and the horse. They looked as if they were having a conversation. Jake noticed too and casually strolled over to join them. Pam and I were out of earshot and could not hear what they were saying. A short time later, Jake left Bree with the horse and came to me and said, "I like Bree, she is a nice little girl and very well-mannered too. You don't see much of that these days," he said glancing over his shoulder at her. "I think she'll look after the filly properly. She's yours."

Jake had spoken so casually that I asked him to repeat what he said, just to make sure that I had heard him correctly. His words took a little time to sink in and when they did, I was speechless and Bree jubilant at the realisation of her dream.

"Beauty," Bree said. "Her name is Beauty."

Ironically, Beauty's birthday was the day before Bree's. She remarkably displayed many traits similar to Bree's, often causing us to laugh.

"Mom," Bree asked in frustration when Beauty was being difficult, "what will I do?"

"Well, Babe, how do you like to be treated when you're in a bad mood? How did I treat you when you were out of sorts?"

She smiled, gave her pony a hug and coaxed her back into a good mood.

Under Pam's guidance and instruction Bree and Beauty became an exceptional team. I admired the young trainer's ability until the day she lost patience with Beauty and hit her across the head with a crop. Although I remained quiet during the incident, I addressed the matter with Bree later on, telling her that I had no idea what the correct procedure was to train a horse, but I knew what I had witnessed was not right.

I also knew Bree held Pam in high regard and felt it important to impress upon Bree that she herself only responded to love and respect and the same principle should be applied to Beauty.

"I will not tolerate any form of rough handling of the horse." I was adamant. "Be firm by all means. But I would be very disappointed if you acted in the way Pam has."

"Yeah, I'm upset about that too, Mom," Bree confessed. "Don't worry, I'll never treat any horse or animal like that, least of all Beauty."

Irrespective of why I was motivated to discharge Pam, she deserves credit for the first stage of Bree's and Beauty's training. Without her knowledge and input neither of them would have progressed so quickly. I explained to Bree that some people would come into her life for various reasons, sometimes remaining for only a short time before they move on. That is what happened with Pam, she had served her purpose and now I had to look for another instructor.

Bree and I agreed that Beauty was definitely a gift. She had given both of us so much pleasure, that I felt humbled by the experience of caring for such a magnificent animal.

'Although I had always been partial to horses, if anyone had told me that I would one day be cleaning up after one, I would have thought them ludicrous,' I wrote in my diary, then stopped and smiled, realising how much I had changed. 'Every morning,' I began, 'rain, hail, or shine, Bree and I would be at the paddock to feed Beauty. Then back in the afternoon to feed her again as well as clean up after her, and none of it ever feels like a chore for either of us. I'm so proud of Bree; she has proved herself to be responsible and very dedicated to Beauty. She adores the horse and it's also evident that Beauty loves Bree. They are great friends and actually play games together. Would you believe that, but when it comes time for work, Beauty gives Bree her best.'

The property where Beauty was agisted was semi-rural. Although outwardly I was every inch a city gal, I have always had a fondness for country life. Deep down, I was just a country gal at heart, easily charmed into oneness with nature.

'There's something wonderful in observing the world around us come to life each morning,' I wrote. 'Everything feels fresh and new, every day gives birth to a new beginning. I have spent many happy hours down at the paddock sitting on the grass, with a proud heart watching Bree and her grand horse working and striving to do their best. Sometimes I feel so very sad watching them, wishing that her siblings could share in the pleasure of their little sister's achievement. I kid myself with the belief that one day this would be possible, knowing that it is highly unlikely.'

Sadly, the bond between Cain and Bree was broken and Bree found it extremely difficult to comprehend the reason behind it. Cain was the brother whom she adored, never dreaming that anything would ever blemish their affection for each other, but it did. Les had inherited from his mother the talent of skilful manipulation which ultimately resulted in the breakdown in the friendship of Bree and Cain. I felt heartsick thinking about them so divided, knowing that if he had left them alone, all my children would have become good friends.

57

The Easter of 1992 became the last of Bree's access visits with Les. He arrived at my door uninvited. I stood frozen at the sight of him standing there in the doorway as my mind darted back to my last encounter with him, recalling the horror of it all. Obviously fear had reflected in my expression and his response was, "I'm not going to hurt you." That statement had become his signature tune on the few times we had met.

Les asked if he could come in. I hesitated then stepped aside and allowed him entry. He walked slowly to the centre of the lounge room and looked around. The unit was small but pleasant. My taste in furniture and talent in arranging it in an appealing way had often won me praise.

I walked past Les towards the kitchen and he followed. I offered him coffee and filled the jug with water, endeavouring to disguise my discomfort, especially since I sensed that he had come for a particular purpose.

"You look beautiful," he said. I asked him not to say that and immediately wished I had just ignored the comment. I had unintentionally directed the conversation to the reason for his visit – reconciliation.

"Friendship is all I can offer you, Les. Nothing would please me more than that," I told him as sincerely as I could, when I really wanted to cut his heart out. I had to be pleasant because he was the main link to my sons. I would have made a deal with the devil to have all my children united and communicating with me again, and he knew that.

Les stood close by me. He seemed disappointed that I did not fall into his arms, instead remaining fixed in my chair.

"Please don't touch me, Les," I pleaded, and slightly cringed when he reached for me. "Please, let's just be good friends. I don't want any more trouble between us."

He backed away silently and leant up against the kitchen cupboards, wearing a solemn expression as he studied me closely. Momentarily I found the courage to look directly at him, while managing to avoid eye contact. Time had not been kind to him. Years of his bitterness had certainly made their mark. Eyes that were once brown had faded to a pale grey and deep crevasses surrounded and encased them. The volume of his hair had lessened notably and gravity played a tug-of-war with his neck. He stooped badly and was overweight. There was no pleasure gazing in his direction so I looked away, grateful that I was spared that dreadful fate. If nothing else, I still had youth and vitality that kept people guessing my true age. And thankfully, when the inquiry was made, I was granted years to my credit.

I looked at the wall clock. It was almost time for me to pick up Bree from the bus stop. I was anxious for Les to leave but he wanted to come with me. We went in his car. The bus was late arriving and during that time Les asked if Bree needed anything,

"Clothes? Chocolates?" he joked.

Initially I hesitated, remembering that anything he gave me would come with a cobweb of strings and conditions attached. Then I saw that it would be to Bree's benefit to let him know that she needed a few things.

The look on Bree's face when she glanced out of the bus and caught sight of Les leaning against his car was one of total dismay. I hurried forward to greet her with a hug and whispered, "It's all right, Babe."

"Are you okay, Mom?" Her voice was full of concern.

"I'm fine, just follow my lead."

Bree greeted Les with caution.

"Your father has offered to buy you a few things that you need. Now we can go into the store and pick up your jacket from lay-by." I tried to sound bubbly and light-hearted. I thought the jacket would please Bree enough for her to feel relaxed, but the afternoon was horribly uncomfortable.

The moment Les left and was out of sight, a sigh of relief came simultaneously from both of us.

"Mom, I was so scared for you, when I saw him there at the bus stop. I didn't know what to do."

"Yes, I know what you mean. I'm so proud of the way you handled yourself today," I said, then told her what had happened before we collected her from the bus. I mentioned that Les planned to take her to up Lightning Ridge. "You'll be away for two weeks," I said, "are you okay with that?"

"I guess so. But do you think he'll cause trouble because you won't be with him?"

"I hope not."

Les returned the following day with Brad, who was on leave from the army. They had planned to go to the movies that evening and Les invited me to join them. I only agreed to go because I wanted to honour the truce I believed was in place, but most importantly Bree wanted me to go. This time she appeared more comfortable. I was not, but disguised my feelings with cunning skill that gave nothing away. I laughed at the boastful stories shared between father and son. It was clear that Les expected me to interact with them and I had more to gain by cooperating. I was aware that every negative move I made would be noted and held against me later on.

As the evening wore on I began to imagine that perhaps a permanent truce might be possible although, as I observed Brad that evening, I did not like the person he had become. Regrettably, he was now a clone of his father and army life seemed to have stimulated his aggression. A melancholic mood overwhelmed me as I knew that my son could have become a totally different person under better circumstances. Aggression was transparently obvious in his body language as well as in his attitude. If he had not been my son, I would not have remained in his company. I thought, 'As a mother I do love him, but I really don't like the person he is now.'

The following morning when they arrived to pick up Bree for their trip away, Les was in a strange mood. Brad had already carried Bree's luggage down to the car, leaving his father standing in the middle of my lounge room, nervously fidgeting with his car keys. The expression on his face was the one he wore just before he was about to explode but I ignored it, hoping whatever was bothering him would pass. I continued with my fussing, making sure Bree had everything she needed for the trip.

I was about to go downstairs when suddenly, without any provocation, Les waved his arm across the room and said, "If it wasn't for me, you would not have any of this," and marched out of the room leaving me baffled and speechless. In puzzled silence I followed him downstairs and said goodbye to Brad and Bree, then walked back upstairs after the car disappeared around the corner.

My mind was in turmoil as I tried to make sense of what Les had meant.

"Surely he could not mean..." Then it hit me. He believed what I owned belonged to him, and his audacity infuriated me. Within seconds of that realisation, and without thinking, I dialled his car telephone and was greeted with a gruff, "Hello."

"How dare you tell me what I have is thanks to you. It is thanks to Stanley, not you. Have you forgotten you gave me nothing?"

He switched the telephone off while I was in mid-sentence. That phone was my only contact link to Bree while she was away.

When they finally returned Bree was upset, complaining that Brad was nasty to her the whole time and Les did nothing about it. She said, "I don't want to ever go away with them again."

I contacted the Family Law Court for advice, telling them what had happened. They told me that Bree was of age to decide for herself. When I told her that, she announced that she intended to spend all of her holidays with me from now on.

When Les called and Bree refused to talk to him he became abusive, accusing me of turning her against him. I hung up on him, refusing to be subjected to his abuse any longer. Brad and Cain called at different times demanding to speak to Bree. Both of her brothers hollered horrible abuse through the telephone at her. Cain went as low as a snake and called his little sister a slut. Bree was absolutely distraught. I had never seen her in such a state as she was that day. She was absolutely broken-hearted.

"Why is Cain doing this to me, Mom? Why is he calling me such awful names?" she sobbed.

I knew why and so did she. Les had set the boys on her like wild dogs as payback. Like trained animals, they obeyed their master.

58

Propped up in bed, in the midst of the comfort of my numerous pillows, I penned my thoughts.

'It was easy for time to slip away without notice when we were down at the paddock. Beauty absorbed our attention completely; she was the perfect antidote to ease Bree's pain at losing Cain's affection, and shows every sign of enjoying all the fuss and adoration we lavish upon her. There was definitely a noticeable difference in Bree, as well as myself, after spending time with Beauty. We truly enjoyed every moment the three of us shared together, even to the point of feeling reluctant to go home at the end of the day. She distracted Bree from the harsh reality of the deterioration of her family, along with the horrible situation that happened at the college.'

I stopped writing and took a moment to reflect. A lot of time had passed since that incident. I shuddered at the vindictiveness of individuals who will stoop to anything to have the last word. I was not referring to Les or to my sons but to Ms Payne, the principal of the college Bree had attended.

* * *

The craft group had gathered together once again, in preparation for another annual fete. The woman who was actually more knowledgeable about craft than Marion did not have the time to dedicate to the group this time. Marion was put out about her leaving because she had not learnt the technique of making a particular doll. In the interest of the fete, I volunteered to teach the grand lady how to make the dolls. Teach her I did, and as expected she took full credit. I did not mind, since it was for the good of our stall and I was just one of many who were not recognised.

The college principal and her attitude were often a topic of discussion at the craft meetings. In the early stages we unanimously agreed that she was a totalitarian, giving no thought or consideration to any opinion other than her own.

The subject of whether the school uniforms should be worn on the day of the fete came up at the general meeting. All of the students opposed the idea and so did many parents. Taking into consideration the success and the attendance rate of the students the previous year, it was in the best interest of the college that it was left as a free dress day. However, true to her authoritarian nature, Ms Payne dug in her heels and refused to relent or even bend a little. Her word was law and that was that.

At Bree's and some of her friends' request, I went to Ms Payne's office to remind her of the promise she made the day I enrolled Bree at the college – to always have the best interest of the students at heart.

"Please allow the students a free dress day," I pleaded with her. "They won't want to attend if you impose the uniform code."

"They will do as I say, and they will attend," Ms Payne informed me coldly.

"You can rest assured that I won't force Bree to go to the fete if she decides not to. I don't believe that you're acting in the best interest of anyone, doing what you're doing. They feel that your decision is unfair. The fete is supposed to be a fun day, not a trial."

The principal tried to force a smile while glaring at me, but it looked more like a snarl. War had been declared between us. Ms Payne had told her little group of partisans that she was going to make an example of me. "I'll get rid of that Emma Jane," she had told them.

Marion was right in the thick of it all, while declaring her allegiance to me. My telephone ran hot for months with up-to-date and in-advance information but I did not trust her, even though she kept me well informed. Faxes and letters went to and from the college to my home in defence of fair play, right up to the actual day of the fete. It was almost comical, but there was nothing funny about events taking place.

I had unwittingly put myself in Ms Payne's line of fire by declaring my support for the students, but continued working with the craft group even though some of the mothers were hostile towards me. I told my adversaries that if they were willing to be dictated to, then that was fine for them, but it was not for me. "When I initially enrolled Bree into this college" I told them, "I was assured by Ms Payne that she would give consideration to students' feelings and opinions, and I am standing firm on the promise that was made to Bree and to me."

"But you're making trouble for yourself and Bree by not giving in," a concerned mother whispered.

"I have always taught my children to stand up for what they believe in, regardless of the outcome. I have read right through the college rules and mission statement, and there's no hard and fast rule in there about wearing uniforms to the college fetes. I've also called numerous schools throughout Brisbane and asked their opinion of the situation, without naming names, of course. I was told that there was always a higher attendance rate of students where a free dress code was applied. That is why they have it, to encourage students to attend the fete. My support goes to the students and that's that. Besides, Bree is proud that I am willing to stand in the students' corner when nobody else is willing to."

Some of them did not understand why I would not back down. The ones I knew that did were too afraid to say so. They thought I was out of my mind, but I did not care what any of them thought, I only valued Bree's opinion.

The day before the fete, I was so busy helping to get things ready that I actually forgot to wash Bree's uniform earlier, just in case she wanted to go. I washed it that evening but it was not dry by the morning. Bree assured me however, that she was not going to the fete and asked if she could spend the day with her friend, who lived near the college. When we arrived at the college Bree offered to help me carry boxes of craft from our car into the class room and set up the stall before she left. Unfortunately, Ms Payne saw her out of uniform on college grounds.

There were several students out of uniform that day and student numbers were down considerably from the previous year. Nevertheless, the craft stall again pulled in the highest amount of money for the day. Ms Payne went out of her way to victimise and make an example of Bree, while other students were excused and did not pay any penalty. Bree was given community service, which she was willing to do during her free Wednesday afternoon, but Ms Payne insisted that Bree do her community service on weekends, knowing that Bree's weekends involved riding tuition and competitions. She actually told Bree that she was a lovely girl and all this was happening to her because of her mother. The woman also broke her professional word and a confidential trust and telephoned Les about the matter, which gave me another issue to deal with.

In desperation, I sent a fax to the Anglican Archbishop detailing the situation and the principal's threat to expel Bree, but he did not respond. I did eventually speak to a representative of the Anglican Church and was told in no uncertain terms that the parents as well as the students will do as they are told. I quickly responded saying, "We pay high fees to have our children educated, not to be dictated to. As a parent I will protect my daughter from dictators that your establishment condones."

Bree was expelled, due solely to the vendetta against me. She was popular among her peers and had been voted class captain. The teachers who were not intimidated by Ms Payne liked Bree and were horrified by their superior's actions against her. They gave Bree wonderful references to take with her to her new school. I sought legal advice and was informed that I could take civil action against Ms Payne. Bree and I discussed it but agreed that she was not worth it. We concluded that someone as vindictive as Ms Payne could not be happy anyway. If anything, we felt sorry for her, knowing that so many people feared her. Fear breeds contempt.

After Bree's expulsion, several other students were also expelled unfairly, and others just left. As it turned out the expulsion was a blessing. Bree went from a small-minded private college to a State High School, where she met and made many lifelong friends and enjoyed her time there right up to the very last day.

Bree thanked me for supporting her. "At least, I can always be assured that you'll stand by me, Mom, and respect what is important to me. Ms Payne obviously did not act in our best interest. She lied and went on a power trip. I'm proud to have a mother who had the courage to make a stand on our behalf when the other mothers wouldn't. Thanks Mom. I'll never forget this. I feel proud that you didn't give in to that bully."

What Bree had said reminded me of the disappointment I had felt the day I stood up in defence of my sister many years before. I never forgot the vow I made that day. Bree felt the trouble was worth it, and so did I.

Ms Payne was eventually replaced.

59

Celeste had returned to the family and was an ally during the saga at the college. She told Les about the deceitful actions of the principal and defused a difficult situation for me. Her return was initiated by my determination not to let another year pass by without mending the rift between us.

* * *

The end of 1992 was fast approaching and Christmas was only weeks away. Bree was basking in the pleasure of Beauty and had often expressed disappointment that her siblings were not in her life to share her joy.

"Mom, I miss Cain," she said. "I just wish we could all be friends. I'd love it if Cain, Brad, Celeste, BJ, you and I could spend time together sometimes. It would be so nice to see them all again. But I guess that won't ever happen now."

I meditated long and hard over Bree's repeated desire to be with her brothers and sister, along with the ache I too felt at being separated from them. I came to the conclusion that she wanted to have her family restored. The sleepless nights that followed were caused by my belief that my hatred of Les was separating Bree from her family.

The night was hot, hardly a breath of a breeze in the air, when I called Les. Sleep had eluded me for many nights as my mind struggled with the idea of calling him and offering to remarry him in exchange for his support to restore my relationship with the children.

My voice broke the silence in response to his sleepy hello. I sat cross-legged in the lounge room, wrapped in a sarong. I made my move under the cover of darkness. My body was damp with perspiration. I was trembling when I said, "Les, it's me. I need to talk to you," then burst into tears, pleading for my children. "I want them back in my life, I ache for them Les, they are my life." I sobbed shamelessly. "Please, help me do that."

"You know what you have to do."

"I'll do anything you want me to do, anything. I'll even remarry you."

Les instantly responded, confessing how much he loved me and would always love me. He told me of the many times he fought to resist calling. "I even considered offering you a thousand dollars to sleep with me," he said.

I was repelled and disgusted at the thought of Les being near me, let alone touching me, but encouraged him regardless. I wanted my children. I told him that I knew he was seeing someone and that he was considering marrying her.

"I don't want to be alone anymore," he confessed. "She loves me."

"She has no idea who you are, does she?"

"She knows about you and that I love you, that's all she needs to know."

"Well, she's not important right now, but we are. Do you want me?"

"You already know the answer to that question, otherwise you would not have called me," he replied.

"You have to say it. Tell me."

"I want you, Bubby."

Feeling more confident, I told him I would call Celeste in the morning to try and mend the rift between us. "Promise me you won't interfere. I also want to spend Christmas Day with all of my children. Do I have your promise to arrange that for me?"

"I'll do what I can. I want to see you."

"Remember, Cain has to be there."

Our arrangements were discreet.

It was difficult for me to call Celeste. Many times during that year I had actually dialled her number, only to hang up the minute I heard her voice. The fear of rejection forced me to drop the receiver. The crazy thing about the rift was that it had nothing to do with Celeste and yet she made it everything about her. I was at a loss, not knowing what to do to put things right. I left her alone that year, thinking that time would heal whatever she was angry about. But instead, it only widened the gap between us.

During our separation I felt Celeste's pain. I sensed that she was pregnant and the baby was a boy and that she would lose him. She did. I could also see that her marriage was about to end. I was totally helpless to comfort her in any way. We were never very close, only because Celeste would never let me into her life the way Bree had. Celeste was intelligent, beautiful and academic, but often stubborn and childish. She allowed her head to rule when compassion was needed, and her heart to rule when common sense was needed.

During her misguided teenage years Celeste unjustly accused me of showing favour to both Cain and Bree over her. Sadly, she had forgotten that she was the answer to my prayers when she was born. I had treasured and taken great delight in her, showering her with love and attention, fussing over her the same way I fussed over Bree when she was a baby. The difference between the sisters was that Bree responded and Celeste did not.

I have a strong conscience where my children are concerned. Whatsoever or whosoever they are or have become they are still my children and I love them regardless. That was why I made the phone call to Celeste, pleading for her understanding.

During those several hours on the telephone we covered many issues. I chose my words carefully, fearful of further rejection and losing yet another chance to see my little granddaughter and family on Christmas Day.

"Look Celeste," I said in desperation, "I'm even willing to remarry your father just to have contact with all of you again."

"No! No!" she said. "If you marry him, I'll have nothing to do with either of you."

Her response came as a huge surprise because I knew that she was seeking his favour.

"I thought that was what you all wanted – to have the family reconciled."

"No. How can you even consider that after all he's done to you?"

"I am desperate Celeste, I'll do anything to have contact with you all again. Anything!"

Her tone was hard and cold when she said, "Cain won't have anything to do with you. His wife will see to that."

"Celeste, I'm willing to try. Perhaps, in time, he will come around."

I was trying to convince myself more than her.

"Well," she said indignantly, "I disagree with what you're doing and believe that you're stupid throwing your life away, all for nothing."

In my heart, I knew that she was right. I honestly dreaded the thought of being anywhere near Les, let alone being married to him again.

Les and Brad arrived at our home together around midday a few weeks before Christmas. This time they were invited, but there was something eerie about observing enemies within the walls of our domain. I stood back and observed them. It was strange how conversation flowed naturally, even though Les followed my every move with lust in his eyes.

Bree was cautious. She looked confused at first, not sure why Les was there with her brother and why I was acting friendly towards him. But her pride in Beauty made her forget her doubt as she asked them if they wanted to go to the paddock to see her.

By the look upon their faces they obviously expected Beauty to be an old nag. Neither of them could contain their surprise.

"Shit," Brad remarked, "she must have cost a packet!"

Bree and I looked at each other and grinned.

"Beauty was not cheap," I said, "but she was worth every cent."

Les walked over to Beauty to pat her but she moved away. True to his personality, he expected the horse to obey him. Bree and I were utterly surprised to see Beauty nip at him when he persisted.

"I'll put a bullet in her head if she hurts Bree," he threatened. Bree glared venomously at him and said, "No, you won't!"

"What did you pay for her?" he snapped and shook his head when I gave him a low fictitious figure. I figured he was surprised that I could afford even that meagre amount.

Back at the house, the afternoon rolled into the evening. Bree said goodnight and went to bed after Brad left, leaving Les and I alone. Les confessed that Beryl, the woman he was seeing, had made him promise not to be alone with me, but he was clearly eager to break that promise. He moved closer and said, "Look at me and tell me that you love me." I did. "With feeling," he said and then started kissing me.

After I had given Les what he wanted, I ran to the bathroom when he was asleep and frantically tried to scrub myself clean. Afterwards I still did not feel any cleaner; I could not wash the feeling of him from my body. My skin ended up red and stinging. I dried myself and went to bed. I could not sleep but lay awake, telling myself that I was a shameless whore for selling myself to Les. I hated myself. I hated Les. I wanted to kill him, but wanted to see my children.

Les slept on a mattress out in the lounge room, unaware of my torment or what I wanted to do to him. I crept out into the lounge room to where he lay. I watched him sleeping soundly, his mouth slightly open. For a few minutes I listened to him breathing, thinking about what I should do. Then I carefully tiptoed into the kitchen, took a large knife from the drawer and went back and stood beside him. I looked down at him again and watched him sleep without a care in the world. My mind raced and my heart beat so fast that I shuddered. My body was soaked in perspiration, my head ached and I felt dizzy. Several times I raised the knife to slam it into his heart. I wanted him to die. I imagined that I had plunged the blade deep into his chest, and that I was soaked in warm sticky blood when I pulled it out of his body. It felt so real that I thought I had killed him. Then he stirred and rolled over. Terrified, I stepped away from him, dashed off to the bathroom and showered again. I could smell blood on me.

'I can't be with him,' I thought as the water trickled over me, 'I know that I will do it. I will kill him.' Thinking about it made me shake uncontrollably. I was an emotional mess.

The air that night was hot and very still. I lay on my bed deep in thought until sunrise, then showered again before taking Bree to the paddock. The light of day highlighted my shame and I avoided Les' gaze during breakfast, finding him even more repulsive. I could not imagine what Beryl saw in him. Perhaps she thought she possessed all the wisdom of the ages and could heal his broken heart. His obsession with me should have strongly indicated to her that his personality was seriously flawed. I also felt that she, like Les, did not want to be on her own in the latter years of her life, but any man who had an album full of photographs of his ex-wife should have set off alarm bells for her.

* * *

Les had shown the photo album to Bree and I when we made the stopover to his place on our way to Brisbane at Christmas of 1991. I looked at it with astonishment when he placed it on the table and slowly turned the pages. A strange look crossed his face when he stared at the images of me captured in times past.

"I look at these all the time, Bubby," he had said. I cringed.

* * *

Brad walked through the front door just as we were finishing breakfast.

"Hi!" he said, then looked at Les and asked, "Are you and Bree ready?"

"Nah mate. Can you take Bree Christmas shopping; your mother and I are talking?"

"Mmm, okay," Brad said, looking puzzled.

After Bree and Brad left I made coffee for something to do, as I could sense Les had something to say.

'How strange,' I thought, 'he's so very predictable.' He displayed an air of cockiness in his manner so I braced myself for what was to come.

"You know, Bubby," he said, pacing the floor, "I'm pretty important down south."

"Oh, in what way?" I asked and sat on the edge of my Edwardian dining table sipping coffee from a china mug.

"I have the power to do favours. Most of them owe me a lot. I own them bastards," he said, "I'm God down there."

He went on to tell me about the people who worked for him, about Beryl's friends and her deceased husband's family.

"The town is small and almost everyone is related in some way to one another. Beryl's husband worked for me before he died. He left her the house and his insurance. She's financially secure." He spoke as though he was talking about the weather.

"Well, now I see the interest," I said. "And all you have is a job."

"I'm tired of living alone," he confessed. "I'm telling you all this because I want to be honest with you if we're going to get back together. We'll have to live there. Can you do that? I want you with me."

I thought for a minute before I said, "I guess so."

"There's something else I have to tell you. As you know I've been going over to Indonesia."

"No," I lied, "I did not know. I wasn't interested in what you were doing, Les," I said in an off-handed manner. I waited for him to continue as it sounded serious.

"Well, I've been having sex with young Indonesian girls."

"Les," I interrupted, "I'm not interested in your sex life. It has nothing to do with me and I couldn't care less."

"But I want to tell you. I want you to know everything," he insisted. "I treated them well," he said, and went on and on. He even talked about his sexual relationship with Beryl and the affair he had with his service manager's wife.

He was not being honest. He was bragging to let me know that young girls were interested in him. He wanted to appear to be a good lover and have me think women desired him.

"Look Les," I said, fed up with listening to his rubbish, "those girls were not with you because they liked you, they were with you because you paid them. You bought them just like you bought me. I really don't care what you do. And as for Beryl and the service manager's wife, there's not much to choose from in a small town. From what you tell me, you're a big fish in a small pond. So who cares? I certainly don't."

I pitied the girls who had to subject themselves to him for a living. My children were the sole reason I had given him permission to touch me for the first time in over twenty years.

"Remember," Les said smugly, silencing me, "you want to have Christmas with the kids."

Christmas dinner was at Celeste and Terry's place. Bree and I were surprised to find Cain and Cindy already there. I had thought they would not come, but hoped they would. My joy turned to disappointment when they left a few minutes after we arrived. Their departure only momentarily soured the day. I knew how to count my blessings. My other children were there.

After Les had left Brisbane, I asked Bree how she felt about Les and I getting back together.

"He could support your riding."

"No way!" she almost shouted, horrified at the suggestion. "Mom, tell me you're not."

"I'm thinking about it. Why shouldn't I?"

"He isn't good enough for you. You deserve so much better. I won't live with you if you do. I'll run away. Please, Mom, don't go near him," she pleaded.

"But I thought you wanted to have your family together again?"

"You're my family, Mom. My brothers and Celeste are my family, but that's all," she said, looking at me. I was bewildered.

It was obvious to Les that no power or persuasion on this earth would make me love him. He remained in phone contact with me during the weeks that followed and we were actually pleasant to each other after agreeing we should not remarry. He was due back in Brisbane a short time later and brought Beryl with him. During one of his phone calls prior to their Brisbane trip, Les took great pleasure in stressing the point that Beryl was several years my junior.

"I've traded you in for a younger model," he had mocked when he first told me.

I welcomed Beryl with a beaming smile and outstretched hand the day she, Les and BJ came to pick up Bree. She was obviously uncomfortable and appeared intimidated by my easy manner towards her.

'Les should have kept his mouth shut about her age,' I thought, surveying her tired features. She was much taller than me. Her silver hair was long. Les had mentioned that she was once overweight and had slimmed down after the death of her husband. I laughed out loud, thinking how much he had stressed the younger woman thing.

"The older model is still the winner," I called out as Les got into the car to leave, remembering his mocking words. He knew exactly what I meant and laughed too, while Beryl looked on bewildered.

"Now Ma, don't be a bitch," said BJ, playfully scolding me as he hugged me goodbye.

BJ had spent most of his time floating in and out of my life, often turning up unexpectedly and departing just as quickly as he had done that day. Although still an enigma, he always remained neutral regarding Les and I.

During the last call to me Les said, "I'm going to marry Beryl. You don't love me, Bubby, she does and she looks at me. You won't. I wanted you to look at me."

I began to weep. "I really hate the idea of my children having a stepmother. I was willing to remarry you to prevent that. They're my children, Les. They're my life. You never wanted any of them. But I did."

"If you'd stayed with me, you could have had everything, but you didn't."

"I wish you would tell them the truth about what you did. I didn't desert them. If you tell them the truth, we could be friends and maybe they'll talk to me. I want all of them in my life."

"You should've stayed with me, Bubby."

"I bet you didn't tell Beryl that you were alone with me, did you? Or any of the things you did to me or the children."

"We have agreed that nothing exists before we got together, so we don't have a past."

"What a lot of shit. Denying what you did to us doesn't make you innocent. Beryl is a fool. You are lying to her and she knows it."

He went silent. Then he said menacingly, "I should have killed you when I had the chance!" The line went dead.

Later that year the children were invited to the wedding but only Brad, Cain and Celeste went. The thought of Celeste going disturbed me. I even tried to dissuade her, telling her that she would only find trouble there, but she was determined to be at the ceremony regardless of my warning. I was not sure what would happen but felt that she should not go.

All of that weekend, Celeste was on my mind, a feeling that something was very wrong nagging at me. On Sunday morning the telephone rang. Celeste was at the other end of the line, crying. She was heartbroken.

"Mom, Mom," was all she could say. "He ignored me. No one apart from the immediate family knew who I was or that I even existed."

She also told me that Cain gave a speech at the wedding, congratulating his father for trading his mother in for a newer model. I was angry that Celeste had not listened to me, angry at Les for treating her so cruelly, and angry that Cain had been so easily fooled into accommodating Les to rob him of his mother and little sister. Les had gone to great lengths to hurt my children in any way he could. My hatred of him left no room for anything else.

60

There were few people other than Bree that I could say that I respected or trusted. Male friendships I had formed fell by the wayside swiftly and became a source of entertainment over coffee with girlfriends. The potential lovers were rated in relation to what I liked about them and whether or not they were worthy of a second consideration. They were not.

Margaret Murray was one of my coffee friends. Her forthright confessions about her past relationships, even though she said she loved the men, never ceased to amaze me. I would never disclose any intimate details about either Luc or Matt because of my feelings for them.

Margaret and her home always seemed to be in chaos. She was eternally worn out and fed up with trying to keep up with her three cute toddlers. They created mayhem. Toys, books, odd shoes and clothing were strewn throughout the house. A stack of dirty dishes sat in and on the kitchen sink. Margaret had to remove a heavy basket of clean washing from the kitchen table and push aside other clutter on the table to make room for four coffee mugs. She apologised for the mess as we sat down, but was too disheartened with her life to really care one way or the other about what any of us thought.

"This place," she said, with a half-hearted wave of her hand, "looks like a bloody café after it's closed."

All of us momentarily went quiet, deep in thought. I surveyed the room, thinking how much Margaret's home resembled my life.

Writing my story had opened up a past that I wanted to forget, and at times it had overwhelmed me. The positive aspect was that deciphering my diaries into readable text forced me to look at my life in a way I had never done before. Doing that filled me with so many regrets, especially when I knew that I had wasted most of my life.

Before we moved, I was alone in the Holland Park unit and Bree was with Les. I picked up Luc's photograph from the china cabinet. Looking at it, I thought how much I missed him and how empty my life felt every time Bree went away. In a moment of self-indulgent pity, I heard Luc's words in my mind, "It's too late for regrets," which made me think about the day I was given the photograph.

* * *

I was in Sydney in 1988, the year following Luc's death. An opportunity arose to visit Luc's best friend Leo and his wife Kate, the woman I had initially contacted when I was looking for Luc's telephone number, only to discover that he had cancer. Although it felt like a lifetime had passed since our last meeting they welcomed me warmly, but when I mentioned the nature of my visit Leo seemed to tense up. He denied any knowledge of Luc being Cain's father.

"You knew. I told you, Leo," I said, handing him a photograph of Cain.

"I don't remember," he muttered apologetically, staring at a younger image of his deceased friend. "No one can deny that he's Luc's kid," he smiled, returning the photograph to me

"Leo, please, I want a photograph of Luc for Cain. One day he may be interested in knowing what his father looks like. Cain has half-brothers and uncles and aunties. They are his real family. If not he, then perhaps his children will want to meet them some day. I owe them that much." I paused a moment to allow my words to sink in, then said, "Luc knew that he was dying."

"He did not!" he snapped. "How would you know that?"

"Luc said that he couldn't afford to come to Brisbane to see me. He also told me he didn't have any life insurance."

Leo was silent. He was watching me wipe my eyes from across the room.

"Love!" Leo called to his wife. "Where are our wedding photos?" Immediately the tension disappeared from the room.

"You wouldn't have recognised him, love," Leo went on to say. "Luc's hair was white. It was incredible how quickly he had aged."

As Leo spoke, I realised Luc thought I would not have loved him if I had seen him like that. He looked handsome as Leo's best man.

With that memory still running through my thoughts, I put the photograph back on the cabinet and then went to my bedroom and lay on my bed. Looking around my room, I could appreciate its serenity and beauty, but the ambience did nothing to ease the ache in my heart. Recalling that day brought me to the brink of hopelessness and I wept uncontrollably. I was emotionally exhausted and my body ached. I fell asleep.

When I woke up I was sitting on a bench in a garden, the same garden where I had walked beside the monk many years before. The sun was bright and felt warm on my skin. I looked to my left. Luc was sitting beside me. We smiled at each other. He took my hand in his, "Everything will be fine," he said, "I will look after you."

Almost twelve hours had passed by the time I opened my eyes again. The encounter with Luc seemed so real that I expected to find him still with me but only his familiar scent lingered in the room.

I clung to that dream for years and longed to be with him, but my devotion to Bree prevented me from leaving.

My life was a vortex as I fought a persistent battle with a depression I endeavoured to hide from everyone. More often than not I felt like an alien, displaced and not knowing where I truly belonged, standing on the outskirts of life, not fully committed to anything or anyone other than my children.

Friends I once trusted had betrayed me. No one really knew me; if they had, they would not have admired me for my so-called strength and wisdom. It frustrated me that I was often told that I was a strong, capable woman, who could handle anything that came my way. No one knew how much living was hurting me or that I only stayed for Bree. Everything I did was for Bree.

At sixteen, Bree had grown into a beautiful teenager; long honey-blonde curly locks and sparkling brown eyes were naturally captivating. When she smiled it was difficult not to be charmed by her.

A month prior to her sitting the year eleven exams, Bree was offered a Level-One Riding Instructors' Course. It was her choice to drop everything in pursuit of the course. The owner of the riding school was her riding instructor, who raised some doubts as to whether she could handle the laborious work in addition to the long hours she would be required to put in each day. She assured him that she could. A dedication to a dream steered Bree though a gruelling ten-hour shift, six days a week, in all kinds of weather. The deduction of her board and the cost of Beauty's feed left her with a meagre sum of twenty-five dollars at the end of each week.

After all her hard work, the promised instructors' course did not eventuate. Bree became disgruntled and tired under the stress of being over worked for little return. At the end of the year she and Beauty left the riding school.

Bree met Sam a short time after leaving the riding school. When she brought him home I knew by the way they gazed at each other that they were in love. Sam stood head and shoulders above Bree, who had to crane her neck to look up at him. His deep voice softened and his green eyes sparkled at the sight of her. I caught a glimpse of Bree's expression and thought how she had grown from a sweet little toddler into a beautiful, confident young woman. She was making so many life-changing decisions, not only in considering her career, but also her personal life.

When Bree and Sam came to me, asking for my permission to live together, I had already adjusted to the idea. Bree told me that she would respect my decision if I said no. It was my desire for Bree to remain at home but there was an inner comfort in knowing that the time had come for her to discover her own pathway. She was almost eighteen and had proven to be responsible at numerous times during her adolescence. I gave her my blessing, with the reassurance that I would be there to support her in whatever she did.

The house Bree and Sam rented was almost bare, but neither of them seemed to notice. They were blissfully happy. An empty house did not matter to them but it concerned me. With donations and gifts and what they eventually bought, the empty rooms were soon filled and together they created a bohemian-style home.

Bree's first year at the riding school had trained her in resourcefulness. Trendy clothes and parties were almost non-existent for her. Her friends drove their own cars and their closets bulged with the latest fashions. The luxuries they enjoyed became Bree's willing sacrifice in pursuit of her dream. That resourcefulness blended superbly with the discipline of shared responsibilities with Sam. A tight budget demanded frugal shopping, budget no-name labels purchased instead of brand name products.

The resilience of Bree and Sam's relationship amazed me, given the stark differences in their personalities and natures. Bree was focused and had always known her direction in life, her nature practical and down-to-earth. Sam was a dreamer. Even with his multi-skilled ability with computers and talent as a musician and artist, he was still searching for his path. The qualities that drew them to each other also became the source of their frustration. Fortunately the merging of the two individual personalities complemented their love for each other, which seemed enduring.

The Level-One course was to commence halfway through the following year. Bree felt refreshed and more optimistic after she and Beauty had rested. She decided to review the prospects for the Level-One Certificate again as she was not satisfied with the job she had.

Remarkably the workload at the riding school, south-east of Brisbane, was not as gruelling for the students or the hours as long as they had previously been. The legitimacy of the course not only eased the workload, it also enabled the students to qualify for a government student allowance.

Bree's natural charm and riding skill had won her praise and popularity among the young clients and their parents at the riding school. The morning I attended a Dressage Day, one of the mothers joined me on the bench seat under a tree. Claire Host introduced herself and began an endless praise of Bree's accomplishments. Her enthusiasm seemed remarkable to me, even though I wholeheartedly agreed with every word she uttered.

I gave Claire an astonished look when she strongly implied that she and her husband planned to offer Bree a position with them at their stables when she finished her training. Claire told me that she and her husband owned a large number of racehorses. She also mentioned that they were aware of Bree's future plans to breed and to train horses, with Beauty's first foal being her starting point.

"I know that it's only a matter of finance, in addition to selecting the right stallion for Beauty, that's standing in the way of Bree starting her project," she said.

Claire made it very clear to me that she intended to offer Bree every opportunity.

"We can help Bree, Emma," she said enthusiastically, leaning closer to me, "and we like and admire her so much. You must be very proud of her. "

The Hosts were impressed with Bree's enthusiasm toward gaining her goals. They knew from their experience as horse breeders that Beauty came from a quality bloodline. When Bree joined us, Claire asked her the name of Beauty's sire.

"God's Walk and the mare was Supreme Court," she said.

Claire knew the sire and told Bree that she had information and a photograph of him that she could have. It was glaringly obvious to me that Beauty was Claire's motivation; more than once that day she had expressed a desire to have one of Beauty's foals.

I was pleased that Bree's life was going according to her dreams. From the time she was a small child she had wanted to work with horses and to ride in equestrian events, in hope of one day representing Australia in the Olympics.

'Perhaps Claire and Bob Host were the ones who could help Bree to achieve that,' I thought after meeting Claire.

'I have an inner comfort knowing that Bree is following her dreams.' I confided in my diary. 'Perhaps now I will be free to leave. When one's life is constantly a combat it becomes difficult to know who is friend or foe. I will probably always live alone if I decide to live. Marriage is a prison sentence. I have done my time,' I wrote, pausing when I thought about a conversation about marriage that I had had with Celeste. After a dinner date with a guy I would say to her in a blasé way, "Ah well, I'll probably end up marrying him." It was my way of saying the guy was a loser, but she assumed that I wanted to be married.

I knew my views were pessimistic, but that was how I honestly felt, and I paid a price for my pessimism. Illness became too frequent for me to dismiss as nothing and I had a second brush with breast cancer. When I realised that the anger and hatred I felt for Les could manifest itself into a disease, it made me review my attitude and frame of mind. I searched for peace but a heavy depression descended upon me. I had a burning desire to get away from my life in Australia. I applied for a position overseas as a nanny but in the middle of making the arrangements cancelled everything, feeling that moving to another country would not change anything. What I was running from was inside me.

After I had cancelled my plans, I confided in Bree about my feelings. So much had changed in four years; Bree and I had moved from a large house into a quaint two-bedroom town house nearby. Celeste had found another reason to distance herself from me again. I had grown tired of trying to live up to her expectations so I let her go. Bree was pursuing a career as a riding instructor and was living with Sam. The one thing that remained unchanged was our friendship, respect and ability to express our deepest feelings to each other without fear or prejudice. Bree listened as I spoke frankly and freely.

"I'm tired of my life, Babe," I began, trying to choose my words carefully. "I'm afraid to desire anything for myself for fear of disappointment. I feel my life is empty and pointless. Most of the time I feel helpless. I look at you and see that you are happy with Sam, which is wonderful and that's what I want for you. BJ floats through life and has never needed me. Brad, Cain and Celeste... well, who knows about them, I certainly don't? I want something for myself, but the very things I want are beyond my reach. I feel sad in my heart. I'm tired of pretending that everything's okay when it isn't. I just want to sleep and never wake up. Do you understand, Babe?" Bree nodded.

"I'm not having a breakdown or anything like that," I said, "I simply feel empty. How I'm feeling isn't your fault. I only hung on this long for you. If I hadn't had you I wouldn't be here today. I love you dearly but I want to be able to do what is right for me. I can see that you have a full and happy life ahead of you. I believe you will succeed with or without me. If

I decide not to continue my life, I want you to understand that I will always be with you in spirit."

Bree listened and allowed me to speak without interrupting. Tears had formed and rolled down her cheeks.

"Yes, Mom, I do understand what you mean, but I've come to realise and appreciate why I was born. I was only speaking to Sam about it the other morning. I know in my heart that I was born to be with you. You're my rock, and I'm yours. Everything I do, I want to share it with you. You're my best friend and my soul mate. I need you in my life. My successes and achievements will mean nothing if you're not there for me to share them with. If anything happens to you then my life too will be destroyed. So be here for me because I need you."

She embraced me, and then we looked at each other and laughed.

"It's okay," I said drying my tears, "I guess I'll have to hang around for a while longer."

I did not fear leaving this life behind. I believed that stepping over the line that divided life from death was simply an extension of life without a physical body. It fascinated me enough to give it more than a passing thought, but my attempt to prepare Bree for what I had intended to do only resulted in her extracting from me a promise to remain with her.

I looked at my world with dissatisfaction, feeling that this was as good as it gets. I craved for more. The nights that followed were long and full of torment as I relived my life over and over again. My mind would not stop. I yearned to rid myself of the hellish nightmares and in desperation called out to God to give me peace.

My renewed belief in God gave me the courage to rummage through the debris of my life, unburdening myself of anger, hatred, resentment and every destructive aspect in me, simply by learning to forgive all that had happened to me. Most importantly, I forgave myself.

Initially it was a daily struggle to overcome my depressing thoughts and allow the positive aspect of my personality to surface. But as time passed, it became simply a matter of changing old habits for new ones.

'No longer is there the jumble of a ransacked room,' I advised my diary, 'everything is now in its place. The table is set ready for the banquet to celebrate my new life. Whatever is in store for me now,' I wrote, 'I will deal with it one day at a time.'

It was not until I decided to eliminate the 'what if' and 'if only' from my vocabulary that I was able to get on with my life, and that meant letting go of Luc.

Like a mountain climber clings to the cliff, I clung to my belief that someone was looking after me. My life depended upon it. That was my strength, without it I would not have been able to move forward or believe that I deserved a better life. My faith had shown me how to embrace life again. Everything was different. My desire to leave this world faded once I understood that it was my destiny to live a long life. That was why Bree was born; so we could be there for each other, and Beauty was Bree's gift.

61

A chance meeting at the paddock where we kept Beauty during Bree's six-month break from the riding school brought about major changes in several lives. Many times before that afternoon Bree and I had noticed a man in his fifties, riding a striking Arab colt along the side of the road. He wore old jeans, checked shirt and a battered Akubra that shaded his face from the afternoon sun

Each time horse and rider passed by Beauty's paddock, we would usually stop what we were doing and watch them. One particular afternoon our admiring stares caught the horseman's eye. He waved and we called out, "Nice horse!" hoping he would stop so we could have a closer look at his horse.

Unexpectedly, he slowly turned the colt and rode towards us, as if he had read our minds. We left Beauty chewing on hay and walked over to the fence. Bree and I said hello in unison, "We like your horse."

Bree was beaming while she stroked the colt's neck and muzzle.

"What's his name?" she asked.

"Shadow," the man said with pride and sat taller in the saddle. He introduced himself, then told us how much of an impact Shadow had made on his life.

Jack Dutchman had recently suffered a heart attack and his recovery was slow. Caring for Shadow was taking its toll on his health. He told us that he was desperately searching for someone willing to be as committed to Shadow as he was. The expression on Jack's well-worn face matched the sadness of his voice, revealing how much the pain of being forced to sell his friend affected him.

"If I had the money I would buy him," I said in earnest. "Your horse would be ideal to breed with Beauty, but unfortunately I don't have it right now." I paused a moment then said, "Perhaps I may know of someone who does. Give me your telephone number and I will contact him."

Driving home Bree said that she would love to own Shadow. I glanced at her and wished that I had the money to make it possible.

"You never know, it could still happen," I said, optimistically determined never to entertain any more pessimistic thoughts. I also had the feeling that Shadow would belong to Bree.

Bree gave me a sceptical glance but did not say anything. She knew me well. If I felt it was possible, then it was.

I called the person whom I thought would be interested in Shadow and gave him Jack's details, but for some reason Jack was unable the times my friend phoned him. Later, I remembered the conversation I had with Claire Host at the riding school, and especially Claire's desire to have one of Beauty's foals. With that in mind I encouraged Bree to go and see Claire and her husband, Bob, and to tell them that she thought Shadow would be the ideal horse for Beauty to start her breeding program. It seemed logical that if Bree gave them a detailed plan of how she would do it, they would in some way work out a deal to purchase Shadow for her. I was not sure precisely how it would turn out, but I knew that Beauty was Bree's trump card.

Although Beauty lived up to her name, she most certainly had a mind of her own and had gained a reputation for being aloof, only taking an interest in her surroundings and people when it suited her. She assumed a position as the alpha mare of the school horses, quickly sorting out the bullies within the herd and displaying superior leadership, courageously protecting timid or insecure horses from the more aggressive ones.

Bree and I were surprised to learn that some people were afraid of Beauty. For example, Bill Walker, who had delivered Beauty's feed for over a year, one day just simply refused to do it anymore.

"That black mare's crazy," he told me over the telephone. "She needs shootin'. I'm not goin' near 'er again," and slammed down the phone in my ear.

I later learned that Bill had entered the paddock with a truckload of uncovered hay and Beauty ran beside his truck picking at the hay. She was not attacking him or the vehicle, just seeing the uncovered hay as an invitation for to help herself. Bill, obviously threatened by her behaviour, stopped the truck and chased her on foot, swinging a knotted rope above his head, which was a declaration of war to Beauty. Consequently, whenever Bill entered the yard, she would challenge him, rearing up in front of the vehicle and slamming her hooves down on the bonnet.

Jeff Wale, a local farmer, also delivered hay. He liked Beauty and appreciated her intelligence.

"I know just how to handle her," he said with a cheeky grin. He threw a biscuit of hay over the fence and while Beauty was busy picking at it, drove into the yard and unloaded the feed.

"Beauty's okay," he said lifting his hat to scratch his head. "Females are happy when you just give 'em what they want, then life's sweet."

Bree would always coax rather than demand anything from Beauty.

I fondly remember her telling me, one day when I had dropped by to see her, about the first cross-country training course they had done that week

"We're supposed to teach our students what we've learnt," she laughed. "While the other girls were taking their horses through their paces, Beauty was totally tuned out. She was not taking any notice of anyone or anything. Then it was our turn. She cantered around the course and enjoyed the jumps. But when we came to the water crossing she stopped dead in her tracks. I directed her to move forward, but she refused and stubbornly backed away from the water, snorting and throwing her head around. You know, Mom, the way she does when she doesn't want to do something," Bree said, and I nodded. "Well," Bree continued, "I put the reins on the saddle, dismounted and walked to the edge of the water. I turned towards Beauty and urged her to walk forward." Bree shook her head and laughed, "I said come on you dick, it's only water. But she was not having any of it. She remained at the water's edge, snorting and carrying on. "Then," Bree said, "I looked down at the water and scooped some up and let it trickle through my fingers. I kept my head down. Beauty stretched her neck so far forward to see what I was doing that her muzzle was resting on the top of my head. Curiosity got the better of the stickybeak and she moved closer. Come on, I urged again and she pawed at the water, splashing me. I splashed her back. She then sat down and pawed the water with her front legs, drenching me. I yelled, 'Get up! Get up!' just as she was about to roll over. Maggie's new leather saddle was on her back. It cost a fortune and I couldn't afford to replace it if it was ruined. We finished the course dripping wet and everyone had a good laugh, and guess who's teaching the watercourse to the students? Me," she laughed.

During another visit, Bree also told me how her friendship with Beauty was firmly established. She was in the lower paddock picking up horse manure, with Beauty following close behind. The school horses were quietly grazing at the far end. Without any warning they scattered in fright, then grouped together and galloped towards her. Beauty whinnied and snorted, throwing her head about in the air. "I looked up," Bree said, "and saw what was happening. The horses were too close for me to run for cover. Before I could do anything,

Beauty had moved in front of me and the horses ran around us."

On the way home, thinking about how Beauty had protected Bree, I recalled the dream Bree had had several years before and realised that the horse in the dream was indeed Beauty.

I also thought that Claire Host's desire to own one of Beauty's foals was as much to do with the mare's personality and loyalty to Bree as with her bloodline. Beauty was an exceptional horse. Although her elegance and conformation might be duplicated with a suitable sire, Beauty had unique qualities for which I credit Bree's love and kindness to the horse over the years. Bree saw Beauty as more than just a horse, she saw her as her best friend.

When Bree told Claire that she had found the perfect horse to sire Beauty's foals that would start her breeding program, she invited Bree and Sam to her home to discuss the matter further with her husband. The Hosts listened with interest while Bree explained her breeding plan in detail. Bob Host was so impressed that when Bree had finished talking, he got up from his chair, left the room and quickly returned with chequebook in hand. When Bob handed Bree a cheque for the amount Jack wanted for Shadow, he said to her, "You can have the receipt made out in your name, on the condition that Beauty's second foal is mine." Bree agreed.

After they left the Host's place, Bree and Sam came to my home to show me the cheque. They were overjoyed and full of optimism and astonished that Claire and Bob were so supportive, but I had known they would help Bree in some way.

Jack also was overjoyed when we told him the good news, amazed at how easily everything fell into place.

"If it's meant to be Jack, then it will be," I told him. He gave an odd look, then smiled and shook his head in disbelief.

Before the sale was finalised, Jack told Bree he would only sell Shadow to her if the horse allowed her into his pen. Before she entered, Jack told Bree and I Shadow's life story.

"From the day he was born," Jack said, casually leaning against the fence, "Shadow has experienced conflict and rejection just like many humans have. His original owner rebelled against a decision his father made to introduce an Arab stallion, Simeon Stav, Shadow's father, to his stock.

"Shadow is a full blood nephew to Simeon Sadik, who was sold to a member of a famous English rock band for well in excess of a million dollars. Even with his prestigious bloodline, the son hated the strawberry roan foal. He said that he was too long in the back and his legs were gangly. As a result, the son locked him and his mother in a small pen and virtually left them to die. By chance Sue, a friend of mine, was looking for a mate for a young filly that had recently lost her mother. She was at the pound to collect a runaway cow and overheard a man asking if anyone wanted an Arab foal."

"The foal was a horrible sight," Jack said in disgust. "He was short and stunted and his belly was swollen from malnutrition. But despite his ugliness the little guy managed to win Sue's heart, and she took him home, naming him Clancy." Jack smiled and shook his head in amusement. "Fancy naming an Arab Clancy," he laughed. "Sue's kindness breathed new life into the little guy's traumatised spirit and he unexpectedly grew into a handsome, high-spirited colt. The idea of keeping a filly and colt together was out of the question. Sue's husband's work commitments took both of them away from the farm for long periods at a time, leaving her inexperienced brother to look after the horses."

"Arabians are well known for their swiftness and intelligence," Jack said with a certain amount of pride. "And it didn't take Clancy long to realise that Sue's brother didn't have a clue. He challenged the brother when he entered the pen at feed time. Eventually, due to the lack of discipline, the colt developed bad habits and became arrogant in the process. Sue's circumstances forced her to find the colt a new home and I was given the first option," he said with a broad smile. "But I told Sue the colt's name had to be changed. It was unheard of to name an Arabian colt Clancy. Kazan was more appropriate," he said, not knowing that the horse's name would be changed again.

Jack had learned about horses during his childhood days. He lived in the Holland Park-Mt Gravatt area during the early sixties, when the neighbourhood was mostly bushland scrub where brumbies ran wild. On weekends he and his mates rounded up the brumbies, penned them and then let them go to be rounded up again the following weekend. They did all that just for the fun of it. He also spent time at the local racetrack, where he raced his favourite mare. The love of horses brought out the natural horseman in him and he was often asked to have a look at horses that were difficult to handle.

"I didn't do anything special," he said modestly, "just patience and kindness was all I exercised. I was more successful with horses than I was with people," he confessed. I detected a note of sadness mixed with regret in that statement.

The more time Bree and I spent with Jack, the more we liked him. 'Jack's bond with his horse reflected who he really wanted to be,' I noted in my diary. 'Unfortunately, when we handle what life deals us, with frustration rather than wisdom, the results can be adverse, causing a lifetime of regret instead of peace. Most of us deal with whatever comes our way in the best way we can. I expect that is what Jack had done – just as I have.'

The past had left its mark. A once youthful and robust frame now walked slowly, ever mindful of the damage that future stress can do. Past memories were reflected upon with a touch of irony in the wisdom of hindsight. Nevertheless, the mateship between Jack and his horse had compensated for some of his unfulfilled dreams.

They spent long hours together while Jack cleared the paddock of potentially dangerous tree stumps. The colt followed him everywhere, watching everything Jack did with a keen interest, and Kazan was changed to Shadow.

Their relationship naturally developed as though they were two horses in a herd, with Jack dominant and having the influence. Shadow, being in the position of the younger horse, submitted to Jack's authority, relying on him for everything. Natural instincts and good social skills are imperative to a horse's survival. Whenever Shadow momentarily moved away from his guardian to investigate another part of the paddock, any sudden noise or movement sent him scurrying back to Jack's side.

The heavy work of clearing stumps for the paddock had robbed Jack of the little strength he had. There were times when he would simply lie where he fell, worn out. Shadow would nuzzle him until he was back on his feet again, the colt's concern and loyalty inspiring Jack to carry on.

Twice daily Jack rode Shadow along the streets and some motorists would slow down and watch them pass, us among them. Shadow's magnificent silver coat shone in the sunlight. Everything about the small horse was awesome and he seemed to be aware of the impact he made. He had gained confidence from the security of Jack's devotion and admiration. Jack continued to ignore the warning signs. He refused to consider that there was anything seriously wrong with his heart when he felt breathless and stabbing pains in his chest. One day the impact of his declining health hit him hard. He struggled to breathe and perspiration poured profusely from every pore of his body as he fell to the ground under the pressure of the heavy weight that had gripped his heart. Shadow immediately sensed something was wrong and came to his aid. He kept Jack conscious by nudging him to get up and licking his face. Jack admits he would have simply lain down and given in if Shadow had not been so persistent.

"I was in so much pain," he said, and his face twisted at the thought.

During the weeks that followed Jack worked with Bree, instructing her how to handle Shadow. He stressed many times to Bree that stallions are dangerous if not handled correctly. "They need to be handled with respect because they are leaders," he said seriously. "Although Shadow is only two and a half, he will soon be a stallion. It's very important for your safety that you understand him."

The teacher went to great lengths to educate his student and demonstrated the ways of working a colt, which resulted in Bree gaining not only Shadow's respect but also Jack's. She obediently followed his instruction to the letter, with great rewards.

The relationship between Jack and Shadow was identical to Bree's and Beauty's. Bree appreciated and respected the bond that they shared, as well as the hardship of Jack's inevitable separation from Shadow. It was natural that Bree would question whether Shadow would accept her in Jack's place, and be concerned that they would fret for each other.

Her fears were put to rest when Shadow finally responded to her commands. Jack took a step backwards after he was satisfied Bree knew what she was doing. A bond of trust began to develop between Bree and Shadow.

Bree was beginning to feel the strain of dealing with the demands of her Level-One exam added to the logistics of caring for two horses twice a day in different paddocks. After putting in a long day at the riding school, she exercised Beauty. Then Sam drove her over to Shadow's paddock, thirty kilometres away, to work with him for a couple of hours. Time lost in travelling left Bree no option than to reluctantly accept an offer Claire and Bob Host made to have Shadow at their property. Their home was only a short drive from the riding school. Initially Bree declined, on a gut feeling that it would not be good for Shadow. She was also reluctant to jeopardise the progress she was making with Shadow by prematurely relocating him to an unfamiliar environment.

Bob Host was considered experienced in handling horses but he would not respect Bree's request to allow Shadow to get used to his surroundings before releasing him with other horses in the paddock.

"Ah, he'll be all right with the other horses Bree, he has to learn to fit in," he said.

The property was large enough to accommodate all the horses in separate pens, but for reasons known only to him, Bob rejected Bree's concerns for Shadow. She felt helpless, overpowered by his authority and fearing the agreement between them would become void in an instant if she in any way defied him.

Bree's work commitments at the riding school demanded her time, in addition to her study. The workload prevented her from giving Claire's daughter riding lessons as often as she had promised and she could not work with Shadow to the extent that she had previously done. She deeply regretted moving Shadow and was concerned that he had not socialised with horses other than with Sue's filly. She also expressed to Bob her concerns about his gelding's unprovoked attack on Shadow while he grazed. Bite marks from the gelding were all over Shadow's body but Bob still ignored her. He lacked compassion for Shadow and saw him as a troublemaker, telling Bree that Shadow would have to learn the hard way, and strongly suggested she was pampering the horse too much.

The week Bree was to sit her exams, she gave Claire Shadow's feeding schedule and handling instructions to follow for the four days that she would be absent. The Hosts assured her they would call her if Shadow became in any way a problem. Every time Bree telephoned them to check on him, Claire repeatedly said, "Shadow's fine, he's no trouble at all."

On the third day Bree told Sam that she was worried about Shadow. He tried to assure her that he was fine. "He'll be okay, baby, don't worry. Just concentrate on your exams," he said.

Bree's feeling of concern persisted throughout the day. She telephoned Sam at work and asked him to pick her up early.

"I have to see if Shadow is okay."

Shadow was at the far end of the paddock when they arrived, facing away from them. Bree got out of the car, and walked up to the fence, calling out to him, "Shadow! Shadow, come on boy." He did not move. She knew something was wrong. He always came running the instant he saw her or heard her call him, but not this time.

Bree walked up to Shadow. He had not moved. She looked at him in wide-eyed horror and gasped when she saw the cuts and bite marks on his back. He spun around and looked at her. Her heart sank at the sight. His handsome face was swollen from cuts and gashes. Bruising had discoloured his once lustrous silver coat. In three days he had lost weight and condition. She could count his ribs. A large haematoma bulged from his chest.

Utterly shocked at Shadow's state, Bree approached him with a handful of hay. "Hey, boy," she cooed, "it's me, I'm here now."

Shadow suddenly lunged forward and took the hay, then backed away at great speed. He was enraged with fear, terror showing in the whites of his eyes. Bree moved closer but he turned and gave her a double strike. She saw it coming and turned sideways, taking the force of the impact from his back legs on her hip. She did not run, but was dumbfounded. Her gentle and loving little horse, her friend who had given her his trust, was battered and bruised and wild with fright because he had been misunderstood and mistreated.

"What have you done to my horse?" Bree demanded when Claire came out of the house.

"Bob beat him with a stick. The little bastard deserved it."

"What?" Bree shouted, shocked at Claire's shameless arrogance.

"He pinned his ears back at him every time he fed him," she smirked.

Sam was standing beside Bree, speechless. He had witnessed Claire's vindictiveness as she justified her husband's cruel, insidious behaviour, and saw that their neglect allowed a larger gelding to do so much damage. They compounded the injustice and traumatised Shadow further by beating him. Disgusted and sickened to their stomachs, Sam escorted Bree back to the car.

"He will be out of here before dark and I'll pay back every cent you paid for Shadow!" Bree said before she got into the car.

"Don't bother," Claire called out, "we'll wipe it off as a bad debt."

In the car Bree broke down.

"I have to call Jack to help me move him," she told Sam. "We have to get Shadow out of there this afternoon."

"I'm so sorry, Jack, I let Shadow down," Bree wept over the phone. "Please come. I need to move him quickly. I am so sorry. He's a mess. I've no one else to call; only you can handle him. I'm so sorry."

Jack arrived with a horse float a short time later. He did not speak. He was angry, but not with Bree. He was angry that Shadow had been so savagely abused. The sight of Shadow almost crushed him. He was calm when he approached Shadow but his old friend reacted in fear and reared up to strike out at him. Shadow came close to hitting Jack in the face when a hoof brushed the rim of his battered Akubra. Jack stood his ground and eased Shadow into the float, but not before a double-barrel strike connected with his chest. The pain of the impact from Shadow's hoofs was as deep emotionally as it was physically for him.

When Jack and Shadow drove away, Bree felt sure that he wept for his mate. Regret lay heavy on her spirit. She felt the responsibility for what had happened to Shadow. Her tears were only for Jack and Shadow.

547

62

I looked up from my writing when Bree and Sam entered my home. They both looked distressed and I asked what was wrong. Bree came in slowly and sat down opposite me at the dining table. Sam was silent and lingered in the background. Bree looked sombrely at me before she burst into tears, sobbing as she struggled to tell me what had happened.

"The vet said that Shadow will be physically and mentally scarred for life. He wants me to have him destroyed. He said that it's the worst case of abuse he had ever seen. He wants to prosecute Bob."

I didn't know what to say. I was horrified. I couldn't fathom the idea of someone we knew hurting Shadow. The room was still. We were all too numb to speak and Bree was sobbing, releasing heartfelt sorrow and regret.

"I should have trusted my gut feeling, but I didn't."

I jumped up from my chair and went to comfort her.

"I don't accept the vet's assessment, Bree," I said with the strength of my convictions. "Shadow will be alright. He won't have any physical or emotional scars. I refuse to accept any of it! You are meant to have Shadow. I feel it. I know it. He will be okay!" I said firmly, as I hugged her and stroked her hair.

Bree stared up at me in silence, just as she used to when she was a little girl. Her face was wet with tears. Her large brown eyes held the hope that I had encouraged her to have. She wanted to believe I was right, and eventually she did. I also knew Bree had to believe in herself as much as she had to believe in Shadow's complete recovery, otherwise neither of them would heal.

Bree held herself responsible for what had happened to Shadow and could not think of him without thinking of how much Jack had suffered too. The weight of that burden absorbed most of her emotional energy.

"I let them down, Mom. I promised Jack that I would look after Shadow and I let both of them down. If only I had trusted my instincts. I felt that something was wrong," she whimpered.

There was no consoling her, even though both Sam and I tried. I said, "It wasn't possible to move him."

Sam came and stood beside Bree, looking down at her utterly helpless. He crouched down and looked into her face. "Baby, you had to study and look after Beauty as well as instructing students. We didn't have another place to move him to. It wasn't your fault."

"I should have listened to my gut feelings. I..."

"Stop that!" I said firmly. "Shadow will be all right. I know it! He will be fine."

Bree pulled herself together for long enough for us to make plans to find a location closer to home where Shadow and Beauty could be together. The property where Jack had taken Shadow was only temporary.

"You know, Mom," Bree said thoughtfully, "what Bob did to Shadow clearly showed me the difference between someone who loves horses and someone who simply owns horses."

Before they left, I asked Bree, almost timidly, "What are you going to do about Bob?" She turned to me, looking exhausted. "Nothing," she said, "I'm not interested in revenge, only in Shadow's recovery. He needs me to focus on him. The universe will take care of Bob, Mom." I nodded, feeling very proud of her because I knew she was right.

Three days had elapsed before I was able to drive to the property to see Shadow. Nothing could have prepared me for the shock of seeing him in such a dreadful condition and displaying a menacing temperament. I wanted to cry and felt my anger rise up. I wanted to give Bob Host a sample of what he had done to Shadow, for him to feel Shadow's pain. What I saw had tested my faith in humanity to its capacity. I hid from Bree the twinges of doubt I felt and began to silently pray for courage. Wanting to believe it, I said confidently to Bree, "Shadow will be okay."

I knew by the state of him that Shadow's recovery would be slow, and Bree would need all the resources she could find to help her. A thought occurred to me while I stood quietly beside Bree, staring in disbelief at the battered, bruised and very dirty colt that vaguely resembled the one I once knew. Shadow was a very proud horse and his appearance would have done little to boost his confidence. I thought that he needed a bath, perhaps a strange thought to have under the circumstances, when the simple task of feeding him was dangerous.

Shadow and Beauty were relocated closer to our homes, which made it much easier to feed and care for the horses. Clearly the incident had affected Bree more than she was saying. Shadow had become very aggressive and almost impossible to handle. Every day, Bree's patience and natural horsemanship were challenged to their limits. Everything she did or tried to do for Shadow was met with aggression. His attitude seemed to enhance her guilt, which consequently had affected her confidence.

The plan to use Shadow as Beauty's sire was now ruined. Bree, Sam and I discussed whether or not Shadow should be castrated; he was far too dangerous as a stallion. We unanimously agreed in favour of castration in Shadow's best interests, as much as for Bree's safety.

Several weeks had passed and Shadow still had not had a bath. It was impossible to get near him for more than a minute. When we fed him, one of us would walk a few metres away from his feed bin and distract him. The other would dash into his yard, quickly tip wet feed into his bin, drop a couple of biscuits of hay and dash back out again before he knew what was going on. It really was a test of skill and not something to look forward to two and sometimes three times a day

Someone had to catch and halter Shadow and have him ready for when the vet arrived on the morning of his castration. I could see Bree was not ready to test her confidence just yet, especially since she had already been on the receiving end of Shadow's fury on a number of occasions. I knew that I would have to be the one to put the halter on him.

Bree passed me the halter before I climbed over the fence. Shadow was standing to the side of the paddock watching me. I walked up slowly to him. He did not move. He was unusually quiet that morning and did not flinch when I slid the halter around his head. Bree and the young woman who lived on the property stood by the edge of the fence line and watched in amazement. The young woman said to Bree, "Your mother is either very brave or very stupid." Keeping her eyes firmly fixed on me, Bree said, "She is praying." Just as I had finished clipping on the lead rope, the vet arrived.

When Shadow regained consciousness, the bonding with Bree had to begin all over again. While he was still groggy from the effects of the anaesthetic, she gently caressed him for the first time in many weeks. Like most males when they are either sick or injured, Shadow was immediately rendered a sook by a tender touch. The discomfort from the operation had made Shadow a little vulnerable to Bree's loving caresses. She was able to bath him. The water calmed him and washed his coat free of dirt and mud. Shampoo foam disappeared under the steady flow and when it cleared, Shadow's silver coat gleamed in the sunlight.

That day we saw the first sign of the power of our faith and a glimpse of Shadow's positive response. His body was healing, with only traces of bruising and scarring. Although I remained outwardly positive, I wondered what his emotional state would be.

The year that followed was nothing short of agony as much as ecstasy for all of us. Shadow's response fluctuated in such a dramatic way that it was frustrating. It was a painful and challenging experience for me to helplessly stand by, merely as a spectator, as my dearest child suffered her crossing from adolescence to adulthood through the initiation of a series of exasperating events.

When the burden became far too great for Bree to handle and it became evident that her beloved Beauty was suffering because Shadow demanded so much from her, she began pleading to be released from having to contend with Shadow.

"I can't help him, Mom," she said downheartedly. "He isn't progressing with me. It isn't fair to Shadow if he stays with me. Beauty is suffering too. I haven't ridden her in ages. She is sad, Mom. It is breaking my heart to see her that way. I have to find someone who can handle a horse like Shadow."

I did not agree with Bree's analogy of the situation. Shadow had come a very long way in her care. It no longer took three people to rug him or to feed him. We were now able to enter the paddock without fear of attack. Contrary to what Bree thought, Shadow was actually calmer in her presence. Her words were spoken out of the frustration of investing so much time and what little money she and Sam had in caring for both horses. They had sacrificed a great deal during that time. Their love, friendship and respect for each other had carried them through the drama.

I told Bree that I would telephone around Queensland to find someone willing to take a troubled horse. I called far and wide around the country, spoke to horse experts and horse handlers of all kinds, and came across one who was interested in looking at Shadow.

"My daughter and I will meet you at one o'clock at the paddock," I said, and gave him the address and my mobile number.

The horse expert arrived and left the paddock before us. The young woman who lived on the property, told us that she had seen the man drive up in a four-wheel drive and stop at the gate where Shadow was standing. She said a man and a woman got out of the vehicle and walked confidently over to Shadow. When they made an attempt to pat Shadow, he pinned back his ears and charged them. They both scurried back to the vehicle and drove away.

The horse expert did not even bother to call and tell me that he had seen Shadow. When I called him, he told me that he had too many horses on his property already and couldn't take him. So much for 'horse experts!' I thought with disdain. So the search continued, but to no avail. Every avenue drew a blank, which confirmed what I felt. Shadow was with the right person and in the right home. I telephoned Bree to tell her.

"You could be right, Mom, but I just can't do it anymore. I'm tired and we can't afford the expense of him either."

"Okay," I said, "I'll take care of Shadow if you teach me how to handle him, until I can find him another home."

Releasing Bree from the responsibility of Shadow was the turning point for her. A burden had been lifted from her shoulders and she was free to give Beauty her full attention.

When we had first moved the horses to the paddock, an electric fence had separated them. Bree removed the fence a few months later, feeling that Beauty could teach Shadow some social skills.

Beauty was Bree's guardian. She could go into the yard at any time. If Shadow ever came too close or seemed threatening to her safety, Beauty would chase him away. Fearing the consequences from Beauty, Shadow behaved and kept his distance.

Now that Shadow was no longer her responsibility, Bree could get on with exercising Beauty. One Saturday afternoon while she was grooming Beauty after a ride, Bree heard Shadow creep up behind her. She ignored him. He came in close enough for her to feel his hot breath on her back but she still ignored him and carried on with the grooming. Shadow gently nudged her with his muzzle. Bree slowly moved her hand behind her back. He sniffed it then rubbed his muzzle and head up against her. Without turning, Bree gently rubbed the side of his face and his muzzle.

"I was ecstatic, Mom," she said, beaming, when she rushed to my place to tell me. "Shadow came to me." It was the sign she had been waiting for. "I can work with him now. He's ready. He came to me."

Beauty would only allow Shadow near Bree, or to follow her around the paddock, if he behaved. 'Things at last seemed to be getting back to normal,' I wrote, 'we've managed to pay the vet bills. Thank heavens for that! Sam has been wonderful. He helped me feed the horses when Bree was ill with the flu. She is so happy and relieved to finally have a breakthrough with Shadow. She has done a fantastic job with him.'

While sharing the paddock, Beauty and Shadow had become good friends. Bree gave Beauty the credit for teaching Shadow manners. As an alpha mare, she taught him that bad behaviour was unacceptable and had banished him to the far end of the paddock until he got the message. He was not allowed within her boundary until he had submitted to her as a form of an apology. The moment he did he was forgiven and welcomed back. Horses are very social animals. In the wild, being a part of a herd is important to their survival.

Once I was sure I had good news, I telephoned Jack. It would not have been fair to call him unless I had. I remembered his heartache only too well.

"Hi Jack," I said, "It's Emma Jane. Want some good news?"

Jack was speechless when I gave him Shadow's progress report.

"But, but," he stammered, struggling to get out the words. "I thought Shadow had been destroyed."

"Oh Jack, I'm so sorry," I said, feeling overwhelmed, "I hadn't realised you thought that, otherwise I would have called you sooner. We would never have done that. I didn't want to say anything to you until I knew for sure that he was okay. Shadow is really okay," I said, trying my best to remain composed. "He's still handsome. Bree has done a great job. Shadow loves her."

"You've made my day Emma, thank you, thank you," Jack was crying. "All I wanted for him was to be well cared for and to be happy. He deserves that much."

Bree was not a 'horse expert', nor did she use any fancy techniques to get results. She was just a young woman with a profound respect and love for her horses. Love and patience were the primary ingredients in Shadow's recovery. He grew into a mature horse, happy and carefree until he died of cancer at age 16.

Those three and a half years that it took to heal Shadow proved to be a test of emotional strength as well as a test of character for Bree. It would be difficult to experience an episode such as this one and not be changed to some degree. I witnessed the struggles and frustrations she had faced and eventually overcame. I also saw how Bree discovered that life was not a fairy tale, as her first seven years were. The reality of it had bitten deep. She felt the sting and was thrown off course for a time, but she recovered.

As a young woman in her twenties, Bree's dream became much bigger than just wanting to be a well-known equestrian rider. Everything had changed. She discovered that the world was larger than an equestrian arena. She wanted to travel and perhaps later return to riding just for pleasure.

63

I sat on the lounge reading a book. My eyes drifted away from the pages as I contemplated the paragraph I had just read. Absentmindedly, I gazed through the window and noticed that dappled sunlight had transformed my ordinary garden into a thing of beauty. While looking at the garden, it suddenly occurred to me that it felt good to be alive. I put the book aside and sat back to reflect over the years, and then reached for my diary. Flipping through the pages I came across the entry I made the day I had spoken to Matt. I finally took steps to find out, once and for all, where he was. I wrote a short letter and sent it to the Navy Department in Canberra, asking them to forward it on to him. I knew in my heart that Matt had survived Vietnam because I could see him clearly in my mind's eye whenever I thought about him.

A short time later I got a call from a naval officer. She told me Matt was married. She could not give me his address but the letter was forwarded on to him as I had requested. The following week was one of great anticipation, as I tried to imagine what he would say and what I would say to him, but he did not call. Disappointed, I was ready to let it go, but my inner voice told me to look for his phone number on the Internet. I was astonished to find it.

When Matt's wife answered my call, I stammered something about being an old friend of Matt's and only wanted to say hello. Although she called him to the phone she did not sound happy.

"Hello Princess," Matt said. I could hear the joy in his voice. "I've often thought about you. I'm so sorry about what happened in Darwin. I was young and foolish and I..."

"It's okay Matt, really," I laughed, "it's okay. I only wanted to know if you're OK."

"There was a lot of love between us darling," he said, "and it's still there. I wanted to marry you."

"I know Matt. You have no idea how much I regret what happened between us. I am so sorry, but all that's in the past now," I said quickly, wanting to change the subject. "Tell me honey, how are you?"

We could not talk for long because his wife was in the next room, but Matt called me on the days he played golf and we were able to catch up on some of the lost years.

"I'm not the same person that you knew, Princess," he said. "Vietnam changed me. We copped Agent Orange and I have this burning sensation in my body all the time. It almost drives me crazy even though I take medication for it."

"I can't imagine that, Matt," I said. His voice sounded exactly as I remembered it. I could never imagine him any different from the mischievous fun-loving guy I knew, even though he was serious, but then I remembered that it had been thirty-two years. We had both changed.

During one of several more phone calls, Matt told me that Les had sent graphic and disturbing letters to him, threatening his life. "They were so disturbing that I reported it to my commanding officer."

"Are you serious?" I was shocked.

"I wouldn't joke about that, sweetheart. My job was top security. I was given a bodyguard, that's how bad the threats were. If he had come anywhere near the base or me he would have been arrested. Les is definitely unbalanced."

I was totally stunned. "I had no idea, Matt. I don't know what to say. I hope you didn't think I knew anything about it."

"To be honest I didn't know what to think."

"My God, I'm so glad I got in touch with you." I sighed with relief.

"Me too, sweetheart."

"Are you happy?"

"I'm content," he said.

"Then you're happy."

"No. I said I'm content."

"I don't understand. What do you mean by that?"

"I've all that I need. I love my children, especially my daughter from my first marriage."

"Do you love your wife?"

"No. I'm fond of her. She's a good woman."

'That would explain her insecurity,' I thought.

"I would have thought that over the years, Matt, you would have been in and out of love many times."

"Oh no, no, I've been fond of some women, but I wasn't in love with any of them. If I was on my own right now, I would be on your doorstep," he said, laughing. But deep down we both knew that would never happen. Although we still had strong feelings for each other, we knew we had missed our chance. Contacting Matt was not about rekindling an old flame, but I was given the bonus of his affection, a recent photograph and two beautiful letters to treasure. I'm happy.

Brad, Celeste and Cain popped into my mind. I organised my thoughts then wrote, 'Many seasons have come and gone since the last time I saw them. They are so far removed from me that they hardly seem real any more. The endless ache of missing them has eased. A verse from one of my favourite books 'The Prophet', written by Kahlil Gibran, jolted me into reviewing my attitude about them. The verse went:

'Your children are not your children, they are the sons and daughters of life's longing for itself. They come through you but not from you, and though they are with you yet they belong not to you.

'You may give them your love but not your thoughts, for they have their own thoughts. You may house their bodies but not their souls, for their souls dwell in the house of tomorrow, which you cannot visit, not even in your dreams.

'You may strive to be like them, but seek not to make them like you, for life goes not backwards nor tarries with yesterday.

'You are the bows from which your children as living arrows are sent forth.

'The archer sees the mark upon the earth of the infinite, and he bends you with his might that his arrows may go swift and far.

'Let your bending in the archer's hand be for gladness; for even as he loves the arrow that flies, so he loves also the bow that is stable.'

Before reading that verse, I had shamelessly thought that because I had given birth to children they belonged to me. Reading and re-reading those words helped me to understand my role as a parent.

Although my children bear the scars of the sins of their parents, I now hope that as they have children of their own, they realise that nobody has all the answers, that their parents are flawed and so are they. Above all, I have learnt that forgiveness was my most poignant lesson. I wonder if they will learn that too.

Many times over the years, I have told Bree that rewards come from the challenges we overcome. Ironically, these days I am a recipient of many rewards. I can now look back at my life with appreciation, with the knowledge that the challenges I have overcome forced me to keep evolving until I became a completely different person, hopefully a better person. I also understand that my mother, Les and Stanley played a major part in making that happen. They tried to convince me that I was nothing without them and they would have succeeded, had not angels crossed my path to give me hope and encouragement to believe in my own worth.

Angels like Dr Pennington, who was kind and made me feel special; my children, especially Bree who gave me hope. She became my best friend and had me clinging to life, when I really wanted to give up. Bree never judged me or deserted me. Her love was always unconditional. Beth, Sylvia and Willy impacted my life with their courage. Although I have not seen them since leaving Victoria, they are dear to me.

How could I have known that for all those years I was subtly being liberated and prepared for the day I dreaded most.

"I want to start travelling, Mom," Bree said, a short time after she and Sam parted. They were together for seven years.

"I'm going to Cairns." I looked at her and saw how excited she was, "I know I'll miss you so much, Mom, but I have to do this now or I'll never do it. I have to do it for me, to have a fresh start."

"Then you have to go," I said enthusiastically, masking the emptiness I knew I would feel without her. The day she left, I was utterly lost and deeply sad. A phone call from her that evening cheered me up.

"Don't worry, Mom, I'll be fine," she said. "You've taught me well."

Later that week I was thinking about what Bree had said about being okay, selfishly wishing that she had not gone away, but then words from The Prophet came to mind. *'Your children are not your children...You are the bows from which your children as living arrows are sent forth...for even as He loves the arrow that flies, so He loves the bow that is stable."*

I tried so hard to be stable, but the first six months Bree was away, I felt lonely. It was the first time we had ever been separated for that length of time. She called me frequently and I pretended to be happy right up until the day she said, "I'm so glad you're my mom. I love you so much. You're my best friend. It's because of you that I'm okay. Thanks Ma."

I was overwhelmed and confessed that I was missing her terribly.

"But I'm really okay," I sniffed. "You always make me feel good. I'm so glad I have you."

Bree's encouraging words made me take a serious look at my life. I really wanted to be happy. I knew that nothing about my life would be different unless I changed it. I wanted a radical transformation.

I told my hairdresser that I wanted to do something really radical, and he asked if he could colour my blonde hair jet-black.

"Go for it," I said, and I loved it.

Although, slim, I was unfit. I joined a gym and began to spoil and take care of myself better than I ever had. I bought new clothes, even splurged and bought my favourite perfume, took up Latin dancing again, went horseback riding, joined a meditation group and started painting in oils again. My 2003 New Year resolution was to be 'happy' and not accept anything other than the best for my life. I took a radical look at the people with whom I associated, distancing myself from those who proved to be less than real friends.

I finally realised that life had not let me down, that I was following my destiny, but was doing it the hard way because I did not trust my instincts. I do now. In the process, I have become a totally different person. My entire outlook has altered. 'Life currents can change in an instant,' I thought, feeling as though I had woken up from a deep sleep with an insatiable appetite for life. There is so much more out there for me to explore, I haven't even dinted the surface. I paused a moment to reflect then wrote, 'I also hope that one day all of my children and I will be friends again. It's possible; I only have to remember how much I have changed to know that.'

Twelve months later.

"Hi Mom," Bree said, "I've got exciting news… The excitement and smile was apparent in her voice.

"Hey Babe," I replied filled with great expectation, "What news?"

"I'm coming home." She almost shouted, laughing and talking faster than usual. "There's someone I want you to meet."

A huge lump formed deep in my throat, and my eyes suddenly went misty. I was still digesting the, 'I'm coming part' and almost missed '...there's someone I want you to meet.'

"What?... Wow! Really? When?"

As I pulled out a chair from the table to sit down, I caught my reflection in the mirror beside the dining table, liking the 'new me', I smiled. "And I have someone I want you to meet."

* * *